CHIMERA'S WEB

CHIMERA'S WEB

A Clockwork Vampire #3

K.H. KOEHLER

The Monster Factory

CHIMERA'S WEB

A CLOCKWORK VAMPIRE #3

K.H. KOEHLER

CONTENTS

I	1
II	30
III	53
IV	82
V	116
VI	154
VII	177
VIII	199
IX	217

X	230
XI	253
XII	270
XIII	285
XIV	303
XV	320

ABOUT THE AUTHOR

Copyright © 2021 by K.H. Koehler

All rights reserved. No part of this publication may be reproduced, stored or transmitted in any form or by any means, electronic, mechanical, photocopying, recording, scanning, or otherwise without written permission from the publisher. It is illegal to copy this book, post it to a website, or distribute it by any other means without permission.

This novel is entirely a work of fiction. The names, characters and incidents portrayed in it are the work of the author's imagination. Any resemblance to actual persons, living or dead, events or localities is entirely coincidental.

Paperback ISBN: 979-8-8692-6638-5

Ebook ISBN: 979-8-8692-6639-2

Cover art and interior design by KH Koehler Design

https://khkoehler.net

No part of this book was created using artificial intelligence.

i

It was the longest day of Mrs. Eliza McGillicuddy's life. It was also her last.

Full of nervous energy, she'd woken early, attended to some of Edwin's professional correspondence, and sent off the new pages of Edwin's latest *Doctor Blood* novel to his editor at Pulped Press. The afternoon passed in a similar blur. But as the hours wore on, she found herself watching the clock almost obsessively, counting down the hours to nightfall.

She realized that she was counting down the time to her own death. At midnight, Mrs. Eliza McGillicuddy would die.

At six o'clock exactly, she closed up the home office in the townhouse she shared with Edwin, Cesar, and Malcolm. She was trembling ever so slightly.

She found Cesar in the kitchenette, polishing and replacing pots and pans in the rack above the stove as he finished the washing up for the night. She stopped in the doorway, leaned on her cherry-wood cane, and noticed how very cute and Susie Homemaker he looked in a red and white checked apron. Beneath the apron, he wore a very starched white shirt and pressed pinstripe trousers as if he had some evening engagement, and when he turned to offer her a fond, close-lipped smile, she saw the front of the apron read in a glaring, blood-red font: BITE THE COOK.

Back when he did much of the cooking, she had bought the apron for Edwin, but ever since Cesar had come to be a permanent fixture in their lives, the task had more or less fallen to him. Not that Eliza minded, since she was a terrible cook, and all Edwin knew how to prepare were curious British cuisines with dubious words like "black" and "pudding" in their names.

She sniffed appreciably at the divine aromas coming from the oven. "Hey, good looking, what's cooking?"

"It's a shepherd's pie, Edwin's recipe," Cesar informed her, smiling with triumph. He was tall and lanky, but not at all weak looking. His hair was cut fashionably messy and his silvery-blue eyes twinkled mischievously.

"One of the better English dishes," Eliza said approvingly.

"I'm one of the better cooks here," he answered with a great deal of confidence—well earned, she might add. Then he added, "Wait...I'm the only good cook here."

They laughed.

He had been a much different person back when they'd all first met. Back then, he'd been human, inclined to close, smooth shaves, perfectly tame hairdos, a generous tan, and razor-sharp security uniforms. He'd changed so much since his untimely death at Edwin's hands. As a baby vampire, he seemed bigger, a little less neat...a little more dangerous.

Eliza wondered if that was intentional or purely subconscious. After all, Cesar was Edwin's Heir and Enforcer, and Edwin was messy and dangerous, as vampires went. Cesar seemed to be trying to emulate his master a little more with each passing day.

"How much did you cook?" she asked, peeking through the oven door.

Cesar wiped his hands on the tea towel tucked into a pocket of his apron. "A lot. I have to keep you and the big, bad wolf fed. Do you have *any* idea how much Malcolm eats in a day? That man is like a machine. A furry machine, but still a machine."

Malcolm Whitby, aka "the big, bad wolf," was Edwin's "hunting dog," the werewolf that acted as his third in command after Cesar. A year ago, he had come to them by way of Edwin's former friend Lord Ian Severn. After Severn was killed—well, *murdered* by Edwin for threatening his Court—Edwin more or less inherited the Werewolf of Whitby. In some ways, Malcolm acted as Edwin's bodyguard and backup Enforcer—except, of course, he didn't have the intimate relationship with Edwin that Cesar did. Malcolm was almost pathologically heterosexual, though she suspected any conflict between Cesar and Malcolm went much deeper than their opposing sexual orientations.

Vampires and werewolves didn't get along. The two men lived together under the same roof, but they would never be what one would call "mates."

Malcolm Whitby had spent centuries in suspended animation, and he was still adjusting to the modern era he'd woken up to. Since then, Malcolm and Cesar had developed a kind of friendly sibling rivalry, like two brothers vying for their dad's affections.

Then a couple of months ago, Malcolm announced that he wanted to attend university. That surprised even Eliza. But Malcolm was a quick study. Cesar cooked Malcolm a celebratory meal that night and served him in one of his cuter, blue-and-white ruffled Betty Croker-inspired aprons. Malcolm, dressed in all-over black leather, sneered at Cesar throughout the meal, and Edwin had to tell them to cut it out.

And so it went.

She looked Cesar over. "Will you be going out tonight?" She tried to sound casual and not at all anxious about being all alone with Edwin tonight.

"I thought I might. Alex asked me out for drinks."

"Alex? Is that someone new?"

Cesar noticeably blushed, something only a very young vampire could do. "Well…yeah."

Eliza grinned. "Is he cute?"

Cesar fiddled with his rolled-up sleeves.

"What's wrong?"

Cesar shrugged. "We met online. He doesn't know about…you know." He turned and nervously rustled his wings—neatly folded beneath the apron strings—as he finished drying the dishes. He was still very self-conscious about his species. Despite the Vampire Bill that had passed in Congress over two years ago, there were still many who did want to see vampires walking around the city. He and Edwin got a good many dirty looks from people when they were out in public.

On impulse, Eliza stepped forward and hugged Cesar around the neck. He was very tall and she very short, so it was quite a reach. She kissed him on the cheek, which was cooler than it looked. She suppressed the strange, knotted feeling in her stomach. What would she ever do without her bestie?

"You'll be fine," she said before stepping back. "You'll be a triumph!"

"You always say that," he demurred, clenching his hands together nervously and looking down at them. "But how can you know?"

They'd had the girlfriend pep talk many times before. "You always are," she said simply and made a shooing motion at him. "So, go get ready for your date. I'll look over the shepherd's pie."

He brightened. "Okay!"

She didn't add that she was far too nervous to eat anything tonight.

***

Eliza escaped upstairs to the bedroom she shared with Edwin. She was leaning less heavily on her cane than in past weeks. She was recovering, but it was a maddeningly slow process. The effects of the stroke she had suffered nearly a year ago lingered on. Only recently had she begun fully dressing herself without Edwin's assistance. She looked forward to the day when she no longer needed a cane to walk or a husband to get her into a dress—which, incidentally, ought to be the following day.

She stopped when she reached the open door of Edwin's upstairs office. He was sitting on a corner of his cluttered desk, speaking into his favorite old rotary phone to his literary agent. They were arguing over some small detail of a contract, but the moment he spotted her, he straightened.

"I'll speak to you later, Gabe," he said, and while Gabriel Dumphrey was still talking, he hung up on the poor man. Edwin turned to face her—this man she had married, this vampire who meant to take her life tonight—and gave her a shy, anticipatory smile and a little wave.

Lord Edwin McGillicuddy was lanky tall and dressed in checked golf trousers, a T-shirt that read TEAM EDWARD, and his favorite pair of red braces. It was his usual "workday clothes," as he liked to call them. As a two-hundred-year-old vampire and author, one would have expected him to be more inclined to wear smoking jackets or dressing gowns as he cranked out yet another *Doctor Blood* novel for his voracious fans and over-demanding publisher, but Edwin was progressive. He had no fashion sense and was likely color-blind, but he was also wide of shoulder and narrow of hip, so she didn't mind it so much.

His face and dark amber eyes were serious tonight, and his auburn hair looked unruly, as if he'd been running his hands through it all day. "Evening, love," he said, and for whatever reason, maybe because he was nervous about tonight or he was only very close to his own past, his Bow Bells brogue was very much pronounced this evening.

Their eyes met and a signal passed between them, both as husband and wife as well as Vampire Lord and Bride. She knew he could hear her heart flitting nervously in her chest even from where he sat. She, in turn, could feel his desire, a low, constant roar like a distant wind over a lonely moor.

"Afraid?" he asked.

"I suppose I am. A little." She went up to him and smoothed down his wrinkled shirt. With him sitting down, she could see him eye to eye—usually an impossible feat with him being so tall and she so short. She studied his bright amber wolf eyes and the gentle but fierce desire simmering there. She felt a faint wind as his wings stirred at her touch.

"Do you trust me?" he asked after some moments of silence.

She nodded. She did, with her life. Even with her soul.

He moved his hands so they rested at her hips and guided her closer until their two bodies touched. His touch was very gentle but hinted at the raw, preternatural power in his arms and body. Ever since she'd nearly died saving him last year, he'd been obsessed with touching her often, as if he wasn't quite sure if she was real. If any of this was real.

And then, sometimes, annoyingly, he treated her like she was made of glass, as if she'd shatter if he wasn't careful in how he handled her. His overly gentle lovemaking frustrated her to no end, and it bothered her even more that he chose to lavish his darker affections on Cesar. It was giving her a jealous bone. Not that he and Cesar were together—because such things were quite normal between a Lord and his new Heir—but that Cesar was now enjoying what they once had.

He rested his mouth near her ear. "Is there anything you want to do? Anywhere you want to go? Anything you want? Anything at all?"

She shook her head. "I told you. I'm ready. I just want to be here tonight with you. That's all."

He leaned back to look her over. Something passed behind his eyes, some darkness. Up until now, their plans for tonight had excited and enlivened him, and he'd spent more hours than she cared to count explaining things to her, painting the details of her life as his newest Heir to her and assuring her of his competence. But as zero hour loomed, he seemed to be getting cold feet.

"Eliza..." he began gravely, "it needn't be tonight."

"If not tonight, then when? Edwin, I made my choice. I don't want to wait. I've already waited a year!"

They had both decided on the time and place of her death, and ever since, they'd been planning and preparing for this night. She had hoped he would do it on their honeymoon. She'd thought the symbolism would be most apropos. But Edwin insisted she be at full strength before he made her his Heir. Thus, they had set the date exactly one year from the day of their wedding. Their first wedding anniversary.

That night was tonight.

She gave her husband her sternest look. "Edwin Oliver McGillicuddy, I said I would do this, and I will!"

Edwin bit his lips. "It's not something one should ever rush into."

"We're not rushing! We've planned for this day. We're as prepared as any two people can be." She stopped and regarded him carefully as she fiddled with the bloodstone on her ring finger, the sign of his promise. "Have you changed your mind?"

He looked appalled. "Of course not." Seeing the ring, he bent his head to kiss the bloodstone. "I want you as my Heir, Eliza, I swear. I always have."

"Then it's quite settled, isn't it? There's no reason to delay the inevitable."

"Yes," he agreed. "You're right, of course." But he continued to look uncertain. "Have you told the others?"

"No." She gave him a determined look. "This is *our* decision, Edwin. Mine as your Bride and yours as my Vampire Lord. I don't want them to worry or to try to talk me out of it. I want this to be our decision alone."

She knew Cesar would approve, and perhaps even her human BFF, Juliana. Malcolm...not so much. One of the first things that the giant werewolf had done on awakening to the Twenty-first Century was to propose that she be his mate, his alpha queen. Malcolm would definitely *not* approve. But this was not Malcolm's decision to make.

She touched Edwin's cheek and leaned forward to kiss him softly on the side of the nose. Then she kissed his mouth. He smelled like the spicy aftershave he wore, and he tasted like chocolate and peppermint. She never understood why he tasted so good, seeing how Edwin was incapable of eating anything but blood. His mouth was very cold, but his goatee tickled her, and that, along with the fierce emotion behind his kiss, warmed her heart.

When they finally pulled away, they were both breathless, their hearts ticking along urgently—her human one and his clockwork mechanism.

Eliza offered her husband her sweetest, sassiest smile. "I'll be waiting down the hall, *my Lord*." She trickled her fingers down his body, then hurried down the hallway to their bedroom and closed the door.

* * *

She dressed in the nightgown Edwin liked best, the silken white spaghetti strap gown with the real pearl buttons that made her feel like some silver screen actress no one had ever heard of before, then added gold hoop earrings and dabbed some perfume behind her ears. She glanced at herself in the full-length mirror on the inside of her wardrobe. Her heart was fluttering again.

The woman in the mirror looked very young, except for her eyes. Those had aged considerably over the years. They looked darker, moodier. Her skin was still a pale brown and her hair very black where it curled in a wild froth around her face. The last year had been very hard on her hair. The power surge from Lord Ian Severn's castle had burned the tips off, so she had begun clipping it into a medium-length afro, her witch's streaking cutting a jagged line of white through it like a bolt of lightning.

The white streak...the cane she still used to get about...it made the tears well up in her eyes. She was twenty-one years old. So, why did she feel like she was a hundred—or a thousand? It didn't seem fair that she'd had to work so hard just to stay alive. And free.

"Stop it, Leeza. You are going to ruin your makeup, girl," she chided herself, sniffing away the tears. She checked to make sure she hadn't. She didn't want runny eye makeup when Edwin walked in.

After she was done fixing herself, she turned to the room and blinked out all of the lights by activating their neural network. A few months ago, Edwin had thoughtfully brought someone in to computerize the whole townhouse. As a techkinetic, Eliza now could control almost every electric thing in it—a sort of living, breathing Alexa. She then lit the candles she had strategically placed around the room to produce a romantic ambiance, then glanced at the clock on the mantel and saw it was going on to ten o'clock.

She felt a surge of nervous energy. They had decided that she would die at midnight. That gave Edwin two hours to prepare himself, physically and mentally. She didn't know if it was enough, or if it was too much. The butterflies in her stomach were getting worse by the moment.

She decided to lie down on the bed, which was something of a relief. About ten minutes later, Edwin let himself into their room and locked the door. He said nothing for a moment until the uneasy silence got to him.

And then: "Cesar went out."

"Yes," she said, "I know. He has a date. Someone named Alex. Is Malcolm home yet?"

"Not yet. I think he's found some mates at university to get a pint with."

"That's good. I'm glad he's making friends."

Edwin watched her in the shimmering, candle-lit dark. "You look very beautiful tonight, Mrs. McGillicuddy."

"Thank you."

"I won't be more than a spell."

"I'll be waiting."

Edwin made his way to the bathroom to prepare himself for bed. She waited quietly, forcing herself not to look at the mantel clock or to fidget. She tried to tame her runaway heart, but it continued to flutter nervously in her chest like a windblown bird trapped in a chimney.

Was Edwin right to be nervous? Maybe she was trusting in him too much? But he had done a fine job turning Cesar into a vampire a few years ago, so that wasn't the issue. He was a powerful Vampire Lord—and hardly a virgin to making an Heir. She was being extremely silly, she decided.

It was nearly eleven o'clock when Edwin finally emerged. He was damp from his shower and dressed in his favorite satin dressing gown, a deep forest green full of embroidery that sparkled absently in the dark. He moved like a wraith as he came to sit on the edge of their bed. He looked down at her lying there and his voice caught. "You're so beautiful that sometimes I can't believe you're real."

She smiled nervously. It felt like it was their wedding night all over again. "I bet you say that to all of the girls. And all of the boys."

"I only say it to you."

"And Cesar?"

He blinked slowly in the dark. "Does it concern you? Our...arrangement?"

She pushed herself up on her elbows, suddenly afraid she had spoiled the moment. "No. I mean, I am a little jealous." She reached out and ran her hand up his satiny arm. "Sometimes, I worry he's getting all the best parts of you."

"I promise he's not getting all the best parts." Edwin smiled a little mischievously. Then he looked worried again. "If it bothers you…"

"It doesn't bother me."

"And, for the life of me, I can't figure out why."

"Do you love me less because you love him, too?"

"Of course not…"

"Well, there you go." Her hand grew still on his arm. "The only thing I don't like about your arrangement is that I know you think you can do things with him that you can't do with me."

He looked appalled. "I've never done anything with him that I haven't down with you."

"That's not true. You do vampire things with him."

"I do vampire things with you, too."

"It's not the same, though."

He sighed. "Why are we arguing about Cesar? Tonight is all about you."

She gave him a pleading look. "When I'm like you, and like Cesar, will you do everything with me that you do with him?"

"I'll do whatever you ask," he answered patiently.

"Oh, Edwin..."

He bent down and kissed her gently and almost chastely on the corner of the mouth while touching her hair. The kiss relaxed her and made her forget for a moment about their plans for tonight. For a moment, it felt like every other night. She took the front of his robe in hand and drew him down on top of her, embracing him and deepening the kiss until she felt his teeth lengthening in his mouth. He moved his hands over her warm curves—still much too gently for her liking—and she began to squirm beneath him.

"Will it hurt? What was it like for you?" she said suddenly. She realized she had never asked him the details of the night he was turned.

He looked sad. "It was Foxley. What do you think?"

"He hurt you."

"Not hurt so much as...surprised me." His eyes turned inward for a moment. "We both knew that my becoming his Heir was part of our contract, but we never set a date. We were supposed to wait until I looked a little older—" He touched his face as if frustrated with his youth, though she'd never really seen him as a child. He was young looking, but he didn't have the air of a child, and certainly not the eyes of one, and no one would ever mistake him as such.

"Of course, Foxley couldn't control himself," he sighed.

She sat up fully and caressed his cheek. "He really did hurt you."

"He didn't make the transition easy, that was for certain."

Her eyes filled with tears.

"Eliza..."

"He really is such a monster!" she said, working hard not to ugly cry over him. Well, she thought, she was certainly a hot mess this evening!

Edwin watched her carefully. "Are you certain about tonight?"

She thought about that for a long moment while she calmed down and the tears stopped. Finally, she said, "Yes. I am." She undid his dressing gown and ran a hand along the hard, familiar plains of his body. He leaned down, covering her, the dressing gown pooling silkily around them both, and kissed the side of her neck.

She tilted her head back to allow him better access. "I know we agreed on midnight, but I want you to do it now, Edwin. *Now*. I don't want to wait a second longer."

He deepened his kisses along her throat, moving to the little mark under her ear. His mark. If this were any ordinary night, he would painlessly open his mark and take only a few small sips from her. They would make it part of their lovemaking. But tonight was no ordinary night. He licked it, making her shiver with anticipation, then stopped as he sat back on his heels and looked her in the eye.

"No. Midnight. That gives you an hour, should you change your mind."

"I won't be changing my mind!" She yanked on the shoulders of his dressing gown in her frustration. "Please, Edwin, do it now."

"I normally do it during sex."

"You make it sound like you've done it a lot."

"Not a lot. Some."

"How many times?" she asked. "Edwin, how many Heirs have you made?"

He settled beside her in bed and sighed as he remembered. "Mouse and Cesar. Oh, and Leo—but he doesn't really count."

"Leo?"

He made a dismissive gesture. "This Russian Prince."

"You made a Russian Prince your Heir?" She cocked an eyebrow at him. "What happened to him?"

"I'm not sure," Edwin said, leaning on the pillows on his elbow and staring at the opposite wall of their bedroom as if remembering. "We lost touch."

"Anyone else?"

"No. Scout's honor." He held up two fingers.

"You were never a boy scout."

He shrugged and smiled innocently at her.

She resisted rolling her eyes. "Well, you didn't have sex with Cesar when you did it. I know that."

"I was in a bit of a hurry then. The Poppets were revolting and the world was ending."

"Did you have sex with Mouse? And with *Leo*?"

"Erm...well...they were...spontaneous."

"Spontaneous?" She sighed. It seemed like every road tonight led to an argument. "Maybe we should have sex."

"Eliza, if you're not sure..."

"Shut up, Edwin." Eliza pushed him down and crawled on top of him, pinning her clockwork vampire to the mattress. He looked pleasantly surprised by her aggression. "I'm in charge now. We're having sex first, *my Lord*," she told him with authority. "And then you will make me your Vampire Bride."

Edwin grinned—evilly. "I love it when you boss me around, my lady."

* * *

Cesar and Alex had agreed to meet at the Lotus Petal in the East Village. It was an elegant little tea parlor, not too snobby, and it specialized in vegan and Indian dishes, Alex's favorite. It was warm and cozy—and not too brightly lit. Cesar hoped all those elements would help put Alex at ease when they finally met in real life for the first time.

He met Alex online six months after becoming a vampire. Back then, he was still in the transitional period between human and vampire, and those six months were the most difficult of his life.

Sensory overload, depression, and an almost all-consuming desire to rip the red life out of every living thing he encountered had driven him to spend way too much time alone in his room playing *Vampire Blade*, a multi-player RPG. He was the best in his guild, and at one point, Alex messaged him to congratulate him on knocking out the big boss in one try. Things progressed from there.

Alex talked Cesar through his period of depression, and Cesar helped Alex through a painfully messy breakup with his cheating fiance. After a while, Cesar felt he could tell Alex anything.

Well, almost anything. There was one detail about his life that he had failed to mention: that he was a vampire. He had no idea how Alex would feel about that. He seemed progressive enough, and he was seemingly a big supporter of the Vampire Bill. Cesar hoped that was enough.

Alex had wanted to hang out with him in meatspace for months. At first, Cesar made lame excuses as to why he couldn't. But as Alex became increasingly suspicious of his cagey behavior, he came to realize their friendship was on the line.

PetriDish666: You're fat, aren't you?
Alucard13: I'm not fat.
PetriDish666: Send a pic.
Alucard13: This is so dumb.
PetriDish666: A pic or you're fat forever. ;-)
Alucard13: *You sent a pic.*
PetriDish666: Holy shit, you're hot!

So he had finally agreed to meet Alex at the Lotus Petal tonight.

Now, he sat at a corner table, fiddling with the multiple tablecloths and assortment of real cloth napkins and telling himself he shouldn't be so nervous. It wasn't like he had deliberately led Alex on. He'd never lied about *any* aspect of his life, that he'd been in the Air Force, worked aboard the *Gypsy Queen*, or that he currently worked as security for Lord Edwin McGillicuddy. He was very open about his family, his beliefs, his sexuality, everything.

He just hadn't mentioned what species he was.

Around eight-thirty, he saw Alex come round the bend and approach the table. He looked charmingly boyish with his hot pink hair and bright blue eyes, exactly like his profile picture. Like a cute anime boy come to life. "Hey, man...I'm really sorry to keep you waiting like this. There was this awful pile up on Fifth and Second..."

Alex stopped when he saw Cesar sitting there. And, for a long moment, both men just stared at each other.

Cesar squirmed uncomfortably, wondering if he shouldn't have used the filters he had on the pic he'd sent Alex. Were his wings shifting weirdly under his suit jacket? Were his eyes dimly glowing in the low lights of the cafe? God, he hoped not.

Finally, Alex took a deep breath and walked the rest of the way to the table.

"How are you, man?" Cesar managed. He stood up and reached for Alex's hand, to shake it.

Alex noticeably flinched at his touch. "I'm...okay."

They both sat and stared at each other as an uncomfortable silence settled in between them like a wall of lead ingots. Cesar played with his napkin and said, "I ordered some mineral water for you. I know you don't drink." Maybe if he reminded Alex of how well they knew each other online, it would put him more at ease.

Alex sat with both hands braced on the table like a man ready to bolt. He said, "You look different than in your profile picture."

"Not too different. Not fat!" he joked, though Alex didn't laugh.

They fell silent again as the busboy brought a mineral water for Alex and a bottle of blood substitute with the label efficiently removed for Cesar. Cesar ignored the bottle and tried to restart the conversation. "I'm really glad you asked me out tonight. It's a nice place, don't you think?"

Alex bit his lip. "I hate to point out the elephant in the room, but..."

"Yeah," Cesar interrupted, looking down at his empty plate. "Okay." He took a deep breath and gathered his courage for the story he had rehearsed. "Two years ago, I met this guy. Well, he's not really a guy. I mean, he *was* a guy once, about two hundred years ago, but he wasn't a guy when I met him."

Cesar twisted his napkin in his lap as he forced himself to continue. "Anyway, to make a long story short, he...well, he sort of made me his Heir."

"This guy," Alex said. "This...vampire?"

"Yes," Cesar dutifully answered. He swallowed hard before continuing. His throat was suddenly so dry. "But there were extenuating circumstances. There were these zombie Poppets who wanted to take control of the world, and this one Poppet who was a real badass chick with a head full of loose gears, and she controlled all of the other zombie Poppets. Anyway, he—this guy, the vampire—was trying to stop her, and he was short on manpower, and he knew I could use a firearm from my military training, so he basically...made me his Enforcer."

Alex blinked slowly. "You're a vampire *and* you're a vampire's Enforcer."

"Well, yeah...but it shouldn't have happened that way. You see, the guy—the vampire—his girlfriend was in trouble, and he needed me to help protect her—"

Alex held up his hand. "This vampire who changed you had a girlfriend?"

"He did. Well, does. Well, they're married now."

Another blink. "He had a girlfriend and he's married now, but you wound up with him?"

"He wasn't married then. And we didn't wind up in bed or anything. We didn't do anything...well, *he* did, but I didn't. I mean, we didn't do anything sexual."

Alex opened his mouth, then closed it. "You said he turned you into a vampire."

"He did. But we didn't have sex."

"So, you're not with him now."

"Well, yeah, I am. He's my master. My Lord. And I'm his Enforcer, like I said."

"So you do have sex with him."

Cesar flinched internally. Why did this have to sound so freakin' bad?

Clearing his throat, Cesar began again. "That's more recent. You see, there were these nasty fairies, and this one Vampire Lord that you would *not* want to meet in a dark alley, and...anyway, that's not important. What's important thing is we defeated the fairies, and then things just sort of progressed."

Cesar winced. He realized he probably needed a backhoe to dig his way out of the hole he was digging.

Again that slow blink. "So, let me get this straight...you're a vampire, a vampire's Enforcer, and you're involved with this other guy. This Vampire Lord of yours. You're having sex with him."

"Well, he is my master, so...yeah."

"Because of these zombie fairies."

"No, there were zombie Poppets first and then evil fairies later on," Cesar explained. "Zombie Poppets and evil fairies. But no zombie fairies...at least, not yet." He laughed far too nervously.

"And you killed the zombie Poppets and the fairies."

"Just the zombie Poppets. The fairies were killed by my master and his werewolf."

"Your master has a werewolf? Is he sleeping with the werewolf, too?"

"No," Cesar stated emphatically. "Absolutely not."

"Are you sleeping with the werewolf?"

"Are you kidding me? I wouldn't be caught dead within ten feet of one of those overgrown fleabags."

An Asian man at a table across from them gave Cesar a dirty look. Cesar assumed he was probably a werewolf and immediately felt bad about what he'd said.

"But you *are* sleeping with the guy. The vampire who made you."

"Not always," Cesar said in a small, hesitant voice. "I mean, it's sort of a casual thing...well, not *casual*, exactly, because I don't have casual relationships, but definitely infrequent..." He looked down at the knot he had put in his napkin and sighed. "Look, Alex, I know I should probably have leveled with you about this stuff before, but...it's really complicated."

"Sounds that way," Alex quipped.

"But...I mean...does it really matter? We talk about this stuff all the time online. You said you'd do anything to ensure the safety of same-sex marriage, people of two different colors, whatever..."

"Yeah, Cesar, marriage between two *people*," Alex said poignantly. "You're not people. You're dead."

A surge of anger made Cesar stand up. "The Vampire Bill passed two years ago. So according to the Constitution of the United States, I'm *people*." His wings rustled in a disconcerting way that made people in the cafe look nervous.

Alex quickly jumped to his feet as if Cesar might fly at him.

Cesar hesitated at the dreadful sight of fear blooming across Alex's face. Things were not going according to plan. He was about to say something to reassure Alex when sudden, chattering, automatic gunfire burst from the kitchen of the cafe.

A kitchen worker in stained cook's whites rolled through the bump doors and jumped to his feet, brandishing a Desert Eagle automatic. Turning toward the wildly swinging doors, he returned fire inside the kitchen.

It was pretty much the last thing Cesar ever expected to happen tonight.

"What the...?" he began but then became aware that a man was standing by his side—the tall, nondescript gentleman who had been sitting across from the Asian werewolf that Cesar had noticed earlier.

He was lean, with a chiseled, determined face. Not a young man, but he moved with lithe confidence. He wore a dark grey business suit and his dark hair was peppered with silver. He looked very everyman, neither remarkably handsome nor very ugly. He was the kind of man you would never notice in a moving crowd, except for his electric blue eyes, which were currently narrowed to burning steel slits.

"Move it!" the suited man roared, and Cesar scrambled under the table while the newcomer leaped onto the seat of his booth, using it as cover as he withdrew a huge, police-issue handgun from some hidden compartment under his suit jacket.

Holy shit! Cesar crawled out from under the table and scurried in a military crawl across the floor, pausing only to make certain that Alex was safe. Unlike Cesar, who had momentarily frozen, Alex had ducked under the table at the first signs of gunfire and taken cover. Good.

As soon as Cesar felt it was safe, he jumped to his feet.

Meanwhile, the man in the grey suit returned fire with his hand cannon, the sound deafeningly loud in the cozy little cafe. Bullets pinged off the woodwork and splintered the colorful pictures of

Krishna and Vishnu decorating the walls. Cesar could barely hear the customers over the chatter of gunfire as they screamed and scrambled to get out of the line of fire.

The man dressed like kitchen staff screamed something in a foreign language and aimed his gun at the Asian werewolf, dropping him in his tracks as the werewolf charged him in human form. The man in the grey suit didn't even flinch. He used both hands to steady his gun as he carefully took aim, squeezing off his shot as if he had all the time in the world.

He was a pinhole shot.

A bullet hit the man in dirty cook's whites in the upper part of his bicep. The shot spun him around but didn't disarm him, and the cook shouted something that Cesar didn't catch, then aimed his automatic at the man in the grey suit. He squeezed off a series of shots, and the man in the suit made a coughing noise and went over the back of the booth when one of the bullets caught him high up, near his heart.

He was brave but outmatched.

Cesar didn't think. Both the werewolf and the man in the suit were down. He knew the guy with the automatic had to be neutralized, and there was no one else in the room who could do it. He stood up and flew at the man with the gun, wings outstretched. The gun went off almost in his face, but the man was startled by the sudden and unexpected vampire attack and his shot went off-center.

Cesar felt the roar of a bullet or two as they tore through his side, but most of the rounds pulverized the wall behind him. He grunted at the pain and his eyes turned all black as his feeding teeth descended. He let out a rattling hiss and the man cursed and immediately pissed himself. Cesar grabbed his Desert Eagle. He wrenched back, and the gun, along with both of the man's hands, came with him in a startling crackle of bones and a burst of blood.

The gunman went down screaming and splashing blood everywhere. Cesar wondered what the hell he was going to do next, but right then, the Asian werewolf stood up. He'd been shot, but he was hardly down for the count. He told everyone to freeze and flashed his badge around just like in the movies.

Cesar threw the gun and the bloody pair of hands still attached to it away and went to sit at a corner table while a stream of backup police arrived. They, along with the werewolf, settled everyone down, took statements, and carted off the gunman bleeding all over the once fine carpeting of The Lotus Petal.

He sat there for a good fifteen minutes, wiping his bloody hands off on the table linens and waiting for the adrenaline rush to wear off. He knew he should probably get the hell out of there, but he was still shaking, and everyone had seen his face. Since there was a vampire registry in this city, he knew he wouldn't get very far.

Cesar breathed slowly in and out, in and out. He did a few mental exercises the way Edwin had taught him. When he was sure he had his bloodlust under control, he checked round the room, but Alex was gone. He guessed his heroic act of saving everyone hadn't won him over.

Around that time, the tall man in the grey suit came round. He looked hurt, limping, a hand pressing a spot under his coat, but at least he was alive.

Cesar sat up, surprised. "Hey, are you all right?"

The man in the suit moved his jacket aside so Cesar could see his torn-up shirt and the bulletproof vest he wore beneath it. "Special Agent Tommy Quinn," he said and reached for his wallet to show Cesar his badge. "I'm with the DEA. Sorry if I gave you a fright, young man. Didn't mean to push you about."

He stopped and looked Cesar over, realizing that maybe he wasn't a "young man," after all. You never could tell with vampires.

"I guess that must sound strange to you. Usually, you give others a fright, yes?" The man smirked at that, and Cesar noticed that when he talked too fast, he had a vague, decades-dead British accent.

"Funny," Cesar said, though he felt no humor. "But I didn't frighten you, apparently."

Special Agent Tommy Quinn shrugged. "My partner's a bloody werewolf and I fight drug kingpins like that opium dealer you took down. Frankly, not too much scares me anymore in this town."

"You should sit down," Cesar said.

Tommy Quinn looked interested. "Should I?"

"You're bleeding."

He touched the corner of his mouth. "Must have bit my lip. Does it bother you?"

Cesar shook his head. "I'm good."

Special Agent Tommy Quinn sat down and grabbed a cloth napkin, holding it to his sore and bleeding lip. Cesar reached for a water glass someone had left behind and pushed it forward.

"Thanks for doing that, mate," Tommy mumbled through the linen. Again, he looked Cesar over, this time with slightly more interest. "Are you sure you're all right? Can I get you a paramedic?"

The adrenaline had worn off, but Cesar continued to feel strangely wired. It was exciting, sitting there and talking to the Special Agent. He was even a little flattered by the man's concern.

A flare of pain caused Cesar to grimace. He rooted around his quickly healing wound before plucking out the bullets—three of them! His body was pushing them from his flesh even as he sat there, and they were starting to itch. He put the bullets, coated in vampire blood, on the table between them.

"Itches," he said, and smiled a little goofily.

Special Agent Tommy Quinn of the DEA laughed.

He was cute when he laughed, Cesar decide. He realized they just might be very good friends before the night was through.

***

"No means no, pup," Malcolm Whitby said just before he punched the punk in the face.

The kid flew through the wall of the tavern where Malcolm and his mates were drinking beer and landed somewhere in the back room where the pool tables and pinball machines were set up. But the punk didn't stop there, crashing into a pool table, knocking the Budweiser lamp askew, and tumbling over the edge.

One of the young guys who took many of the same classes as Malcolm turned to him and said, "Jesus, Malc!" and then made a hasty retreat while one of the servers reached for the phone to call for the police. This being a Friday night, he and Malcolm, along with some of their friends, had dropped by the popular college hangout after a long week of classes. They'd spent most of the evening talking about their upcoming finals or the rave on Saturday. Then the young punk showed up.

Malcolm knew he was trouble just from the look of him. Like Malcolm, he was big and burly. Like Malcolm, he wore a long leather coat, but also a gang bandana. He walked with a swagger. None of these things made the punk inherently disagreeable in Malcolm's book. But when he started to harass one of the bar girls, Malcolm decided to intervene. He finished his beer, got to his feet, walked to the punk, and punched the guy straight into the next room.

Now, Malcolm waited. He stood just over seven feet, his half-plaited hair falling raggedly to his shoulders while he watched the slowly swaying Budweiser lamp cast shadows across the back room.

The guys in the bar stood wisely back while the girls looked like they wanted to jump his bones. It was flattering, but Malcolm was only worried about what the punk would do next.

Then someone—some *thing*—issued a long, loud belly growl from behind the pool table, and everyone currently in the room backed out as the floor faintly vibrated with the noise. The bartender stopped dialing 911 on the bar's old rotary phone and dropped the receiver.

Malcolm stayed as he was, a mountain of black leather that would not be moved as he faced the intruder. Again, a low, rattling growl echoed out over the small, dim room. But, this time, it came from Malcolm, and it sounded like a muffler being dragged across asphalt.

Although a punk had flown across the pool table and landed in a dark corner, what stood up now was anything but that. The huge, bulky, hunchbacked creature was nearly eight feet tall and covered in wiry grey fur. It looked neither human nor animal, though its snout was filled well beyond capacity with teeth as large as a dinosaur's, and its claws clicked together like giant ceramic hooks. The sound of bones breaking, popping, and resetting themselves as it shifted filled the room like kindling on an open fire. Rolling its bloodshot eyes ceilingward, it roared defiantly at Malcolm.

Malcolm stood unfazed...and then, just for the hell of it, he began to laugh. "You're naught but a pup, lad. A beta, at best. Who is your alpha?"

The creature ignored the taunt and moved forward, walking on its knuckles like a giant ape. It seemed cautious at first, but then it lunged at Malcolm with remarkable agility.

Long before the werewolf reached him, Malcolm moved like greased lightning, meeting the werewolf halfway across the room. The creature howled in anguish as Malcolm snagged its furry throat in one enormous and suddenly beclawed hand. And even though the creature in its current form towered over Malcolm by a good foot, it whimpered like a hurt kitten.

"I asked ye a question, lad," Malcolm bellowed, bearing his own teeth, which were suddenly as big as scythes in his mouth. He flashed his stormy greenish eyes at it.

The creature rolled its terrified gaze to meet Malcolm. It squeaked out a response in a voice neither man nor animal and then promptly pissed on the floor at Malcolm's feet.

Malcolm looked down at the urine stains on his cowboy boots, growled with disapproval, and casually threw the werewolf into the nearest wall.

"Scamper back home, pup," he said in a soft, reasonable voice, "and tell ye master that the Werewolf of Whitby doesn't take kindly to threats. If he has something to say, he may say it to me face."

Whimpering, the werewolf tottered and then rushed for the back door, crashing through it with a splinter of wood. Beyond that came the sounds of garbage cans clanking as it barreled through them and into the street, followed by the screeching of cars and a scream or two as passersby darted out of the way of the retreating werewolf.

Malcolm casually returned to the bar and ordered another round of Hair of the Dog from the Wood, the only ale in the bar that came close to good English stout. The girl he had saved came over to ask Malcolm to sign her forearm as if he was a celebrity. She also asked him if he had a girlfriend, which he did not.

***

"Dear god, Edwin...!" Eliza cried and clutched the bedclothes around her in great swaths as Edwin drove her crazy with his tongue and a little nibble of teeth in just the right places. He knew what she liked. "Are you going to do it? When are you going to do it?"

"I'll do it when you stop asking, lovey."

He kissed and loved on her as if it was their first time. She was so warm and alive, and he wanted to revel in his wife's aliveness since it would be the last time for them.

Tomorrow, she would be just as cold as he, and though the sex would be just as good, maybe even better, it would also be different. She would be his Heir, his creature. His responsibility, just as Cesar was.

She told him to bite her.

He ran his open mouth over the delicate column of her throat. He sensed her pulse beating there like the wings of a butterfly. He tasted her blood even through the thin sheen of her skin. He closed his mouth over her pulse, fully meaning to bite into it as he had never bitten her before—

—but someone pounding insistently on the front door downstairs stopped him.

Edwin paused, his teeth denting her skin, and Eliza issued a growl of frustration. "Keep going, Edwin. Make me yours. Make me your Bride."

And he tried to...but the knocking only grew more insistent. The visitor was now slamming his fist on the door and yelling something angrily, and no one else was home to answer the door.

Bloody wanker!

As much as it pained him, he released her and sat back. "I better find out what's going on."

Eliza groaned as she turned to face him. "Do you have to?"

"Won't be a moment, love." He cupped her face and kissed the side of her nose. "Keep it warm for me."

Grabbing up his dressing gown, he darted with nearly preternatural speed from their bedroom.

* * *

When the shouting started, Eliza, alerted, reached for her discarded robe, slipped her arms into it, and started downstairs.

Down in the foyer, Edwin was saying, "You must be bloody kidding me!"

"I have the warrant here, Mr. McGillicuddy."

"It's *Lord* McGillicuddy, and I don't bloody care what kind of paper you have!"

The police officer in the doorway muttered something unpleasant under his breath.

Eliza frowned as she came up behind Edwin. "What's all this about?"

Edwin stood blocking her while a big, burly police officer dangled an arrest warrant in his face. Three more officers stood behind him as if they were all afraid that Edwin would put up a fuss. Edwin looked decidedly pale—or paler than usual, anyway.

"Go upstairs, Eliza," Edwin said, staring at the collection of men. His voice was short and commanding. Not like Edwin's at all. "Now."

"No! What's going on?"

"Upstairs, Eliza, now!"

"No!" she insisted, trying to squirm past him.

"Ma'am," the first officer said in a grim, no-nonsense voice, "I have a warrant for the arrest of the Poppet Alisa Book, the property of Lord Michael Summersfield. You are Alisa Book, correct?"

The words hit her like softballs, rendering her mute for a moment. They both knew this day might come—the day she was discovered to be a runaway Poppet. Lost property. A vampire's glorified sex doll. But after all they had been through, and in her tyrannical desire for freedom, she had somehow convinced herself that that day would never arrive.

She stuttered on a response. "I most certainly am not!" She had to force her voice out. "My name is Mrs. Eliza McGillicuddy, and I am the wife and Courtesan of Lord Edwin McGillicuddy…"

The big officer pulled forth a small silver device shaped like a makeup compact. But when he opened it, it revealed a cone of light and a hologram of the woman in question.

It was she, Eliza, though the rendition was from a few years ago. She barely recognized the thin, cringing, waifish girl she had been: Alisa Book, the Courtesan of Lord Michael Summersfield. She had changed so much that she barely recognized herself.

"Edwin…" she began in a panic, grabbing his arm with both hands as tears sprang to her eyes. " *No!* Edwin, don't let them take me…!"

And he tried to do just that. He dragged her back, but the officers muscled into their home, waving iron bobbies in Edwin's face, weapons quite effective at killing vampires, though it hardly fazed him. He got her to the foot of the steps and was pushing her up hem before the big officer took the baton to him, staving him over the head before ramming his iron weapon under Edwin's chin, pinning him to the wall of the townhouse—*their* home, the home they had made together.

Edwin choked and began to burn. He let go of her arm. One of the other officers pulled her around, pinning her arms behind her back and snapping a pair of chainless cuffs around her wrists even as she screamed for them to let her go.

Her distress galvanized Edwin and, wild-eyed, he began to resist, which resulted in the remaining officers closing in on him with their awful iron bobbies, their arms rising and falling over her husband's prone form as they beat him to the floor.

Eliza screamed and fought all the way to the police cruiser parked in the curb outside.

| ii |

London, England, 1824

The lad sitting hunched on the floor of the stone cell was seventeen or eighteen years old, by Lord Henry Foxley's estimation. He was tall and lithe and had that scraggly, underfed look that Foxley had come to associate with the commoners of this land. His clothing was much like the boy himself—dirty, torn, and haphazardly patchworked together.

According to the story Foxley had gotten from the bailiff, the lad worked at a whorehouse. He watched over the doxies for the master of the house and probably did some light prostitution himself. He had killed a bloke in a hand-to-hand skirmish only the day before.

Such things were quite common in this realm, but how he had killed the man had piqued Foxley's interests. The boy had killed a powerful judge using the bridle and riding crop the judge had been using to discipline his doxy. When the girl's cries had grown too loud, the lad had intervened. He had used the riding crop to beat the man to near unconsciousness, then squeezed the life right out of him using the reins of the bridle as a garrote, his rage so great that he had actually broken the man's neck in the process.

Foxley had gone to see the mutilated remains just to confirm the story. The bloke was an overfed mountain of a man of over three hundred pounds. The lad who had killed him was less than half his weight. Foxley was bloody impressed!

"You are he?" Foxley asked with some interest. "The man to be hanged this evening?"

The lad sat there, clutching his updrawn knees, staring right through Foxley. He said nothing in response and seemed to be lost in a fugue state.

"What did it feel like to kill a man with your bare hands, lad?" Foxley persisted. "Did you enjoy it? Did you come whilst doing it?"

No response even to feign outrage. Foxley was afraid the lad was of such low intelligence or was perhaps in such a state of shock that he would never speak again. But then the lad lifted his head, and Foxley saw the eyes of the murderer to be hanged tonight.

Beneath the curtain of his unwashed, dirt-matted hair of indeterminate color, those eyes were cunning and of such a startling, unnatural wolf-amber, like fire behind church glass, that they seemed unnatural. Dark, unhealthy rings lurked beneath the lad's eyes, giving him an undead look. Foxley decided he liked the lad's eyes very much.

He was much too thin, of course—half-starved, really—but there was a wiry strength about him that appealed to Foxley's aesthetic.

"You ain't alive. Farking corpse," the lad said, slurring his words through his Cockney accent so badly that Foxley had to strain to understand him.

Foxley laughed at the boy's audacity. "The same could be said of you, lad, in approximately..." He consulted his pocket watch for dramatics. "...two hours."

He expected to see fear, horror, the reaction of a sane man about to die, his life cut off so early on that he never even saw his twenties. But the lad behind the bars was not sane. He didn't look afraid, only resigned, tired. Tired of life. Tired of being hungry and hopeless. Tired of struggling. Tired of trying.

Foxley inhaled the foul stench of the prison and sifted a myriad of information through his senses. The lad was young, strong, and certainly not hard on the eyes. He would clean up beautifully—assuming Foxley cared enough to work through the layers of the city's grime. But he was almost finished already. If the hangman's noose didn't take his life tonight, the syphilis that he'd picked up in the whorehouse most certainly would, and not in some very distant future. He had two, three years, tops, by Foxley's estimation. Starvation and the toxicity of this city would erase the lad as if he had never existed at all.

Foxley gave it approximately two seconds of thought before making his decision—a snap decision on his part, but he felt in his gut it was the right one. "Would you like to live forever?"

The boy laughed. It was a hard, contemptuous sound at least a decade older than his years. His thin shoulders shook, and then he began to cough hoarsely. Foxley scented the blood in the lad's sputum and imagined his disease slowly eating its way through his young body—unknown to the lad, of course.

The lad wiped a drop of blood off his broken lips. "You offering, guv?"

Foxley leaned against the bars of the cell and smiled nicely, being sure not to show any teeth. "What do you think?"

"I think you're a farking kid playing. Some waif in fancy dress."

Foxley smiled widely at that. The lad caught the gleam of his teeth and flinched noticeably. "Oh, my child," he said with facetiously large eyes. "If only you knew. I'm older than this structure." He rapped on the ancient stone wall of the jail. "Older than this nation. I was alive ten thousand years before your primitive, red-haired, flesh-eating ancestors ever crawled out of the bogs and cooked their first meat. And I'll be here ten thousand years after England falls."

The lad finally looked afraid. Foxley had gotten his attention. Good.

He continued by saying, "I've sailed countless seas. I've conquered a billion people. I've killed and consumed a million more. One day, I will be a million years old. Ten million. A billion. I will outlive this land, this planet, this reality that you know. Then, one day, I shall go to the stars and conquer other people, other nations, other realities."

The lad shivered at his words.

"I am impervious, unstoppable." Foxley smirked. "I am time itself. And, tonight, I am your god…or the closest thing you're ever likely to get to one." He paused to let that sink into the lad's hard and uneducated head. "Maybe one day you, too, can be twelve thousand years old. A godling standing at my side, conquering nations, bending human beings to your will. Why not consider it? What else have you to do with yourself?"

Foxley left then, returning a mere ten minutes before midnight, when the hangings were scheduled to begin. The lad was standing at the bars now, his eyes narrowed with suspicion as he considered Foxley's offer.

"Why me?" he asked at last.

Foxley brushed invisible lint from his tailcoat. "Well, it certainly isn't your level of education, of which you have none. Or the way you smell, like a dog that has rolled in its own shit. Do you want the truth? Of course you do. Then the truth is shall be." Foxley leaned forward and clutched the bars of the cell.

The lad shifted back, clearly horrified by the unnatural sight of him.

Foxley licked his lips. "You're young and beautiful, and I love young and beautiful things. That's the main reason. The most important reason. But you're also a remorseless killer, and I like things that kill without remorse. I like owning them. I like using them."

For the first time, the lad looked less sure of himself, his swagger failing. He grew paler still if that was even possible in this cold, soulless city of white-skinned, starving people. "Is that what you'd have me do? Kill?"

Foxley let the moment linger on. Around them, the prisoners to be hanged prayed or cried for their mothers or otherwise committed themselves to their final absolutions. And then: "I would have you do whatever I choose. That's the deal, my small, trembling child. When you become mine, you're mine forever. I'll do with you whatever I wish."

He wet his lips with the tip of his tongue, enjoying the pale look of horror washing over the lad's face. He even touched the crude wooden cross under his ragged shirt, as if that would or could save him.

Foxley knew he looked small and harmless until he smiled. Until then, he was the young, blond, grey-eyed ragamuffin. And then, when his victims saw that ageless, godlike look—that look that said they would die, and not swiftly and not painlessly at his casual hands —they usually shit themselves just before they gave in. Some men had gone mad just looking on Foxley, the unnatural juxtaposition of a youthful face and ancient, reptilian eyes.

But not this one. He looked at Foxley defiantly, a young man who had stared into the face of death too many times to care one way or another. Foxley liked that about him, too. It had been centuries since anyone had dared to go toe to toe with him.

"Do we have a deal?" he asked.

The lad didn't answer at first. He just watched as the Head Executioner took a large, burly fellow from the cell across from his and walked him out to the town center where he would be hanged for the entertainment of the crowd. Foxley knew this child he was speaking to was wondering why he hadn't chosen that man, as tall and strong as he was. Foxley waited. Despite his great size, he screamed and cried to God the whole way. He threw himself to the dirt floor and offered to give himself over to the Head Executioner if the man would only grant him one more hour, one more minute...

Foxley paid the man's dramatics no mind. He was not here for that sick, pathetic creature. He wanted the beautiful, heartless murderer standing just beyond the black iron bars. Suddenly, he wanted this one very much...and he always got what he wanted.

He waited and watched, his eyes pinned to the starving lad with the wolf eyes. The lad watched as the condemned man was led away. He touched the wooden cross around his neck once more and then turned to him. "Aye. All right. Whatever you want, guv."

"Excellent," Foxley said. "You'll make a lovely Heir, my sweet. And one day you may even be my Enforcer, perhaps a Lord yourself." He slid his hands over his waistcoat and up his throat to his lips as a myriad of possibilities flitted through his imagination. Foxley had a very vivid one, indeed.

"Your name, lad," he commanded. He could taste the young man's blood already in the back of his throat.

The rangy child swallowed hard, his Adam's apple bobbing. Foxley smelled the fear on him, the terror of entering unto this death-in-life, but it was already too late. He had made his decision to be damned and live rather than to be damned and die. Foxley knew he was not the type to renege on a contract.

Parting his cracked and nervous lips, he said, "My name is Edwin Oliver Wodehouse McGillicuddy."

* * *

Two minutes after Tommy let Cesar into his apartment, Cesar had Tommy up against the wall of his flat over the barbershop on

Delaney Street (Tommy said he'd gotten an excellent deal on it) and was contemplating eating the man alive.

Tommy breathed out a belated, "Oh dear," and then could say no more as Cesar started kissing his throat and gently nipping at the tender, jumpy skin under Tommy's chin.

Cesar had spent perhaps half a minute scanning Special Agent Tommy Quinn of the DEA's apartment—it was a clutter of old furniture rubbed raw with use, dusty knickknacks, framed pictures, and piles of unfolded laundry—and the other half deciding what to do with Tommy.

The force of the collision knocked Tommy into the wall by the bookcase, shaking the books and collectibles and knocking some stuff down. Tommy didn't seem to mind. He groaned and hooked his fingers into Cesar's shoulders, which caused Cesar to ease himself back momentarily.

"Sorry," he said breathlessly. "It's been a while. Didn't mean to scare you."

"It has been a while," Tommy agreed, looking pleasantly surprised. "But I'm not scared."

"Good." Cesar smooshed the man against the wall, cupped his face, and kissed him, but the pressure of Tommy's rig got in their way.

"Sorry about that."

"And here I thought you were happy to see me," Cesar joked as Tommy unclipped some buckles and struggled out of his DEA-issued shoulder holster. He gently set it and his firearm on a nearby desk.

"Try again," Tommy said, and Cesar did.

Cesar groaned. "You *are* happy to see me."

Tommy laughed. He had a deep, faintly mocking laugh. The laugh of a man who had seen much and suffered more. Cesar decided he liked it as much as the rest of him. He kissed along Tommy's jawline, then attacked his throat once more, kissing and licking a path to his ear. Tommy tasted like aftershave, honest sweat, and blood...life. He nuzzled into the man's warm skin.

"Bloody Christ, you don't fool around!" Tommy groaned, skittering uncertainly in the mess of books gathered around their ankles.

To save Tommy's balance and pride, Cesar grabbed him and turned, propelling him back until they reached the opposite wall of Tommy's cramped little living space, where an old, nicked secretary squatted in one corner. It was covered with unopened mail and sported a lovingly framed picture of a much younger Tommy and a pretty young woman. Both of them were dressed in late 1970's wedding attire. Cesar pushed Tommy down, cupped his cheeks, and kissed him hungrily.

Tommy tasted like bad cop coffee and peppermint and heat and life. He was delicious.

As they made out, Cesar's attention fell upon the wedding picture again. "Pretty girl," he said as Tommy kissed his way along his jaw, making him groan in delight.

"Maggie. We were together thirty-two years," Tommy managed in gulps of breath. He ran his fingers up and down Cesar's back, exploring his vampire wings straining under his suit jacket. "She died four years ago."

"Sorry. Is this awkward for you?"

Tommy looked up at him, his stormy grey eyes sincere. "No. I loved Maggie. Nothing we do here tonight will ever erase my memories of her...or my love." He slid his hands around Cesar's hips. Cesar could tell the man was learning his way around vampire physiology.

"Have you ever...?" Cesar stopped at the awkwardness of the question. "What I mean to say is..."

"Have I ever been with a man? In college, many, many years ago. And only briefly."

"I was going to say a vampire, but yeah...that, too."

"I've never been with a vampire. This is a new experience for me."

"But you're not afraid."

"Should I be?" Tommy asked, drawing back.

Suddenly, with just a few words, Tommy was transformed into more than a simple lay, a one-night stand to feed Cesar's insatiable hungers. He was a man, a husband, a widower, someone who had had dreams, a life.

"So, why a vampire now?" Cesar asked in return.

Tommy was silent a long moment as he considered, and then, "I...don't know. It was time." He pulled Cesar close. "Any more interrogation questions, my dear, or can we just fuck already?"

Later, Cesar decided to be more upfront than he had been with Alex. "Yes, I'm younger than you," Cesar explained when they were lying together in Tommy's unmade bed. "I was made a vampire two years ago when I was twenty-four years old. I'm twenty-six now, but I'll always look twenty-four. I'm also the Enforcer of the vampire who made me. No, you can't catch vampirism by sleeping with a vampire. No, I won't hurt you...unless you ask nicely." He glanced at Tommy with a gleeful smile. "If you have any other questions, Special Agent..."

"No," Tommy laughed, "I think that's everything." He seized Cesar by the cheeks and kissed him passionately, running his tongue fearlessly over Cesar's sharpened eyeteeth. "If you're like this on the first date, my fanged friend, I can't wait to see what our second one is going to be like."

Cesar glanced around at the mess they had made of Tommy's flat. He smiled evilly. "I'm not sure the room will survive it."

* * *

"She's quite beautiful. And graceful. She dances ballet perfectly, sings opera, and she can even crochet. I think you'll find her quite to your taste," Miss Gracey, the headmistress of the Pine Valley Scholomance said.

The older Poppet giggled nervously like a coy schoolgirl when she realized she'd made an accidental funny. *Quite to your taste. Oh my!* She walked quickly and confidently down the quiet, antiseptically clean halls of the Scholomance, trying to keep up with her guest, Lord Michael Summersfield. He didn't look at her at all, but Miss Gracey periodically stole glances at the tall Vampire Lord at her side.

For a dead man, he looked quite alive. And delicious. He was slim and gorgeous (but, really, what vampire was not?) with soft, pointed features and long, graceful limbs. His hair was perfectly black and styled up to the minute, and his eyes were perfectly blue and brilliant in his lean, no-nonsense face. His dark grey power suit clung to every perfectly molded inch of his body, and the pure white wolfskin coat he wore over his shoulders Mafioso-style swung dangerously as he moved.

She usually preferred a more rugged type, but she knew how the Vampire Lords were. The old ones looked and acted like giant animated dolls. It was almost a fetish with them—to see who could look more perfect and fabricated, less like the human they once were and more like a beautiful caricature. It was something that had briefly bothered her when she first met Lord Summersfield in the head office. He was stiff and almost surreal (and, of course, she worried that the coat might be real werewolf fur—oh dear!), and his fingernails were rather long and his teeth uncut, but despite these things, she certainly wouldn't have complained if Lord Summersfield wanted to park his bedroom slippers under her bed.

He looked down at her with the bored, disinterested eyes of a true Vampire Lord, and Miss Gracey blushed and quickly looked away, her thighs squicking in a most unladylike fashion! There was a rumor that Lord Summersfield was empathic. He was not able to pick up on actual thoughts, but he was nonetheless sensitive to emotions and intentions. She dearly hoped she wasn't being obvious! He was very good-looking, but also an important patron of theirs, and Pine Valley, located in upstate Vermont, only produced young Courtesans and Courtiers of the first water for Lord Summersfield's Court. It wouldn't do to ruin their very lucrative arrangement!

"Right this way!" Miss Gracey said, hurrying on ahead.

She felt both disappointed and relieved when they finally reached Miss Dahlia's room. This was always a moment of great expectations for Miss Gracey.

All Courtesans and Courtiers were born *in vitro* in the Biocell Labs. They were then each dutifully trained up to please his or her future Lord—and Miss Gracey was no exception to that rule. But unlike almost all Poppets, Miss Gracey's mind had been "misdesigned" (the polite terminology) by the ones who created her. When her Lord discovered she could make her own decisions without consulting him, he had sent her back to the Scholomance posthaste. Miss Gracey was then stamped as "damaged goods."

Poppets returned to the Scholomances where they had been trained seldom came to good ends, and Miss Gracey's choices had been limited, at best. She was either to be used as genetic stock and/or spare parts in a lab or they would need to find some position for her. Miss Gracey, being the resourceful type, made certain her predecessor, Headmistress Adeline, took an unfortunate tumble down a long flight of stairs. Thus, Miss Gracey became the new

Headmistress of the Pine Valley Scholomance at the ripe old age of twenty-one. She had held the position for over ten years, and she had helped to train up legions of young Courtesans and Courtiers to better serve their vampire patrons.

She laughed nervously as she unlocked the door with her master set of keys. "Here we are!" she called brightly.

Miss Dahlia's room was done up in great swaths of white—white curtains, white carpet, and a massive, four-poster bed with fluffy white valances. One whole wall of the room sported a mural of a spring garden, complete with hummingbirds and bees fluttering predictably around pale, almost anemic, pastel flowers. All of Miss Dahlia's dolls and toys were white, as were most of her clothes. It was a strange predilection on the girl's part, but one Miss Gracey had indulged, as it made her more manageable—not that Miss Gracey had trouble with any of her girls because she most certainly did not!

Miss Dahlia was seated at a round blond tea table in the shadow of the mural, dressed in a long, white chiffon dress, her hair done up in white ribbons. On the serving tray sat an ornate white and silver teapot and four tiny white porcelain teacups with tiny pink roses on them. Miss Dahlia, it seemed, was having "tea" with her dolls and her favorite stuffed dog, Mr. Snoop. It was her favorite pastime.

Miss Dahlia, on noticing her visitors, waved sweetly to Miss Gracey. "Have you come to have tea with my dollies, Miss Gracey?" she asked.

"Why yes, we have, my dear," Miss Gracey consoled her.

Miss Dahlia smiled. She was fourteen years old but had the mental capability of a child of four. She could not read simple words, nor even do a child's puzzle the way the other Courtesans and Courtiers could.

Lord Summersfield swished past Miss Gracey, leaving the stink of wolf fur in his wake, and approached the girl. Miss Gracey felt a catch of worry in her throat. Lord Summersfield moving through the virgin whiteness of the room toward the girl made her think of some great predator about to fall upon a small white dove lost in the shadows of a forest.

The Vampire Lord frowned with concern as he pulled off his kid gloves and bent to examine his Poppet-to-be by seizing her chin and jerking her face first to one side and then the other. "What's wrong with her? She seems overly simple."

Miss Gracey hurried to stand by Lord Summersfield's side. She stuttered on a response. "I thought you wanted her designed that way? 'The simpler the better.' Those were your instructions," she reminded him.

Lord Summersfield narrowed his electric blue eyes as Miss Dahlia instinctively flinched away from the vampire's pointed-nail touch. The girl clutched Mr. Snoop like a furry shield, squishing him against her ample bosom. She looked on the verge of crying. She had perfectly white porcelain skin and perfectly black hair. There was a natural blush on the apples of her cheeks, and she had huge eyes and huge breasts, all made to Lord Summersfield's specs.

Lord Summersfield crumpled his face as if he smelled something bad. "I expect so. But can we do something about her wardrobe? She looks like a child bride."

"But Miss Dahlia likes the white."

Lord Summersfield's thin lips pressed together with disapproval. "Well, I do not. Dress her in royal blue—or, better yet, red. I like red."

Miss Gracey was momentarily puzzled by Lord Summersfield's erratic manner, then reminded herself that it was a Vampire Lord's prerogative to change his mind. They, the Poppets, served an important function in society. They were the recipients of the Vampire Lords' passion, their lusts, and, sometimes, their darkest rage. It was their calling. Through their sacrifices, the rest of humanity could sleep easy in their beds, knowing no vampire would visit them or wreak havoc. In that way, the Poppets were the world's greatest sentinels. Without them, the world would not survive the vampires' endless, undying hungers.

Miss Gracey forced herself to smile cheerfully. "Perhaps you would like to see her dance, my Lord?"

Lord Summersfield looked less than enthused. But, before he could respond, his cell phone went off. Ignoring Miss Gracey and his new Poppet, who was now crying softly into Mr. Snoop's fur, he snatched it up out of some secret compartment in his suit and flipped it open.

He turned and stomped away from the two Poppets. "What is it? I'm indisposed at the moment."

He stood there, tall and stormy grey, and listened for several moments, his face showing no emotion. Only the very old ones could do that. Only the very old ones had so little humanity left in them.

Miss Gracey wrung her hands. She hoped Miss Dahlia's condition wasn't going to spoil their arrangement. If he refused Miss Dahlia, the Poppet would have to remain here, either to be recycled for genetic material or put to work in the Scholomance. And considering how simple Miss Dahlia was, she would likely be less than useless.

"Yes, all right. I shall be there as soon as possible" came Lord Summersfield's suddenly animate voice. "No...*no*, you will do *nothing* until after I've seen her."

Lord Summersfield snapped his cell phone closed and turned to face Miss Gracey, making her flinch with the hungry, intense expression on his face. "Have the girl and her belongings loaded onto my Hummingbird and sent to my estate. I have business to attend to in New York."

"My Lord?" Miss Gracey asked with cautious optimism. "You will take her, then?"

"Yes...whatever." For the first time, real emotion seemed to animate Lord Summersfield's stone-white face as he glanced at a distant wall—not seeing the wall but something far beyond it. She detected a lust and excitement so powerful that it made Miss Gracey cringe to see it. "It seems the police have found Alisa Book!"

***

Cesar came awake quickly and decisively. He knew it was very early morning, not quite sun-up. His internal vampire clock had likely roused him even though it was unnecessary. With UV protection blanketing the city, he could move about anytime day or night without the fear of the sun setting him ablaze.

He sat up, surprised with himself. He'd had lovers in the past, of course, in the time before he was a vampire, but he'd never actually *slept* with any of them. He never liked the idea of staying over at a stranger's home and waking up in an unfamiliar bed, but this morning was different. He rolled over, feeling happy and satisfied, and reached blindly for Tommy beside him.

He was gone.

Cesar frowned, wondering if he'd only imagined last night...their laughter, their conversation...their love...and he immediately turned over and scanned the room.

Tommy's bedroom was old and comfortable, full of all of the stuff that a married couple collects over the years—photographs, afghans, curtains, and furnishing long out of date. The idea made him sad. It made him wonder if he would ever have an opportunity to collect a house full of old useless things with someone one day.

A dangerous thought, he reminded himself. He wasn't so naïve as to believe he would just find someone one day as Edwin had, settle down, and have a family of his own. Despite being social creatures, vampires were mostly lonely and unhappy. They could have no children—not *real* children, anyway—and their relationships with humans, inhumans, and even other vampires were precarious, at best. Cesar was quickly learning why Edwin was so adamant about protecting Eliza. He had waited over two hundred years to meet someone like her, and he knew, just as Cesar did, that he would never find anyone like her again.

Tommy, dressed in pajamas and a robe, was perched in a window seat on the far side of the bedroom, a cup of tea in his lap. He was observing the street. The busy scurrying of New York cabs and cars burned like little fireflies in the early morning darkness. Glancing upward, he traced the contours of the airships and gyros in the distant skies with his finger on the windowpane, the floating ships winking with their own constellations of lights.

"Tommy?" Cesar's voice was a little hoarse, a little uncertain. "Is everything all right?" Perhaps he'd been too rough on the man last night...

"I love this city," Tommy said, sounding distant and dreamy. "I love that we get the national movie releases first, and I love the tree all lit up in Rockefeller Center at Christmas. And cheesecake in New York is the best in the world."

Cesar sat quietly, listening.

Tommy smiled. "We should do a midnight cheesecake run. That's so New York."

"I don't eat cheesecake," Cesar said, not without regret.

"That must be hard." Tommy turned and glanced at him with pity. "What's it like?" He sipped his tea. "Do you regret it, being what you are?"

Cesar thought about that. "Not really. My Lord is a good man. I got very lucky. I guess I just exchanged one set of complications for another."

Tommy nodded as if he truly understood. "My partner Tanaka talks like that. Not about being a werewolf, mind you, but about being a DEA Agent. The long hours, the wife never knowing if you're coming home in one piece." He pressed his lips together. "Do you love him...your Lord?"

Cesar didn't even have to think about that. "He's my Lord. He's in my blood. I suppose he's more a part of me than anyone will ever be." Then he realized what he'd said and added, "But...what I am doesn't limit me to just loving him. I mean, he's married and very happy, yet we manage to care about each other anyway. I supposed that doesn't make any sense to humans."

Tommy smirked. "Vampires are not naturally monogamous creatures. No, I get that. I think it's an important adaptation of their —of your—great longevity."

With the dull glow of the early morning city behind him, Cesar could almost see the sharpness of the bones in Tommy's face. He didn't think much about it. He just said the first thing that came to mind. "You're sick, aren't you?"

Tommy raised his eyebrows. "Is that a vampire power of yours?"

"Not really. I had an uncle who was sick, my mother's brother." He swallowed. He'd never talked to anyone about this, not even Edwin. "It was the reason my mom came here to America from Guerrero before I was born. That's in Mexico, by the way, one of the poorer regions. She brought her brother here to America for treatment for his HIV. That's how she met my dad here. She worked as his cleaning lady. So I know when folks are sick."

"What happened to your uncle?"

Cesar rubbed at the back of his neck as he remembered. "He hung on for a few years, but he was too sick. After I was born, Mama and I would visit him whenever we could get away from my dad."

"Your father didn't approve of you seeing your uncle?"

"He didn't approve of my uncle being gay." Cesar swallowed hard. "Uncle Luis died when I was six years old. I was there when it happened. I was with him."

"That must have been very hard for you. You're awfully brave."

"Not really," Cesar admitted. "He was my mom's only family. I wanted to be there for her…and for him."

Tommy nodded. He returned his attention to the window. He was silent for a long time. "It's in my pancreas," he finally said.

Cesar swallowed again. Hard. His heart was beating very fast. "Are you getting treatment?"

Tommy laughed. "My friend, you don't recover from pancreatic cancer."

Cesar shuffled forward in the bed so he was resting at the foot of it. "You could be treated. It could extend your life. What have the doctors said?"

Tommy waved it off. "Six months without treatment. Nine months with. But who wants to spend three months of your life being systematically poisoned by chemo and radiation?"

Cesar felt his pulse jump. "Tommy…"

"Well, there you go, with your fear and your pity. And people like you wonder why people like me don't want to talk about it."

Tommy had a point. "I'm not afraid of these things."

"No, I suppose you wouldn't be, would you?"

"I'm already dead."

Tommy guffawed at that. "I forgot. You seemed so…alive tonight."

Cesar ignored the obvious double entendre. "Did I hurt you? You should have told me. I could have hurt you."

"You didn't hurt me."

"Is that why you wanted to be with a vampire? Do you want me to do something for you?"

Tommy looked at him directly, unblinking. Bravely, like his Uncle Luis. "I wanted to be with a vampire tonight because that vampire was you."

They watched each other from across the room.

Finally, Cesar asked, "Does it hurt?"

"It's rather dull and uninteresting, if I'm being honest."

"There must be something you can do..."

"I'm tired, Cesar. I'd like to come back to bed now, please."

"Then come back to bed."

"You won't talk about this anymore? Because I'm tired of the subject."

"I won't talk about it unless you want to talk about it."

"Excellent." Tommy stood up and set his cup of tea down on the window ledge. His smile was sad and more than a little lustful as she shucked off his robe. "Cesar, stay with me tonight. Today. We'll make love again, and then I want some cheesecake. And we won't speak of all of this rubbish unless I choose to. And you won't be sad, and I won't be ill. Understand?"

"Yes," Cesar agreed as he welcomed Tommy back under the covers. He rubbed himself against Tommy's warmth, wrapped his wings around him, and felt a small part of his heart die inside him.

* * *

"I want to see my wife immediately!" Edwin demanded, virtually climbing over the desk of the sergeant on duty at the police station.

The sergeant looked bored by Edwin's theatrics. "I told you. She's not here. Besides, the Poppet is *not* your property. Preliminary DNA scans show she has identity nanobots that indicate she belongs to Lord Summersfield." He turned his computer screen so Edwin could see the report he'd been reading off. The desk sergeant looked both bored and annoyed by the whole affair. "Perhaps you can speak to Lord Summersfield about the property..."

"She's not property!" Edwin tried to grab the man, but Malcolm Whitby, standing behind him, threw his whole arm around Edwin's chest to slow his momentum. And even then, it jerked him Edwin immediately released his hold on the desk. Despite Malcolm's rough manhandling, Edwin didn't want to accidentally hurt his Dog of War, pull his arm out of the joint or anything. The enormous werewolf in dusty black leather was loyal to a fault, and he knew, under it all, that Malcolm meant well.

But even Malcolm's intervention wasn't enough to incite the cops—no lovers of inhumans, Edwin knew. Two soldiers in the room with them pounced forward, prepared to restrain Edwin. Letting go of his master, Malcolm stepped between him and the charging cops and easily palmed the faces of the officers closing in on Edwin.

The officers quickly backed off.

"Enough," Malcolm growled low, and both men slowly backed away, looking terrified and reprimanded. One grabbed his gun and pointed it at Malcolm, who refused to move out of the way. Malcolm being Malcolm, the big werewolf would happily die for him.

The desk sergeant stood up to break up the conflict, but he looked reluctant to make any move against the vampire and the werewolf standing in his station. Edwin, his eyes fully black now, bared his razor-sharp teeth at the man. It was taking everything in him to stop himself from ripping the bloody faces off these clowns.

The sergeant snorted in fear. "Git out of here, you fucking grotties."

Grotties. That was the more recent racial slur for the inhumans. Grotesqueries. Grotties.

Edwin sucked in a breath to get his impulses under control. Slowly, his eyes returned to normal, though he didn't move an inch. "She is my wife, you bloody git!" He stepped forward and saw the desk sergeant cringe. "Where is she? Where did they take her? Tell me at least that!"

After Edwin got the info from the officers, Malcolm took pains to guide his master from the police station without causing any incident that might get them arrested. Wise man. His eyes were cool and fierce as they stepped out together onto the street.

"We will get Miss Eliza back, my Lord," he promised, looking determined. "Make no mistake. We will rescue her."

* * *

Eliza huddled on a bunk in an isolated cell, watching the door. She had just recently been transferred to Lord Michael Summersfield's gyro, the *Marie Antoinette*. She would periodically smooth her nightgown down over her legs or otherwise tug at her shawl. Otherwise, she did not feel inclined to do anything but watch and wait.

The Chief of Police had given her the shawl when he realized his officers had pulled her from her home without even giving her a chance to dress properly. He looked extremely uncomfortable with the whole affair. He was a human being stuck in the middle of nasty vampire business, and it was clear he did not like it, that he considered this above his pay grade.

She had begged him to let her see Edwin before she was loaded onto a Hummingbird bound for Summersfield's ship, but he said that wasn't possible. He was obligated to return her as lost property to her vampire master—and post-haste. She figured he only wanted her out of his sight.

Lost property. Like she was a cell phone or a pocketbook. She almost felt sorry for him. Almost. She knew her presence was a disturbing reminder that some forms of legal slavery persisted in America.

After she arrived aboard Summersfield's ship, she was walked to a small room with an examination table and a one-way mirror. It reminded her uncomfortably of an interrogation room. There, a white-coated medical doctor from Biocell, the multi-billion dollar pharmaceutical company that designed Poppets for work down in Poppettown or for pleasure for Vampire Lords who could afford them, stepped in to speak to her.

He used small words and spoke slowly. She thought about calling him a wanker. That's what Edwin would say. But what good would it do? If Biocell realized there was something wrong with her brain, that the chemical lobotomy she should have been born with hadn't taken, they might take her back to the labs and do things to her. And if they learned about her abilities as a techkinetic, she would definitely go.

So, Eliza just kept her mouth shut and nodded at the appropriate times.

The doctor gave her a full body examination. She had forgotten how mortifying and dehumanizing such exams were—or maybe she just hadn't realized it all those years ago when she was a young Poppet at the Scholomance. By the end of it, she felt no part of her body was hers any longer.

After that, the doctor assured her that everything would be fine, that she would be well cared for and promptly returned to her master. She'd nodded, tried to look interested, and worked on not bursting into tears.

Now, she stared at the locked door, wondering what was next, wondering what she could do to escape—if anything. She was a techkinetic. She could spring every lock in the ship, create mass pandemonium, and escape...but escape *where*? They'd never let her get off the ship alive, especially if she showed them what she could do. They'd probably shoot her before she got to the loading bay. Her one real hope was that maybe Edwin could plead her case to the High Vampire Courts. All of that was in his wheelhouse, not hers. For the first time in her life, she had to trust that Edwin would save her.

She flinched when she heard the cell being unlatched. A nurse pushed it open. He looked cowed like a dog that someone had beat into submission. He stepped inside, muttering something apologetic under his breath, but then was pushed forcibly out of the cell by a tall, thin figure in a long, white wolfskin coat.

The moment the vampire was inside the cell with her, Eliza's breathing stopped, her body turned to lead, and her mind went blank with a mass of white static terror. She had to clench her legs closed or risk peeing herself with fear. Here was the living embodiment of all her nightmares. The one persistent shadow lurking at the back of her mind for the past three years. The one danger left unchallenged. The nightmare she could not bear to face.

The thing that owned her, body and soul. The thing that had made her, that had once bent her unmercifully to its will. The thing that had frightened her, scarred her, and changed her forever.

Lord Summersfield smiled hungrily. "Alisa," he said. "It's been a while."

| iii |

Six weeks later

"Hey, man, help a brother out?"

Cesar, surprised, looked over at the homeless man sitting under the eaves of a project on West Fifty-Seventh Street. The man smiled hopefully back at him and held out one grubby hand. He was a thin black man in his mid- to late-fifties, by Cesar's estimation, though it was hard to tell. He was probably much younger than he looked. Another derelict castoff of society. He was dressed in three coats, with a worn brown scarf coiled around his neck and a ragged watch cap pulled down to the level of his eyes.

Cesar looked around at all of the other New Yorkers passing in determined waves around him and wondered how these people—these humans—were able to look upon one of their own in such a deplorable state and feel nothing. They were treating him like a piece of landscape. But that was the essential difference between humans and vampires, he decided. The vampires mostly hated and envied each other, but they always had each other's backs in a firefight.

And then sometimes they didn't. Since Eliza had been taken from him, Edwin had first appealed, then pleaded, then finally threatened the High Courts to get her back, but it was all a big legal nothing burger. They kept telling him the same thing over and over: Michael Summersfield had commissioned Eliza. There were documents. Records. She belonged to him. But if Edwin wanted a Poppet, they could certainly arrange it. It just couldn't be Eliza.

Of course Edwin didn't want a Poppet. He wanted Eliza. But no one cared about what a minor Lord wanted—particularly one with no political or social pull.

"Chile...you got some change? I just wanna coffee," the homeless man said, sounding a little more desperate. "Promise I ain't buyin' no liquor with it."

"Y-yeah, of course." Cesar dug out a ten-dollar bill from his wallet and passed it to the man.

The bum snatched it up, but not before his hand touched Cesar's.

Cesar felt a strange spark, like a static electrical charge after crossing a scratchy rug. He jerked his hand back reflexively.

The bum grinned at him with brown stumps of teeth. "Thanks, man. You a real brother."

"I'm not your brother," he said, sounding more defensive than he'd meant to. He didn't know why, but he'd decided he didn't like the bum very much. Something about the man made the little hairs on the back of his neck stand up. He liked that the bum had touched him even less.

The incident, though not uncommon in this city, bothered him all the way home.

The townhouse seemed darker and quieter these days. Cesar went down the hallway, briefly glancing into the office where Eliza used to work, a spike of despair stuck deep in his heart like a thorn. He missed her terribly. He felt like one of his limbs had been ripped off, and, so far, nothing he or Edwin had done had made the slightest difference.

He found Malcolm in the kitchen, building a hero sandwich, heavy on the meat, for himself. "I'll have dinner done in a jiffy," he said and reached for the apron he kept on the hook near the stove. He wanted to try to keep a sense of normality in their little family. It was the only thing he could think to do, given the circumstances.

Malcolm turned, stuffing the sandwich in his mouth, and said, "No worries. I'm more than capable of looking after my own needs, lad."

Cesar stood there, trying to think of a suitable comeback. He had nothing. Given the situation, there was no joy to be had in irritating Malcolm, and he knew Malcolm felt the same way.

"All right," he said, giving in and putting the apron back.

Malcolm dusted some crumbs off his shirt and fixed his coat, the one he usually wore when he took his Harley out.

"Going out?" Cesar asked.

"Aye. A date."

Cesar considered that. It did not seem like a vary Malcolm thing to do, under the circumstances. They all knew how he felt about Eliza, and that no woman could compare in Malcolm's eyes. Maybe he was wrong?

Before Malcolm left the apartment in a swirl of long, black leather coat, Cesar said, "How is he doing?"

Malcolm shrugged one big shoulder. "How do you think?"

After he was gone, Cesar picked out a bottle of blood substitute from the refrigerator and went to sit in the dark of the sitting parlor for a half hour. When he'd sufficiently gathered his thoughts and courage, he stood up and prepared to face his master and ask for the biggest favor of his life.

* * *

Malcolm had lied to Cesar about his date. Well, not exactly *lied*. But he'd definitely taken the truth for a little ride round the bend.

The girl he had rescued from the werewolf had invited him to a pop-up rave—but only as a friend, seeing how she had a girlfriend. The rave was located in the basement of an old church in downtown Brooklyn, not far from the pub where Malcolm encountered the beta wolf. Although he was hardly in the mood to engage in merrymaking, he was also interested in learning more about the local pack the beta belonged to.

Malcolm didn't know what to expect when he arrived, but the rave reminded him of the many sumptuous fetes he had attended while he lived in the Court of Lord Ian and Lady Catherine Severn. There were colorful costumes, live music, food, and drink. The glass ball hanging over the dance floor made a mosaic over the faces of those dancing in the crowded, sweaty room. His college friends certainly knew how to party.

He felt shy at first, but that didn't last. The girl who had invited him pulled him into the circle of her friends and, soon enough, he found himself mingling, drinking, and generally enjoying himself like a soldier wolf who had died gloriously on the battlefield and gone to Valhalla to celebrate in the hall of the gods with Fenrir and Tyr. A beautiful human girl even taught him to dance; she said he was very limber.

For the first time in weeks, he found he was having the time of his life. And then he encountered another werewolf and everything changed.

* * *

"Mr. Snoop said he wants to speak to you, Alisa."

Eliza, sitting stoically in the ladies' parlor with her needlework in her lap, looked up from her latest project.

Dahlia stood in the doorway of the room, cradling her white plush dog. She was small and delicate like a little alabaster doll. She was staring at Eliza in that hopeful way she had, her eyes huge, blue, and doll-like.

Eliza set her petit point aside and said, "Is Mr. Snoop feeling all right tonight, Dahlia? She doesn't hurt anywhere?"

Dahlia had to stop and think about that. Of all of the Poppets who lived aboard Lord Summersfield's gyro, Dahlia was by far the prettiest...and the simplest. Even the other Poppets, not exactly rocket scientists, avoided her, which Eliza thought was pretty hypocritical of them. But life among Poppets was like that. There was no cohesion among creatures with few thoughts in their heads. The Poppets' chemical lobotomies wouldn't allow for organization or much contemplation. Eliza knew from experience that with time, they adopted a volatile, almost pack-like structure, like dogs trying desperately to climb to the top of the heap, though Eliza wasn't sure what the prize was supposed to be.

"Dahlia?"

Dahlia stared down at her feet. "Mr. Snoop's tummy hurts."

Eliza felt a spike of dread, followed by an equally powerful surge of hatred for Summersfield. "Does his tummy hurt enough to visit the sick bay?"

Before Dahlia could formulate a response, another of the Poppets, an older, smarter one named Nathalie, bullied past Dahlia and stepped into the room. "Alisa! I need to speak with you immediately!"

Eliza went back to her petit point. "I'm right here and there's no need to yell, Nathalie."

The girl stomped her feet angrily. She was tall, blonde, and willowy like some fairy princess. Summersfield had favored her for some time and it showed in both her ego as well as her contempt for the others. But now her status was in question. Dahlia was replacing Nathalie in his affections, and Nathalie had just enough brains to realize it—and a need to rage at someone because of it.

She stopped in front of Eliza's chair and slapped at her petit point. "You took my blue ball gown!"

"I did not take your blue ball gown," Eliza answered neutrally.

Nathalie leaned forward, her bright green eyes small, sharp, and mean. "I saw you looking at it! You took it, and now you're lying about it! You know that gown is our Lord's favorite!".

"I know no such thing, and I did not take your gown." Eliza knotted the row she had just finished and began a new one.

Nathalie slapped at her hands and Eliza dropped her needle. "Tell me where it is or so help me, Alisa, I'll scratch your eyes out!"

Eliza said nothing, only continued to watch the distraught girl. She couldn't find it in her soul to hate on Nathalie. It was like being cross with an abused pet that was misbehaving.

Nathalie made a move to lunge at her.

Eliza silently ordered the lights out in the room, which startled the girl. She slipped from her seat and came around Nathalie in the dark. She was standing behind Nathalie when she ordered the lights back on, and now, she had the girl in a safe and relatively painless restraining hold, an arm around her shoulders and another just below her waist to keep her from kicking or dancing backward onto Eliza's feet.

Nathalie screeched and tried to shake off Eliza's hold, but Eliza was larger and older than the girl, and her time on Earth had helped her to build up some muscle and fat, making her more powerful than any stick-thin Poppet who lounged around all day, looking pretty but atrophying from lack of exercise. Eliza released her hold across the girl's shoulders but twisted her arm behind her back, pinning it.

Eliza put her mouth close to Nathalie's ear. "I do not have your ball gown, and you will cease accusing me of theft or passing around gossip about me. You know absolutely nothing about me, girl, and be thankful for that!"

Nathalie whimpered in response.

"Now, you will return to your quarters and search for your missing gown. I'm sure you'll find it there, amidst your hundreds of other gowns." She turned and pushed the girl toward the door.

Nathalie stumbled a few steps before catching herself against the edge of a chair and spinning around. She looked ready to say something, but Eliza clenched her fist at her side and made the lights in the room flicker ominously. The girl glanced around, then fled, thoroughly spooked by Eliza's performance.

In retrospect, it was probably unwise of her to flaunt her power so. If Summersfield found out, god knows what he would do to her. But she didn't know how else to handle the constant catfights that broke out amidst the many jealous and insecure Poppets.

After Nathalie was gone, Eliza realized that Dahlia had slipped to the floor of the ladies' parlor and was clutching the wall, crying softly against the flocked Victorian wallpaper. Her dog lay on the floor, momentarily abandoned. Eliza had forgotten how much Dahlia hated the dark. It was always dark in Summerfield's quarters, and Eliza knew the girl would never fully recover from her first encounter with their Lord.

As if any of them could. She looked at the young girl, only fourteen, weeping and murmuring her comforting mantras against the wall, and was horrified to find she felt almost nothing. She had been here six weeks, and already her mind was turning to all static emptiness. She supposed it was her brain's way of coping with her situation, her mind turning off all emotion in order to prevent an overload. Staying strong and almost emotionless was the only way she would ever survive this ordeal.

She recalled her first day back aboard her master's gyro. Summersfield took her for a full tour of the ship, walking up and down corridors and in and out of rooms, pointing out all of the things he had changed while she'd been "lost on Earth." He'd kept his hand on her elbow, pinching her bones as if afraid she might bolt.

Eliza had looked blindly at the sumptuous, over-decorated rooms, saying nothing and trying desperately not to sob or shriek or fall to her knees. She didn't want to make a fool of herself. *If I can only retain my dignity, I can get through this. He can take my body and my blood. He can't have my dignity.*

Then they reached his personal quarters. Summersfield, looking like a dark, wrathful god in his charcoal business suit, his blue eyes fiery, and his face lean and carnivorous, dragged her into his bedchamber, the place she feared more than hell itself. He pushed her up against the wall, his big hand encompassing her throat, and started interrogating her about her years of freedom down on Earth.

Eliza made small noises of confusion. She couldn't answer any of his questions. She was too afraid.

He touched her then, and that, finally, broke her. She started screaming hysterically and wetting herself like a child as the sheer horror of her existence crashed down around her. Thankfully, her histrionics stopped him from asking her any further questions, though she was ashamed to admit she would have said anything if he would just stop *touching* her. With just a few strokes, he had reduced her to a mindless animal.

"Obviously, you were very well cared for by your…husband," he said, trying to sound concerned, though his voice dripped with ice. He looked her over critically. "I wonder. What did that Cockney bastard dog do with you the whole time?"

He shook her like a rag doll against the wall, his rage at Edwin substantial.

She started to fight then and instantly regretted it. It was the opportunity that Summersfield had been waiting for.

He backhanded her onto the bed. His blow packed incredible power, and Eliza actually blacked out from the impact of it. When she came to a few moments later, Summersfield was ripping her garments off her shoulder. Enraged, he bared his teeth at her and struck like a viper. His teeth went deep into her shoulder muscle. It was nothing like Edwin's love bite, and she screamed as Summersfield drank and drank. Blood loss quickly weakened her, and soon, she didn't care about the pain, or about the fact that he was probably killing her.

He didn't, though. Fate wasn't that merciful to her. Instead, he stopped and drew back, her blood pouring from the corners of his mouth and from between his viper teeth. It dripped all over her neck and face.

"Despite everything, you're still so sweet, Alisa," he growled, his voice barely human, his eyes all black and wild. "If you still had a blooding bracelet, I wouldn't need to be doing this to you. We'll need to look into that tomorrow, won't we?"

She moaned, unable to do anything but lay there and bleed.

"For now, though, you'll serve your master, Poppet." Then he was hurting her, subduing her. Eliza was too weak to fight, too weak to do anything but lay there and let the monster do what he wanted to her.

The memory of it made her sick. The following night, a technician from Biocell arrived to surgically attach a new blooding bracelet to her left wrist, not that the bracelet would keep Summersfield from biting her elsewhere. He didn't often use the bracelets that would have allowed him to feed off his Poppets from a sterile, eternally open wound without needing to bite them. Summersfield enjoyed feeding *au natural*, claiming the blood was sweeter when not filtered through technology.

She wondered if he would call her to his bed tonight. It had become her daily terror, the reason she feared the night. The constant feedings were making her dizzy and sick, and she knew she was making increasingly poorer decisions, like how she had handled the Nathalie situation.

When she bent to help Dahlia up, she felt a wave of dizziness. She hurt from her bruises and the multitude of half-healed bite wounds on her body. Her body couldn't produce enough blood to keep up with her master's demands. As a result, she felt constantly weak and depleted.

Tears sprang to her eyes. A part of her prayed that Summersfield chose another Poppet tonight, even though the thought made her feel terrible. She was stronger than the Poppets here. She could handle him well enough; she knew they could not.

"Come along, sweetie," she said, helping Dahlia to one of the chairs in the sitting parlor.

"Mr. Snoop!" Dahlia said with teary, panic-filled eyes. She had left her stuffed dog in the doorway.

The trip back to get Dahlia's dog left Eliza winded and aching. She sat down in a rocker next to the terrified girl who was now clutching her toy and talking to herself. She hung her head. "Easy, baby. See, your doggy is fine."

Dahlia sniffed and clutched the dog to her ample bosom. "Thank you for rescuing Mr. Snoop, Alisa. The other girls think you're mean, but I like you a lot." She started sucking her thumb.

Eliza sighed tiredly at the girl's revelation. Nathalie was behind all of this. It was obvious that she needed a long-term plan to deal with the girl, maybe by scaring her enough to back down. Then she realized that Nathalie wasn't the problem. The other Poppets weren't her enemy. None of them were hurting her.

"Jesus, I'm getting as bad as they are," she whispered under her breath. She clutched the armrests of the rocker. She had to get a handle on this. She had to learn to control her temper, to fight the animal growing inside. She wasn't Alisa the Pleasure Poppet. She was Mrs. Eliza McGillicuddy, wife of Lord Edwin McGillicuddy. She had to remember that.

"Edwin." It was a battle to keep the tears from pouring from her eyes. Edwin was a huge, open, bleeding hole in her heart that she could not deal with at present, not on top of everything else. As she was being dragged away from him, he had promised to find a way to free her, to get her home. But now, six weeks in, she found it was hard to keep the faith, and she was growing increasingly angry that she had let Edwin give her that hope.

"Who's Edwin?" Dahlia said, abandoning her thumb and her dog to look at Eliza with great attention. She and Dahlia had arrived aboard the gyro together, and ever since, Dahlia had developed an almost pathological attachment to Eliza. She wanted to be with her constantly, even sleep beside her at night. It made Eliza feel so very sorry for the girl. When she got out of here—if she ever did—how would Dahlia cope?

She smiled as serenely as possible at the girl. "Lord Edwin. He's a knight in a fairy tale, Dahlia. One that will come and rescue me one day."

"I've heard of fairy tales," Dahlia answered vacantly. She stared at the walls as she struggled to recall details. "I like the story about the mermaid. It reminds me of the fishy."

Eliza smiled. "*The Little Mermaid*," she said. It was a favorite of Dahlia's. She watched the movie over and over, especially when she was afraid.

"Can you go with me to see the fishy today?" Dahlia asked.

Eliza grimaced. She was in no condition to make the journey, but just seeing the joy it brought to Dahlia's eyes made her want to try. "We'll go after lunch. When I have more energy," she said.

"Yay, fishy!" Dahlia said, springing to her feet.

Later that day, she and Dahlia made the trip down to a lower level of the gyro. She wished she had her cane. Her stroke, as well as the constant blood loss, was doing her no favors, but Summersfield told her that first day that he wouldn't tolerate a crippled Poppet, and if she didn't learn to walk on her own, with grace and with style, he would recycle her for genetic material.

He was making her learn to walk without it, just as he was controlling all of her meals in his mad desire to make her as slim as possible. She hated it, hated the way it reduced her to a *thing*, a possession of no more value than anything else aboard his gyro. He treated his collection of exotic pets better.

Together, she and Dahlia took the glass elevator down to the floor where their master kept Moira in a huge tank in the center of one of the many ballrooms. Dahlia enjoyed the glass elevator, commenting on all the Poppets and ship personnel she saw along the way. Then the doors shushed open, and it was thankfully only a short walk before they reached the ballroom.

Moira's massive tank took up almost a quarter of the huge room. It was so large it operated as its own ecosystem, complete with kelp beds, coral reefs, and even a miniature castle that acted as Moira's home and the place where she could hide when she wasn't in the mood for visitors. But she was feeling friendly today, and when Eliza and Dahlia walked up to the tank, she darted out of her castle and swam to the glass to see them.

Moira was such a beautiful siren. She had a lean brown body that graduated into a slim, long orange and gold fantail that flicked vibrantly against the glass of the tank. Her yard of glittering yellow hair drifted in the water like a shining veil of gold filaments. Her sharp blue eyes were old and wise. It was said that Moira was at least three hundred years old, but despite her years in captivity, she always looked on Dahlia with kindness and Eliza with interest.

She put one webbed hand upon the glass separating them and spoke to both of their minds, a trick of the siren-kind.

Welcome, my friends. It's been a few days.

"Is has," Eliza agreed. She could have thought the words to Moira, but the siren seemed to like the sound of people's voices, maybe because she was alone so much of the time.

Dahlia waved her dog's paw at Moira and said, "Mr. Snoop says hello, Moira."

Hello, Mr. Snoop, Moira answered. *You and Miss Dahlia are looking exceptional today.*

Then she turned her attention to Eliza and said, *You look pale, my little love. Have you been eating and resting?*

"Yes, of course," Eliza answered brightly. There was no reason to burden Moira with her problems. Summersfield kept the siren as a prize to show off his power and status to the other Vampire Lords when they visited. He had caught her off the Caribbean when she was only a young pup. However, she was not a thing to be dominated sexually, because Summersfield would never get in the water with Moira—sirens were known to eat vampires, werewolves, and humans alike. As a result, Moira hadn't known the open ocean since she was three years old. Eliza thought how very sad her existence must be, having never known freedom or seen any of her own kind since she was a child. Summersfield kept her like a pet in an aquarium.

Don't be sad, Moira told her, frowning. *You mustn't be so sad, Eliza.*

Don't call me that. Don't call me Eliza, she told Moira as she experienced a spike of unreasonable anger. She didn't like how the siren could get inside your head, how she knew things about you.

It's your name. It's the name you've chosen for yourself, little love.

"I'm not that person right now," Eliza told her. "I don't want to be that person right now! I'll be Eliza when I go home to Edwin."

She swallowed down a sudden wave of nausea. It never seemed to go away anymore, even when Summersfield didn't summon her. She wondered how much damage he was doing to her with these nightly feedings.

Dahlia didn't notice, having moved to the other side of the tank to look at the lobsters crawling along the bottom, Moira's main source of food. But Moira noticed. She stroked her webbed hand down the glass separating them and said, *You should rest more, little love. Your condition is a precarious one.*

Eliza lifted her head. "What?"

Moira's hand drifted down the glass so it now rested near the middle of Eliza's body. A look of concern mixed with serenity filled her face and made it seem almost beatific. There were stories that Moira could detect sicknesses in humans who approached her tank. That and other things.

A terrible, festering worm of fear dug deep into Eliza's brain and heart. She stepped away from the glass. She had decided this little field trip to see the "fishy" was a mistake.

Moira tracked her with her old, reptilian eyes. *You feel him, don't you?*

"You're insane, Moira," she snapped, wondering why this was upsetting her so badly when it was patently impossible. She was a Poppet; she didn't even have a working uterus, and Edwin was a vampire; his seed had been dead for centuries. It would have taken something beyond a miracle to make them conceive a child together.

She decided she didn't want to stay here any longer, talking to an obviously crazy siren. She went to gather Dahlia, and, together, the two of them returned to the Poppet's quarters.

She was feeling extremely ill by then, and after seeing Dahlia off to her own quarters, she retreated to her room. She dropped down onto her knees on the floor of her private bath and heaved generously into the toilet.

"Alisa?"

One of the other Poppets, a male named Sascha, stepped into the bathroom, having overheard her retching from out in the corridor. "Are you all right, Alisa?"

Sascha wasn't a bad person, as Poppets went, but Eliza knew he'd stomp on her in a New York minute to get to the top of the heap if he saw the opportunity. You couldn't trust Poppets any more than you could trust vampires…or sirens.

"I'm fine. I think I had a bad shrimp for lunch." She wiped her mouth with toilet paper.

* * *

"Edwin, can I talk to you?" Cesar asked, stepping inside his Lord's private office. The room was dim, the lights off, and the only illumination came from the stripes of city lights bleeding through the blinds on the windows, but Cesar's eyes penetrated the gloom easily enough. He almost didn't recognize the place.

When they all moved in together just over a year ago, Eliza had assigned rooms to everyone. With four people to consider, the townhouse had become pretty cramped, but she knew the importance of them acting like a proper Court, and they managed to make do with the rather limited space. Eliza and Edwin had their own room, and Cesar had his. Malcolm had set himself up a fairly impressive personal space in the renovated basement. But no one had suggested that anyone take the smaller guest bedroom, which doubled as Edwin's office, the place where he wrote his pulps. Part of that was due to the respect they had for their Lord. As head of their small Court, Edwin needed a place to retreat to when his thinking became too complicated or there was some issue to resolve. The other reason was more pragmatic—Edwin was a disorganized slob and no one wanted to try to reclaim the space, not even Eliza, a notorious neat freak.

But when Cesar stepped inside and looked around, he realized that Edwin had been extremely busy over the last few days. Books had been returned to their shelves, his desk was clutter-free, the carpet vacuumed, the dust shields over his book covers and favorite gangster movie posters dusted, and all the woodwork polished to a shine. Presently, he was in the process of reorganizing all of his files in the two big file cabinets against the wall, a pencil clamped in his teeth.

"Edwin," Cesar said, softer now. "Are you all right?"

Edwin removed the pencil and slipped it behind his ear. "Bit busy, love. Come back later."

"I really need to talk to you."

"And I really need to freshen things up. Eliza is going to pitch a fit when she comes home and sees this mess."

Cesar stared at the shampooed carpet. He doubted Eliza was going to see it for a very long time. "Edwin..."

"Bloody hell, what?" he shouted, slamming the filing cabinet closed and rounding on Cesar.

Cesar held his ground in the face of Edwin's anger. He knew it wasn't for him. Since this whole debacle began, Edwin had talked to a sheer battalion of attorneys and High Court officials, but no one was being optimistic about Eliza's situation.

He looked his Lord over. Edwin's clothes were rumpled from sleeping in them, and his waves of chin-length, mahogany hair disheveled from running his fingers through it. He was gaunt from lack of food, and the dark rings under his eyes spoke to the bad sleep he was getting—when he slept at all, which wasn't often. He looked so worn and somehow shrunken since losing Eliza.

Cesar felt his heart go out to his master.

"I'm sorry," he continued in a small voice. "I didn't mean to irritate you. I was just concerned. And I brought this." He held up the bottle of blood substitute.

"Honestly, I'm not very hungry." Edwin straightened up and blanked his face of all emotion as he smoothed the wrinkles in his shirt and adjusted his braces. Cesar knew he was trying to be the strong, proud Vampire Lord they needed, powerful in the face of adversity.

Like I can't feel his pain. Like it isn't a part of me.

Cesar set the bottle down on his desk and went to Edwin. He slid his arms around his master's waist, sinking slowly to his knees before the man who had made him what he was. He meant the gesture to comfort Edwin, but it was also a formal gesture among the vampires, Cesar had learned. A way for Cesar to remind Edwin that despite everything he was enduring, he was still the Lord of his little Court, and he still had responsibilities to them all.

Edwin stroked his hair, his body visibly relaxing as he responded to the little gesture.

"It'll be all right, my Lord," Cesar said. Normally he wasn't so formal, but he sensed Edwin needed this right now. "You'll figure things out. You always do."

"I think you have far too much faith in me, lad."

"You handled the crisis aboard the *Gypsy Queen* and all that business at Lord Ian's castle all right. You'll find a way here, too." He drew back and smiled up at the man who was his teacher, father, brother, lover, everything to him.

Edwin's usually fierce amber eyes softened, and all the passion and affection he felt came flooding into them. Cesar climbed to his feet and slid his hands up the back of Edwin's neck. He leaned close to embrace him.

Edwin sighed. Cesar could feel his mounting desire, but also his reluctance.

Cesar drew back and said, "Too soon?"

"I expect I feel a bit guilty, is all," Edwin admitted, running his fingers absently along Cesar's jaw. "I shouldn't be enjoying myself while Eliza is with...him."

"You still need to eat. If you won't drink from a bottle, at least drink from me."

Edwin gave him a surly look. "Whelp, I'm not some child who won't take his mother's milk..."

"I want to help you." Cesar undid his collar. "I want to feed you. Let me." He stroked Edwin's cheek. "It comforts me too."

When Edwin didn't protest, Cesar took him by the hand and led him to the smoking couch with its soft, buttery mahogany leather, the place where Edwin had been sleeping for the past six weeks because he wouldn't sleep in his bed without Eliza. Cesar knew that because it had fallen to him to wind up his master's heart in the morning.

Once they were comfortably seated, Cesar lay down in Edwin's lap and worked the buttons of his dress shirt open, shrugging the material down around his shoulders. He had managed to hang onto his natural Latino tan despite his vampirism, and his golden-brown hair, a gift from the German side of his family, made a pretty contrast—or so Edwin had told him.

Edwin watched him, his eyes greedily drinking in Cesar's slim, muscular chest and exposed throat. Cesar reached up and hung an arm around Edwin's neck, urging him to lean down so Cesar could kiss him. He tickled Edwin's eyeteeth with his tongue until they lengthened to dangerously hungry hooks of ivory.

"There you are," Cesar said with a smirk.

Edwin sighed tiredly.

"We'll get through this. But you'll be useless to Miss Eliza if you don't eat and keep up your strength." Cesar added with a charming smile, "Besides, what vampire can resist this?" He turned his head and ran a finger down his own neck.

Edwin snorted. "You really do have an exaggerated idea of how sexy you are."

Cesar smiled and wiggled a little in Edwin's lap, which just made them both laugh. "I have a nice ass and you like my blood. Be a shame if you let it go to waste."

Edwin's eyes blinked black. It was all the invitation he needed. Less than a second after the words were out of Cesar's mouth, he seized the side of Cesar's face to keep him still. Edwin's strength was enormous, fueled by days of hunger. He leaned down and sank his teeth deep into the private spot behind his ear. The bolt of pleasure was sudden and intense. Cesar writhed beneath him, luxuriating in the flood of pleasure that Edwin's fierce and beautiful mouth could bring.

Edwin drank him, pulling the strength and energy from his body in a way that left Cesar moaning and twisting in his lap as the first brutal surge of *El Mal de Amor*, Edwin's sexual power, rolled over him like a storm. The force of it bowed his back and made his fingernails sink an inch deep into the plush leather of the sofa beneath him.

"Uhh..." he said, all the articulation he could muster. "Christ...that feels...so...fucking...amazing."

Edwin moaned a response and licked along the edges of the wound, then bit him *again*. This time, the wave of *El Mal de Amor* was so intense that a bolt of pleasure ripped through Cesar from top to bottom, making him cover his mouth so his scream didn't bring the neighbors running to their door. He felt like his soul was literally being torn from his body and sent floating.

Edwin moaned out some endearments, but Cesar barely heard. He'd seen vampires move things with their minds. He'd seen them control armies of lesser beings. But no power he'd ever encountered could compare with the sheer brute force of *El Mal de Amor*, the Lovesickness. Even after Edwin had stopped sucking on the wound and simply licked at it, Cesar could do little more than whimper from the sensations electrifying his blood and heightening his senses. Kings and emperors had thrown their fortunes at Edwin's feet just to spend a night with him and experience a moment of this rare, shivering euphoria.

All was silence and darkness for a while. He saw a universe full of stars and aether and darklight, and he experienced a deep, thrumming devotion to Edwin that bordered on the religious. For a while, Edwin was Lord, god, and master in both his mind and his heart. He would have done anything he asked.

With time, his senses finally returned to him and he found himself sitting in Edwin's lap, cuddled against his chest like a small child, with Edwin smoothing his hair back. "You back with us, lad?"

"Yes," he croaked. He felt warm and safe. But his voice creaked with weakness.

"Are you all right?"

He smiled a little goofily. "I feel wonderful. How long was I out?"

"Two hours."

"Wow." He straightened up as he recalled his reason for being here. "Edwin...?"

Edwin kissed the top of his head. "What is it, love?"

Cesar took a deep breath. He tried to remember all the little details of his argument, the thing he had come here to discuss with his Vampire Lord, but the Lovesickness had scrambled his thoughts and he had to think hard to remember what it was he was supposed to say. "I need to ask you something, and you're probably not going to like it."

"Why don't you try me and see?"

Cesar looked earnestly into Edwin's face. "I...this is hard to say."

"Just say it. It can't be that bad."

"I...I want to make an Heir."

There was a lengthy silence. Then Edwin said, "That's not possible."

Cesar felt a stab of anger. "Why?"

Edwin gave him a sympathetic look. "You're far too young to make an Heir. Maybe in a hundred years. Two hundred..."

Panic broke over him then. "I don't have two hundred years. Tommy doesn't have two hundred years! I need to do it now, in the next few weeks."

"Tommy," Edwin said. "That's the bloke you've been seeing."

Cesar took a deep breath and explained about the cancer, about his hopes for making Tommy his Heir. He hoped he was appealing to Edwin's better nature—or, at least, his own sense of separation from Eliza. But he soon learned how wrong he was.

Edwin's eyes remained remote. "No. I'm sorry, love. Not possible."

"Please, Edwin," Cesar said, clutching the front of his shirt. "This is important. He's the one. Tommy's *the one*..."

"You're barely three years old in vampire years, Cesar. You don't even know what *the one* is..."

Cesar glared at him. "I'm old enough to know love when I see it. I love Tommy, Edwin. I'm *in love* with Tommy. You *have* to let me do this..."

"I said no."

He thought maybe he hadn't heard right. Hadn't he just given himself to Edwin? Tears filled his eyes. "I thought you, more than anyone, would understand..."

But Edwin cut him off. "You're too young to make an Heir. Only a Lord can make an Heir, and I'm afraid to say that you're no Lord, lad. Maybe in a hundred years..."

"But...why?"

"It simply isn't done. It's not allowed."

"Now allowed?" Cesar said much too loudly. "What is that? Another stupid and outdated vampire rule? Then you make him. Make him for me, Edwin..."

"No."

Cesar just stared up at his master for a long moment while the pain and the anger festered inside him. *"Why?"*

Edwin looked impatient at last. "Two reasons. Number one being that Tommy wouldn't be blood bound to you. He'd be bound to me. He wouldn't be your lover anymore, Cesar. He'd be mine—"

"I don't care if he loves you more than me! I just don't want him to die!"

"—and the other thing is, I just can't handle another Heir right now."

Cesar snorted back the tears in his throat. "What about Eliza? You were going to make Eliza your Heir..."

"Eliza was a special case."

"And Tommy isn't?" Cesar wanted to claw at Edwin's heart, dig it out by its mechanical roots until he felt what Cesar felt. His voice and horror had reached a fever pitch. *"How is Eliza more important than Tommy?"*

Edwin schooled his face to remain blank and emotionless. He was very good at doing that when he needed to. "I think we're done here," he said coolly and started getting up, pushing Cesar away.

Cesar held onto his hand even as Edwin dumped him unceremoniously to the floor on his knees. "You have to do this for me!" Cesar cried, clutching it. "You have to! I have no one else to ask!"

Edwin looked at him. Finally, his eyes were cold and remote, the eyes of a true Lord. "Cesar," he said, "I'm your master. I don't have to do anything I don't want to." He pulled his hand away and turned to leave the room.

"If you don't help me, I'll find a way," Cesar sobbed after his Lord from his place on the floor. "So help me god, Edwin, I'll find a way!"

* * *

It was near midnight when Malcolm became aware of the other werewolf.

He was showing a girl an English country dance that went remarkably well with the Billy Idol remix the DJ was playing when the little hairs on the back of his neck stood up. Naturally, he assumed it was the beta creeping around, but when he sniffed the dense air of the crowded room, he realized the scent was not the same. It was...sweeter, somehow.

Excusing himself from his dance partner, he followed the scent, weaving in and out of crowds of people drinking, smoking, or dancing. Several girls and even a few guys tried to persuade him to dance with him, but he had eyes only for the werewolf moving among the humans.

Near the wall of the church, he caught the sight of long hair as a lithe figure moved with almost preternatural grace through the crowd. A flash of eyes made him pick up his speed.

Now that he had spotted the werewolf, he was enraptured.

The creature ducked out a door and into the delivery alley located behind the tavern next door, near the loading docks where cargo was unloaded daily. Malcolm followed but stood very still in the shadows, making certain to stay downwind of his prey. He was sure his friend knew he was here somewhere, but he didn't want to find himself at a disadvantage—cornered or hunted.

Then he started moving again, following the scene of the wolf. It took him down a few alleys and into a more private part of the piers where some buildings were clustered together. Behind it was a stand of carefully cultivated elms in late spring bloom.

Once he was under the cover of the trees, he stripped, carefully folded his clothes, and tucked them and his boots away under a tree. He took a deep breath and stretched, his brown, moon-kissed flesh shivering in the dark, and let the shift flow through him. He had been shifting a long time; thus, he did it silently and efficiently, going from man to animal with a shiver and a blur.

He was a big wolf. A giant among giants. He was ebony black, a shaggy, muscular shadow with chartreuse eyes. He trotted silently down another alley, his senses on full alert. The polluted city wind bristled his long, shining fur. He could smell the stink of rats in the sewers, fast food cooking nearby, and rotting humanity far off. He tasted the spring rains that would visit the city in a day or two. The lone cry of a pigeon out long after hours made him prick his big, triangular ears up.

He was alert but not concerned. It excited him, this encounter. He turned a bend and stalked into the open, taking the new wolf by surprise.

Startled, it looked up at him from where it was pawing around a fat, freshly killed sewer rat. The new wolf, a white female with handsome black markings around her fierce amber eyes, raised her head and snarled at him, showing off her impressive teeth. Her wrinkled-back snout was painted prettily with her prey's blood.

Malcolm was unperturbed by the female's reaction. She was a big wolf, an alpha from the sweet, meaty scene of her. Such a wolf could potentially hurt him if he let her, but he was not without strength—and charm. The bloodied rat looked delicious, but he was more interested in the female.

The female stood over her kill, her body as stiff as a board, head low, ears flat, tail out straight to show she meant business. Her ruff bristled, and again she snarled, a deep belly growl that vibrated through the asphalt under Malcolm's paws. Her voice ended on a high, whining note that told him to go his own way.

Malcolm wagged his tail and panted in response. He had not yet met an alpha female in this city, and he was not about to be dissuaded by such a fine creature.

The female pointed her ears at him. The gesture told him she didn't want to share her meal, but she was not averse to sharing his company. The reaction lifted Malcolm's heart and spirit. It would be nice to be with one of his own kind.

It had been a long time since he'd communed with such a beautiful alpha. Lust, excitement, and loneliness drove him on. He took a few steps toward her, head up, tail wagging, confident in his step. The female barked once, sharply, as he closed in on her. She was telling him she was interested, but only if he respected her boundaries.

Malcolm grunted an acknowledgment. She was an alpha; thus, she was only willing to mate with another alpha who respected her space but who also wasn't afraid of her. Instead of approaching her carefully, he trotted up to her confidently and snapped at her ears.

The female wolf backed away, allowing Malcolm to bolt down her kill, bones, fur, and all. It was an old game and not one that humans understood clearly. They saw cruelty and barbarity where there was none. Malcolm didn't want the kill; he wanted the female. The female was interested in her kill, but she was now more interested in knowing if Malcolm dared to steal it from her. By doing so, he had proven that he, too, was an alpha, and worthy of her affections.

Tail high, the female trotted down the alley from which Malcolm had come. He followed after, and once they had escaped the cluster of buildings, he discovered her in the stand of trees, sniffing his clothing. She wanted to know his human scent; that was a good sign. It encouraged him.

He closed in on her, sniffing her from nose to tail. He licked her snout and she returned the gesture, licking inside his mouth the way a pup will do with its mother, looking for food. She was interested.

He rested his chin atop her head and held his tail high like a flag. After that, she whined and rolled over, rubbing herself against the dirt, playfully biting at his mouth. He nosed her belly, then jumped on her. She wiggled out from under him and took off down the street, keeping to the shadows so they would not alert any humans. Malcolm pursued her, watching her tail flicker like a silvery flag as he kept pace with her.

They moved in and out of the alleys and byways of the city. When they came upon a small park, they played and rolled in the grass. Malcolm showed off, snorting and barking, then followed the female down to a duck pond to drink. Soon, they were off again, chasing each other through the dense pines and over the springy, cold ground, scooping up whatever prey they came across in their travels—squirrels, chipmunks, moles. When their bellies were finally as full as their hearts were light, they found a quiet patch of thick spruce pine needles to mate in. They mated first as wolves, then as humans.

The female was a tall, leggy black woman with lush white curling hair and black eyes. They didn't speak as humans. Neither of them was interested in human speech. Besides, in only the short time they'd spent together, they already knew each other intimately. Through sight, smell, and touch, they both knew they were alphas;

they both knew they were lonely and seeking. They knew all the important things.

Malcolm lay beside her in the tall grass, listening to the insects buzzing around them, stroking her face with his human fingers. As the sun broke between the tall buildings, Malcolm and the female shifted back to wolf form, licked each other's mouths goodbye, and took off in separate directions. Tonight was another full moon, another night to run, eat, and mate.

Malcolm was looking forward to seeing the female again.

He drove home on his Harley with a song in his heart and, for the first time in too long, a smile lingering at the edges of his lips. For the first time in too long, life was looking up.

* * *

Summersfield's gyro wasn't nearly as grand as Lord Foxley's. It hung above the Earth, a modest satellite, barely amounting to a quarter of the size of Foxley's *Gypsy Queen*—a frequent point of contention between the two vampires.

But then, Summersfield wasn't as old as Foxley. He'd gained his Inheritance during the Eleventh Century. He had yet to collect the ridiculous wealth that Foxley and the other old ones had. Foxley's gyro, when Eliza and Edwin were aboard it, had been like a whole other world made up of streets, buildings, and microneighborhoods. It housed some of the most prestigious corporations, casinos, and television stations in the world.

The *Marie Antoinette* was modest and compact, host to only a small number of corporations. It had no hotels or entertainment parks. Summersfield did not allow tourists on board. There were no gambling halls, no shops, no real commerce. As a result, getting what Eliza needed had been difficult but not impossible. She'd palmed it while down in the sickbay, fetching stomach upset medication for Dahlia from the sympathetic ship's doctor. Eliza was very good at stealing and concealing things on her person; a year down in Poppettown had taught her sleight-of-hand.

To her relief, Summersfield had not summoned her to his quarters tonight. He had chosen Dahlia, but no part of that made her feel any better. Poor Dahlia. She knew the girl would be inconsolable tomorrow.

Eliza sat in her window seat in her room, teacup in hand, looking out at the clouds of aether gathering around the ship. A bird smacked against her window and then bounced off, starling her. It only served to remind her that Dahlia's spirit was being systematically broken even as she sat here, sipping tea and feeling grateful to have stayed under their Lord's radar tonight.

"What kind of a person am I?" she wondered aloud.

She was troubled by the way she seemed to be talking to herself these days. Perhaps she was mad. The idea did not entirely displease her. If she went mad, she wouldn't feel anything at all. Or so she hoped.

She started crying spontaneously. She was sore and tired and so homesick that she felt like she might die from it. She missed seeing Edwin in his terrible, mismatched clothes, Cesar's lopsided, boy-next-door grin, and Malcolm's grim and loving gaze. She missed her boys, her friends, her life. And now...and now there was *this* horror to face.

She finished her tea, then forced herself up and into the bathroom. She rummaged through her linen closet, finding the item she had palmed from the sick bay. She pulled the dipstick out and looked it over. Funny, but this was the one dilemma she'd thought she'd never have to face. Despite the legal abuse of Poppets, as well as a lifestyle that was degrading at best, the Poppets never had to worry about human issues like these.

Until now.

For the first time in her life, Eliza wondered about the possibility of a Christian God. She decided one had to exist. There was no way life was this cruel and calculating without someone in charge, someone who hated her with every fiber of His being.

Ten minutes later, she stood looking down at the color strip, squinting and waiting for the purple line.

Waiting to see if mad Moira was right after all.

| iv |

"I take it your master doesn't know you're here," Mr. Stephen said when Cesar deplaned the Hummingbird.

The light, ground-to-gyro craft was parked in one of the many flight slots in the hangar of the *Gypsy Queen*, and the two men were surrounded by the bustle of airport traffic. Cesar grabbed his overnight bag from the boot and climbed down the ramp to face Foxley's main Poppet manservant head on.

His footsteps slowed as he approached the other man, his overnight bag slung over a shoulder. "No," he said in a somber tone of voice. He glanced around the massive hangar and watched the Hummingbirds and other light craft coming and going, carrying dignitaries, security staff, and VIP tourists on and off the giant floating vampire paradise that was Lord Foxley's whole world—the *Gypsy Queen*, the world's largest gyro.

He felt a dull stab of nostalgia. Only three years ago, he'd been head of this hangar, the man in charge of security for this part of the gyro. Well, back when he was a soldier...and a *man*.

Back then, he'd only mixed with Poppets of low status, those that worked the casinos and the ones employed to give the tourists a roll in the sheets. Sometimes, one took a fancy to him, but never in his wildest dreams did he ever believe he would be living this life, navigating the dark corridors of vampire politics as one of the undead. And he'd never known any of Foxley's inner staff personally. He'd certainly never spent any time with the likes of Mr. Stephen, who was perhaps the most powerful Poppet on Earth, politically speaking.

Cesar was impressed by the man. For such a powerful Poppet, Mr. Stephen was remarkably well composed, handsome, but not staggering so, and strangely...lordly, in presence. He was a tall man, fit and well muscled, with looks that reminded him of actors who played bit parts as gangsters in old Edward G. Robinson movies. He wore his dark, tailored, form-fitted suit well.

Mr. Stephen gave Cesar an up-and-down perusal, but his face betrayed no reaction.

"You plan to stay the night?" he asked formally.

"If it's no bother."

"That's for Lord Foxley to decide."

Cesar tried on a lopsided grin. "You sound less than enthused, Jeeves."

Mr. Stephen shrugged, not insulted, as he climbed into a sleek, spacey EV that resembled a high-end golf cart. Cesar got in beside him, throwing his overnight bag in the back.

"I'm merely curious about your business with my master," Mr. Stephen said, surprising Cesar with his candor.

Not waiting for a response, Mr. Stephen started the vehicle and they drove out of the hangar and into the warren of bright white service corridors that made up this part of the gyro. One looked the same as another, and there were no signs on the walls to indicate where they were or where they were going. Cesar realized he was entirely at Mr. Stephen's mercy. He'd forgotten how confusing the *Gypsy Queen* could be if you had no idea where you were.

"I'm not here to assassinate your Lord, if that's what you're worried about. I just want to talk to him."

"I don't worry about my Lord being assassinated. Many have tried over the centuries. None have succeeded. I rather doubt you'll be the first, whelp." Mr. Stephen smirked.

Cesar bristled at being brushed off so easily...and by a Poppet, no less. Annoyance made him cocky. "Are you so sure?"

"My master would not have allowed you to call an audience with him if he thought you were up to nefarious purposes."

Mr. Stephen's gumption was impressive. "Pretty forward-thinking for a Poppet. I could kill you now, stuff your body into a ventilation shaft, and then go hunt down your Lord, you realize."

He'd meant it as a joke, a poor one at that, but immediately regretted running his mouth in such a flippant way. What if Mr. Stephen believed him and threw him off the gyro? He'd worked very hard to get a message to Lord Foxley without Edwin knowing, and he couldn't afford to mess this up.

But Mr. Stephen quirked an eyebrow, not impressed. "I have a seventh-dan black belt in Aikido, so anytime you want a go, baby vampire."

"Your Lord lets you study martial arts?"

"My Lord lets me do whatever I wish."

Cesar was impressed. Eliza once said that Mr. Stephen was like her, a Deaf. That is, he could not plug into the simple, common Hive mind the other Poppets had. He hadn't believed her until now. But Eliza was right. Mr. Stephen was an extraordinary Poppet not only capable of higher thinking but also functioning under his own will.

"There many like you?" Cesar asked.

"What's that, whelp?"

"Deafs? That's what Eliza calls you guys."

"I'm the only one of my kind aboard the *Gypsy Queen* that I'm aware of."

"Must be lonely."

"Not really. I attend to Lord Foxley's needs. It keeps me busy."

"Foxley's down with that? A Poppet with free will? One he can't control?"

Mr. Stephen smiled a secret smile. "He finds me fascinating. And I have not found him to complain about my service."

Cesar got the distinct impression that there was a lot more between Mr. Stephen and Lord Foxley than just a Poppet and his Vampire Lord. "You're in love with him, aren't you?"

Mr. Stephen lost his smirk momentarily. "My feelings for my Lord are none of your business, whelp."

Bingo. Cesar had landed a hit on Mr. Seventh-dan Black Belt. Figuratively speaking, of course.

He smiled. "He will never return your affections, you realize. He's still hung up on Edwin, even after a hundred years."

"Edwin is Lord Foxley's favorite Heir. He holds rank over me." Mr. Stephen sounded so robotic, like he had to force the words out.

Cesar almost said something more, maybe something a little bit mean, but they were passing a No Admittance sign, and Cesar realized they were treading into the private sector of the *Gypsy Queen* that scarcely anyone on board ever saw: Lord Foxley's personal offices.

They passed three security checkpoints. Each time, Mr. Stephen had to run his electronic access card and endure a retinal and fingerprint scan. Eventually, he and Mr. Stephen left the EV behind and climbed into a cylindrical, stainless steel elevator. Mr. Stephen took an old-fashioned key from his pocket and set it into a slot beneath a button with no discernible markings on it. "Only one of its kind," he explained proudly.

The steel, windowless elevator moved both vertically and horizontally. They rose and fell, shot left and right through a series of unseen vacuums. Soon enough, Cesar realized he had no idea where they were headed or where Foxley's inner sanctum was located, which was probably the idea.

After a few more ascents and descents, the elevator stopped and they were deposited into a long, dimly glowing white corridor with neither windows nor markings, just like all of the others. They might be anywhere aboard the *Gypsy Queen*, he realized.

Mr. Stephen crooked his finger. "Follow me, whelp."

He followed Mr. Stephen down several twisting corridors until they reached a nondescript room with no windows like the corridors but lit with soft uplights. It was outfitted with a white wrap sofa and glass tables. Generic watercolor paintings of sailboats covered the walls. It looked like a glammed-up version of a hospital waiting room.

"Stay here. Do not go wandering the halls. Wait for Lord Foxley," Mr. Stephen instructed.

Cesar offered his lopsided grin. "What if I don't listen and take off?"

Mr. Stephen smiled sinisterly. "Why not do it and find out?" He then exited the room.

Cesar didn't, though. He had no idea what might be out there, and this mission was too important to act foolishly or to test Lord Foxley's patience. Cesar waited one hour, then two. He kept glancing at his watch, stretching his legs, walking the room, and flexing his wings under his dark brown bomber jacket. At this rate, Edwin was likely to phone him to find out why doing some light downtown shopping was taking so long.

Then again, maybe not, he thought bitterly as he paced the room for the hundredth time. Edwin was more than happy to take advantage of his body and his blood, but as for showing Cesar the attention he had before he'd lost Eliza...well, he fell short there.

He was so utterly consumed by his legal dispute over Eliza that he hardly knew anyone else existed at this point.

Finally, he yawned for the first time. He sat down on the sofa and pressed the heels of his hands to his eyes as a stab of guilt assaulted him.

"You're not being fair," he told himself.

If Tommy had been taken, he'd feel the same way. Hell, he loved Eliza, would have done anything for her, and he couldn't stand the idea of Lord Summersfield keeping her...hurting her. But he also knew they had to approach this from a practical standpoint.

There was nothing they could do for her at the moment, and everything they could do for Tommy. Except that Edwin could care less about Tommy—the one downside to living with an emotional wrecking ball like Edwin McGillicuddy. If you weren't his most beloved, you were almost nothing to him.

A door slid open behind him and he heard a soft voice say in a casual tone, utterly without accent, "Oh. You're still here."

He started getting up to turn and face the man stepping into the room, but he said, "Don't get up."

And he couldn't. He really, really couldn't. It was like he was a stone statue, incapable of moving. He couldn't even wiggle a finger or blink an eye.

Lord Henry Foxley was a bloodkinetic. He'd forgotten that. He could hold a person's blood immobile, and since blood ran throughout his body...and not just any blood, but Edwin's blood, which was, in fact, Lord Foxley's...

The man in question came around the chair and looked at him. He was dressed in equestrian gear—a soft, wine-red, velvet jacket, white breeches, and shining black, knee-high boots. He carried a crop. But he didn't smell like a horse as Cesar expected. He smelled like sex. A lot of it.

He looked like a twelve-year-old boy. Cesar had forgotten that, too. He looked on this...creature...with the face and body of a young, blond boy and the silvery eyes of an ancient reptile, and he heard a small whimper catch in his throat.

Lord Foxley pulled off one soft kid glove, then the other. "Don't bother trying to fight it, whelp. You can't. Not until I say. But you can speak."

"I..." Cesar realized he had no idea what to say. He swallowed and his throat clicked. All the arguments he had rehearsed on the ride up to Foxley's gyro had dried up in his throat. "Oh, god."

Foxley smiled. It was an ugly, stomach-turning sight, those old, pained, ancient, wise eyes...the disproportionately young body. It was like the eyes of God had been sewn into the guileless face of a child. It turned Foxley's visage demonic. "It's very difficult to look upon me, isn't it? Surreal? Nightmarish."

Cesar swallowed against the knot of vomit in his throat. The words that popped into his mouth surprised even him: "Your master was an animal."

Foxley's smile grew. It wasn't a real smile. It was the kind of smile you perfected over the millennia to reveal nothing except what the other person expected. "He was. Unlike your master. How is Edwin, little whelp?"

The question took him off guard. "Edwin is...Edwin."

Foxley narrowed his demonic eyes but kept his smile in place. "You should know that were Edwin not your master, if we didn't have him in common, I would not have entertained this audience. Remember that. Does Edwin know you're here?"

Cesar shook his head—or tried to. "No...this has nothing to do with him. He's not a part of this." He said it with more bitterness than he intended.

Foxley's succinct smile grew with delight at the news. "What do you want? What have you come here to ask of me?"

Was he psychic that he should know that Cesar was here to beg assistance?

"You're wondering how I know." Foxley's voice was a mere sibilant hiss. "Of course you are. And no, I'm not psychic, little whelp. Empathy of any kind has never really touched me on an emotional or psychic level. The humans would call me a sociopath if they cared enough to study me. But I know people. Call it the gift of having lived twelve centuries among the humans."

"I'm not human."

"No, you are not," Foxley agreed. "You're like Edwin. And like me. Thus, I understand you in ways no one else does. I understand things about you that you're not even aware of." His smile slipped, but only a little. "Now, tell me what you want, grandson."

Cesar sucked in a deep breath at the words. How to begin? He thought of a dozen openings and then dismissed them all.

"I'm losing interest."

"H-help. I need your help!"

Foxley turned and paced across the suite. Cesar found it easier to breathe and speak with the creature turned away from him. "Details," Foxley said, his voice low, bothered, as he turned his crop irritably in his hands.

Cesar knew he had but seconds before Foxley threw him off the gyro...or worse. His whole dilemma tumbled out of his mouth. He tripped all over himself trying to explain his impossible situation, then realized he probably didn't make a whole hell of a lot of sense, not that Foxley had any trouble following him, it seemed.

A half a minute after Cesar stopped babbling, Foxley turned those terrifying eyes on him and said, "For what reason should I make this Detective Thomas Quinn my Heir?"

"No one else will help me. Edwin won't help me..."

Foxley looked bored. "For what reason should I make this Thomas Quinn my Heir?" he repeated.

Cesar finally picked up on what Foxley was saying and said, "I'll pay you."

Finally, Foxley looked interested. "How much?"

"Whatever you want."

Foxley put his smile back on. "Whelp, you have no idea what my bite is worth."

Cesar bit his lip and picked his words carefully. "Y-yeah. That's true. But there has to be something I can offer in exchange for your help. There must be *something* you want that I can give you."

"I'm twelve thousand years old. You have no idea what I want."

Cesar kept staring at the floor to avoid Foxley's eyes, but now he looked up. The sight of the vampire sent a bolt of fear right through him. He went back to looking at the floor. "E-everyone wants something. Even you."

"And what do I want? Your body? Your soul, perhaps?"

The words made Cesar's skin crawl. "Whatever it takes. I'll give you whatever you ask."

"You should take care with how easily you offer yourself, grandson. Someone may take advantage of you"

Cesar squirmed. Things were not going to plan.

"You must care very deeply for this man," Foxley said almost whimsically.

Cesar swallowed against what felt like a walnut stuck in his throat. "I love Tommy. I'm willing to do anything to save him."

"Anything."

"Yes," Cesar answered with more confidence. Then he nodded. "Anything at all."

Foxley moved in a sleek circle around the sofa until he was standing directly behind Cesar. The little hairs on the back of his neck stood on end, and he desperately wished he could turn his head or shift away, but he couldn't. Foxley wasn't touching him, but his very presence made Cesar's entire body hum with a kind of negative, unspent electricity as if Foxley might pounce on him at any moment. He, of course, would be helpless to defend himself. Foxley could probably kill him with a single thought. Make his blood or his brain explode, maybe turn them to fire. He was sure the Vampire Lord was capable of that and much more.

Foxley's voice came low, so low that Cesar had to strain to hear his whisper. "You're a very young vampire. Do you know what you are, whelp?"

Cesar frowned in confusion. "I..."

"You don't, do you?"

"I don't understand."

"What are you?"

Again, it took Cesar a moment to understand the gist of Foxley's question. He recalled what he had done during the battle at Whitby Hall, the way he had shifted his form. "I'm a...a..." Truthfully, he had no word for what he was.

"Chimera."

"What?"

"The word you're looking for is 'Chimera.'"

Cesar shook his head. "No, there was only one Chimera...Edwin killed him."

Chimera was the vampire who had shot Edwin through the heart all those years ago and nearly killed him. Were it not for Foxley's clockwork mechanism, Edwin would be fifty years in his grave. He was the same Chimera that Edwin killed only a few years ago when Mad Maria attacked Foxley's gyro and turned his Poppets against him. Even then, Chimera had been hunting Edwin in a futile effort to finish what he had started.

Foxley's cool breath touched the side of his neck. Cesar's pulse jumped. "Chimera isn't a vampire, grandson. It's a subspecies. And there are more than one—though, interestingly enough, all are all connected."

"I'm not...I mean...how do you know that?"

"You don't know what you are. Neither does Edwin." Foxley sighed like a teacher forced to put up with a less than apt pupil. "There was never just one Chimera. There are two—or there were, anyway, before Edwin destroyed one of them. The greater and the lesser. The Lord and his Heir."

Cesar swallowed that down. It was like a jagged pill in his throat. "So...which did Edwin kill when all that went down two years ago?"

"I do not know. If it was the Lord, then he has brought down upon himself the wrath of the Heir. If it was the Heir, then he has then the outrage of the Lord still to face. Either way, the one who remains will not rest until he has destroyed Edwin and everyone he cares about."

A thought occurred to Cesar. "Is it...the remaining Chimera that tipped off the police about Eliza's true identity?"

"The creature has been biding its time, waiting to strike. And he will when he is prepared to deliver the killing blow."

Cesar trembled slightly at this revelation.

Foxley came back around to the front, leaned down, and eyed Cesar critically up and down. "Like them, you are a Chimera. Only the third I've ever encountered in twelve thousand years. What a very special little whelp you are."

Cesar couldn't swallow or he would.

Foxley smirked in that artificial way. "Has the remaining Chimera contacted you yet?"

Cesar shook his head. "N-no."

"I think he has, though perhaps you didn't recognize him for what he was."

Cesar thought back to the homeless man on the street who had spooked him. There had been other strange encounters over the years, but he couldn't honestly say if they were natural or not. The very idea made his head swim.

"Why would...? I mean, that makes no sense. Why would the Chimera contact me?"

"With only one left in the whole world, why would he not?"

Cesar didn't know what to say to that.

Foxley started pacing across the room. Except it made Cesar think of a big cat with too much energy and too little space to expend it. After a moment, he touched his ear and said to someone else, "Bring it in."

A minute later, Mr. Stephen returned with a leather portfolio under his arm. He set it on the glass table before Cesar and then exited the room without saying a word.

Cesar found he could move the upper portion of his body. He looked at the portfolio in the leather binder, afraid to touch it. But after a few minutes, curiosity spurred him on. He couldn't be certain, of course, but the loose-leaf pages in the binder looked like some kind of contract.

"It is a contract," Foxley assured him, using that weird almost-telepathy again. "And I'll explain the terms so there is no mistake as to what we want, the two of us. You, Cesar, will agree to act as my Enforcer for two hundred years. In return, I shall grant you, within limits, what you ask. After we've both signed this contract, I will interview Detective Thomas Quinn as a possible candidate for an Inheritance. Understand: The decision to make Detective Quinn my Heir or not ultimately falls to me. Your terms, however, are non-negotiable. You, Cesar, will act as my Enforcer regardless of my decision. Do we have a deal?"

Cesar stared down at the neat stack of papers. "So, I'll need to work for you for two hundred years?"

Foxley looked at him keenly. Cesar expected something sarcastic, but the Vampire Lord seemed deadly serious. "That is the price you will pay to have me make Detective Quinn my Heir. As a bonus to you, I shall also protect you from any advances made by the remaining Chimera. After all, you will be part of my Court. You will be my Enforcer. And, as Edwin already knows, I always look after my own."

"But Tommy will be yours, won't he?" he said, remembering what Edwin said when he'd turned down Cesar's request.

Tommy wouldn't be blood bound to you. He'd be bound to me.

"He'll belong to you," Cesar clarified.

"And to you. You and the detective will join my Court here aboard the *Gypsy Queen*. How you two conduct yourself whilst here is of no concern to me—though, of course, as my Enforcer, you will have considerable power and influence, and you will have the station to make certain vampires and Poppets your exclusive property. You may take Thomas, or any other member of my Court, as your exclusive, or nonexclusive, lover."

Cesar thought about that for a long moment. "But...I'll have to leave Edwin's Court."

"You cannot serve two Courts." Foxley gave him a shrewd look that made Cesar's hair want to curl a little. "I cannot alter the fact that Edwin is your Lord, master, and maker, however, this contract"—he tapped the folder—"trumps his influence over you. You will become my Enforcer—in effect, my exclusive property. Two hundred years—really, hardly a blink in time for those like you and I. After that...well, you two can then decide if you wish to continue to work for my Court or strike out on your own. However, by that time, I expect you will likely have become your own Lord and will want to establish a Court, which will be your right."

Again, that smirk. "My Heirs and Grand-Heirs always come to power so fast."

"You wouldn't force us to stay after two hundred years?" Cesar asked.

"Read the contract, child."

Cesar bit his lip. "During this interview...you won't hurt Tommy?"

"My interviews are not designed to harm anyone, merely to test the physical and emotional fortitude of potential Heirs," Foxley explained. "I will ask him questions. You may be present during the interview process."

Cesar stared down at the contract. He was torn, utterly torn. A part of him experienced a gnawing concern at getting into bed—physically and politically—with Lord Foxley. Good sense told him it was a bad move. A terrible move. But on the other hand, what choice did he have? Tommy had six months of life left, if that. And Cesar wasn't sure he could find another Vampire Lord on Earth, never mind one he might convince to do this deed.

"Can I read over the contract?"

"You have one hour, and then I withdraw the offer." Foxley left the suite.

Cesar sat alone with the contract for the next hour, reading and re-reading it. He could find no subterfuge, no loopholes, and no obvious trickery. It was all very straightforward and written in layman's terms rather than legalese. It encompassed everything that Foxley had explained, no more, no less.

He realized this was his decision, and his alone. To join Foxley aboard the *Gypsy Queen*, along with Tommy...or to remain on Earth with Edwin, without Tommy. The idea sent a dull spasm of panic into his heart.

He reread the contract.

* * *

The following morning, Malcolm stepped into the kitchen and noticed Cesar looked rather troubled. He stood at the stove in one of his ghastly aprons, turning pancakes that only Malcolm could eat, saying nothing.

Malcolm moved to the counter to pour tea into his thermos for class. Normally, he enjoyed the vampire whelp's silence, but today he sensed that something was different. Cesar looked a million miles away.

"I'll be out tonight," he told Cesar as a courtesy. "No need for dinner."

Cesar nodded but said nothing for a long moment. Then he blurted out in a forced way, "I'll be out for a bit myself today."

"Seeing your lover?"

"Something like that."

Malcolm waited, but no further information was forthcoming.

Malcolm flared his nostrils, sifting various scents through the air—the tea on the counter, the pancakes on the stove. He could even smell the printing ink from Lord Edwin's office. Naturally, Cesar gave off little to no scent. Malcolm could not scent vampires out the same way he could humans. Still, he knew something was troubling the young man.

He thought about asking, then decided it wasn't his place. His main concerns were Edwin...and Eliza. He wolfed down a pancake, then took his cup of tea down the hall and knocked on Edwin's office door.

"Come."

Malcolm said, on entering, "I've met a woman. An alpha."

Edwin sat up on the smoking couch. As far as Malcolm could tell, he'd been staring at the closed blinds on the office windows, the old black rotary phone in his lap as if he were about to make a call, or perhaps was waiting on one. There were loose papers all over his desk again. Malcolm perused them quickly—legal documents—before turning his attention fully on his Lord.

These days, it wasn't unusual for their Lord to pass in and out of these strange fugues. Sometimes, he caught Edwin sitting in a chair, saying and doing nothing for hours at a time.

But today he tried to look interested as he turned his golden eyes on Malcolm. "Steady on?"

"An alpha," Malcolm repeated. "I believe she may be head of her own pack. Which one, I don't know. But I intend to find out. I intend to take it."

"The alpha?"

Malcolm sipped his tea. "The pack. Whether the alpha aligns herself with me is still to be seen."

Edwin quirked an eyebrow, obviously impressed. "That's balls, old boy."

"None of this is about me," Malcolm explained. He considered his argument a moment. "No Vampire Lord on Earth commands a pack at present. It is...how do they say it now? Antwacky?"

Edwin, suddenly interested, swung himself around to a sitting position in order to fully address Malcolm. "I think you mean antiquated...obsolete. But aye, I get your meaning."

Edwin eyed Malcolm carefully before getting to his feet and approaching him. Their Lord was perhaps sloppy and chaotic at times, but Edwin McGillicuddy was no mental slouch. He caught on right away to what Malcolm was saying.

Malcolm automatically started going down on one knee as his master approached, but Edwin waved the formality away. When Edwin was standing in front of Malcolm—he was only a little shorter than the werewolf—he said, "That would make you a Dog of War with his own pack working in a vampire's Court."

Malcolm smiled. "Aye."

It was, to put things plainly, unheard of for modern vampire Courts to command packs, though things had been different in Malcolm's day. His former Lord, Ian Severn, had commanded the ragged, tired remnants of the Bloothorne Pack for decades before the Sidhe in East Anglia finally wiped it out. For Edwin to command a pack of War Dogs would be an enormous boon to his power. It would elevate Edwin's Court to what had once long ago been referred to as a "Congress."

Congresses didn't exist any longer. Such powerful alliances between vampires, werewolves, and other inhumans made governments too nervous, and the High Courts had started breaking them down decades ago. But if he and Edwin could resurrect the tradition and establish a powerful Congress—the most powerful on Earth, currently—it would give Edwin the leverage he needed to challenge Lord Summersfield's Court without Edwin needing age or longevity behind him. Malcolm thought they might then have a prayer in crushing the other Lord and saving Eliza.

They didn't say these things explicitly, but the concept passed nonetheless between the two men. In essence, Malcolm was asking his Lord if he was confident enough to take on a much larger Court, and Edwin silently nodded. Malcolm knew that Edwin was tired of vampire bureaucracy, the endless phone calls and paper chasing that led nowhere. He also knew that despite being a pretty "smart cookie," as they said today, Edwin had little head for war moves. He was a loner by nature, not given to strategies of these types. That was where Malcolm came in as his Dog of War, his general.

It was time to be proactive.

"You're doing this for her," Edwin finally said. "For Eliza."

"I love her," Malcolm confessed. There was no point in lying about it. Edwin already knew how he felt about Miss Eliza.

"'Tis a dangerous game we play, Malcolm of Whitby."

"I would do anything for her. And I will do anything to bring her back home."

Malcolm waited to see how Edwin would react to that.

Showing no reaction at all, Edwin stepped forward and put his hand on Malcolm's arm. "If you bring me wolves, I shall care for them. They shall be part of my Court as you are, wolf."

Malcolm, still holding his teacup, dropped to one knee and inclined his head even though he knew it wasn't strictly necessary. Edwin didn't hold with many formalities. But the centuries of sleeping under Lord Ian's castle had not dulled the edges of Malcolm's etiquette. "You honor me, my Lord."

Malcolm, in bowing and inclining his head, was offering Edwin his neck. His life. It was a ritualistic thank you, an act of submission. He didn't mind. If they could retrieve Miss Eliza, he would be whole again. "You will, of course, need to make the final play. The challenge to Lord Summerfield's holdings," he reminded his Lord. That was the one thing Malcolm couldn't do for his Lord.

"Aye, I understand."

"And so, you understand the danger to us all."

If Edwin lost, he would forfeit all he had to Lord Summersfield—including them, his Court. It was a complex and dangerous gambit.

Edwin didn't respond to that. Only: "Go get that alpha." And he patted his wolf's burly shoulder.

And so, late morning found Malcolm crossing the campus on his way to his philosophy class, a satchel of books across his shoulder, when the alpha female found him. He had just found his place in the lecture hall when the female walked in, gave him a heavy-lidded, sloe-eyed look, and moved up the walkway to a place just behind him. He could barely concentrate on the lecture while he dreamed of talking to her. The next hour dragged.

But as he stepped outside the lecture hall, she said, "You're a natural alpha."

He turned to face the female alpha wolf. She looked different than she had last night. More refined...but no less wolfish. She was wearing a bustled green gown that fell to her hips with wide-legged slacks beneath and a thick, fluffy scarf around her neck, possibly to cover up his love marks. Her silky white hair was done up in a proper coiffure, but tendrils had drifted down around her lean face and large, dark eyes.

She offered her hand to Malcolm, who took it. "It's good to finally meet you, Malcolm Whitby." Her voice was deep, slightly smoky. Malcolm enjoyed its low, businesslike pitch and timbre.

He bowed over her hand. "I'm pleased to make your acquaintance, my queen."

It was a deliberately formal way of addressing an alpha, but he wanted to use every charm he knew of to get into her good graces. The touch of her hand sent a shiver of anticipation down his back and made his wolf eyes want to come out, but he controlled himself.

"Very gentlemanly," she complimented him. "Old-fashioned. You may call me Anjou. Anjou Lacroix."

"Thank you, my queen." He brushed a light kiss over her knuckles and smiled. "You've found me rather quickly."

"You weren't difficult to find, Malcolm Whitby." She narrowed her snapping blue eyes. "There are not many men in the city of New York like you."

"Indeed."

"I love your accent. Cornwall?"

"North Yorkshire."

"Will you accompany me to tea?"

"Aye, my queen."

A half hour later, the two of them were seated in a little tucked away tea parlor in Brooklyn Heights, sipping Earl Grey and sampling biscuits, Lust had made them both hungry, and between the two of them, they quickly made short work of two platters. He showed her every courtesy, and he minded his etiquette and manners as if she were, truly, a queen. She was very much the alpha, eating openly in a show of vigor and hunger. Her eyes never left his face.

"Not many wolves acknowledge the old ways anymore," she said, chewing carefully on yet another chocolate digestive biscuit.

"I'm a very old wolf," he answered.

She laughed at that. "You look like a pup."

He didn't feel like a pup, but he didn't correct her. There was no way he could explain the unusual circumstances of his being here without going into excessive detail—something that might make him sound like he was quite mad.

"I meant no offense," Anjou explained. "I mean only that you look young."

He reminded himself that people were different now. By the time he was fourteen years old, he was engaged to be married and was already the Dog of War of a powerful vampire. His mate birthed his first child when they were both only sixteen. Today, though, the wolves—indeed, people in general—were not in such a hurry to grow up. "I'm not offended. But I am older than I look."

She didn't press for details on that. "What pack do you hail from, Malcolm Whitby?"

"Bloodthorn. In East Anglia."

"I don't know that pack."

"It's since gone extinct," he explained.

"I'm sorry!"

"And yours?"

"Youngblood. But we just call ourselves the Bloods."

Malcolm didn't know the name, but he wasn't about to let that put him off his game. Hers might be a new, young pack, but young wolves were a boon. Fresh blood was the strongest and most enthusiastic.

"I must assume you've come to me because you mean for me to challenge the old alpha," he said to be straightforward. "May I ask why?"

Anjou took a dainty sip of tea and swallowed. Unlike Vampire Courts, wolf packs were matriarchal by nature. The queen remained the head of her pack for the duration of her life, or until she chose to retire. She usually split the important decisions of pack politics between herself and her king, but it was her ultimate right to replace the alpha male if she deemed it necessary. The balance was subtle but worked well to ensure there was a strong, healthy collective. The pack might appear to look to the king for guidance, but the queen was his rock and the true power behind his throne.

Anjou's current alpha might have committed any number of offenses to lose favor with her. He might have been unfaithful to her, or just expressed weakness in some way. The younger pack members might be questioning his authority. If that was the case, then he, Malcolm, had the opportunity to become Anjou's champion, her potential new alpha male.

It was a lofty, honorable position—to be queen-chosen. Sometimes, the queen chose a new mate from her existing pack, but it wasn't unusual for her to look outside. Anjou's reasoning was her own, but the human part of him couldn't help but be curious about her reasoning.

"You question my motives," she said. "That's good. You're not a wolf to run blindly into dangerous situations."

He shook his head of long, half-braided hair. "Not true, my queen. First, I assess, and *then* I run blindly into dangerous situations."

She grinned at that. "Joseph and I were very young when we founded the Bloods, just children ourselves, but since then, Joseph has made a number of poor decisions regarding the pack. I was willing to overlook it at first, but he has become increasingly selfish and insecure, and that is rubbing off on the others. One of our young males was harmed due to his...insecurities."

He wondered if that was the young beta he had thrown into the wall of the pub a few weeks ago, the one who had challenged him. "Joseph's wolves have been watching me," he guessed, recalling the surprisingly violent encounter.

Her eyes widened. "His wolves attacked you?"

Malcolm shrugged. "It was only one wolf, hardly a beta, no bother."

She looked impressed. Malcolm felt his excitement edge up a notch.

"It's understandable," he said. "He's marking his territory."

"But you haven't run away," she pointed out.

Time for the truth. "I don't run, Anjou. I mean to take this territory. And you...if you will have me, my queen."

Her heart, beating steadily until now, started to thunder in her chest as her excitement increased. He heard it—and he reveled in the sound. "Joseph, however, is not weak like his betas," she explained. "He's led the Bloods for years."

"But not well, or you wouldn't be seeking me out," he observed.

Anjou inclined her head, accepting that. "He's not a wise leader, but he is a forceful one."

"I'm not bothered," he told her honestly. "Has he hurt you?" *That* bothered him. A lot.

"Not so much that I can't handle him."

"He should not be hurting you," he said low, almost a growl. "Only an insecure wolf would threaten one of his own for no reason. And never his queen." He sipped his tea, his elongated teeth clinking against the edge of the teacup. "It's wrong. Perverse. *Human.*"

She nodded, understanding him completely. "You're not afraid, are you? I knew you were a brave wolf when I first saw you."

"I'm brave when the cause is right." He wanted to temper his responses with humility. He knew she would appreciate that. On impulse, he took her hand and kissed the pulse in her wrist. "And you're a very desirable cause, Anjou."

She blushed at that.

They talked a little about their human lives. Anjou said she was studying to be an architect—but not at this college. At CCNY. Malcolm was impressed that she had come all the way across town to seek him out. She said there were twelve members in their pack, including two new pups, which she was responsible for. Malcolm explained that he was currently between packs but was connected to Lord Edwin McGillicuddy's Court and that he worked as his security detail. He knew that information was vitally important to their growing relationship. She might not like it, but he wanted to be upfront with Anjou Lacroix.

Human beings lied. Vampires wallowed in those lies. But a true wolf was an honest wolf.

Anjou sat over her tea and thought about that for some time. Wolves and vamps tended to avoid each other in this day and age. They existed on different ends of the morality spectrum. Malcolm felt the first gnawing bites of true concern.

Finally, she looked up and said, "You're...a vampire's wolf? A Dog of War? I thought they abolished such positions centuries ago."

"They are...uncommon." He did not explain that he came from a time when being a Dog of War was still a position of power and honor. To serve a great Vampire Lord was to be a great wolf. So much had changed.

During the long centuries of his sleep, the wolves and the vampires had grown distant like two continents drifting apart. The wolves had become insular and distrustful, and the vampires eccentric and perverse—strangely human. It was almost unheard of today for a wolf and a vampire to share the same space, never mind a Court. He supposed that he and Edwin were indeed a very odd couple.

Anjou bit her lip. "So, should you become alpha of the Youngbloods, we will all then be extensions of Lord McGillicuddy's Court? Do I understand that right?"

He nodded. "You are correct. And under his protection."

She sat back with a worried look in her eyes. "I'll be honest, Malcolm. Vampires frighten me. And I don't know much about Lord McGillicuddy. He's young, isn't he?"

Malcolm never missed a beat. "Lord McGillicuddy is a strong leader. The Youngbloods have nothing to fear from him and everything to gain from his power and influence."

She turned her head slightly as if she was unsure whether to believe him or not. She flared her nostrils, scenting him to see if he spoke the truth. "He was Lord Foxley's Enforcer once, wasn't he? That's certainly something to fear. Lord Foxley is a monster."

"He's not his Enforcer now. He's his own Lord, and a good one, with an Enforcer of his own. I trust him."

She scrutinized him. He didn't mind. He only spoke the truth. And she had the right to be cautious. Even though an alpha female was the technical head of a pack, she was only as strong as the male she set as her figurehead. If Anjou chose the wrong champion, it could only weaken her pack.

Malcolm patiently sipped his tea while Anjou contemplated his words. Then, a true alpha, he went for the direct approach, no games. "Anjou, if you want me to challenge Joseph for alpha status, I will. But if you distrust me, then we can have no future together."

She looked at him very seriously. Then she laughed. The transition was sudden and jarring, but the sound was pure and delightful to him. "You talk like we've known each other for years, Malcolm Whitby. Like we're some old married couple."

"I feel we have known each other for a long time, Anjou Lacroix."

Anjou took his hand and squeezed his long, powerful fingers. "Yes. I feel that too."

He could tell she had made her decision as queen of the Youngbloods.

"If you wish to challenge for alpha status of the Youngbloods, Malcolm Whitby, I will honor the conquering male. I will submit to him as his queen."

After that was established, he poured her more tea from the ornate china teapot on the table between them. "I will be honored to challenge for the position, my queen."

And just like that, it was done. The challenge set. And he or Joseph might die for it. Most challenges were to the death, but Malcolm put that out of his mind.

Anjou offered him a demure smile. "Come back to my loft, Malcolm. I want to mate with you again. I enjoyed our time together last night."

The tea forgotten, he stood up and brought her fingers to his lips for a quick swipe of a kiss. "Yes. I want that too."

But they only got as far as the alley behind the tea parlor before Malcolm felt his wolf rise. He turned to Anjou, boxing her against the wall. His hand completely encompassed her hip as he dragged her to him, kissed her breathless, then breathed into her. She was tall, hearty, not skinny, but easy for him to handle. She fit in his arms as if she were born to be there. He held her easily and tasted her wolf in her kiss. It rose steadily along with her lust—and his.

"You're a lovely wolf," he told her and lifted her slightly so her back was to the bricks

"And you're a fine young man," she growled, her palm to his cheek as she kissed him.

He mated with her more roughly than he had intended, but she didn't complain, kissing and biting at his mouth the whole time until their blood mingled in their mouths. Her teeth were sharp and her nails pierced the back of his neck and snagged in the plaits in his hair as she gripped him.

"Are you mine, my fine, strong wolf?" she asked near the end.

"Aye," he panted. "I am whatever you need me to be, my queen."

"You'll make a fine wolf king," she said in the moments before they came together, growling their release into each others' mouths to keep from howling at the full moon rising steadily over the city.

* * *

It was another Summersfield fete. He enjoyed putting them on, they lasted for days at a time, and they were utterly exhausting to Eliza.

Usually, Summersfield threw them whenever he had a visiting VIP aboard the *Marie Antoinette*, an opportunity for him to show off his power and status, but he'd been known to throw one randomly for no reason at all. The music, sex, champagne, and blood flowed freely at his parties. Something, he even had a reason to celebrate—like a new Heir or Poppet.

This fete—or *crush*, as he preferred to call them—had been put on ostensibly for her benefit. A welcome home party, he stated the night before while Eliza lay exhausted and aching in his bed. She no longer experienced terror at Summersfield's hands. She'd given up fighting him days ago. It was easier just to give in, and she had perfected learning to disassociate while he was using her body and blood to satisfy his needs.

Usually, she studied the ceiling tiles—whatever ugly, morbid picture he'd had the servants put up in his chambers that day. The more terrible the better, she had decided. She liked the dancing devils or the gods and monsters at war. It made her feel like she was floating down into a deep, cavernous hole in another dimension, looking up at the heavens where eternal conflict waged. She would sometimes make up stories about what was happening.

And it helped. Because she needed to behave and maintain her cover. There was Dahlia to consider.

Summersfield knew how she felt about the young Poppet. He felt it—empathic that he was. The one time she'd resisted, he'd warned her that what she was suffering would be nothing compared to what Dahlia would experience if Eliza continued to try his patience or managed to run away again. He said he'd tear the girl limb from limb, and the price and waste of her be damned. Then he would move on to the others and systematically destroy one Poppet a day until she was found and returned.

It was his promise and his warning. He was not going to lose "his Alisa" again.

As she stopped at the top of the winding, *Gone With the Wind*-style staircase and stood there in her long, midnight blue gown, a glittering butterfly mask upon her face—it was a masked crush, after all—she felt her heart lurch. Then it started beating double-time.

Lord Summersfield was waiting for her. He was standing at the bottom of the stairwell in one of his luxurious Brioni tuxedos, his dark hair slicked back and shining in a way that made it look like plastic. His blue eyes were cool and reptilian, devoid of all emotion.

She never did understand that about him—how he could be so well tuned to other's needs and intentions yet harbor almost no empathy of this own.

As she looked upon him, waiting for her at the bottom of these steps, she realized something. He was utterly gorgeous—and horrifying. Because he was so in love with himself, he had refused to wear a mask even at his own masked ball, and he had no less than four Pleasure Poppets of various genders flitting around him like brainless butterflies, all of which he was ignoring.

Tonight, he had eyes only for her.

Eliza swallowed against the sickness in her belly, thankful for the mask. Her latest bout of vomiting had left her piqued in the cheeks, and Summersfield was likely to notice. She didn't want to be noticed tonight. She desperately hoped his attention went elsewhere. For her sake. For the sake of...the little one inside of her.

Oh, sweet Jesus, she thought. How had this happened? How in hell could she be pregnant? The very thought appalled her, terrified her, and left a kind of white static coursing through her body. She didn't want a baby, not a *vampire* baby. She didn't want this now. She didn't want this *ever*. And yet, this thing lived inside her.

"Alisa..." Summersfield said in a low, deceptively soothing voice and swept out a long arm, indicating that she should begin her descent.

She climbed carefully down the stairs in the long, cumbersome gown, terrified she would fall, hurt the child...*the child she did not want! The...thing...inside her.*

Was it even a child? What if it was some misshapen creature? A monster?

And then she felt even guiltier at the thought. How could she think that way? How could she and Edwin ever conceive of a *monster?* Yet she had no name for it...the...half thing...growing inside of her.

Edwin's child. It's Edwin's child...

"You look ravishing, my dear," Summersfield said as she joined him. He raised his arm for her and she set her hand on it properly, trying to avoid the almost arctic cold he always put out. Edwin was never this cold. It was less like Summersfield was undead and more like he was a metallic statue, something that had never lived at all. Something that ate all of the heat out of the living.

"Thank you, my Lord," she said in a soft voice, keeping her eyes on the floor.

He walked her into the banquet hall, accompanied by the annoying flock of beautiful, brainless Poppets. She sighed to herself. Moira's tank had been moved here so Summersfield could impress his guests with his exotic trophy. Moira floated near the wall of the tank, her hand upon the glass. She was gazing upon Eliza in that soft, pained, hopeful way she had.

Over the past few weeks, a strange belief had taken hold of the siren. Poor Moira thought Eliza was some kind of *savior*. She believed that Eliza would deliver them all from Summersfield's hands. Somehow, that made it all the worse.

She looked away and noticed there were cushions scattered all over the floor, trestles piled high with platters of gourmet food, and Poppets and lesser vampires dancing to old ragtime music being pumped out of invisible speakers in the ceiling between all of the glittering, diamond chandeliers. Everyone was in evening finery and wore dazzling masks that would come off as the night wore on and the alcohol and the lust continued to flow. It was to be another long affair, days before she'd be allowed to sleep properly or be by herself.

They walked the banquet hall for hours while Lord Summersfield targeted various high-ranking vampires. He talked about the health of his stock portfolio, his latest purchases from India and the Far East, what redecorating he had going on aboard the gyro, and, of course, Eliza.

"She's a novelty Poppet. She thinks on her own and has her own will. She even cries real tears when you hurt her," he told one tall, thin vampire who looked like a lizard in human clothes.

The vampire stood much too close to her and said with a leer, "Impressive, old boy. Where *did* you purchase it? I should like to own one of these 'thinking Poppets.'"

Eliza twisted this way and that, hoping for a reason to leave the party, or just to sit down. Walking in five-inch heels was making her feet smart, and she didn't know what she would do if she grew ill again.

"I'm hungry," she whimpered in a way that she hoped made her seem like a simpering idiot. Hopefully, the tall, thin vampire would forget all about her and move on to greener pastures. Maybe Summersfield would even let her rest her swollen feet.

But Summersfield stubbornly ran her out for another hour. When she finally complained of hunger for the third time, he grumbled something under his breath, deposited her at the head table, and sent one of the servants to fetch her a plate of food. Eliza slumped at the table and watched the Poppets and vampires slow dancing. A few vamps had begun pawing up the Poppets. It was only a matter of time before the masks came off and the mass orgy started.

One of the servers set a platter of food down in front of her. The smell of the braised meat, which once would have delighted her, only left her stomach churning. "Please take it away," she said, turning toward the tall man at her side.

He was wearing a serving tuxedo and a devil mask, but she immediately recognized his tall, lanky, but sinewy form. His dark mahogany hair was pulled back into a tight queue. She'd know *him* anywhere. Her heart thudded thickly in her chest.

Their eyes met from behind their respective masks. She almost gasped something out, but he put a long finger to his lips, then motioned for her to follow.

Glancing aside at Summersfield, who was presently dancing with a high-ranking Vampire Lady, Eliza surged to her feet with renewed energy and slipped between the twirling couples, following the man across the ballroom and down one of the adjoining corridors. They turned left, right, and left again. The crowd of people thinned out.

He turned into a random room, and she followed, closing the door behind her. It was an empty office of some kind. But she hardly noticed; her eyes were all for the stranger standing before her.

Ripping away her butterfly mask, she said his name. Tears sprang to her eyes and she wondered if she was dreaming this.

Edwin removed his devil mask and gave her a once-over. "How are you, lovey?"

"Oh, god, Edwin!" She ran to him and threw herself into his arms. For long moments, she could do nothing at all. She couldn't speak, cry, or move. She could only cling to him and tremble. She breathed in his hair and skin, rubbed it against her cheek, and clutched him.

It seemed to go on forever, and yet not nearly long enough. Soon, her arms tired and he slowly lowered her to her feet. She looked up into his dear, familiar face and realized she'd been crying all along and there were tears and snot all over her face.

"Edwin...Edwin..." She couldn't stop crying or saying his name as if he might vanish like a dream if she did not.

He clutched the back of her head and held her against the front of his tuxedo, against the hard, familiar planes of his body. He kissed her ear, the side of her face. "It's all right, love. I know I've taken too long. But I'm here now. I'm going to take you home..."

His words melted into her fuzzy brain only very slowly. But when they did, she pulled back. She stared up at him and said. "No, you can't!"

"Eliza," he said patiently, "it took a lot of work just getting through security here. But I've made a decision about what we're going to do. We'll go below to Poppettown. We'll join the Red Doors—"

The Red Doors. The secret Poppet underground railroad...

"I can't!"

He looked at her, confused. "I'm not leaving here without you."

She shook her head, scattering tears. "I can't leave Summersfield's Court!"

He took her hands. His eyes looked bloodshot as if he'd been the one crying all this time. "If you're worried about Summersfield, don't be. We'll go underground, you and me. We'll stay there until we're safe and Summersfield gives up. Or we'll stay there forever. I don't care as long as we're together—"

"I can't, Edwin! I just can't!" She sniffed at the sobs gathering in her throat and tightening her chest. "If I leave his Court, Summersfield will torture and kill his Poppets. He'll kill them all...!"

Edwin shook his head in disbelief. "I don't care about them..."

"I do!" she sobbed. "Their blood will be on my hands! I can't, Edwin, I just can't!"

He dropped her hands and looked at her angrily, but she knew his anger was for Summersfield and this impossible situation. "Eliza...listen, love, I can't get any help from the High Courts. I can't get help from anyone! This is all I have, the only thing I can do..."

She was crying again. She hated crying so openly in front of him like this, but she couldn't help herself. "And I can't go and abandon the others to that monster. I can't be happy knowing they'll be tortured and killed because of me..."

"Summersfield won't kill his Poppets," Edwin insisted. "He's bluffing, Eliza. He's just trying to keep you from running away again."

"He'll kill them," she said in a cool voice. "I know he'll kill them. I know what he's capable of. He broke Derek's arm and left him to suffer without medical care for just looking at him the wrong way. There is no limit to his cruelty. Yes, Edwin, he *will* kill them."

Edwin's face darkened as he reached out and carefully traced a small bruise across the bridge of her nose, the lingering vestiges of Summersfield's latest fit of temper. "And I leave you like this? Leave you to be brutalized by that son of a whore...?"

"No," she said in a softer and much more controlled voice. She gave him the strongest, most stubborn eyes she could muster. "You stay with me for as long as we have. Until they come looking for me." She took his hand and led him toward a narrow sofa in the corner.

Lying scrunched up on the narrow cushions, she touched him with gentle, exploratory fingers as if to re-connect with him. He didn't respond much. She suspected he was afraid of hurting her, touching her in some way that would aggravate a bruise. She had plenty of aches and pains, but she didn't care about that. She didn't care about the pain with him here beside her. "Please, Edwin..." She tugged at the front of his black jacket. "Hold me? Make love to me?"

But he shook his head. "He'll smell me on you. Then he'll hurt you again. He might even kill you."

"Edwin, please..."

"I know what he's doing to you, how he is hurting you..." he whispered darkly, almost but not quite against her lips. "Our blood-link? Remember? I can feel your pain. I can feel how much he's taking from you. It's depleting me, too..."

"I can handle him! I can take the pain!"

Edwin's eyes blinked black. He was angry...no, he was raging mad. "You shouldn't have to *take it*, Eliza." He sat up suddenly, his hand on her arm, ready to drag her away. "I'm taking you from here. I don't care what he does to the others. And if he tries to stop me, I'll kill the bastard."

Eliza pulled away from him. "And I said I'm not going!" She'd started to cry. She covered her face. "You won't win. He's too old. Too powerful."

"I have power, too. I made vampires cringe when I worked for Foxley," Edwin insisted, even though she knew it was mostly bravado. Edwin was barely more than two centuries old. Lord Summersfield, a thousand years steeped in his power, would crush Edwin like an insect in a fair fight.

"Can't you just hold me, love me? Does it have to be an ultimatum?"

He stuttered on a response, then reached for her again. Slowly, she melted against him and, together, they lay there a while, just holding each other. He pushed her hair off her face and kissed her forehead. She thought about all the things she could say, the things she could tell him, and the one thing she knew she should tell him about—but she knew him. She knew that would only send him into a mindless rage that would end with the both of them dead.

He couldn't know. Not now. She didn't need him spiraling.

He was watching her, looking hopeless, and this was not what she wanted in their brief reunion. So she said, "Tell me about home, Edwin. About Cesar and Malcolm. Tell me everything. Quickly!"

"Everything." He kissed her hair.

She snuggled against his chest and just breathed a sigh of relief. Five more minutes. That's all that she could manage before Summersfield came looking for her. Five minutes of lying here in heaven. It felt good to be home—even if it wasn't forever.

V

Club Mischief, London, 1923

"He's a prince, and he has quite a fortune stashed away somewhere. Do you like him?" Foxley asked.

They were standing close enough to the string quartet that no one else in the room to hear them. Around them danced flocks of half-drunken British Aristocracy in black tie and sequined flapper dresses, many growing rowdier as the endless champagne flowed and the night wore on.

Leave it to Foxley to wonder about a young fugitive's fortune, Edwin thought without surprise.

Foxley's lust for young, succulent prey was exceeded only by his raging desire to expand his already nearly Byzantine empire. He already controlled half of London, and there was nary an opium den, house of prostitution, or gambling den that did not filter neatly into his coffers. And wherever Foxley could not outright control a business, he had Edwin run protection for it.

All for his dream to one day own a giant floating city in the sky, Edwin thought, standing beside him.

He believed Foxley might be a little touched in the head. More recently, his master revealed his schematics for a gigantic dirigible he planned to call the *Gypsy Queen*, a ship unlike any in current existence. Not a ship, he corrected himself. A floating mini-planet, vampire-made and vampire-controlled. Edwin had come to realize that either Foxley was a mad genius or he was simply mad.

He brushed aside a couple who had bumped into him accidentally. The man's tuxedo was all askew, and he had one hand on the exposed breast of the young woman in his arms, a woman who was giggling wildly.

"Oh dear, pardon us, Lord Foxley!" the man said to Edwin.

Edwin gave the couple a dismissive glance that made them quickly turn away as if he'd thrown an ice pick at their faces.

Edwin did not correct their error. When he and Foxley attended these lush, drunken affairs, they sometimes switched identities for fun and/or for profits. Foxley looked much too young to be a Vampire Lord and Edwin much too Lordly to be his Heir and Enforcer, and, so, it amused the two of them to play with people's minds.

It also helped strengthen the mystique about Foxley Industries and helped propagate many half-truths across polite London society. Such subterfuge was both amusing and useful. Just last week, a disreputable moneylender had stalked and attacked Edwin, thinking he was Lord Foxley. Edwin had dispatched the man quickly, leaving everyone none the wiser. When one ran a crime organization as large and varied as Foxley did, it helped to shroud oneself in a bit of mystery.

"They say the prince is a hapless fop. What do you think, my Heir?"

Edwin studied the subject of their conversation. The man in question was a young, slim thing of seventeen or eighteen years, dressed in a brushed black tuxedo. He was making the rounds of the socialites with a great deal of false bravado. He was blond and pretty, hair freshly cut to mirror the most recent trends, and cheeks as vibrant as apples. His eyes, though…they were shadowy green and told the tale of his woes—travel, misery, hunger, oppression.

And beneath all of that—desperation. A dangerous combination, because, as Edwin knew from experience, a desperate man will do almost anything.

The boy laughed and played the debutante well, but there was an age and darkness in his soul that drew Edwin's attention like a magnet drawing metal filaments. He wanted the boy for the same reason that anyone has ever wanted anyone—the dangerous thrill of being overwhelmed, of losing oneself in another, of literally biting off more than one can chew. The irony of the thought brought a small but sinister smirk to his lips.

Edwin sipped his wine, tasting the almost metallic tang of it far back in his mouth. "A prince, you say?"

He'd never had a prince before, though Foxley had had occasion to send him to the bedchambers of various kings, queens, emperors, and princesses in his attempts to expand his ever-growing empire. Edwin never took offense. Seduction was his forte. It was what made him dangerous and a formidable Enforcer. Plus, bedding his prey was a great deal of fun.

"Nicholai Leonardo Romanov. Leo, to his friends." Foxley smiled secretly, making his normally young, guileless face take on a strangely masklike appearance. Foxley, for one brief second, looked demonic. Edwin recognized the hunger, wisdom, and greed in it. Foxley, like Edwin, wanted the boy, just not for the same (and admittedly ignoble) reason Edwin did.

Edwin thoroughly enjoyed studying his master in these rare moments when he dropped all pretenses. But the look quickly vanished, and very soon, he was once more the young charge standing with his tall, devastatingly handsome, red-haired guardian.

Edwin licked his lips. "Why is he important?"

"He's the bastard offspring of Nicholas II."

"You jest."

"Look closely and you will see it in the boy's delicate cheekbones. The curve of his smile."

Edwin watched for a few minutes to affirm that, yes, indeed, the boy did bear some vague resemblance to Nicholas II. He knew because the Czar and Czarina had hosted a lavish gala ball only a few months before their execution at the hands of Yurovsky and the Bolsheviks, and during that time, Edwin had had an opportunity to get to know the couple quite well.

"How did he escape the slaughter?" Edwin's interest was fully piqued now. He had never had a Russian fugitive prince before.

"Leo was being used as kitchen labor," Foxley explained. "The result of some midnight tryst between Nicky and one of the chambermaids, or so the story goes. You know how it is."

Edwin grunted. Such arrangements among the royal households weren't uncommon. In a way, he wasn't all that different from Leo Romanov. Neither of them had had a father who had acknowledged them. Both of them had suffered as outcasts. Of course, Leo at least knew who his father and mother were. Edwin, because of the circumstance of his birth, hadn't a clue and never would.

He snatched a fresh champagne flute off a passing tray. He was suddenly very thirsty. "Go on."

"The night of the execution, Yurovsky sent him away, thinking he was nothing. His uncle, who knew better, smuggled the boy to Kaluga, then to Switzerland. Eventually, he escaped the borders and traveled here to the Empire. He's been here almost a year."

"He's certainly fitting in," Edwin said, taking a long sip of his champagne. He licked his lips and slightly pointy teeth.

"So you *are* interested," Foxley said with a knowing smile.

Edwin shrugged, trying not to appear too enthusiastic. The young, bastard Russian prince was comely and troubled-looking.

Edwin was bored and hungry, and pickings among the British Aristocracy were slim tonight. It was a potent combination.

"I wouldn't mind a drink." He set aside his empty glass. "And what's in it for you, old boy?"

"I want to see you happy and satisfied, my young, handsome devil."

"I'm sure."

Foxley gave him those comically facetious eyes that he so often did these days. "*Where* is this cynicism coming from?"

Edwin smirked, his eyes never leaving the young prince. "It's been 169 years, Foxley. You never do anything without good financial reason. What's the game?"

"You're counting the years?" Foxley said, sounding insulted. "Prisoners count the years, Edwin."

Edwin ignored the jab. "A fugitive prince hardly seems worth our while. He can't have that much on him."

Foxley pressed his lips together with displeasure. He only did that when Edwin trumped him in some way, which was becoming increasingly frequent. "If you must know, the boy's uncle smuggled out a number of highly valuable works of art from the Imperial House."

"Ah. It all comes clear," Edwin said as he smoothed his cravat.

"Are you still interested?"

"Aye. But I think you're a shark, old boy."

Foxley snorted at that while Edwin melted into the crowd to mingle.

The band started playing a waltz. A comely young woman in a short, white dress and glittery silver tiara came over and asked him to dance. Edwin waltzed her around the ballroom floor, trying to catch the eye of the young Russian prince, but Foxley's words—his accusation—bothered him more than he'd expected it would.

Why had he baited his master? Wasn't he a loyal and devoted Heir? Hadn't he done everything that Foxley asked him to do? It was almost like Foxley did not trust him—as if he were waiting for Edwin to betray him. They were having an increasing number of these acerbic exchanges.

Foxley watched him from across his room, his eyes following Edwin's every move.

He's jealous...insecure, Edwin thought to himself as he expertly dipped the young woman. They were brothers in arms, father and son, Lord and Heir, and Edwin loved his master as any proper Heir should, but he was no one's fool. Edwin knew that in Foxley's heart of hearts (if Foxley could be said to have one) that he wanted more. He wanted everything—Edwin's heart, his soul, his desire.

The problem for Edwin was that it was impossible to desire someone like Foxley. Love he could manage. Devotion? Yes. Foxley had given him eternal life and a purpose. But desire? How did one desire someone—some *thing*—as monstrous as Foxley?

Even barring any mere physical barriers that could conceivably be overlooked, there were other issues to consider. His greed, for instance. The bloodthirsty avarice that caused Foxley to rip through the bodies and souls of everyone who stood in his way. The human wreckage and cold, forgotten graves that Foxley left in his wake could pave a thousand battlefields several times over.

The thought made Edwin feel, increasingly, the weight of his years. Perhaps Foxley was right to suspect him. Edwin was contracted to serve Foxley for two hundred years. That indentured servitude would end in just over a quarter of a century. Already, Edwin was his own Lord. He never realized how much he was looking forward to striking out on his own, doing things his own way.

He chalked his restlessness up to becoming his own Lord much sooner than either of them had anticipated—sooner, really, than any vampire had any right to be—but now he wasn't so sure. He was afraid he was just tired of Foxley, tired of the carnage, and eager to be away from him. Sway from this life, such as it was.

But you're his Favorite, he reasoned. Foxley had given him everything he wanted, everything he desired. As long as he sat in Foxley's shadow, he wanted for nothing. Foxley had saved him from the noose, from hunger, disease, and death. Mortality. Foxley had made him a godling on Earth as he had promised. Edwin knew he was an ingrate for having such traitorous thoughts, but he couldn't shake the feeling that despite it all—all of Foxley's proclamations of love, all of his little gestures of generosity—his master was using him like he used everyone else in his life.

"You're beautiful," the woman tittered, drawing his attention back to the present. She was staring up at him, mesmerized by him. That was another point of contention between the two of them. Foxley could never get that look, not if he wielded all the money and power in the world. Edwin was enthralling this human just by thinking too hard and spreading too much glamour about.

"Are you a vampire?"

"Yes," he answered nonchalantly, trying to tone down his power.

"Oh, my. I saw a cinema about a vampire just last week. *Nosferatu*. Have you seen it?"

"I'm afraid not."

"It was a right jolly show, but he didn't look like you. He was ugly." She looked up at Edwin with big, doe-like eyes. "You can bite me if you want. Feed on me. I don't mind." She stopped dancing to pull down her dress and offer him a plump breast.

"Thank you for the offer but I must decline," Edwin said evasively. For some reason, the thought that this pathetic little creature wanted him to victimize her just made him sad. Foxley said he was sentimental. He often complained that Edwin didn't put the proper emotional distance between himself and his victims. He was probably right.

He was relieved when, moments later, one of the help interrupted him to tell him a guest had invited him to a game of English billiards. He disconnected himself from the drunken, vampire-crazy woman and followed the servant into the billiards room.

As he stepped inside, he noticed that the Russian prince was there, selecting a cue from off the wall. *Leo the Green-eyed Lion*, he thought poetically as he looked the boy up and down. He was certain that Foxley had made all the appropriate arrangements for this liaison.

"I expected more players," the young man said in his heavily accented English. He moved nervously toward the billiards table as if expecting assassins to pour out from behind the potted plants in the room.

Edwin wondered what it had been like for him to learn his entire family had been executed in the basement beneath his feet like rats in a nest. Did he mourn the passing of the family that had refused to acknowledge him or had he celebrated their destruction? Whatever his reaction, Edwin felt a pang that such a young man should know such darkness early on in his life.

"Perhaps they heard I was playing," Edwin said, trying to lighten the mood.

"Are you that good?" Leo asked archly.

"I can be extremely motivated when the prize is worthy."

Leo's eyebrows lifted at that. "That could be construed as extreme arrogance, you realize," he responded, deliberately sparring with him.

Edwin's pity turned to admiration. They called him the Prince of Hell for good reason. Most mortal men were too frightened of him and his reputation as an Enforcer at Foxley's Court to talk to him, let alone challenge him like this, but this boy seemed inoculated against such fears. Perhaps he had seen too many horrors in his homeland—or, more likely, he simply didn't know he was playing with one of the most dangerous men in the Empire.

Leo put down five pounds. Edwin raised the ante to ten.

The men came around to string. Both came close, but Leo's ball came back to balk, and he started the game. Edwin didn't mind. He stood aside and admired the sinewy strength in Leo's back and shoulders and the careful fit of his trousers as he leaned over the table. He potted two balls before Edwin took over.

Leo glanced nervously around the room.

"No assassins."

"Pardon me?" Leo's lean, pretty face piqued.

Edwin finished potting a ball and indicated the room. "There are no assassins here unless it's one of them." He indicated the suits of armor in the room with them, standing silent sentinel under gaslight sconces.

Leo laughed. "Do you think anyone ever wears them?"

"You should check."

Edwin waited while Leo checked each suit. "Nothing. It would seem we are safe for the moment." He laughed again to cover his nervousness.

"I'm not an assassin," Edwin assured him. *At least, not tonight,* he silently added.

"I didn't ask," Leo said, picking up his cue.

"But you thought it."

"I would be very surprised if you were," Leo said, bending to their game.

"Why is that?"

"You don't look like an assassin."

"And, pray, what does an assassin look like?"

"Not you. You look like one of those American actors. Rudolph Valentino or Douglas Fairbanks." Leo missed his hole and exchanged places with Edwin.

Edwin deliberately brushed against the young man's shoulder as he took a new position. "I'm far more interested in *le petite mort* anyway."

"The little death," Leo said archly. "You're Foxley's."

Leo's statement surprised him.

Edwin potted a second and third ball before dignifying that with an answer. "If you believed that, you would not have stayed here to play me."

"Maybe I was curious," Leo said. "On the ton, they call you the Prince of Hell. The Devil. Are you? The devil, I mean."

"Who calls me the Devil?"

"Everyone in London."

"It's obvious"—Edwin stopped to pot a fourth ball—"that you've been speaking to the wrong people."

"There were devils in St. Petersburg. Many of them."

"And did you escape them all?"

He expected Leo to shy away from his affront. Instead, the little prince narrowed his icy green eyes and, much like Foxley, his face was transformed. Edwin had no doubts that Leo had done whatever was necessary to survive the horrors of his existence. He might look it, but he was no innocent.

"No, but I did tame most of them."

They locked eyes, and, suddenly, Leo smiled, again the little flirt, and went to gather them both drinks from the wet bar. He offered one to Edwin. "The master of the house has very good vodka."

"You're not afraid?"

"Of losing my ten pounds?" Leo said. "Yes, very." He knocked back his drink, the ice clinking against his teeth.

The vodka highlighted his coloring and made his face ruddier. His hair glistened like gold when he bent to the balls. He stretched in a slow, deliberate, catlike way. It occurred to Edwin that things were all turned around. He wasn't here to seduce Leo. It was Leo who was the seducer.

Again, he felt a pang. It had no name, though it masqueraded in many faces. Hunger. Loneliness. Frustration. Guilt.

I want to be free, he thought, which was a very strange thought for him to have, especially while he was working. He had never known true freedom until he had met Lord Foxley.

Leo cursed in Russian and turned to face Edwin. He leaned against the table, canting his body in a way that was unmistakably inviting. "Missed."

"I hadn't noticed," Edwin admitted.

Leo blinked slowly with his big, green eyes. "You are not such a fearsome player, after all, vampire."

"And as a devil?" Edwin leaned forward and set his hands on the billiards table, boxing the young man in. He was suddenly intoxicated by the heat and scent of the human in front of him. He felt his usually silent pulse quicken within him.

Leo gave him a hungry look that would have made any vampire proud. "They are only fallen angels, yes? Not so frightening." He brushed Edwin's lapels, then took a handful of his shirt and pulled him forward so they were pressed against one other—Edwin's chill against Leo's warmth. Edwin was taller, but only by a little. Leo leaned up and teased Edwin's lips apart, shivering when he sensed the sharpness of Edwin's teeth.

Edwin slid his arms around Leo's waist and kissed him. He kissed his eyelashes and the side of his neck, but very lightly, with a tenderness that surprised even him. Leo made delightful little mewling noises as Edwin nibbled his way to the edge of Leo's collar. Leo turned his head, giving Edwin his throat. He purred like a little lion.

Leo tasted like heat and life. Sweet, salty, and succulent. The small, pulsing vein at the base of his neck seemed to sing against Edwin's tongue. "Do it...yes...I want to feel it," Leo said before sliding into his native tongue and saying other things that Edwin couldn't follow.

Unable to hold off any longer, Edwin struck like a snake, sinking sharp, painless teeth deep into the rich, red velvet wellspring there. The boy let out a cry as *El Mal de Amour* took him to a place he had never been to before.

Edwin drank and drank. Leo's warmth filled his mouth and aching, empty belly in a way the vodka never could. Foxley wanted him seduced. And Edwin only meant to drink until the razor-sharp edges of his never-ending hunger were sated, but time quickly lost all meaning. Leo kept moaning and urging him on, whispering to him in the soft, perverse language of lust.

Before Edwin even realized it, Leo's warmth began to wane.

Edwin, his heart beating frantically in his chest and Leo's stolen blood washing like the ocean in his ears, forced himself to back off, to let go. Dread filled the good warmth inside him. He was shaking and barely able to stand. The boy—Leo the Green-eyed Lion—lay empty and defeated on the billiards table, gasping for breath. His fingers clenched at empty air and his eyes had a frightening shine to them while the last of his blood washed into the velvet of the table.

Edwin was no virgin, but, somehow, he'd lost himself tonight. Not for the first time, and yet, this was a hundred times worse than the times before. Worse than the carnage he'd wrought in times past. The boy had struggled so hard to flee his oppressors—only to come to this.

Death at an assassin's hands—just one that had loved him.

"Leo," Edwin said, his voice full of tears, his heart breaking into small pieces inside of him.

* * *

I'll take Summersfield down. I'll take his Court. Just give me time.

That's what Edwin told Eliza just before he left her. He'd wanted to challenge Summersfield right then and there in the middle of his masked crush. He didn't want to wait and make Eliza endure any more than she had, and if he somehow managed to take Summersfield down, by High Court law, he'd own Summersfield's Court, the *Marie Antoinette*—and all of the Poppets aboard her.

But Eliza begged him not to. She insisted he wasn't ready.

"He's a thousand years old. You won't win," she'd told him.

Her words made Edwin's pride smart. He might be young, but he was much stronger than most vampires his age. He insisted he could outmatch Summersfield even though he secretly had his doubts. Summersfield had never lost a challenge. Even Foxley avoided the Vampire Lord like the plague. In the not so distant past, Edwin recalled Foxley altering his plans just so his and Summersfield's paths did not cross. Foxley was not afraid of Summersfield, exactly, but he was nonetheless leery of the younger vampire's ambition.

"I don't understand why everyone is so bloody afraid of the tosser," Edwin said angrily. "He's not even as old as Foxley."

Eliza seemed reluctant to say, but she finally blurted out, "He's an empath, Edwin. A powerful one. He knows what moves you'll make even before you do it. It's like his superpower—the reason he's never lost a challenge." She sighed tiresomely. "I shouldn't have even told you that. Somehow, he'll know I said something. Then he might punish someone just for me telling you."

She trembled in his arms. "You should leave as soon as possible. The longer you stay, the more he becomes 'aware' of your presence aboard the ship. And if he finds you..."

"Is that the reason you're so afraid of him?" he asked. He was stroking her hair, speaking low.

"I'm not afraid of him, Edwin. I'm *terrified*. I heard that after Derek, I, and the other Poppets got away from his Court, Summersfield went on a rampage and destroyed every Poppet he owned and replaced them out of a fear that others would leave him. He took it as a personal affront." She drew back and shook her head, tears streaming down both cheeks. "And I know it isn't just some rumor, because I don't recognize a single Poppet on board this ship. I won't be responsible for that happening again—and it will if you challenge him and lose. He'll kill you, Edwin, and then he'll kill every Poppet in his Court, including me."

He didn't know how to respond to that. The situation was fucking impossible. But then, Eliza kept insisting she could handle her situation, and that Edwin needed only to stand down. Unfortunately, it wasn't in Edwin McGillicuddy's nature to stand down on anything—particularly in a situation like this.

Now, as he made his way down the long industrial staircase to Poppettown, he replayed his options in his mind, as limited as they were. He was dressed in a dirty, wet, flowing black raincoat that made him feel like *The Shadow*, and as he listened to the belching of the city's huge steam-powered machines surrounding him in the dark, he thought yet again about what he could do to undermine Summersfield's power. How did one destroy someone who could get into people's heads? Who could anticipate your every move?

He reached the large, vault-like door and spun it open...

I'll take his Court. Just give me time.

It had become his entire focus now. His reason for existing.

Minutes later, he was making his way out of the basement of a derelict tenement building and standing on the street, surrounded by the ramshackle, mismatched architecture of Poppettown, the slum where so many runaway Poppets, fugitives, and general ne'er-do-wells called home.

He lit a cigarette and considered his surroundings. It was a lawless land, and it looked like it. The huge steam machines that powered the city of New York rose up and up into the infinity of a metallic sky, creating a miasma of grinding gears and steamy pollution. Down here, the workers who kept the city running lived in miserable little crooked buildings made of bricks and debris, their facades dressed in graffiti, and their tin roofs pitted and rusted by a century of humid, low-hanging precipitation. The random buildings squatted together, windows broken, looking like children's blocks that might topple over anytime. Elsewhere, there were coldwater flats, sleazy pawnshops, bars, gambling halls, and plenty of houses of ill repute.

People rushed about him—humans, vampires, Poppets, refugees one and all—as he stood among the foot traffic and hailed a cab. No law enforcement paroled these wet, eternally dim streets. The law, such as it was, was dictated by the most powerful crime organizations in current power. Most New Yorkers found the place appalling when they had the misfortune of finding themselves down here. And some barely knew it even existed. But the overall decay and danger of the place barely touched Edwin.

In a way, these were his people, his kingdom. A boy of the Bow-bell, it was simply his East End of London dressed up in another skin.

A cab pulled to the curb, and the driver, a handsome black man who also happened to be a simpleminded former Pleasure Poppet, looked him over with hazy eyes. "Where you goin', mister?"

"Starlight Casino. Know it, mate?"

"Why do you want to go there?" He might be simple, but Edwin had the impression that the man recognized him for what he was and was doing vampire math in his head. Was it worth taking on the fare with the milky skin, bright auburn hair, and wolfish yellow eyes—a member of the species who had undoubtedly abused and humiliated him? Perhaps he should just drive away.

Edwin waved a hundred-dollar bill under his nose, deciding it for him.

The Poppet immediately perked up. "Everyone knows that joint. Get in."

Ten minutes later, he was standing outside the casino. It had once been an ugly redbrick warehouse, one of a thousand in this part of Poppettown, but the owners had dressed it up in lights and paint so it looked more like a carnival sideshow. Inside, the dregs of society swarmed. The lobby was full of whores and pickpockets. Giant lighted signs advertised different game rooms, several peepshows, and an "erotic massage parlor."

Eliza had worked in this dump as a laundress soon after escaping Summersfield's Court. Both she and her childhood friend Derek had their hours in here—Derek turning tricks and making a fortune, something Eliza could never bring herself to do, not after what she had experienced at Summersfield's hands. The thought darkened Edwin's mood considerably, and he had to make a conscious effort not to let it show on his face.

A woman clad in only body glitter stood at the entrance of the massage parlor, beckoning to him. Beside him stood a huckster, busily calling out to passersby. He was telling them what they could expect from the most beautiful and exotic Pleasure Poppets in the world—and all of it for less than twenty dollars! He even handed out menus with going rates scribbled haphazardly on them. Places like this were more likely to cut your throat and steal your cash, but Edwin put on a smile and went up to the huckster.

"And what can I do for you, young man?" the huckster said cheerily, so caught up in his own game that he was unaware that he was speaking to a two-hundred-year-old vampire. "A brunette, perhaps? No, I can see you would prefer a lovely redhead..."

Edwin cut him off. "I'm looking for a guy. A cowboy, to be exact."

The man leered at him. "We have cowboys...we have Indians..."

"I want a specific cowboy. A Snake-Eyes named Derek Wall."

The huckster's face grew guarded and he lost his bravado. "Trust me when I say that Derek Wall would not be interested in your company, young man. Clarissa, here, on the other hand..."

Feeling tired and more than a little put out, Edwin reached out and snagged the huckster by the tie. He let his eyes go all black so the huckster could see, finally, what he was dealing with.

The man froze, and suddenly, the smell of wet trousers hit Edwin's sensitive nose. "Derek," Edwin said in a much less friendly tone. "Which room?"

Minutes later, he was standing at the door, knocking. He waited exactly ten seconds before his patience unraveled, his rage and desperation exploded, and he gripped the doorknob, ripping it and the door off the hinges and tossing it aside like driftwood.

Inside, two naked girls screamed and bolted from the king-sized bed in the suite. Derek sat up, took one look at Edwin, and pulled an old-fashioned Colt from the holster under his bed. "You," he said menacingly and cocked back the trigger.

"Hallo, mate," Edwin said, stepping inside.

He was impressed. Somehow, Derek Wall managed not to shoot him all through his brief explanation for his being there. He did eye Edwin as if he'd lost his goddamn mind. When Edwin finally finished his story, Derek surprised him by reaching for his gold silk robe and tying it on as he got out of bed.

Derek stood up, eyes narrowed, the gun held loosely in one hand.

Edwin was fairly certain he could draw Belle from the back of his trousers at about the same time that Derek squeezed off his first shot. At this range, they would most likely hit each other, Derek would die, and Edwin would either live or die, depending on whether Derek managed to hit Edwin's clockwork heart. However, none of those scenarios was beneficial for his plight. Or for Eliza.

Derek, standing there half-dressed in his robe and cowboy boots, gave him a surly look and said, "No."

Edwin thought maybe he hadn't heard right. "But...it's Eliza...Alisa. Summersfield has her. We can work together to get her back. If you organize the Red Doors..."

"I said no, Edwin."

Edwin stopped speaking. He'd had high hopes that Derek would respond on a wholly primal level to Eliza's predicament. After all, long before Eliza was his, she had been Derek's. They'd grown up together in the Scholomance. He was her first love, a huge part of who she was today, and Edwin knew he would always have a piece of her young heart—even if he was loathed to admit to it.

But Derek didn't seem to feel the same way. He pressed his thin lips together and stared at Edwin with shadowy eyes. "The Red Doors? I don't think so. The Red Doors don't mobilize except for a just cause."

"But it's Eliza."

"Just so."

Edwin stared at him, struck speechless for a full minute. "Derek, mate, you know Summersfield. You know what he's doing to her..."

A shadow passed across his handsome face. "Everyone who has ever been a Poppet at his Court knows what he does, and everyone who knows also understands what he's capable of."

Edwin opened his mouth but Derek cut him off. "Summersfield slaughtered a hundred of his Poppets on the day Alisa and I ran away from his Court. He ripped them to bloody rags, and I know that isn't just some story. I've seen the pictures he took."

"He took pictures?" Edwin's fingers were just itching to get around Summersfield's throat. Refocusing on Derek, he said, "Help me, and I'll take him out. I'll make him pay for what he did."

Derek laughed as he took a step forward, still brandishing the gun. The darkness and madness in his eyes spoke volumes. Summersfield had damaged him beyond repair. Eliza once said that Derek feared nothing in the world more than the Vampire Lord that had owned him. For Poppets like Eliza and Derek, Summersfield was the ultimate bogeyman, the thing to be feared above all other things. Even Foxley didn't elicit the primal terror among the Poppets that Summersfield did.

"You will never beat him in a fair fight, Prince," Derek proclaimed. "Summersfield is an invulnerable monster."

"Nothing is invulnerable," Edwin insisted. "Everything has a weakness."

"Not him. Not Summersfield," Derek continued to laugh madly. "Now...get out."

Edwin started to turn, then stopped and swung back around. "Why?" His voice cracked with desperation. "Why would you turn your back on Eliza?"

Derek's expression remained stony. "Alisa made her choice. She chose you even knowing the danger it would put her in. She always knew Summersfield might find her, and still, she chose you."

Edwin felt his teeth slide down as anger took him. He clenched his fists, his fingernails cutting into his palms. "You won't help us—help her—because she hurt your fucking pride?" He almost leaped forward, but Derek lifted the gun and leveled it at Edwin's head.

His next words left Edwin cold.

"She made that bed she's sleeping in. Now she must lie in it. Get out, vampire."

Edwin thought about compelling the man—all it would require would be one bite and Derek would be his. At least for a time. But Derek, perhaps sensing his intentions, squeezed off a shot that exploded into the woodwork an inch from Edwin's ear.

Edwin shook his head, his ears ringing. When the tinnitus cleared seconds later, he heard a rush of feet on the stairs as the bouncers made their inevitable way up to see what the gunshot was about.

"Next one goes into that robot heart of yours, you undead freak," Derek said, his voice as dead and toneless as an assassin's. "Or whatever thing passes for your ticker."

Two giant bouncers appeared in the doorway behind Edwin. They started forward but then hesitated when they saw the gun in Derek's hand. "There a problem?"

"No problem," Edwin said, holding Derek's dead gaze. Raising his arms to show he was unarmed, he slowly backed out of the room and made his way down the stairs.

Out on the street again, Edwin stood for a long moment in the gutter, watching traffic and despairing. Although he had an iron in the fire with Malcolm and the Youngblood Pack, he wasn't fool enough to believe that was anything but a Hail Mary. This had been his ace in the hole, his secret weapon. If he could get the Red Doors behind him, he knew he could weaponize half of Poppettown. It would make him an incredibly powerful Vampire Lord. But he couldn't do that without Derek. And Derek…well, he'd shown Edwin his true face.

It surprised him, but there was no help coming from the underground.

For the first time in his life, Edwin had no idea where to go from here. He felt lost. Alone. So, he reacted not at all when, a few minutes later, a black limo pulled up to the curb and the back door opened to reveal a bulky werewolf in a tailored white suit, guns crisscrossing his chest under his jacket. He indicated the car. "Get in, McGillicuddy," he said.

Edwin, rousing himself, looked up at this curiosity. "And why should I do that?" he asked just to be a smartass. He was feeling rather self-destructive at the moment and didn't care if the gangster wolf tried to shoot him in the street. In fact, he hoped he tried. At the moment, he was in a mood for some good old-fashioned fisticuffs.

"Get a load of the pretty boy here," the werewolf said to someone in the backseat with him. "He don't wanna get in the car, Master. What do I do?"

The person in the car with him sighed, then got out on his side. It was a tall, slim vampire, which struck Edwin as odd. Those of the fanged community did not usually hang out with those of the befurred one. The vamp was dressed in a long, brushed, dark red coat with faux fur along the sleeves and lapels. Edwin spotted sparkling golden hair and green eyes like a cat's. He spoke with a decade-old Russian accent as he leaned over the roof of the car.

"Please ignore my large friend here and come with me, my Lord," Leo said. "I may be able to help you retrieve your wife."

***

Eliza sat quietly beside Summersfield in his personal theater box. She was dressed in an opera gown of royal blue and lavender. Dahlia, dressed in red, sat beside her, her little hand clutching Eliza's in a death grip. She was whimpering because Summersfield hadn't allowed her to take Mr. Snoop with them tonight. Down below on the stage of Summerfield's private theater, a collection of Poppets were performing *A Streetcar Named Desire*, his favorite play.

Halfway through the second act, Eliza felt Summersfield's arm stretch across the back of her seat so he would play with Dahlia's midnight black curls. Dahlia sat stoically in her seat, looking as motionless as a doll, though tears glistened on her cheeks. At one point, she had whispered that she wanted Mr. Snoop, so Summersfield told her that he had burned Mr. Snoop in the ship's incendiary and that Mr. Snoop was no more, which caused Dahlia to scream so shrilly that Eliza feared she might have gone deaf with the sound.

Even now, it haunted her.

After Edwin left her, she made a promise to herself that she would look after her own welfare and that of the...baby...inside her. She would make that her priority. She had to! But now she saw how impossible it was to keep that promise. She had no doubts that Summersfield planned to terrorize Dahlia tonight, to break her down as he had broken down hundreds of Poppets before her.

She couldn't let that happen. She couldn't be this selfish. If she let it happen...well, that would make her as bad as the evil creature sitting beside them. Eliza was strong. Stronger than Dahlia. Moira said she was their champion.

Perhaps, she thought, it was time to be proactive. Time to stop crying and despairing...

She needed to divert Summersfield's interest away from Dahlia. But now? And, honestly, how much could she endure? How many times could she put herself in Summersfield's way before his hunger killed her?

It seemed an impossible situation.

Down below, the aging Southern belle Blanche DuBois went through her caricature of motions in the play—exaggerated sighs, cries of distress, and fluttery hand movements. And slowly, as she watched, Eliza came to realize something. The character of Blanche really knew how to run men out. They consistently fell for her histrionics and came away convinced that they would be her savior. It made them feel good about themselves. It placated them.

Eliza, because she was different from the other Poppets, had grown up used to being the leader, the motherly figure, the one all of the other Poppets looked to for guidance. As a result, she had never learned to play the femme fatale. She had never learned to *lie* properly. She had striven for honesty in a world that was not at all honest.

Now things had changed. Aside from Dahlia, the other Poppets disliked her, feared her, and refused to have anything to do with her. Once, she thought she could organize them into some kind of coup, but she had since given up that idea. They were too simple, too set in their ways. *Too broken.*

Perhaps it was time to approach her predicament from a different angle. She needed to turn the tables on Summersfield, and that would require a bit of theatre.

In the dark, she slid her hand in a friendly manner over Summersfield's leg. She felt him stiffen in surprise—he wasn't used to her or any Poppet making the first move. But she took a few deep mental breaths and cleared her mind of all of her bitterness, anger, and despair. She would never be able to pull this off if she didn't force herself to feel what she was conveying.

"Alisa..." he said after a moment, his voice reverberating in the dark. It was a dark, chocolaty voice, the kind of voice that made both men and women alike swoon.

She made herself remember what he'd been like before she'd gotten to know him, the little teenage crush she'd had on him at the Scholomance when she first looked upon him, her future Lord. He'd been so tall, dark, and mysterious, like the heroes in the books she liked to read. It wasn't until later that she learned what a monster he truly was. She let herself feel that dull tingling sensation from years ago, as repulsive as it was.

"I never liked that name," she confessed, but not in her usual vapid, higher-pitch Poppet voice. Not in the tone of the simple Poppet she'd been pretending to be up until this moment.

"Really." He sounded interested and not at all surprised. He did not turn his head, but she sensed she had his full attention. "Perhaps you will tell me what I should call you instead."

She turned her head and fixed him with an honest look. "I prefer Eliza."

"The name you chose for yourself. Where did you get it from?"

"Eliza Doolittle of *Pygmalion*."

"The little flower girl who takes elocution lessons from Henry Higgins so she may one day take on polite London society." He nodded as if immensely pleased by her confession.

"It's one of my favorite plays," she told him. "Edwin and I saw it on Broadway last year. The Music Box Theater. It inspired the film *My Fair Lady*, as well as countless other adaptations."

He finally turned to her and, in the dark, their eyes met. She narrowed them to show she was no simple Poppet.

Summersfield already knew, of course. He had always known. Smirking, he picked up her hand and kissed the pulse in her wrist, which jumped under his cold lips. "My lady, it is good to finally meet you. What else can you teach me?"

* * *

The call came into the DEA's office just before noon on his last day of work. A man fitting the description of a suspect they'd been tracking for months had been spotted on the pier, going into a warehouse. Shots were fired and a passerby had called it in.

Tommy Quinn hung up the phone and turned to Tanaka, who was wolfing down a corned beef sandwich at the desk across from him. "Looks like Frankie Abbot is moving down at Pier 8. Wanna drag his sorry ass just for old time's sake?"

Samuel Tanaka raised his bushy brows. "I thought you were going to take it easy, this being your last day and all. But hell yeah. I'm in."

Tommy, grinning, got to his feet and reached for his suit jacket, thrown over the back of his seat, the same chair where he had sat and filled out police forms for the last twenty-five years. "Call for backup," he told one of the younger cops before flying out of the bullpen.

Together, the two of them suited up in body armor in the locker room, checked their munitions, slipped their badges around their necks, and took Tommy's old sedan down to the docks the way they had countless times before over the many years of their partnership. Several black and white backups trailed behind them at a safe distance.

Normally, Tommy, as senior partner, went in first, but as he climbed from the car, a sudden, sharp pain in his back made him clutch the roof and bend at the waist. The pain quickly subsided, but when he looked over at Tanaka, he spotted the concern stamped across his partner's face.

"You okay?" Tanaka asked, coming around the car.

He hadn't told Tanaka, or any of his other coworkers, about his diagnosis. The only one in the department who knew about the cancer was his captain and one of the girls down in HR, and he'd had no choice in that matter. He'd had to be honest about his reasons for early retirement, and he'd needed all of his insurance papers up to date.

"Getting old, I think," Tommy joked.

"Well, I already *knew* that." Tanaka smiled with easy familiarity and pulled his piece. "I'll take lead this time." He moved to the door of the warehouse, leaving Tommy no time to protest.

Not for the first time, Tommy feared that Tanaka might know more about his condition than he was letting on. Not specifics, mind you, but being a werewolf and all, he was surely picking up on subtle cues. For almost two decades, they had shared each other's company, celebrating their victories and consoling one another on their failures. They had spent more time together in Tommy's car than they had with their respective wives. When Maggie died, Tanaka spent a week sleeping on Tommy's sofa in a show of camaraderie, and, these days, Tanaka's wife Betty invited Tommy to dinner every Sunday afternoon. Tanaka knew him better than anyone.

Tommy leaned against the car, waiting to see if the pain would return. When, mercifully, it did not, he moved into position behind Tanaka.

Tanaka's ears pricked up in a physical way that had surprised Tommy the first time he had seen it. Now, though, it was as commonplace as the way Tanaka chewed with his mouth full.

"What is it?"

"Absolutely nothing." Tanaka signaled that he was going in.

Tommy nodded, thankful the adrenals in his body were blocking out any pain the cancer might be throwing at him and covered his partner with his weapon.

"Detective Sam Tanaka, DEA," Tanaka said as he kicked in the door and quickly cased the area with his gun. It was dark and seemed to be unoccupied from what Tommy could see from his position. He cautiously moved into place beside his partner to examine the darkness—and that's when the lights were flipped on and a chorus of voices cried "Surprise!"

Tommy was gobsmacked. "You son of a bitch," he said when he found he could speak. He put his gun away.

Tanaka laughed as he put his piece away. "We knew it was the only way to get you here, old man."

The warehouse was decorated with streamers and balloons, and there was a gigantic banner that read WE WILL MISS YOU, TOMMY! strung across the length of the warehouse. Over two dozen tables were set up, complete with crystal glassware, top-notch silverware, and bottles of champagne for everyone. Maybe a hundred people were standing there, cheering and waving at him. Some held their phones up as they took a video of his stupid, surprised face. Even a live band had been hired, and they immediately started playing some old ragtime tunes—Tommy's favorite.

The time, effort, and dedication put into his retirement party was humbling. It made Tommy's eyes sting. A long row of longtime friends and coworkers paraded up to him to wish him well. He was hugged and kissed and his hand shaken almost straight off. Then Betty Tanaka—a professional party planner, and he should have remembered that, he thought—led him to the head table, which was packed with catered food, streamers, balloons, and gifts.

"I hope you're hungry," Tanaka said, sounding apologetic. He clutched a glass of bubbly in his big hand. "As usual, Betty overdid it."

Betty playfully boxed her husband's ear.

Tommy couldn't find it in his heart to tell Tanaka and his wife that their efforts were thoughtful but in vain, that the cancer was making eating a nightmare of vomiting and indigestion, and that these days, he was on a strict regimen of soups and liquids. So, instead of concentrating on such depressing issues, he loaded up his plate, accepted a tall glass of champagne, and joined his friends—these people he had worked with, struggled with, laughed with, and bled with for more than twenty years of his life—and pretended that everything was okay.

One by one, his old friends and colleagues from over the years visited his table and exchanged stories with him. "So, I guess Frankie Abbot will forever be the brass ring that got away," he joked with Tanaka.

"Naw," his partner said. "We picked his dumb ass up early this morning. The little shit held up a Stop 'N Go and got his ear blown off by the counter guy, who had a shotgun." He raised his glass to Tommy. "Consider it my gift to you. Now, Harry Mancini, on the other hand..." Soon, he had launched into the story about the mobbie that got away when they were both still fresh and wide-eyed from the Office of Training.

It was like two and a half decades of his life painted on a huge animate canvas, not that Tommy minded. The camaraderie he felt that day would never leave him, he knew. These stories...these lives...they made him what he was, and he cherished them. They made him happy, almost as happy as he'd been with Maggie. These people had been with him even as Maggie died by inches. They were his family or the closest thing he had to one.

Tommy wasn't a man given to sentimentality, but he realized he loved them, one and all. By nightfall, he was drunker on the atmosphere around him than on the meager alcohol he had drunk throughout the party. The only thing that could have made this celebration any better was if Cesar were here to celebrate with him, but no one knew about that part of his life. The thought rounded out his sentimental mood. It gave him something to look forward to that evening.

Eventually, the Captain came around to offer Tommy a formal commendation, a gold badge on a wood plaque with his name on it that would hang in City Hall in recognition for all of his years of service. The local newspaper showed up to take his picture, and then his friends sprang the last—and best—surprise of all, an all-expenses-paid holiday for two to the Caribbean, which the whole office had chipped in for. He and Maggie had vacationed in the Caribbean a few years before she died of ALS. He was touched that so many of his friends remembered.

"I hear you have some young sexy thing you're hiding away," Tanaka joked while everyone getting ready to leave came round to hug him once more. Tanaka shook Tommy's hand, a playful spark in his eyes. "I'd be lying if I said I wasn't a little bit jealous."

"You old dog. Betty would kill you."

"I heard that," Betty said from afar, ears pricked to their conversation, and both men laughed.

Tanaka surprised him by pulling him into a rib-crushing hug. Tanaka wasn't exactly the touchy-feely type outside of his werewolf pack, so this was definitely suspect. When they finally pulled back, there were tears in Tanaka's eyes.

"Now, don't be like that," Tommy joked. "They'll put you in retirement soon enough."

The Captain appeared one last time with his retirement papers, and, together, they walked out to Tommy's car. "Are you going to be all right?" he asked, his voice low, discreet.

Tommy knew the man as a brusque, no-nonsense type who seldom inserted himself into other people's lives. Their relationship was nothing like in the movies. They didn't banter or rub each other the wrong way. Tommy was a dependable agent and followed the letter of the law. No Dirty Harry antics. The captain generally let him get on with things with a minimum of interference. The two men had great respect for one another, but now Tommy saw how uncomfortable he was. His condition did that to people, reminded them of their own mortality, and that was perhaps the worst part about it. For all the good camaraderie, an ill man was still something of an outcast.

"I'll be fine," he lied, then indicated the folder in his hands. "Thanks for taking care of the paperwork. And thank you for the holiday."

"How will you manage? Further down the line, I mean."

"I have that all taken care of, so no worries."

The oncologist had estimated Tommy's time around three months of quality life before he'd need an in-home nurse or hospice care. But considering the thudding, persistent ache in his back, Tommy thought it might be much sooner. Still, he wanted to see the tropics one last time with Cesar. He just wasn't sure he'd be coming back from it.

They stopped at his car, and the captain turned to face him. He put a friendly hand on Tommy's shoulder. "You're one of the good ones, Tommy. The best I ever had. If you need anything..."

"I'll let you know," Tommy said with a practiced smile. "Really, Frank, I'll be fine. You know, I might even beat this thing. Then you'll have to take me back. Imagine that." He laughed, and Frank laughed, too. The two men shook hands, then Tommy got into his car, which Betty had stuffed with leftovers, and drove home.

Ten minutes later, he pulled into his designated spot in the complex's underground park garage and cut the motor. He sat very still and stared into the darkness for a long moment. And just like that, he threw himself the biggest pity party he'd ever had. First, he cursed, then he cried, then he punched the dashboard until he feared he'd set off the airbags. Afterward, he felt rather ashamed for all of his childish rage. He'd thought he was past this. Just like Maggie and the ALS, he had to play the cards he'd been dealt.

"Bloody tosser," he told himself in the mirror, hating his red-rimmed eyes and the dark, unhealthy shadows lurking beneath them. His face looked gaunt and as grey as his suit, and his skin was thin like parchment ready to tear away from the surface of his skull.

He could see jaundice steadily creeping into the whites of his eyes. For the first time, he looked bloody sick.

"Bloody, bloody tosser." That's what his father said whenever he was pissed drunk at the pub and angry at the world.

Taking a deep breath, Tommy put himself back together. He smoothed his hair, straightened his tie, and wiped the tears away. Pain ticked down his back, gently and persistently. He felt an irrational jab of disappointment in himself. The pain was breaking him down in a way nothing else in his life had. It made him want to curl up somewhere, preferably in the company of someone he loved, and sleep, dream. Bloody dying had made him sentimental and lonely.

Once he was calm again, he got out and went upstairs.

The last time they'd been together, Tommy had given Cesar his key. It was the first time he'd done something so rash, but now he was happy he hadn't held back as he would have in years past. The lighting was low when he stepped into his apartment. Cesar had lit candles and set them on random surfaces so the entire apartment glowed warmly and romantically. The homey, comforting smells of dinner wafted from the kitchen, bringing back memories of Maggie warming his dinner in the oven when he came home late from work.

"Oh good, you're home," Cesar said, stepping out of the kitchen in an apron that boldly read WILL COOK FOR SEX.

Tommy laughed at the apron. He didn't have the heart to tell his friend that he'd been eating all afternoon. So instead, he forgot all about that. He went into Cesar's arms, letting the vampire cradle and kiss him. It felt good to taste him, to feel the steely, supernatural strength of Cesar's arms around him, keeping him safe.

"You look tired," Cesar said when at last they came up for air.

"I am. A little. Is that apron for real?"

"Absolutely," Cesar grinned. "But, first, I made dinner. Cornish hens and stuffing. It's a specialty of mine."

Tommy swallowed hard. "Could we bypass that for dessert? Ice cream? I have a bit of a sick stomach tonight, I'm afraid."

Cesar looked concerned. "Sure."

Instead of the kitchen, they retired to the sofa in the living room. The vanilla ice cream that Cesar fetched him tasted bloody good. They watched *America's Next Top Model* together. It wasn't until recently that Tommy had come to appreciate ice cream and popsicles. It seemed like the only food that didn't irritate his perpetually angry stomach.

He noticed the carefully set dining room table and felt a pang of guilt. "Are we celebrating?"

Cesar curled up around him on the sofa. The way he was able to manipulate his sinewy but well-muscled body was a sight to behold. He put a hand on Tommy's chest, and Tommy felt his heart flutter at the weight. His trousers were suddenly very tight. His stomach might be a ruin, but at least some things were still working right.

With a little smirk that Tommy had come to associate wholly with Cesar, the vampire said, "I have good news for you."

Cesar's smile was so contagious that Tommy smiled back. "You plan to throw me to the floor and roger me tonight. Vampire-style."

"Well, yes...that...but something more than that. It's about the cancer."

Suddenly, the good mood he was feeling dissipated. Tommy set his ice cream aside. "We talked about this. We said we wouldn't discuss it."

"You don't have to die," Cesar said.

After more than twenty years of police work, Tommy was rather astute at reading people. He could tell Cesar had been the type of child to rip his presents open first thing on Christmas morning. He was impetuous and headstrong. Subtlety and patience were not his strong suit, but that was partly what made Tommy love him as much as he did. His nervous young energy was contagious. He really did love this vampire boy, but he still didn't want to discuss the cancer. Not tonight.

Tommy started saying something to that effect, but Cesar cut him off.

"I *know* what we discussed, Tommy. I've been thinking about it constantly. But you don't have to die. Not now. I have it all arranged."

Tommy gave his lover a dubious look. "Arranged?"

Nodding, Cesar jumped to his feet and started pacing while he launched into his explanation like some hyperactive kid who'd eaten too many Pixy Stix. From his place on the sofa, Tommy tried to follow everything that Cesar was saying. He watched the vampire circle his apartment, but within seconds, he was lost and begging Cesar to backtrack. Cesar was so animate that he didn't even seem to realize he was falling all over himself.

"No, not *Edwin*," he said to one of Tommy's many questions, gesturing wildly. "Edwin's *master*, Lord Foxley. He's agreed to interview you for the position of his next Heir. I have it all arranged. You just have to show up for a brief interview and answer a few simple questions. I'll be there as well, so you won't be alone."

Cesar hesitated, his eyes lit up. "It won't be difficult, and I have Foxley's word you won't be harmed. Also! I promise being made an Heir is nothing like you see in the movies. It's quite pleasurable, the whole process—like having your first ever orgasm."

Tommy opened his mouth, then closed it.

Cesar grinned at him. "And I just know Foxley will approve of you. You're too good of a cop for him to say no, so you don't have a thing to worry about..."

Tommy held up a hand. "Stop. Just stop."

Cesar did, though he continued to stare at Tommy. Slowly, the color drained from his face as he realized something was wrong. His lips trembled as he forced the next words out. "What's wrong?"

With effort, Tommy stood up. He smiled as he seized Cesar's cheeks in his hands, hoping to soften the blow. "I appreciate your concern, Cesar, I do. It touches me. And I don't want you taking this the wrong way—though, I suspect, you probably will—but...I don't want to be a vampire. I love you, truly, but I don't want to be one of you. So I'm afraid the answer is no."

Cesar stared at him, blinking in confusion. "I don't understand."

"What's not to understand? I want to spend my remaining time with you, but when it's my time, it's my time."

Cesar's eyebrows knitted together as he processed Tommy's words. "But that makes no sense. There's a way for us to be together forever. Why wouldn't you want that?"

Tommy let his hands fall to his sides. "Let me try and explain. I want to be with you as long as I can, but I don't want to be a vampire. I've never wanted that, and what we have isn't about that."

Cesar hung there a moment, utterly confused. Then his smile returned. "You've just never really thought it through..."

Tommy sighed. "I have, in fact. You'd be surprised what you think about when you get a diagnosis like mine. But, ultimately, I'd rather die as a man than live as a vampire. Do you understand?"

Another second passed. Then: "You're not thinking straight." Cesar's voice had gained a frantic octave. He was animate again, but for an entirely different reason. He clenched and unclenched his fists. "I arranged this for you! For us!"

"And I'm grateful for your efforts, truly, but the answer is still no." Tommy clutched Cesar's face, trying to calm him. "I know this is difficult for you to accept, my dear, but you have to try. It's my body, Cesar, my future, *my* decision. Understand?"

The remaining color drained from Cesar's face. "No...no, I need a reason. Give me a reason...!"

Tommy sighed. This was going down just about as badly as he had expected it would. "How about I give you two? Number one, I've dealt with vampires on occasion in my line of work, and I know you lot have a great deal of complicated politics. I want no part of that..."

"They're not complicated—" Cesar insisted, but Tommy pushed on.

"And number two, as silly as it sounds, I was raised in the Church of England, the Anglican Church, and our catechism believes that a man who is turned to vampirism has no soul."

"That's ridiculous!" Cesar exploded. His eyes suddenly darkened and Tommy could see his teeth lengthening in his mouth, though he suspected Cesar wasn't aware of it. "Those are stupid, bullshit excuses, Tommy!"

"Maybe to you..."

Cesar grabbed Tommy's arm too hard, completely unaware of the unbelievable strength in his hands. Tommy cried out in pain and surprise, which made Cesar release him too quickly. Tommy skidded on the carpeting and went down hard, just missing the sofa and landing in the space between the sofa and coffee table. The impact on his tailbone was hard and jarring, and he grunted from the pain.

Tommy watched Cesar's wide, terrified eyes clear and return to their usual pale silvery blue. Looking frightened, he bent to him. "T-Tommy...I'm sorry!"

Tommy snatched his hand away. "I think you ought to go."

"I didn't mean..."

"I know you didn't," Tommy said in a soft, subdued voice. He wasn't angry. He felt too sorry for Cesar to feel anger that he'd overstepped. Tommy was by no means happy that this had happened, but he wasn't going to make a big deal of it, either. Something else the cancer had given him—an innate inability to dwell on minor offenses.

He clawed his way up and onto the sofa cushions. "Please, I'm not cross, but I want you to go right now. We'll talk later."

"No, Tommy...I..."

"Later, Cesar. Please."

* * *

They met at an outdoor café on Broadway. Malcolm was sitting at one of the sidewalk tables, a cup of tea and some biscuits in front of him, when the werewolf suddenly appeared, pulled out a chair, and sat down opposite him.

From the rough look of him, Malcolm could only surmise that this was Joseph, Alpha of the Youngbloods. The man was huge, as large as a wrestler, maybe bigger, and dressed in a shirt with the sleeves torn away to reveal twin canvases upon which were scrawled primal tattoos. Malcolm estimated his height as even with his own, about six-five, but Malcolm was sure Joseph outweighed him by at least fifty pounds, all of it muscle. He had a military bearing, hair cut short and bristly, jaw set stubbornly. His brutish face bore several scars, and only one of his eyes focused properly. He smelled strongly of wolf; it was obvious the older alpha carried his beast very close to the surface of his skin.

If Malcolm were younger, he might have been frightened of Joseph, but Malcolm had faced the Sidhe, one of the most dangerous creatures in the world. He thought he could take this alpha.

"You must be Anjou's new boy toy," Joseph said. "The Scottish werewolf." His voice dripped with sarcasm.

Malcolm met the man's eyes squarely. He usually had very good instincts when it came to meeting new people. For instance, upon meeting Eliza for the first time, he knew she was a tremendously strong and smart woman, and Edwin, her husband, a good man—or as good as vampires ever got, anyway. Malcolm immediately and thoroughly disliked Joseph. The man gave off an air of brutish indifference. He was a bully, and Malcolm did not like bullies. "English, actually," he corrected the alpha.

"Well, hallo there, guv'nor!" Joseph said in a deplorable Oliver Twist-esque accent. He looked Malcolm up and down. "No pinky in the air? What if the Queen finds out?"

Malcolm set his teacup down, unperturbed. "Her Majesty the Queen is a striga. She has little to do with the werewolves or their ways, I'm afraid."

Joseph flashed his wolf eyes. "Muscling in on a man's territory. A man's woman. I ought to knock your block off right here and now, boy."

"Man?" Malcolm answered, unmoved by Joseph's bluster. "And who might this 'man' be? All I see before me is a spoiled child used to getting his way."

Joseph's face crumbled even as Malcolm detected the snick of a switchblade under the table. He smelled the oiled steel and realized Joseph had edged it very close to Malcolm's genitalia.

A wolf, and he required a human weapon!

Malcolm harrumphed, unimpressed. "Now then, that would cause quite a stir, would it not?" He glanced about the busy street. "You would be arrested. And it would hardly endear you to Anjou."

Rage boiled in Joseph's mismatched eyes. "What has that bitch been saying about me?"

Malcolm sighed and sat back, pinnacling his fingers under his chin. "I will say this one time only, wolf. If I discover that you've harmed Anjou or any of her pack members, our challenge will take a very dark turn, indeed."

Joseph sat forward in his seat. "What the fuck does that mean?" The blade pressed against Malcolm's immaculate and professionally pressed trousers.

Malcolm moved much faster than any man, and most wolves, could, reached under the table, and snagged his rival's balls through his jeans. Predictably, Joseph jarred in his seat, shocked and surprised by the act, and dropped the blade, but Malcolm didn't let go.

Malcolm smiled and finished the tea in his cup with his other hand. Then his voice growled forth, too low for any human within earshot to hear: "It means I kill you, child, cut your chest open with my claws, and eat your heart out. Do you understand me?"

Joseph opened his mouth and then closed it several times like a fish suffering from lack of air. Malcolm tugged at his rival's sensitive equipment, then let it go and got up. Joseph squirmed around in his seat uncomfortably, then seemed to recover. He bounced up, set a card on the table, and told Malcolm he expected to see him in the ring.

"Very well," Malcolm said, taking the card. "And may the best wolf win."

vi

Take me with you today. Let me show you what I can really do.

That's what she'd told Summersfield that morning as she lay beside him in his bed, the sheets rumpled around them. She was still a little stunned from last night. Following the theater, she had gone willingly with him to his suite, and, once inside the dark, humming rooms that made up his personal suite—a place very few people aboard the ship ever saw—she told him to wait for her.

She'd had no idea if he would listen to her, but he seemed amused by her audacity and went to sit patiently on his divan. She found a wall of books in the adjoining room and picked one out at random—*The Odyssey*—then returned to the parlor and sat down at his feet and started reading to him. He'd found it utterly delightful.

It didn't stop him from taking her to his bed, but he was uncharacteristically gentle with her. It was hard to play along, of course, but Eliza discovered that if she worked at it, she could imagine herself as an actress in a play, following stage directions. It wasn't her, she decided. She wasn't Eliza. She was this character she had created for his benefit. And hers.

The next morning, she watched him rise and dress. He said he had an important board meeting with his stockholders. Afterward, though, he would take her for a walk in the artificial park he had created mid-ship. Then they would go to lunch.

She sat up, crawled to the foot of the bed, and delivered her lines like a starlet. "Take me with you. Let me show you what I can really do."

He looked at her, eyes narrowed in suspicion, nostrils flared. She wondered if she had lost all the ground she'd gained last night. So she upped the ante.

"The board meeting is about the missing investment funds, correct?"

Now, Summersfield actually looked shaken that she should know that.

She added quickly, "I hear things from the servants. You think one of your own people is draining the corporate account, and you're right. But if you rely on your empathy to discover who it is, you'll never get to them in time before they move all of your funds out of your accounts. Now that they've been found out, they're going to move fast today. You know that, right?" She hoped the logic appealed to him. "I can get you their name."

Summersfield moved closer to her. She edged back in the sheets, clutching them against her chest, afraid he would leap upon her. But he only smiled as he loomed over her. "You think you can do that, eh?"

She forced herself to sit up straighter. "No, my Lord. I *know* I can." She smiled. "I can communicate with electronic devices. Use a meeting room with a docking table and I'll prove it. I'll prove *myself.*"

His face changed not at all, and she wasn't sure if he believed her, but just before noon, he returned to collect her. He looked at her doubtfully as she took his arm. But Eliza smiled up at him and said, "You'll just have to trust me."

When he walked her into one of the formal meeting rooms with its giant, wireless, phone-charging table, she knew she had him. His stockholders were already seated, waiting for their Lord and CEO to show.

Sweeping the room, she noted that the men and women all had their phones properly docked. One of Summersfield's little quirks was that he never allowed the use of cell phones during his business meetings. He didn't like people's attention wandering off him. It was one of his many conceits. As a result, most of his people liked to dock their phones and recharge them during these incredibly long and boring meetings.

He sat at the head of the table and she took the spot at his right-hand side. No one paid her any mind. It was their Lord's prerogative to keep a Poppet nearby in case he grew hungry. She was the living equivalent of the pitcher of water and glasses on the serving tray at the center of the granite-topped table.

The meeting lasted a little over three and a half hours. During that time, Eliza kept her hand under the table as she touched the underside where the docked cell phones were. Sometimes, Summerfield's eyes moved to her, but she continued to smile nicely and vapidly in appropriate Poppet fashion.

When the meeting was concluded and everyone got up to leave, she set her hand on his shoulder to keep him seated. "Look at your tablet," she whispered.

"This better be good, Eliza." Looking unimpressed, Summersfield picked it up and swiped through it. He looked increasingly confused. "What is this?"

She said nothing, just let him examine all the new data that had filtered down onto his device. As she suspected, he wasn't exactly the sharp tool when it came to tech. Had had employees for that. So she explained. "I cloned all of the phones docked at this table and put a copy of each of your shareholder's phones on your device. It's a lot of stuff to go through and it'll take you some time, but I think you'll find a clue as to who is moving your funds around."

He scrolled for a while before looking up at her with a cynical, almost fearful, eye. "And you can do this how?"

"I'm not sure. It's a power I recently acquired. Something to do with my unique biology. But this is just the tip of the iceberg of what I can do for you."

She leaned down and looked into his eyes while commanding the lights in the room to flicker—not erratically but in a predetermined and easily recognizable pattern of Morse code that spelled out his name. When they came back up properly, Summersfield was still staring at her in that strangely emotionless way he had, but he had gone a few shades paler, if that was even possible.

She had done it. He was hers.

* * *

Edwin followed Leo Romanov up ten flights of stairs. He was dead and even he was winded by the time they reached what he thought was the basement level of a warehouse on a pier in the lower Bronx. Leo took a device no larger than a cell phone from his pocket and hit a button that caused a large panel to slide back in the ceiling. Spreading his wings, he shot upward and into the dimly lit warehouse far above, making it look simple.

Edwin stayed down below a long moment, looking up at the hole. He didn't fly. Never had. He wondered how he was going to do this when Leo suddenly threw down a rope ladder. His face appeared over the edge. "I remember."

Grumbling, Edwin scaled the ladder and found himself in the massive warehouse full of lights. The big werewolf climbed up after him. The ceiling arched upward maybe fifty feet, resembling the ribbed dome of a cathedral. Computer panels and lit screens took up one whole wall of the warehouse. Opposite that was a cozy seating area. After briefly glancing around the high-tech surroundings,

Edwin followed his Heir to the small collection of tables and chairs and saw there was piping hot tea waiting for them.

"Nice digs," said Edwin. "You live here?"

Leo nodded once as he sat down in a wing chair. "My associates and I. *Da.*"

Edwin glanced at the big bruiser who didn't seem to want to wander more than a few feet from Leo at any given moment. "Is he your associate?"

"That is Hugo, my ship's engineer."

Edwin looked the huge man over. Hugo glowered back at him but said nothing.

"Hugo has heard the stories about you, Edwin," Leo explained. "He thought you would be bigger."

Snorting, Edwin went to sit down but decided to keep Hugo the werewolf in his peripheral vision at all times. "Ship's engineer," he mused, then turned to Leo. "You have a ship?"

Leo smiled over the edge of his teacup. "You're surprised?"

Edwin refused the tea that Leo indicated was his. "I shouldn't be. You're resourceful."

Little had changed with Leo. He was still the beautiful blond youth with the large green eyes. The sight of him tore a small and very deep hole in Edwin's heart. He thought about all they had meant to one another once and never would again.

"There you go, getting sentimental, my Lord," Leo mused. "As if things haven't worked out for the best." He smiled, but it was bitter and wistful, and the sight of it encompassed everything left unsaid between them.

Following the incident in the game room in Club Mischief in 1923, Edwin was faced a dilemma. Normally, after such an incident, he would have fetched Foxley's cleanup people who were tucked away in all of the major cities, and they would have discreetly disposed of Leo's body. He had done it dozens of times before. But this time, Edwin couldn't bring himself to do it. He couldn't treat Leo like an unfortunate mistake. He had seconds—if that—before Leo passed on from blood loss. So, Edwin, following his heart, opened a vein in his wrist and made Leo drink him while massaging his throat like he was a sick kitten.

It was the first time Edwin had ever tried to make an Heir. He didn't know what to expect.

Leo continued to lay there on the billiards table, looking quite dead. Maybe he hadn't done it right? Or maybe he needed more time? Edwin wasn't sure. He only had broken bits of memory from the time Foxley turned him.

Not knowing when else to do, Edwin threw Leo over his shoulder, climbed out a window, and hurried down to the street, where he hailed a cab. Thankfully, the cabbie just thought his mate was blackout drunk and happily drove them into the heart of London. Edwin told him to stop at a random hotel—a sleazy-looking joint that didn't look like anything Foxley would frequent. Edwin paid for a room and took Leo up, staying with him all night.

Later, Leo woke up, confused and hungry—and Edwin got a crash course on how to care for a baby vampire. It was difficult, made more so by the fact that Edwin had no experience in caring for anyone but himself. Compounding things further was the fact that he couldn't let Foxley know about Leo. If Foxley found out what Edwin had done, he would most assuredly destroy his Heir in a fit of jealousy. Edwin knew his master all too well. Foxley wouldn't want Edwin's attention diverted away from him. And Edwin had decided he couldn't bear to part with the vampire he had made.

Leo was his Heir. Leo was his.

The very next day, Edwin bought tickets aboard the *SS California*, which was sailing for New York, and he and Leo ran. Foxley followed them as Edwin expected he would. And, over the next few decades, he and Foxley would play a long game of cat and mouse with Edwin only a few steps ahead of Foxley at all times. Most of the time, Edwin felt like Foxley was running him out, playing a game he knew he could easily win. Probably the bastard could reel him in at any time, but he seemed to be enjoying the chase.

The next forty-some-odd years were terrifying, infuriating, and extremely tiring. The Second World War, and the chaos that followed, seemed to delay his capture and confuse the agents that Foxley sent after him. By the time the 1960s rolled around, Foxley had grown tired of the game, tired of Edwin's insolence. He sent the assassin Chimera to retrieve Edwin and bring him home—with force, if necessary. Thankfully, Edwin and Leo had since parted company and there was only Edwin to punish.

Just before they saw each other for the last time, Edwin and Leo broke their bloodlink. It was a difficult spell, and it demanded they both bleed themselves out completely and replace their blood with that of several victims, mostly criminals they found in the seedier parts of town—not that that made the process any easier to stomach. After they made certain they shared not a single drop of blood between them, they made a pact that they would never contact each other or, indeed, see each other, again. It wasn't safe. Foxley could turn a wormy eye on Leo at any time and use him as leverage to bring Edwin home. So this sudden little reunion had come as something of a surprise to Edwin.

"You're concerned," Leo guessed.

"But not displeased. I've missed you." Edwin's heart was heavy. There was something about your first Heir—much like your first-born—that was unique and special. But the circumstances of their lives had not made it a pleasant experience for either of them.

"I missed you for a while. And then I did not," Leo admitted. "That sounds cruel—"

"No. It pleases me to know you've been happy. You have been happy?" Edwin sat forward.

Leo smiled wistfully and his eyes drifted. "I have been happy and I have been sad. Very sad. I had a companion for a while, but he passed on in 1989."

"I'm sorry," Edwin said because he was. "I'm sure it was hard."

"But not unexpected. He was very old. We were together for thirty-two years."

Edwin frowned. He remembered a depressive episode he'd experienced in 1989 that lasted months. It must have been the remnants of his and Leo's bloodlink. They might not be together any longer, but their blood still recognized one another's pain and always would, it seemed. "You didn't turn your companion?"

Leo shrugged. "It would not have been fair to him...and it would have put me in a vulnerable position."

Edwin had never really thought about it that way. Did Eliza make him vulnerable? He had wanted to turn her. But was it fair to her to alter her life so completely? He wasn't so sure now.

"You are sad now. I feel it," Leo said, reading the ragged fragments of their bloodlink. "It's why I am here. I know what you are going through, my Lord."

Edwin lifted his head and indicated the warehouse. "Then you must know this isn't safe. If Foxley finds out..."

Leo muttered curses in Russian. "I do not care what Foxley knows or does not know. I only care about what you are experiencing because I know something of the pain."

Edwin sighed. Regardless, he couldn't put Leo in danger this way. He started to get up, but Leo motioned for him to stay.

"I owe you. I must help you, my Lord."

Edwin laughed. "You owe me? After what I did to you in that billiards room?"

Leo gave him wise eyes. He seemed unperturbed by Edwin's statement. Perhaps he enjoyed being a vampire. The thought never occurred to him. "Was it done in malice?"

Edwin was surprised by the sob that caught in his throat. "I don't know, Leo. I'm not sure it matters. The results were the same, regardless. At the very least, what I did to you was dome in selfishness." He took a deep breath. "I wanted you and I took you."

Leo cocked his head. "But you are not that man any longer, *da?*"

Edwin stared at the floor. "Perhaps. Or perhaps I am more that man than I have ever been."

"We are all timeless and yet changing inside." Leo indicated the warehouse whose lights had begun to flicker. A low, almost subliminal hum had begun under Edwin's feet. "Time makes us who we were always meant to be."

Edwin swallowed hard, absorbing Leo's wisdom. Finally, he said, looking around, "What is that? What is this place?"

Leo's eyes sparkled. "Shall I show you what I have become?"

***

They went up a long, spiraling, iron staircase, then up another. A third one followed. Each level was similar, though each seemed more packed with crates and equipment than the last. It didn't take Edwin long to realize that they were moving through the levels of a cargo hold as they might on a great ship. And his suspicions were confirmed when they came upon a level with round, riveted porthole windows. Edwin approached one, rubbed away the grime, and saw the distant mist of cumulus clouds closing in on all sides of them.

"We're in a ship," he said. "We're flying."

"Earlier, we were stationed in an underground hangar, but now we are flying, *da*," Leo explained. He motioned Edwin to one last staircase, the longest one yet. When they reached the top, Edwin spotted two men with guns standing on at a large porthole door open to the bridge of the ship. The men saluted Leo crisply.

As Edwin and Leo stepped into the navigation room, the guard outside announced, "Captain on the bridge," and all of the people stationed at their computers stiffened. The ones standing at the helm saluted Leo.

It was a motley crew. Not all of the members of Leo's Court were vampires. Some were shifters, and there was even a woman at the helm who was close to eight feet tall, stark white, and dressed in soft red armor, her long white hair coiled atop her head. She turned to glare at Edwin, and her alien black eyes and unnaturally long slit of a mouth startled him.

A full-blooded Fae!

She was unlike what he had faced in East Anglia last year. The Fae there had been watered down with human interbreeding. They were Sleepwalkers, only able to assume their true forms during an altered form of consciousness. REM sleep, Eliza had explained. And still, they had been dangerous as hell.

"This is Narissa, my chief navigator," Leo said, introducing them.

Edwin was sure to stand at least five feet away from Chief Navigator Narissa, though the Sidhe seemed to take no offense. She did harrumph to her captain. "Funny, I thought he would be taller."

Leo put a hand up to hide the smile on his face.

Peeved, Edwin stepped forward to meet the woman head on, though he didn't extend his hand. He knew better than that. Fae, even half bloods, had the unique power to pull the lifeforce out of all living things with just a touch, which was probably why Narissa was wearing fingerless leather gloves.

He looked at the navigational screen she was working over. "What is that?"

Narissa turned to the screen. "Us. It's a bird's-eye view of the *Queen Anne's Revenge II*. We are entering the airspace over Baltimore, where we'll refuel the *QAR2* before continuing on to Glasgow."

He was surprised by how quickly they had covered the space between New York City and Baltimore. But, considering the *QAR2's* design, it made sense. It was a small, compact gyro, less than five hundred feet in length, obviously created for speed and high maneuverability. He studied Leo's ship on the screen. Its torpedo-like shape, the air scoop fin that ran along its spine, and the forward thrusters located beneath the ship gave it an especially shark-like appearance, though it bore no markings or flags. He knew enough from listening to ship talk from Foxley to know that usually indicated it was a decommissioned vessel or an unregistered airship.

A jolly roger, in other words.

"What's in Glasgow?" Edwin asked. He'd finally realized he was aboard a pirate vessel, and that they were going places he wasn't comfortable with.

Narissa turned and gave him a grin that split her face entirely in half in that creepy way of the Fae. "The question is not what's in it, but what isn't...but will be again!"

***

The thin, bare-chested satyr lifted the ogre over his head as if the creature was made of feathers and threw him easily across the room. The ogre smashed into the chain-link fence separating the pit fighters from the circle of bloodthirsty onlookers, bounced off, and rolled to the blood-splattered cement floor of the warehouse. The crowd immediately started to scream their approval, and not a few tried to reach in and scratch at the big man's bare back where he lay on his face, barely conscious, blood dripping from both pierced nostrils. Some screamed for his death.

Malcolm wasn't sure if the audience was trying to get him to stand up or wanted to kill him.

He felt a spike of nausea. It certainly wasn't unheard of to fight for sport in his day—and werewolves often had to prove themselves among their rivals—but such fights were always conducted privately, not for entertainment purposes. There was nothing to be had in death.

The people of this era were surprisingly bloodthirsty.

The satyr raised his arms and screamed victory before leaping to the top of the fallen ore and stomping his head to bits with his hooves. The savagery of the attack caused Malcolm to take a few steps back. Blood dotted his motorcycle boots. Around him, the people screamed and cheered.

He almost turned to leave, but what passed for a referee stepped out of the roaring crowd and moved to the center of the pit—he had to step over the ogre's now very dead body—and rang a big bell he was carrying. "Your champion, Yog-blogsoth!" He held up the satyr's bloody, half-wrapped first while the creature grinned from one long ear to the other. Meanwhile, his fans went wild beyond the chain link.

I'm too old for this nonsense, Malcolm thought as he tried to push his way past the crowd behind him. He would find another way to build his pack. Nothing, but nothing, was worth this. But the crowd hemmed him in, holding him in place. He was about to use force if necessary to cut a swath through them when the referee announced the next two contenders.

"We have quite a show for you tonight, folks! Next for the Octagon—Big Joe Black of the Youngblood versus Malcolm, the Werewolf of Whitby!"

More hollers and whoops rose up even though this lot could not possibly know who he was.

Malcolm turned and saw two members of the staff dragging the ogre's body away—it left a wet, red stain on the cement—while Joseph waded through the crowd on his way to the pit, hungrily eating up the praise of the onlookers. He was dressed in gladiator armor and a black fur cape, and he swished his way to the center of the pit as if he owned the place. Once there, he tilted his head back and roared, then centered his eyes on Malcolm to make certain everyone in the warehouse knew exactly who his opponent was.

Malcolm didn't care if turning away made him look weak. This was strictly blood sport without purpose or meaning, and he would have no part of it. He knew Miss Eliza would agree. And she certainly would not approve. She would be appalled to see him here tonight.

But Joseph's next words stopped Malcolm dead in his tracks.

"Challenge is set and match, Malcolm!" Joseph said just loud enough to be heard over the screaming crowd. "And if you do not meet me toe to toe, Anjou will pay the price."

Malcolm turned back, a spike of anger making his teeth grow in his mouth. "That was not part of the deal!"

Grinning, Joseph made a come-hither gesture. "It is now!"

Bristling, Malcolm started toward the pit, the audience pushing him along as if afraid he might bolt. When he reached the gate, a beautiful vampiress dressed in sexy red leather grinned at him with her saber teeth and pulled it open, welcoming him inside the chain-link barrier.

Inside, Joseph waited for him, a lopsided grin on his face.

Malcolm eyed him up and down while he removed his long jacket and then his shirt. Several of the women and even a few of the men in the audience catcalled Malcolm, but he ignored them. His attention was wholly focused on Joseph as he tried to spot a weakness in his rival. So far, he hadn't noticed anything obvious.

The referee indicated that both men should approach him, and when Malcolm and Joseph were only inches apart, the man announced that there were no rules within the confines of the pit.

"I know," Joseph said. "Let's get on with it." He grabbed the referee by the shoulder and reeled him in so he could bite the side of his head. The little man screamed bloody murder while Joseph pulled his ear off and yanked one of his arms out of the socket. His bell clanked as it fell to the concrete.

Malcolm lunged toward the little man, intending to pull him away from Joseph and out of danger. But it was a ruse. Joseph let him go and turned on Malcolm. And now Malcolm was at a disadvantage as he was trying to carry the injured man out of the pit. Joseph grabbed his arm and turned, wrenching Malcolm's arm back at a painful angle. Malcolm grunted and dropped the referee, who landed on the concrete and rolled away.

With a laugh, Joseph's grip tightened, and, applying hardly any effort, he lifted Malcolm and threw him the length of the pit.

Malcolm was shocked by the other werewolf's power and ferocity. Hitting the fence made his already injured shoulder smart, and as he went down, he fell into a pool of blood left behind by the last opponent. Trying to stagger up, he slipped and fell to the ground again.

The crowd screamed in either delight or horror, depending on which fighter they had laid their money on.

Joseph did a brief victory lap while Malcolm checked himself to make certain he had no serious injuries. His shoulder was partially dislocated, but he was able to click the bone home with a hard shrug of his shoulder. It hurt, but years of shifting made such an injury more of an inconvenience than a concern.

He stood up, being careful not to slip in the blood again—it was splashed generously across the floor—and turned his attention on his opponent.

The other werewolf had returned to the center of the pit and was waiting for him. He'd ripped some of his armor off in strategic places so he could partially shift into his man-wolf form. Joseph was a huge, bulky wolf. Lots of gym muscle. It made him good to look at, but Malcolm wondered what his maneuverability was like. Calling on his wolf, Malcolm let his other self fill his form. It bumped his height up to almost eight feet. Wrinkling back his gums, he showed his enormous scythe-like teeth and gave Joseph a deep, rumbling belly growl.

Joseph, who had been posing for his fans, suddenly turned and gave Malcolm a careful up and down appraisal. Malcolm didn't see fear, exactly, but there was certainly caution in the way Joseph moved back toward the edge of the pit.

Malcolm approached him, letting the wolf in him guide his moves. He trusted his wolf and knew it would be able to match Joseph's attacks if he could just stay calm through it all.

For Miss Eliza. I'm doing this for you, my lady...

The two werewolves suddenly clenched. For Malcolm, it was like grabbing a tree trunk wrapped in fur. Malcolm felt muscle over muscle over rock-hard bone. He squeezed the other man and tried to throw him, but Joseph was too heavy. Before Malcolm knew what was happening, Joseph inclined his head and bit Malcolm's shoulder.

Malcolm roared and used all of his strength to push Joseph back. The act tore a bite of flesh from Malcolm's shoulder and pain immediately flared down his back and into his arm. Malcolm whined and clutched his wound while Joseph stepped back, blood oozing out from between his huge teeth. Blood was spurting from his wound as well, and Malcolm immediately gripped it tight to control the bleeding.

Joseph used the distraction to smack Malcolm back a few steps. Malcolm stumbled until he hit the chain link, where the people were screaming and poking at him with sticks and small knives, telling him to get back in the ring and fight like the pit dog he was.

Bu Malcolm only blinked, the pain from the bite wound making him feel ill and blurring Joseph's image. He had both furry, heavily muscled arms raised over his head while he roared with victory. Malcolm chastised himself. He was losing focus—losing the fight. He had to do better than this. He was no pup. He had fought larger and meaner opponents than Joseph. But it had been ages since such savagery was necessary. And Malcolm had learned to live and enjoy the Twenty-first Century. He was a pacifist by nature.

Not now, though. He couldn't be weak. Not with Miss Eliza's life and freedom hanging in the balance.

While Joseph taunted him, Malcolm looked up at all of the people. Amidst the unfamiliar faces, one stood out. Near the back of the room, he spotted Anjou, who had just slipped in the door of the warehouse. Her face was painted with worry.

Something happened. The sight of her brought him an inner peace he had never known before. With Anjou, he could have a mate. A wife. He could have another chance at a family. A pack. He could *belong*.

With a grunt, he straightened up and centered himself. Joseph was brutal and clever. He would need to be more so.

He moved toward Joseph. Strangely, his thoughts turned to his master, Lord Edwin. Now, there was a guy who didn't play by life's rules. He didn't just bend them, he broke them in half and then beat his opponent over the head with them. Malcolm recalled how the vampire had fought while they were taking out the Fae last year. *By any means necessary.* Malcolm was no lover of vampires, but he admired his master's gumption and ingenuity.

Malcolm growled, his voice ending on a high warning note. It drew Joseph's attention around to him.

"Ready to go again, pup?" Joseph asked, his voice muffled through the big teeth in his mouth. He wasn't even looking at Malcolm; he was staring up at his adoring fans, reveling in their screams.

Malcolm released his hold on his wound. It was still bleeding, but not as badly. The pain was good, he found. It kept him focused and alert. He cracked his neck and shoulders and strode forward.

Joseph laughed as he beckoned. "Come to me, pup. I want to break your back like kindling."

When only a few feet separated them, Joseph did when Malcolm expected he would—he lunged, jaws gaping wide to snag Malcolm by the throat. Malcolm, staying calm throughout, did something he knew his master Edwin would do. A slippery fellow, Edwin always used his head. Malcolm ducked to the side and grabbed Joseph by the arm as he sailed past, twisting him sharply to the side.

A sharp crack echoed through the warehouse, indicating that Malcolm had likely broken Joseph's arm. He didn't hesitate, following through by wrenching Joseph's arm back at an impossible angle. The move not only aggravated the broken bone but flipped Joseph's entire body over. Joseph went ass over teakettle and landed with a grunt on his back on the cement.

Still holding Joseph's arm at a bad angle, Malcolm dragged him around, then, with a harsh snap, jerked him to his feet almost as if they were ballroom dancing. He then rammed his shoulder into Joseph's clavicle and lifted him briefly over his shoulder before power driving him into the floor again. It was a move he had seen professional wrestlers use on television.

Joseph howled with pain.

Malcolm, actually enjoying himself now, threw himself upon Joseph, his meaty forearm slamming into Joseph's neck. Joseph grunted and passed out.

Getting to his feet, Malcolm spied Anjou cheering for him almost louder than anyone else here. Raising his head, he howled his victory.

"Kill him! Kill him!" the crowd was screaming as one. He saw the madness in their eyes. They wanted this bloodshed.

But he was an honorable wolf and, under these circumstances, death was not necessary. It wasn't something Edwin would do. Malcolm had defeated Joseph appropriately.

Despite the crowd's demands for Joseph's death, Malcolm started shuffling back away from Joseph's prone figure...and that's when Joseph turned his head and clamped his jaws on Malcolm's ankle, sinking his teeth in deep.

Malcolm screamed in pain and fury. He didn't think much about it. Reaching down, he snagged Joseph by the upper and lower jaws and started prying his mouth open. The tensile strength in Joseph's jaws was powerful, but the pain had amped Malcolm's strength, and after only a second or two, he had Joseph's jaws wide open, Malcolm's blood pooling from between those jagged teeth. The sight set the beast off inside Malcolm, and he followed up by dragging Joseph's jaws wider and wider until he heard a click and knew the bone had split.

Letting go, Joseph dropped to the concrete, whining in pain through his broken jaws. After a few seconds, he managed to scrabble up on his hands and knees, his jaw all askew, and scurried away in defeat, leaving Malcolm the clear winner of the battle.

The crowd screamed in delight, but Malcolm had already left the pit.

Later that night, as Malcolm lay satisfied in Anjou's arms, the cheers and roars of the crowd still echoed in his ears.

***

Leo gave Edwin a quick tour of the ship.

The *Queen Anne's Revenge II* might be compact, but it had many floors. After he took command of the ship, Leo turned the former dining halls, game rooms, and grand sitting parlors into an assortment of staterooms and cargo holds. Edwin spied the old woodwork, and some of the chandeliers were still intact. But the furnishings were long gone, replaced by large machinery, packing crates, fuel tanks, and even animal pens.

"This place is like Noah's ark," Edwin remarked as Leo led him to his captain's stateroom, which was located off the helm. On the floor below them, he'd spotted some queer-looking exotic birds in cages. And, as they entered Leo's room, one of them greeted them, a pink cockatoo on his perch who kept saying pirate stuff like, "Arr" and "Shiver me timbers!" It was cute.

Edwin played with the bird while Leo explained.

"We transport everything aboard the *QAR2*." Like Narissa, he pronounced it "Quar-2." It had taken Edwin a moment to catch on.

The door they'd passed through didn't want to shift closed all the way, so Leo swore and kicked it, then slid it fully closed with his shoulder. He turned to Edwin with a half-smile. "Old ship. Used to be the *Lady Luck* before we...uh, borrowed her and re-christened her."

Edwin knew that name. "That was a floating gambling hall back in Prohibition Days. I think Foxley owned it at one point. But she was shot down during World Word II after the Allies confiscated her to carry warheads."

"Shot down, not destroyed," Leo informed him. He patted the door like he was assuring an aged pet that it was still loved.

It explained the extensive renovations to the lower levels and the old-fashioned-looking rooms with all their furnishings ripped out.

"Actually, this old heap is falling apart, but she does what we ask her to do…mostly." Leo turned to flip on some lights. They flickered problematically before turning all the way on.

The cockatoo said, "Host the mast, matey!"

The captain's quarters had been extensively renovated. It reminded Edwin somewhat of Lord Ian's updated castle on the Whitby moors. The walls had been outfitted with runner lights, and computer stations were snugged into corners. A huge, heavily gridded windowpane that probably served as a visual navigational panel took up one whole, slightly rounded wall. A cockpit station was attached to that wall.

"You can control the whole ship from here," Edwin observed.

"If need be," Leo explained. "There are override capabilities. But I did not bring you here to show you my antique toy. Follow me."

Leo started down a side corridor with Edwin following. The captain's quarters were vast and composed of a small mess hall, a lounge, and several tiny staterooms. At the end of the hall was another door that required a security card—the captain's personal sleeping quarters. Edwin knew it belonged to Leo because he recognized many of the works of art on the walls from his time when he was on the run with him. Leo had described many of them beautifully.

Edwin moved closer to Leo's bed to admire the large, exquisitely painted portrait of the royal Romanov family hanging above it.

"Oh, you won't be getting me there," Leo said, surprisingly Edwin with his archness when he realized where Edwin was standing. "I will go nowhere near your mouth again, my Lord."

"No." After a guffaw, Edwin indicated the picture. "I was just looking at this. You keep it above you when you sleep?"

Leo looked at it for a long moment. "To remind myself that I am alive and they are not."

Edwin had forgotten how embittered Leo had been when they first met, angry with the world but especially Czar Nicholas. He had not treated his mother well and had put Leo away in the shadows to cover his shame.

Edwin indicated Leo's extremely dead family. "You realize if you had been acknowledged, you would be dead now just like the rest."

Leo gave Edwin a droll look. "I am dead, my Lord." Which was a very good point.

After he locked the door to his stateroom, he shifted the rug at the foot of his bed and opened a hidden hatch in the floor. Flipping it back revealed a narrow wooden staircase. Diffused, blue-ish light from below was splashed across the room and the portrait of the dead Romanovs. Leo started down with Edwin following, and when Leo requested he close the hatch, Edwin found a rope and pulled the trap door shut behind him.

The hidden hold was quite large, boasting a number of thick metal structural supports from floor to ceiling. Runner lights, similar to those above, lighted the walls as he descended behind Leo. It was outfitted like a barracks with comfortable chairs, benches, and bunk beds. Bookcases covered one whole wall with an eclectic collection of books. Edwin recognized a few of the *Doctor Blood* novels he had written.

Leo said something in the Fae language that Edwin didn't understand, but softly and gently as if he were trying not to spook someone.

Edwin steeled himself as he reached the bottom of the ladder.

Two figures stood in the middle of the room, clutching what looked like homemade rag dolls. They were small, child-like, though that didn't mean anything in Edwin's experience. Fae could look like a lot of things. The two creatures hidden away in this hold had greyish skin and black hair and eyes. They were a combination of ugly and cute.

Edwin stopped ten feet away to give them—and himself—plenty of space. Experience had taught him that Fae tended toward short, violent tempers, and he didn't know what these two were capable of.

Leo showed no hesitation. He went to them and knelt, whispering something to them in the complex language of the Fae. It sounded a little like Upyrese, the ancient language of the upper Vampire Courts, but more musical in tone. But that made sense, seeing how the Fae were the distant cousins of the vampires.

The two Fae answered him in whispers and moved closer to him so they were tucked under Leo's arms in a way that suggested they trusted him. Leo then turned to Edwin and explained, "This is Asia and Aletta, selkies stolen by poachers from their home in Loch Fyne and then bought and exhibited by Lord Milford and his Court. Just recently, we infiltrated Milford's gyro and liberated them."

Edwin, surprised, looked the two selkies over. "You liberate Fae from a vampire's Court?"

"It's what we do. Fae, Poppets, and sometimes valuable treasure..." Leo shrugged and grinned. "The Vampire Lords never report their losses because they are terrified of the bad PR it will cause them, seeing how it's often illegal contraband they collect.

Plus, vampires are prideful beings and cannot stand to lose face to one another."

Edwin laughed at that. Leo was spot on. He then knelt to make himself seem less threatening to the Fae who were studying him with their huge, wary eyes full of sparkling ocean light. They were Fae, yes, but Edwin had always liked children.

After a second, the selkies moved forward to touch him with just their fingertips. "So, what's the gig, then?" Edwin asked Leo.

"Help me get these two beautifies back to Loch Fyne and I'll lend you my ship and crew to free your woman."

vii

Eliza hadn't been to the Poppets' level of the ship in weeks. How many, exactly, she wasn't sure. Time had ceased to have any relevant meaning to her.

Each morning, Eliza woke in Summersfield's bed, dressed, and then accompanied him to all of his business dealings, whether they were formal ones like meetings with his shareholders or casual fetes to welcome a visiting VIP aboard his ship.

During the board meetings, he insisted she gather intel for him. Afterward, they took lunch and spoke of his plans for the evening, which were usually a party, dancing, or some theater event. In the afternoon, they went back to finish any remaining meetings or flew out to observe his holdings. In the evenings, she returned to Summersfield's private quarters, where her eveningwear was invariably waiting for her. Once her personal lady's maid had dressed her and redone her hair, her last stop was to join Summersfield for his evening rounds and entertainment, which usually took her late into the night.

Being Summersfield's Favorite was exhausting. Yes, he treated her better, letting her rest when he realized he'd run her out too long, and he was no longer limiting her meals or draining her blood. He had even given Eliza her own private quarters (adjacent to his, of course) and Brianna, the lady's maid, who proclaimed that

Eliza's every wish was her command. But the weeks were flying by, and the pregnancy was taking its toll on her.

She was tired no matter how much she slept. The morning sickness had thankfully passed, but her breasts were becoming increasingly tender, she had near-blackout headaches some evenings, and there was a growing metallic taste in her mouth she couldn't explain. She probably needed prenatal vitamins, but there was no way she could sneak those without tipping Summersfield off.

She needed to end the pregnancy before he found out. But now that Summersfield had decided she was his Favorite, there was no way she could do that without him noticing. He hovered over her constantly. She was now valuable to him and his business. And if she angered him in some way, what then?

She couldn't risk his wrath. And having Brianna around was also a risk. She was an incessant gossip and knew every detail about everything going on aboard the *Marie Antoinette*. She was particularly keen on what drama was occurring between the Poppets, and Eliza couldn't trust that she wasn't reporting back to Summersfield. This morning, Eliza learned from her that bedlam had broken out down below.

With Eliza gone from the Poppets' quarters, Nathalie had resumed her place at the top of the pecking order and had begun tormenting any Poppet she saw as a threat to her authority. Currently, she was turning her fury on Dahlia, not because she perceived the girl as any kind of threat, but, Eliza supposed, she saw Dahlia as an "Eliza proxy." Nathalie thought she was hurting Eliza by zeroing in on Dahlia. And she wasn't wrong.

No matter what Eliza did, nothing seemed to get any better.

As Eliza came in from her afternoon duties and sat at the foot of her bed, she suddenly realized she needed a good cry. And she did. She dropped to her side, clutched a pillow, and cried into it. These days, it was both a relief and a necessity. She had to cry herself out regularly so she could go back to her usual empty performances for Summersfield. It was the only way she would get through this evening's misery—another soulless crush Summersfield was throwing just to impress a visiting Vampire Lord.

She heard Brianna's light footfalls in the antechamber and quickly sat up, wiping her face. She then reached for a tissue from the box on the bedside table to blow her nose. She was almost back to normal "zombie mode" by the time Brianna swirled into the room.

"Evening, miss!" Brianna called as she pushed her cosmetics cart ahead of her. She was always annoyingly upbeat. It was as though Brianna never had a bad day.

Were Brianna a Poppet, Eliza could at least understand it. But she was human.

I wonder how much he pays her.

Because Brianna loved to talk, Eliza had gotten to know the woman quite well. She was a former Hollywood makeup artist, and a very good one. She used to do touchups for stars such as Angelina Jolie and Margot Robbie between takes.

"How are you doing tonight, miss?" Brianna asked, looking into what had to be her blotchy, miserable face.

Eliza smiled her always empty Poppet smile and told Brianna she was lovely and it was such a nice evening. That usually got Brianna talking about the weather while she dressed Eliza and re-did her makeup—safe subjects. She never wanted to say too much to Blabbermouth Brianna. She knew it would all get back to Summersfield.

"I hear the master has something special planned for you tonight!" Brianna insisted while she painted Eliza's face. "What a lucky little Poppet you are!"

"How is Dahlia?" she asked as Brianna worked on pinning up her wild hair with an antique comb. She hated the condescending tone of the bitch's voice and had to force herself not to grind her teeth.

"The same. Hysterical, most of the time. Or so I've heard." And Brianna said it in that disgustingly happy voice of hers.

Eliza felt her heart squeeze inside of her. She couldn't understand how Brianna could find any of this amusing.

But then, she reminded herself, they were all only Poppets to her. Not real people. She supposed that for many humans like Brianna, it was like watching a bunch of pretty animals trying to interact with each other. Their foils made for interesting conversation later on.

"Miss! You will ruin your makeup!" Brianna cried in horror.

Looking into her dressing table mirror, Eliza realized she was crying and smearing her mascara. God, she looked terrible, drawn and angry, with dark rings under her eyes. Brianna, ignoring her distress, went to work wiping away her smeared mascara and then deftly reapplied it. She worked quickly.

"The master wants to see you immediately, so we must look our best," she announced pertly. "Here are your instructions." She passed Eliza the closed envelope with Summersfield's wax seal on it. It was the same ritual she did every night.

After Brianna was done and gone, Eliza sat staring at her unnaturally wide, horribly traumatized eyes in the mirror, then looked down at the envelope. Ripping it open unceremoniously, she read the contents, then frowned.

No fete or theater tonight. Summersfield wanted to see her next door in his chambers. That would have terrified her once. Now it was de rigueur. He probably wanted blood and sex, the same as every night. She might not even get something to eat first, dammit.

Lifting herself from her seat and smoothing down her long, almost diaphanous white gown—she realized it made her look like a virgin sacrifice, which is probably why Summersfield chose it—she went next door to see what the "master" wanted from her tonight.

The main lounge was empty, so she followed the clanking noises to the kitchen at the back. It was not a room widely used here. Summersfield could eat none of the food prepared on board the ship, and he certainly wasn't about to prepare any of it himself, even for his guests. But there she found him in his modern, industrial-sized kitchen, carefully dicing vegetables and potatoes. He even wore an apron.

"Eliza!" he said cheerily, waving her over.

She had a brief moment of shock, followed by one of complete heartbreak. The scene reminded her of how Cesar used to prepare all of their meals in the townhouse. She missed him and their cramped, overfilled townhouse. She even missed how he used to verbally spar with Malcolm over dinner. She missed her vampires and her werewolf. God, it felt like a lifetime ago.

Swallowing the knot in her throat, she soldiered on, carefully approaching the counter.

"Have a seat," Summersfield said, indicating a bar chair pushed against the counter where guests could watch the cook work. "I will have your dinner ready in no time." He looked down at the mess he was making on the cutting board. "Er...well, it will be done eventually, at any rate." He smiled a little goofily.

Watching him carefully for any sudden moves, she climbed into the bar chair and then just stared at him wordlessly. The harsh uplights did him no favors. It made his skin look like chalk and his hair as black as coal. At least he had washed out the oils he used generously to slick it back during board meetings. But now she understood why he used it because his hair stuck out in weird cowlicks like he habitually ran his fingers through it.

"Do you want me to cut?" she asked after watching him struggle for several moments with the carrots and the chef's knife.

He stopped and stared at the cutting board for a moment as if trying to decide if he should get angry with it or not. "No, I have this."

She watched him prepare the carrots and onions for the mutton roast he was making. Once it was all in the high-end wall oven, she said, "You know that will take a couple of hours to cook."

He turned, wiping his hands on a dishtowel. "That's fine. It will give us time to talk."

The tone of his voice frightened her.

He read her fear easily. "It's nothing terrible, Eliza, please relax," he explained as he got some well-iced wine out of the fridge and a bottle of blood substitute for himself. He carefully set two stem glasses down on the count. "I thought we could use a little privacy tonight—and it's only good things I wish to talk to you about."

His tone of voice made her stomach flip over nervously anyway.

As he poured her glass, he gave her a long, sad look. "You think me a monster, don't you, Eliza?"

She looked at the glass before picking it up and taking a small sip. He might have put something in it, of course, but she doubted it. After all, he didn't have to drug her to make her do what he wanted.

She couldn't taste any alcohol in the wine, which was odd. "I think you are what you are," she said truthfully.

He nodded. "A monster."

"We can all be monsters at times."

He smiled tight-lipped, not offended. "You are always so diplomatic. Perhaps that is why I find you so intriguing. That and your intellect. I should have it measured. I have never seen a Poppet so inclined to intellectual matters. You would make an astute businesswoman, Eliza."

"Perhaps you should teach me if I'm going to be hanging around the board rooms like this." She'd meant it as a joke, and she was surprised when he laughed.

Summersfield raised his glass to her. "I'm glad you are the way you are. It is good to talk to someone who can stand toe to toe with me. There aren't many who can, you know."

A thought occurred to her. She had never heard of anyone on board his ship claiming Summersfield as his or her Sire. "Don't you have any Heirs?"

He shook his head as he sipped from his glass, which was properly opaque to prevent anyone from seeing the viscous red liquid inside. "No…well, that isn't entirely true. I did try once, but I wasn't…satisfied with the results, one might say."

She didn't ask what had become of his Heir, but she could imagine it pretty well. Instead, she steered the conversation in a different direction. "When was that? When you were young?"

He gave her a penetrating look that made her squirm. "I haven't been young in a very long time, Eliza."

"Ah." She could see she had piqued his interests.

He blinked slowly. She could see the concentration on his face as he reach back very far for the details of that time. "Once, long ago, I was an infantryman at the Battle at Brudek. It was a minor battle that took place between Henry III, King of the Romans, and Bretislav I, Duke of Bohemia. The battle occurred in the Palatine Forest in what is now an all but forgotten part of the Czech Republic. But I was not officially a part of either army."

She waited, and he continued without a prompt as she expected he would.

"I was sent along with other infantrymen by the King of Hungary to offer support to Bretislav's tiring troops. It was how we poor peasants made a wage back in those days. They were starving times, and I was one of many poor peasants who needed to bring coin back to my family. I was eighteen at the time, my name then was Mihaly Nyari Mezo, and I had a wife and four children to think about."

She tried to digest that. She'd had no idea he was Hungarian or that he'd been married and had had children. He just didn't seem the type. But then, she reminded herself that men and women married young back then, and most suffered through short, miserable lives that only ended in one of three ways—famine, war, or disease. She touched her stomach. And if you were a woman, you usually died in childbirth or under the hand of an angry man.

"The battle was short and brutal. And nothing of consequence. No one even learns about it in school anymore, which is a shame. I died in that battle." He turned away and gave her his back while he refilled his glass.

She studied him carefully, finding it hard to read him suddenly. After his glass was half-filled, he said, "You want to know how I died. And how I was reborn."

"If you want to talk about it."

He turned back and leaned on the counter. After a few sips, he said, "There is an ancient tradition of scattering flowers over battlefields where many soldiers have died. Most historians believe it is an attempt to cut the smell of the rotting flesh of dead men until the bodies can be removed and properly disposed of. But, in truth, a greater problem is vampires."

She shivered a little.

"In those days, they were savage animals. They often came out at night to pick over the bodies until they found a soldier near death but not quite there yet. Then they would steal his blood and flesh—a form of scavenging. The flowers are scattered about to ward the vampires off, as some are allergic to special kinds. But since the only flowers that are generally available near battlegrounds are wildflowers, it is a haphazard gesture at best what flowers will prevent vampires from getting to any who have not yet died.

"I remember the girl who was scattering the flowers over the field around me even as I lay there, not quite dead, a Roman knife in my side. She was young like me. And I remember the flowers. Purple marsh gladiolus. I still recall the stink that filled my nostrils, how it seemed to amplify the rot of dead men all about me."

Eliza swallowed hard. Her throat was parched but she had almost forgotten the wine. "Is that...how it happened?"

"In a way. I was dying from blood loss when one of the soldiers—I don't even know which side he'd been fighting for—suddenly appeared. He stood there over the tiny flower girl who was presently drinking the dregs of my blood. I saw him draw his sword and behead her. I expect he meant well, but it bathed me in her blood, and I died with her black, bitter lifeforce between my teeth. I must have swallowed it in my death throes because my next memories are of digging my way out of the mass grave where I and my comrades had been buried."

Eliza, despite herself, felt her heart tick in her throat. She couldn't imagine something so horrible. The nightmare of realizing that you were buried alive. Assuming, of course, he was even telling her the truth. For all she knew, he could be repeating the plotline of some obscure vampire movie she had never seen.

But she didn't think so. He seemed a bit too giddy and unguarded tonight to be his usual cagey, slimy self.

He went on to tell her other stories about his experience as a young vampire with no master. She had heard of vampires left masterless and how they usually went mad. He spoke of wanting to return home, but after learning through difficult, firsthand experience the extent of his transformation, he decided it was better to let his wife and children believe he died on that battlefield. His decision made, he stowed away aboard a seagoing vessel and traveled to other lands, preying on the ship's crew at night. He said that Bram

Stoker interviewed him and used many of his personal experiences in his drafting of the novel *Dracula*.

"The *USS Demeter*," she said.

"But of course, that was a fictional Russian ship—and not the one I traveled on. It wasn't even Russian. And there was no Mina or Lucy. All of that was made up for reasons of romance in the novel."

"Then, you've never had a Mina." She saw a look pass across his face similar to the anger he often displayed. She had offended him.

He edged back. "On the contrary, I have had *many* Minas in many different lands."

His statement was so insistent that she sensed he was lying. He might be a thousand years old and an astute businessman who had built an empire floating in the air, but she sensed he had always been a hopeless social cripple. She wondered if anyone had ever really loved him—or even just *liked* him—including his human wife and children.

The night wore on. The more he drank, the more he talked. The roast burned in the oven, but she didn't tell him that. She was more interested in his stories. The way he slurred his words and cursed his fate interested her. His whole life had been one of sadness and loneliness. As she suspected, he had never really had a healthy relationship with anyone. He'd become a soldier and had decided to fight in a war that he had no dog in because he hated his life and wanted to escape his responsibilities as a husband and father. As a vampire, he learned to terrorize those who crossed him or to clumsily seduce those he needed something from. He had spent his coveted eternity spilling selfishness and anger all over everyone he met.

When he realized it was late and she hadn't eaten, he tried to rescue the roast, but as he attended to that, she picked up his phone, calling for room service. He dropped the roast in the sink and went back to talking about himself and his many conquests, his favorite subject.

She found herself feeling a little sorry for him. Michael Summersfield was a small, damaged man, and the course of his life had been hard. His tribulations had made him harder still. Because of his bloodline, or lack thereof, the other top vampires mostly shunned him as some kind of social pariah. Even Foxley, himself an outcast, would have nothing to do with him, which embittered Summersfield to no end. Summersfield considered Foxley an insufferable snob—and a few other choice words in languages she couldn't understand. He had a past not unlike Edwin's, and yet, Summersfield was a lonely, bitter, spiteful creature, fashioned by accident and allowed to run amok. Even his friends, those he had, were there simply to use him or to be used by him.

They were all parasitically feeding off one another, and they would stab each other in the back—and probably in the hearts, too—given half a chance. What a miserable, pointless existence vampires had.

"But you will make me great," Summersfield slurred, leaning on the counter now. His eyes were large and dilated, and the first ticks of concern were going up Eliza's back. "You *are* making me great, which is pretty ironic, I suppose. That trick of yours...all that data you've collected...I'll be able to manipulate the stock market soon...and I could blackmail the High Vampire Courts with all of their dirty laundry..." He laughed idiotically. "I can be great, truly great, and it will all be because of you, Eliza. You are my magic charm."

He reached out to stroke the jagged, lightning-like white stripe in her hair. His touch made her catch her breath.

"How do you do it, pet?" he asked much close to her face.

She could smell the blood on his breath. And the stinking ambition. "I don't know."

He snorted irritably. "Him...McGillicuddy...does he know? Did you do it for him? Is that why that little snot-nosed punk is so powerful now? Is that why everyone seems to revere him? Or, at least, to talk about him?"

His eyes wandered. Thankfully, he seemed to lose track of his thoughts. "The High Courts secretly fear him, you know. Edwin Snot-nosed McGillicuddy! They talk about him like he has some measure of power to unbalance the system. A two-hundred-year-old brat whose only claim to fame was being Foxley's lapdog for a while!"

His attention snapped back around to her. "I can't stand it...the idea that he put his hands on you. That he had you in his bed when you're my property. You were always my lucky charm!"

Summersfield punctuated that last with a slam of his fist on the Grecian marble countertop, putting a long, jagged line into it.

Eliza jumped but kept her mouth shut. They were descending into dangerous territory. If she said or did the wrong thing, he might just kill her tonight. Her hand went, once more, to her belly, where she rubbed it, a gesture she'd found herself doing rather often of late.

He didn't seem to notice or care about the damage he'd done to his expensive kitchen countertop. He kept his greedy eyes centered entirely on her, making her sweat under his venomous gaze. "You don't belong to him. You never belonged to him! I made you! I made your greatness, Eliza!"

She didn't respond, just breathed steadily in and out to keep from panicking and saying something stupid. There was no point in defending her choice of lover and husband. And she wasn't about to discuss Edwin in any kind of detail with him no matter how he baited her. For one thing, it wouldn't make her situation any easier.

For another, Edwin was hers and hers alone. It was the one thing Summersfield couldn't touch or be a part of. And he seemed to know that.

He stopped stroking her hair and tangled his fingers in her curls. She stopped breathing, terrified he'd rip her head right off. He could do it, too. But he turned his head down and took a few deep breaths as he worked on getting his temper under control.

When he looked up, she saw the anger had fled his eyes and he was smiling like the good little sociopath he was. "You are so beautiful. So precious to me. I have a gift for you, Eliza. Two, actually."

He untangled his fingers and turned on his heel to step into another room at the end of the hallway. When he returned, he was carrying Mr. Snoop, which surprised her. She thought he had destroyed the toy. He set the stuffed dog down on the counter in front of her.

Eliza opened her mouth, then paused, confused.

"It's for Dahlia," Summersfield explained. "I have decided to move her into our private quarters. She'll be your companion Poppet from now on. I know the two of you are close." He stopped, his hands shaking a little. She wondered what that synthetic blood was cut with. He looked all coked up.

"I...I don't know what to say, sir," she said, trying to sound contrite.

This situation was about the worse thing she could imagine happening. She had done all this miserable shit over the past few weeks so Dahlia would be safe in the Poppets' wing, not so she could be moved into Summersfield's shadow. He'd only terrorize her more, she knew. But she couldn't say any of that.

"And that's not all." He reached under the counter, took out a professionally wrapped gift in dark chocolate paper with a white ribbon, and set it down next to the stuffed dog. "This one is entirely for you, my pretty pet."

She looked at it a long moment, afraid to touch it. But when she saw he was getting increasingly squirrelly, she grabbed it up and slowly unwrapped the white ribbon, terrified something horrible was inside.

Vitamins.

She looked at the bottle. Prenatal vitamins.

"You didn't know I know, but I do." Summersfield stared at her with those huge, hungry Belladonna eyes. He was almost swaying like a cobra. He leaned over, completely invading her personal space, and put a hand on her abdomen. "I can hear its heartbeat, you know. It's healthy. Another miracle. In all my days as a Vampire Lord, I have never heard of a Poppet with child, and yet there you are, Eliza. Amazing me once more."

She felt numb. She set the bottle down and just stared at it, trying desperately to hold back the tears of horrified dread that were threatening to fill her eyes and spill over her cheeks. All her nightmares realized.

"Don't be frightened. I'll be with you through all of this." Summersfield nodded sagely, his voice soft. "The first time I heard its little heart beating, I understood why you were created. I understood everything."

He smiled. It was a mad, holy smile. "For me, Eliza. God made you for me so I will have a second chance at a family. The little one will be mine in a way nothing has ever been mine before. My child. My Heir! And this time, I will be the father I have always been meant to be. This time, I will protect what's mine with my life, if necessary."

***

Edwin spent the rest of the day familiarizing himself with the layout of the ship, including the extensive weapons barracks. Leo had to attend to the mid-flight refueling, so Hugo the werewolf showed him around. They started with the converted casinos carrying stock—most of it contraband (he explained that at the moment they were carrying antiviral medication to parts of India and Africa where the meds were too expensive for the common people to afford) and moved their way down to the barracks full of rescued exotic animals, and, finally, the engineering level, where Hugo hung out most of the time.

The man was huge and moved barrels of crude oil around like they were Legos. He was also extremely proud of how he had updated the ship's engineering and computer system, though the vast machinery he pointed out and the inner workings of the dirigible were mostly lost on Edwin, who didn't have the skill to fix a broken toaster.

It depressed him. Looking at it all reminded him of how much Eliza would love this ship, and that in turn left him feeling anxious and melancholy. He wasn't sure if he was going to be able to hold onto his patience and complete Leo's mission to deliver the selkies before moving on to the rescue mission that Leo promised they would tackle next.

"Where does that go?" Edwin asked, pointing to a narrow metal staircase that twisted upward and then out of sight.

"Service stairs to the forward deck," Hugo explained before losing interest and started to explain about his improvement to something he called the forward envelope.

Later that night, after the sun had gone down, Edwin found another of those twisty staircases and followed it up to a vaulted door in the ceiling. Twisting the wheel, the door gave way to fresh air and a star-filled night sky.

Climbing out of the hold, he found himself topside, a large, wrapped walkway that went around most of the upper part of the ship. The forward deck, he supposed. It was freezing cold at this altitude, but he didn't care. It was invigorating, and he was slowly discovering he had a touch of claustrophobia. He couldn't imagine hiding away all day in this flying tin can, and he didn't know how the crew endured it. He walked to the edge of the safety rail and leaned on it. It wobbled precariously like everything else on the ship.

He saw darkness and cloud cover, with a few twinkling lights shining between to indicate civilization was down there somewhere. The height and speed they were moving at made him feel slightly nauseated.

When he looked back up, he spotted the ship's navigator, Narissa, standing at the helm. She was staring north through a pair of large, electronic goggles. When she twisted around to look at him, he saw special calculations racing across the goggles' lenses. They reminded him of field glasses such as a surveyor might wear. Holding tightly to the rail, he made his slow way out to her.

"How long before we reach Glasgow?" he called to her.

Narissa grinned widely in that creepy way of the Fae. "We'll be there by morning, vampire."

"The ship is moving that fast?"

"One hundred and twenty air knots," she announced, sounding quite pleased by the ship's performance. "The *QAR2* is one of the fastest gyros in the world. Even faster than the *Gypsy Queen*."

"Impressive."

"We should see the Sky Palace by mid-morning tomorrow." She sounded excited about that. Then, rethinking what she'd just said, she added, "I guess *you* won't see it till tomorrow evening, what with the sun melting your pretty face or whatever it does."

Narissa chuckled at her own poor wit. "Either way, She Who is Three will board us early tomorrow, so be on your best behavior tomorrow evening when you crawl out of your coffin, vampire. She Who is Three has a poor temperament for cagey vampires."

Edwin ignored the barb. His skin was crawling. "Who is 'She Who is Three?'"

"We don't say her name. It may summon her." Narissa went back to surveying their progress, or whatever it was she was doing.

But her comment bothered Edwin. So he went below and pounded on Leo's door.

"Come," he said from inside.

Edwin found the door to the captain's quarters sticking and had to slide it open with his shoulder. When he stepped inside Leo's stateroom, he found him making vampire love to a Pleasure Poppet pinned against the wall by his bed. Edwin immediately turned to give them their privacy, but Leo said, without breaking the rhythm of his lovemaking, "Stay. I will see to your needs in a moment, my Lord."

Shrugging, Edwin went to sit in an overstuffed chair by the electric mantel and waited while Leo finished up. His Heir's lips were rouged with the Poppet's red blood when he turned away and fixed his clothes. He then asked the gorgeous young Poppet to get into his bed. The Poppet obeyed him without question, his eyes full of love and worship for his captain.

Leo turned to give Edwin a half-smile. "Hungry, my Lord? Marco still has blood aplenty to share."

He looked at Marco, who was giving him a long, come-hither look. "You have Poppets aboard the ship?"

"We liberate them, too, when we can. And some have chosen to join my crew. Marco is my..." He turned to give the beautiful young creature a long look. "...my special one."

Edwin raised his brows at that. "I'm happy for you, Leo. Truly. But can we speak alone?"

"Anything you want to say can be said in front of Marco. What is troubling you, my Lord?"

"Tell me about the Sky Palace. And about She Who is Three. I feel like I'm missing vital information here."

"Ah, that." Leo reached for a handkerchief to wipe his lips. "Can I interest you in some bottled food? I have some in the kitchen." And he headed that way.

Edwin got up to follow, but before he left the room, Marco called out to him.

"You're him. Lord McGillicuddy?"

Edwin backed up a step. "Aye?"

Marco threw back the covers. "My bed is always open to you and my throat your wineskin, my Lord."

Edwin sighed and joined Leo in the kitchen.

Before he even had a chance to open his mouth, Leo said, "I offered to help you get your Bride back for entirely selfish reasons, I'm afraid. I did hope my crew would keep their mouths closed until we had reached the Scottish shore, but it's apparent that that is not in the cards." Leo went about fetching a bottle of blood substitute from the refrigerator and two glasses from the cabinets. He set them down on the counter in front of Edwin. "You may as well know. I'm using you."

Edwin took the glass that Leo offered him. He had a heavy but resolved heart. "I figured this was about calling in your chits, but I have to admit I'd had hopes it was more. "

Leo smiled that heartbreaking smile that made him want to do anything for the beautiful young man. "I am quite the scoundrel these years, you. Part of my Inheritance, *da*? But, if it makes you feel any better, Lord Edwin, I really do miss you. It has pained me greatly to be apart from you for this long."

"Me, too." Edwin took a long swallow of Leo's house brew. He wasn't offended. In fact, he was more impressed by Leo's gumption.

He didn't expect his little Russian prince to be so cutthroat. "What do you need me to do?"

"Tomorrow, we will be entering Scottish airspace. As soon as we do, the Sky Palace will be alerted." Before Edwin could ask for more details, Leo added, "That's the gyro of the local Fae and their queen, the Morrigan. The other Fae call her the 'She Who is Three' that you are asking about. *Nyet*, I have no idea why, so please don't ask me that. You may ask Narissa, if you dare."

"I'd rather not," Edwin answered drolly as he pulled himself up onto the counter to sit. There were no stools. Leo joined him there, and, rather unexpectedly, leaned on his shoulder.

"We will be boarded. It is more of a courtesy than anything else, but if we do not bow to the Faes' tradition, we will come under considerable scrutiny. They may find a reason to criticize us anyway, seeing how the Fae are not exactly...fond of vampires."

"That's putting it mildly." Edwin drank down half the glass in one gulp. He was hungrier than he realized, and he started wondering about Marco's offer of his throat. Blood from a Poppet was so much more nourishing than this bottled trash. "So, what do you need from me?"

Leo gave him a worried look. "I had hoped you might act as my negotiator, seeing as you have had extensive dealings with the Fae. I know what happened to you last year in East Anglia. It's made you the talk of the town, so to speak."

"I see tongues have been wagging amidst the Courts."

"Everyone is talking about what you did. You wiped out an entire village of Fae. No vampire has ever been able to do that."

Edwin held up a finger. "Number one, they were half-Fae. Sleepwalkers. They only became Fae at night. Number two, I had help. A lot of it. From the Bloodthorn Pack, the vampires of Castle Whitby, and from my Eliza. She was the real hero of that dust-up, waking the Golemi from a thousand years of sleep—"

Leo cut him off. "That may be so, but the story has evolved several times over. They are saying you defeated the All-Father Corcoran in battle."

Edwin shrugged. That was true enough, but he'd used pretty desperate tactics to do it. And truth be told, Corcoran had gotten pretty close to ending him.

"The tongues that wag also say you have wolves to call. No vampire has had that power in centuries. They call you the Prince of Wolves now, you know."

Edwin rolled his eyes. It was better than the Prince of Hell, he supposed. "Best you not believe all that tripe."

"Are you saying it isn't true?" Leo smiled a challenge. "Are you not the Keanu Reeves of vampires, my Lord?"

Edwin laughed at that. It was simply too rich. "So, you want me to talk to this Fae. This Morrigan."

"*The* Morrigan. And she is no mere Fae." Leo thought a moment. He did that sometimes when he was searching for the proper English words to use. "She is of a pure bloodline in the Court of the Unseelie. The most powerful Fae in the Western world. Maybe the most powerful who has ever lived."

Edwin grinned to cover his concern. That sounded a tad worse than Corcoran. "And you want me to negotiate passage from this...the Morrigan."

"That or kill her."

Edwin laughed, then realized Leo was being perfectly serious. "Bloody hell!"

Leo looked worried. "We *must* deliver those selkies to Loch Fyne before the next full moon or the two will be landlocked forever. They will lose their powers. Besides, I promised."

He narrowed his eyes and finished his drink. "Promised who?"

"The other Selkies. Asia and Aletta are...important to them."

Leo was being cagey, which was his right as Lord and captain of this ship, but Edwin didn't like surprises. "Important...how? Educate me. I really do need to know everything, Leo."

Leo pinched his green eyes closed. "Important like...the last two mated pair in existence. Essentially, the future of the selkie species hinges on them getting back to the sea and making more selkies someday. And if I don't get them home, well...the other selkies may have promised a...difficult situation."

"Difficult...how?"

Leo's eyes shifted away. "All right. They promised to do things if they don't get the little ones back."

The blood substitute turned bitter in Edwin's mouth. "What things?"

Leo's mouth twisted this way and that. Finally, he said, "Storms? Bitter seas? Something about worldwide plagues..." Leo squirmed. "The phrase 'End of Days' may have been used."

It took Edwin a moment to digest that. "They are going to declare war on everyone on land if the selkies aren't returned?"

"Pretty much the size of it, *da*."

Edwin sighed and closed his eyes. So he had to negotiate with the queen of the Fae for passage across Scottish airways to deliver two selkies before the lords of the sea destroyed everyone on land. And he had to do that with a powerful Fae queen probably not liking him very much due to his terrible reputation as a killer of the Fae. And all of this so he could finally get back to rescuing Eliza.

Edwin jumped down. "Fark!"

Leo jumped at his outburst, which Edwin had aimed at the ceiling of the stateroom.

Edwin sighed and hung his head. "I think I need that drink from Marco now."

| viii |

She woke in the middle of the night and turned over in bed.
The dim blue runner lights in the room washed over Summerfield's face. He looked almost peaceful, almost beautiful, in sleep. Eliza reached out and brushed some of the problematic hair off his forehead.

He didn't stir. But then, for the moment at least, he was dead to the world in every sense of the word.

She moved her hand down to his throat and spanned her fingers across the place where his carotid artery would be flowing, were he alive. The runners in the room flickered, quickly and erratically, before coming back up and stabilizing into longer, stronger beats. After a few moments, she realized she could match the fluttering of the lights to her own heartbeat. Closing her eyes, she could feel the rhythm and flow of the electricity moving in the walls and floors of the ship. Every little current seemed to respond to her calling, and she sensed, down below and in other parts of the gyro, the machinery acting just as erratically as the lights were in here, in Summersfield's inner sanctum.

She breathed in and the power came to her. She breathed out, and it flowed out of her fingertips and snapped through the countless wires of the ship, going places dark and unseen. With a little effort, she found she could reach deep into the ship. She might even be able to crash it if she was determined enough. Crash it and kill them all. The idea both appealed to and appalled her all at once.

When she finally opened her eyes, Eliza was surprised to find a swirling blue ball of lightning crackling over Summersfield's throat where her hand was hovering. It wasn't large, but it was powerful. It could fill all of his cells, make his blood boil, and burn his flesh to a crisp. She could kill him with it. All she had to do was push the power into his body, into his heart, and make it explode.

She could end all of this.

She could end him.

But, she knew, she would pay for it. The High Courts would execute her for her crime. And that was the best-case scenario. More likely, the lab that created her would imprison her and take her apart piece by piece until they fully understood what was wrong with her. And they would absolutely take the baby.

Her baby. She would be condemning that small life to an existence in a tank, studied for the eternity of its life. Eliza might deserve her sentence, but he—or she—did not.

It didn't deserve what was to come.

She stared into the ball of lightning, mesmerized by it.

"Trust Edwin," she told herself.

But it was so hard. She was slowly losing faith every day. In her darker moments, she imagined him giving up on her and moving on from this impossible situation. She imagined being here for the rest of her life, however long that was, waiting for a prince who would never come to rescue her. She could imagine despairing, a broken Sleeping Beauty stuck forever under a spell.

"You don't trust the prince. You trust the monster."

It was a funny thought to come to her, but somehow she knew it to be true. Edwin was both the prince *and* the monster. Maybe more monster than prince, if she was being honest. And he didn't play by the rules. He never had.

He wouldn't leave her. He wouldn't give up on her.

She believed that. She *had* to believe that.

She let the ball of lightning dissipate. Slowly, the lights in the room returned to normal.

In that moment, she felt bereft, but she felt her decision was right—even though she had no reason to believe that.

Lying back down, she lifted her hand over her face and watched the electricity dance over her hand and skip between her fingertips. She had to give Edwin more time before she acted. She had to let the monster find a way to save her.

"Daddy is coming for us, baby," she whispered, touching her belly. "He will save us both. I hope."

* * *

It took some doing, but Edwin managed to dig up a sunblock suit from the *QAR2's* deep storage. He had to knock the dust off it as it had not been used in some time—not since the Seventies, at least, he wagered. Back then, scientists had begun perfecting UV protection over major cities in small parcels to prevent the mass immolation of its vampire population. Those smallish circles of protection gradually grew, connected, and, eventually, satellite projection came to protect the undead in all the major urban areas and even some of the rural.

But in the years before such technology, sunblock suits were a necessity for his sort if they planned to step out on a sunny day. This one was made of obnoxious yellow fabric, with a full gaiter to cover his face up to the eyes and a large fedora to offer protection from the top down. The coat and trousers were overlarge and resembled something he'd worn during his zoot suit years, but it would do.

It would *have* to do. He had no intention of lounging around in bed until the sun went down. He couldn't afford to lose precious time. He had to talk the Morrigan into giving them passage through Scottish airspace—and, hopefully, not killing them all.

"Are you sure you want to do things this way?" Leo asked as he stepped into the stateroom where Edwin was dressing. He looked worried. "The Morrigan is willing to wait until nightfall for negotiations to begin. She's told us as much."

"Eliza may not have that long. I've wasted enough time." Who knew what she was enduring? Still, Edwin hoped like hell there were no tears in the tacky, plastic-feeling material. The suit was heavy and hot as hell. Not good for his maneuverability, either. He pulled the gaiter up and turned to look in the mirror. He looked like the Shadow—if the poor bastard had fallen into a vat of yellow paint.

Narissa, who had followed Leo into the room, nudged her captain aside and started to laugh at him.

Edwin glared at her in the mirror, grabbed his goggles, and said, "Lead the way, mum."

His formality made Narissa grimace, but she turned on her heels and started down the hall to the air chute that led to the docking bay.

The whole ship was riddled with chutes, which Edwin had discovered long after climbing far too many stairs to get to different levels. Leo, who was a little claustrophobic, didn't use them, but Edwin had no issues with jumping into one to get somewhere on the quick. They were even a little bit fun. This time, though, he had to share it with Narissa, which put them almost up against one another in the narrow tube while the lift (which could go in almost any direction like Willie Wonka's glass elevator) ascended to the deck. Since they were doing a mid-air docking, they would be meeting the Morrigan on the forward deck—and in the glaring light of morning as the sun rose over the hazy Scottish Highlands.

Watching Narissa move as far away from him as possible in the tight space was sort of entertaining. "Blimey, you really hate vamps," he said just to annoy her.

"I like some vamps. I don't like *you*," she answered, blinking down at him balefully from her eight-foot height. "You kill Fae."

"Only Fae who annoy me," he answered and watched her wince.

The chute slowed as they approached topside. Leo used the small, tinny speaker inside the confines of the casket-like space to announce that a small craft from the Sky Palace was on its way and would dock in the next few minutes.

Narissa, dressed slightly more elaborately in a long cape over her armor, answered, "Standing by, Captain." Her eyes never left Edwin.

She and Leo exchanged a few more words as the docking procedure began, Leo handling all of the controls from the safety of the bridge. A few seconds later, Narissa lifted her chin and said to Edwin, "Goggles up, vampire."

Edwin put the heavily tinted UV-protection goggles on. At this point, he was covered head to foot, though he remembered reading somewhere that sunblock suits weren't perfect. More like ninety-seven percent effective. After half an hour of direct sun exposure, things were apt to get a bit dodgy.

For the first time, he wondered if he would survive this. He hadn't exactly scripted anything he planned on saying to the Morrigan.

"Begin ascension," Narissa said to Leo, and a panel slid open above them, sending down a sword-like ray of pure yellow, vampire-killing sunshine.

It was probably more psychological than anything else, but Edwin thought he felt the sunlight trying to worm its way under his suit as the platform began rising to the level of the deck. Every inch of ascension made the sunlight feel a little bit heavier on his shoulders like someone was adding small but potent weights. He hadn't expected that. He realized he'd grown overly accustomed to the city of New York being protected round the clock by UV satellites.

Even with the tined goggles on, the light was so bright that Edwin had to squint just to see shapes moving through what looked like molasses on fire. Narissa knocked his hat sideways as she started across the deck toward the transport ship, and Edwin quickly grabbed it and straightened it without realizing he wasn't wearing his gloves.

He immediately felt like he was suffering the worst sunburn of his life and stuck his slightly smoking hands into his pockets. There, to his relief, he found a pair of gloves to go with the suit. Grumbling, he pulled them out and started after Narissa across the deck.

The docked ship was a large, oval-shaped transport that looked like an alien, streamlined version of the Hummingbirds that most gyros used for off-ship travel. It was made of a substance that resembled dark red glass, with an elaborate, brassy, scrollwork design all over it, giving it the look of a fancy Faberge egg.

"Nice ride," Edwin said, pushing against the sun to reach the ship.

"It's a chariot," Narissa explained, sounding extremely proud of it. "They are only used by Fae royalty of the Unseelie Court." She kept her wide, excited eyes pinned to it, her hands almost trembling in anticipation. Edwin recalled Leo saying something about Narissa being one of the captives he had freed from the Vampire Courts. He knew they were notorious for stealing exotic pets (and people), usually at a young, impressionable age. Maybe this was the first time Narissa, as an adult, was seeing her people.

The chariot was humming and hovering in the air when a portal on the side opened and a long ramp formed on that side almost like the craft was made of a shifting molecular structure. Blimey, Eliza would have loved this, he thought—and, once more, he felt a deep pang of sadness followed by low-grade panic. He wondered how she was faring, though he suspected she wasn't doing well. The dull waves of pain and frustration echoing down the umbilicus of their bloodlink suggested as much.

He expected a lot of pomp and circumstance surrounding the arrival of "She Who is Three." Instead, a small retinue of bodyguards appeared, followed by the queen herself. The Morrigan.

Like Narissa, the Morrigan was unnaturally tall and slender. Eight feet, at least, though it was difficult to tell her actual height because of the endless reams of snow-white hair piled atop her head. She was dressed in something that resembled a short Celtic wedding gown, stark white with mechlin lace. Under that, she seemed to be wearing black military trousers and knee-high boots. Military badges glinted on the front of her tunic, and a simple twist of branches that seemed to move slightly slithered through her hair.

She was most assuredly one hundred percent pureblood Fae. Her face was a perfect oval and her eyes huge and stark black in her alien face. Her mouth, though, was little more than a small red slit cut in her lower jaw. Edwin had seen that slit grow and grow in those of her kind. He had seen it full of small, white, perfect, shark-like teeth.

The moment the Morrigan alighted on the metal plating of the deck, she spread her wings, which were glassy and translucent and resembled those of a giant dragonfly. She barely fluttered them, and suddenly she was floating toward the crew of the *Queen Anne's Revenge II*. And Edwin swallowed hard.

Normally, the Fae moved in a slightly hunched, long-limbed way that was nearly surreal to watch. Edwin suspected it came from walking through a world not designed for such tall, thin creatures. As a result, they reminded him of marionettes in old traveling shows being jerked this way and that. But the Morrigan drifted toward him.

As she approached, he subconsciously straightened up to seem taller, her small, hoofed feet in their custom boots dragging along the deck plating of the ship. Before he could do or say anything, Narissa shot ahead of him and got down on one knee to bow to her queen. Moving aside her cape, she produced a rather frothy collection of roses, which she held up in greeting. Not the kind of stuff you'd get at a florist, either. These looked homegrown, orange and yellow and imperfect, full of thorns. Edwin suspected Narissa had grown them herself on the arbor on the ship. Maybe she had even grown them for this very purpose.

She held the roses out to her queen but kept her head bowed low. "My liege, it is good to finally meet you," she said in the garbled tongue of the Fae, which Edwin was able to understand only because of its similarity to Upyrese. "I am Narissa, your servant. And though you surely do not know me, I pledge to you my hands, my words, and my life."

The Morrigan, hovering in place, looked at the roses a long time before taking them in her arms. The moment she touched them with her long white hands, Edwin saw the small buds bloom all the way open, darken with decay, and then die. After a few seconds, all she held were thorny sticks in her hands, which she dropped.

He looked at the mess of dead roses on the deck.

"Stand, child, and tell me your story." When she spoke, the Morrigan's voice seemed to echo with many voices, which Edwin figured made sense, since she was the "She Who Was Three."

Narissa stood and began to speak in a stammering, unsure voice, her eyes pinned to the dead roses. She spoke about being taken as a small girl from her mother and forced to work in the vampire Courts as a servant and a soldier. Tears filled her eyes when she recalled how Captain Leo had smuggled her out of a lifetime of slavery. He was a good man (for a vampire), she said, and he had earned the trust and dedication of his whole airship crew.

"And you have made your life here among the vampires? You are their...servant?"

"I..." Narissa narrowed her large black eyes. "I suppose, my liege. I have given the ship's captain my loyalty in exchange for his help in freeing me from the Court that once held me captive. But, in truth, I am no one's servant but yours. If you could only find your way to—"

The Morrigan stopped Narissa's speech by reaching out and touching her chin. She used her long white fingernails to force her face up. Narissa, tears shining unspent in her eyes, looked hopefully upon her queen. She obviously expected something—words of comfort or maybe something more ambitious. Maybe for her queen to invite her to join her people aboard her vessel.

But all that hope was dashed when the Morrigan said, "I sense you are tainted, girl. Tainted by bloodshed. And tainted by our cousins, the Dark Fae. You stink of vampire, and you are no child of mine. Go back below to your captain who owns you."

Narissa gasped. Her entire body began to shake and her unshed tears suddenly spilled out onto her cheeks.

The royal guard seemed to hold their collective breath as they watched. Edwin couldn't look away.

Narissa, desperate, reached out to the queen of the Fae, but the Morrigan ignored her, floating back a few steps. Narissa choked at the display, then, tilting her head skyward, she released such a scream that it made Edwin's hair stand on end. Scrambling up, she stumbled away from the Morrigan, rushed right past Edwin, and leaped into the chute that would take her below and out of sight.

Once she was gone, Edwin turned back to the Morrigan, who was watching him keenly.

"What the fark was that?" Edwin said.

The Morrigan blinked her large, black eyes at him. Her wings flickered, perhaps in irritation. "Ah, Dark Fae. The one who wishes to negotiate a temporary truce." She smiled in an ugly, knowing way. "You look...chagrined."

"Bloody hell, you're a right cunt, ain'tcha?" Edwin blurted out.

The Morrigan started at his outburst, then said, "What did you say, vampire?"

"You heard me. You're a bloody heartless cunt!" The words just tumbled out of his mouth the way they usually did when he was angry. It wasn't one of his finer moments, he knew, but as a Gaelic vampire, he felt he had the right to share a piece of his mind. He gestured wildly at the dead roses scattered about. "She grew those flowers for you! She wanted you to acknowledge her, rescue her, you stupid cow! Don't you get that? She wanted you to take her home to her people. And you just told her to fuck off? What the hell's wrong with you?"

The Morrigan's eyes filled with rage, and her tiny mouth became even tinier as she sucked in her cheeks in indignation. "How dare you talk to me in such a way, you shadow...you pathetic excuse for a Fae creature! You are naught but a small leech on the throat of the world, vampire!"

Edwin laughed at her, which shut her up. "Bloody hell! You can't even throw shade right! And I'm supposed to negotiate with *you*?" Blowing out a breath, he took a bold step toward the bitch, which, to his surprise, backed up in concern. The royal guard came to attention and started moving forward, but the Morrigan motioned them back. Leo said Edwin had a reputation as the Fae Killer. Maybe the Morrigan knew that?

He certainly hoped so! Taking another bold step toward her, he shoved a finger almost but not quite into the place just beneath her breasts (he couldn't quite reach them, hovering as she was) and said, "Listen here, cow. We are on an important mission to deliver two creatures—two *Fae creatures*, I might add—to their people at the shores of Loch Fyne. And we are on a *very* tight schedule. So here's the plan. Shove off and let us pass or you're going to make me mad. And trust me, darling, you do not want to see me mad!"

The Fae queen loomed over him, eyes wide as if she could not believe he was talking to her with such audacity. She looked poised to explode...but then, seemingly to remember his reputation, she smiled instead. In that soft, echo-y voice, she said, "You are he. The one they call the Prince of Hell who murdered a whole village of Sleepwalkers?"

"Lord Edwin McGillicuddy, mum," he stated. "At your service."

That once-small smile spread across her almost featureless face. "Funny. I thought you'd be taller."

He bristled. "Funny. I thought you'd have better manners. Were you born in a barn? Come to think of it, you probably were—"

She cut him off. "I should have you arrested and tried as a criminal in the Unseelie Court for what you have done to my people."

Edwin did not have time for these trivialities. He reasserted himself as best he could, covered as he was from top to bottom in yellow plastic, with a gaiter mumbling his words and goggles over his eyes. "Arrest me later. Try me later. Let us by or...or I'll be forced to do something you won't like."

She looked unimpressed with his bluster. He wondered if he'd cocked things up and good, but after a few breathy seconds, she waved one of her guards over. From him, she took a long box and presented it to Edwin.

He looked at it suspiciously.

"I assure you, Fae Killer, it is not a bomb."

It took some fumbling to get it open, what with the heavy rubber gloves he was wearing. While he did so, he noticed how hot his arms were growing. He had a feeling that if he didn't get out of the killing rays of the sun soon, he might start sparking like a Roman candle.

Inside the ornate box was an old-fashioned-looking key, quite elaborate, gold with jewels encrusting it. It was about the last thing he expected to find. He held it up in question.

"The key to the Sky Palace." The Fae Queen grinned. "You look about as fearsome as Paddington Bear, vampire, but if you are as powerful and fearsome as they say you are—and your admirers seem to think it's true—then you should have no problem taking my Green Man in a fair fight one on one in the White Room."

He had no idea what she'd just said, so he improvised. "It's a challenge, then. A fight."

"Correct. And if you win, I will wipe your blood debt off your record, and you and your crew will continue on your journey unmolested by my Court. Lose...well, we have janitors for *that* job."

Edwin stood there silently as he considered. He had no idea who or what "the Green Man" was or what a "White Room" might be, but he had been able to take on and defeat Corcoran in a rather unfair fight just last year. How much more difficult could it be to take on *one* Fae in some kind of fairy Fight Club?

He clenched the key as an idea spread a smile across his face—though, of course, the Morrigan couldn't see it. "Fine. I accept your challenge. But one change of terms. If I win, the *Queen Anne's*

Revenge II doesn't just get free passage. Your Court also joins my growing Congress. If you agree to that, we have a deal."

The Morrigan's eyes widened in surprise. It was the first honest and open expression of shock he had seen on her face. "What did you say? Your...Congress?"

"Correct." He cleared his throat and stood tall.

"No vampire has been the Lord of a Congress in five hundred years. It simply is not done."

"I'm a bit of a wild card. You'll need to get used to that," Edwin explained. "If I win, you and your crew are mine. I mean, unless you're afraid your 'Green Man' may not win—what with me being the Fae Killer and the Wolf King and all that jazz."

He hoped he'd laid it on just thick enough to entice her, and it seemed he had. The Morrigan suddenly smiled from ear to ear, which made Edwin question this move of his. She seemed just a little bit too eager. What wasn't she telling him?

"I accept your terms, Dark Fae. Join me tonight, and we will see what the great Fae Killer has in him."

* * *

Another crush.

Eliza wondered if Summerfield ever grew sick of throwing them.

That answer would be *no*, she noted as she watched him waltz around the ballroom with Dahlia in his arms. This was one of his formal black-tie affairs, everyone dressed to the nines. The theme was Disney Princesses, and every lady was expected to emulate a Princess in her dress and mannerisms. Dahlia was currently dressed as Sleeping Beauty, complete with a fiber-optic ball gown that changed colors from blue to pink and then back again as she was spun around the ballroom.

It was a chintzy and stupid theme, Eliza thought, but at least Dahlia was smiling tonight and having fun. She had been moved to Eliza's quarters two days ago and given back her Mr. Snoop. She was satisfied and calm. She slept every night curled against Eliza's back.

A footman in formalwear and a powered wig stepped up to Eliza to ask if she wanted anything off the buffet table. Her heart tripped a moment, remembering Edwin's visit, which seemed very long ago now. But it wasn't Edwin.

"No, I'm fine," she told him, not feeling fine at all.

Summersfield had asked her which Princess she wanted to be, his gift to her. She had chosen Tiana, the Princess from *The Princess and the Frog*. She was Eliza's favorite. But at the last moment, Summersfield changed it to Cinderella, and she was forced to stuff herself into a tight, flouncy blue ball gown that she hated. It was a small insult, but it left her smarting. She couldn't even be the Disney Princess she wanted to be. Time and again, Summersfield dangled little bits of freedom in front of her and then snatched them back.

The waltz ended and Summersfield made his way back to the head table—and her. These days, he hung over her day and night like she was some prize he was scared of losing. He invaded her space all of the time, and he liked to feel up her belly, which left her incensed. Sometimes, he talked to the baby as if it was his own. Only Edwin had the right to such privileges.

But, of course, Edwin wasn't here.

Looking across the room, she spotted Moira in her tank, lying against a glass wall, both of her webbed hands touching the glass. Her eyes were full of trouble. Eliza knew the siren sensed something terrible was about to happen. Hell, she had said as much earlier in the night, and that didn't make Eliza feel any better about tonight.

She was wondering what indignity Summersfield was going to heap upon her next when he rapped a butter knife against his glass to get everyone's attention. "Thank you for attending the Princess Ball tonight, my friends," he said in his rich baritone as he stood up. The way his white cream tuxedo and black hair sparkled under the forced lighting had all of the women in the ballroom fluttering. He moved to the front of the hall, just under the decorative weapons on the faux flagstone walls. "I know I make rather a habit of these soirees, but I assure you that tonight there is a reason to celebrate!"

He turned to look at Eliza, sitting at the head table. That made her heart jump in her throat. She did not want to be the center of attention.

"Tonight, I am celebrating a very special and important lady in my life." Nodding to the orchestra to play a low tune, he took a small gift box from the pocket of his tuxedo. His guests oohed and aahed as he slowly made a show of heading toward Eliza, the box on full display. "I also know I've been making a habit of giving you many gifts of late, Eliza, my love. But I simply cannot help myself. I must spoil you!"

He looked at his guests, all of this carefully choreographed, and they responded with polite laughter and some sighs from the ladies in attendance. Nathalie and a few of the other Pleasure Poppets in costume glared at Eliza with resentment.

Summersfield, oblivious, smiled down at her. Beneath his white tux, the shirt he wore was dark red satin. Under the garish lights, it looked as if he was bleeding from the throat and wrists.

He unwrapped the gift himself, revealing a ring box, which he held up for everyone to admire.

Now, her heart was beating even harder. She looked at Moira, whose eyes were full of terror for her. She almost couldn't swallow as she looked back up at the terrifying box.

Oh, god. Summersfield was going to one knee before her. As he did so, he opened the box.

Eliza felt like she was going to throw up.

Inside shone a large and exquisite red diamond set in a ring of white platinum, a thick band that reminded her strangely of a manacle.

A Covenant ring, similar (but not the same) as the one Edwin gave her last year when he asked her to be his vampire Bride. She had lost his ring when she was arrested; the police sergeant had pocketed it, and she knew in her heart of hearts that she would never see the ring again. Not unless Edwin could find it on the black market.

This one was larger and more garish. It made the tears well up in her eyes. She missed Edwin's humble bloodstone on her finger terribly.

"Eliza...I wish for you to wear my Covenant ring. I wish for you to be my Bride as recognized by the high Vampire Courts."

She just stared at Summersfield, trying to keep from bursting into tears. Around them, the room had fallen into silence. She knew from her education as a Courtesan that this was very much the equivalent of a man proposing marriage to his future wife—except it was a Vampire Lord proposing a covenant to a Favorite Poppet. The promise that one day—one day soon—Summersfield would make her his vampire Bride.

The idea was too horrible for her to contemplate for long. She couldn't imagine being bound to him for an eternity. She'd rather be dead.

The room held its collective breath, and all eyes were on them. In the endless seconds that followed, she knew everyone could have literally heard a pin drop. Thankfully, no one questioned her tears. They probably thought she was overwhelmed with happiness.

Summersfield's smile slipped just a little as the silence stretched out. "Eliza, please...say yes," he insisted.

Her heart clenched. She had no choice, even in this. But she would not willfully agree to be his Heir. Not this! It would be the ultimate betrayal of her marriage to Edwin and her vows to him to be his future Bride. She wanted to scream in Summerfield's face. She wanted to knock the ring away. But fear had her now—fear and the spotlight—and only an irrelevant sound squeaked out of her parched throat.

Summersfield looked around the ballroom in embarrassment and said, "Such a nervous, surprised Bride."

More polite laughter.

"Eliza..." he whispered, his voice slowly growing hoarse from anger and humiliation. His eyes slid sideways, centering on Dahlia as if she couldn't figure out what that meant.

She wanted to say no—she should have said no—but she was a coward, a terrified little coward. An awful little Poppet. And instead, she moaned out a little "Yes" instead.

Summersfield, looking satisfied, slid the ring rather forcibly onto the ring finger of her left hand. Then he swept her up into his arms and spun her around to the hearty cheers of his friends and Court.

The band started playing a lively ragtime number as he dragged her into the center of the floor to dance with her, his new Favorite and future Bride.

Eliza felt dizzy and sick. She wanted to die, but she was denied even that. She didn't say anything, just listened to the roars of celebration going up around her.

Later, Summersfield's friends came up to congratulate them both and the Poppets made empty celebratory sounds. Some looked relieved to not be her. Others were envious of her "good fortune" at netting a vampire. Dahlia grabbed her hand and asked her if this would make her Dahlia's mother. It was all Eliza could do to keep from screaming and screaming until she was hoarse.

And yet, through it all, she smiled.

From behind her, she felt Summersfield's hand on her bare shoulder and heard him whisper, "Soon, the three of us will be together forever, Eliza—you and I. And the babe."

| ix |

En route to the Sky Palace, Leo looked over from his place in the cockpit of the aging Hummingbird he was piloting and gave Edwin a dirty look.

"What?" Edwin said from the passenger seat.

"I thought you were going to handle that."

"I did handle it."

"By invoking Thunderdome?"

"*I* didn't invoke Thunderdome. That twat invoked Thunderdome!" Edwin insisted, clenching the armrests of his seat. Fast Hummingbirds zipping through the air were not his thing and never would be.

"But you agreed to it. You agreed to fight her Green Man."

Edwin scowled. "What was I supposed to do, Leo? Back down and run away? How would we have reached Loch Fyne, then?"

Leo started throwing up his hands, then wisely put them back on the cockpit controls, much to Edwin's relief. "You could have tried...something. *Negotiated.*" He sighed tiredly. "I don't know why I expected anything else. This is you we're talking about, after all."

Edwin's eyes slid over. "What does *that* mean?"

Quickly changing the subject, Leo said, "Why is Narissa crying her eyes out in her stateroom? What did you say to her?"

Edwin let go of the seat just long enough to jab a finger at his Heir. "*That* is not my fault. That cow did that!" He was about to add more about the cocked-up encounter when the shuttle suddenly beeped. Edwin grabbed his seat. "What the hell is that?"

"Relax. The computer is just telling us we're approaching the Sky Palace."

A few seconds later, a voice came in over their hailing comms, giving them docking instructions. They slid easily—much too easily—through an open docking door and into the ship's hangar. While they did so, Edwin got a good look at the palace from their video capture.

It was pretty much what he expected. The Sky Palace wasn't a gyro by definition. It was certainly as large as one—it might even be larger than Foxley's *Gypsy Queen*, he thought—but it was a stationary rig. It was so large that he seriously doubted it could move efficiently except for some basic defensive maneuvers. The Fae had either used some kind of primitive magic to rip a whole shining white castle and its underlying mountaintop out of the ground and levitated it or—and he was more inclined to believe this—they had designed the gyro to look that way. Whatever had happened to bring it about, the satellite was a gigantic structure of white stone so reflective that even at night, the moonlight shone off it like it was made of ice. It was actually difficult to look at the structure for long—probably part of its defense system.

"Bloody hell," Edwin said, impressed by its many towers and turrets and the massive chains keeping the rig stationary and floating high above the Scottish farm country that lay hundreds of feet below. He looked at the key in his hand. Since they were inside the docking bay now, the ship whirring down, it was pretty obvious to him that the key the Morrigan had given him was merely symbolic, a sign of her "welcome."

According to the docking instructions they were given, they were to wait for an escort. Thus, Edwin and Leo sat there side by side for a time in the dimness of the silent ship. Eventually, Leo said, "How the hell are you going to fight the Green Man, whoever that is?"

Edwin decided to be perfectly honest. "No idea. Guess I'll have to figure it out as I go."

"Your modus operandi."

"Do we need to clear the air?"

Leo laughed. Then, taking a deep, long breath, he let it out and made such a shout that Edwin nearly jumped in his seat. He said something in Russian that Edwin couldn't follow, then added in English, *"Why? Why did I go with you into that game room? Why did I let you seduce me? (Something something Russian) Why in hell was I such a damned, stupid fool? Why?"*

He looked over at Edwin with wide eyes. Edwin looked back. He had no idea how to respond except with, "Steady on?"

Leo kicked at the Hummingbird for good measure before throwing open the cockpit and getting out. Edwin followed.

A much larger retinue of royal guards was waiting for them in the hangar, a huge but modern-looking docking station with many ships coming and going. The walls gave off a faint, pulsing white light.

After Leo had composed himself, they started moving through the crowded, busy station. Edwin recognized a great many of the Fae, but some were so unique that he had no names for them. His cousins were many and varied, unlike vampires. Most of them turned to glare at him. Some mumbled things to their friends before skirting away.

Edwin was the Killer of the Fae. He supposed that, at least on the Floating Palace, he was strictly persona non grata.

The queen's guard, who were made up mostly of the tall, white Fae he was most familiar with, commanded that he and Leo follow them out into the corridors of the rig. Edwin didn't see the Morrigan, though a man in military uniform suddenly appeared and beckoned that they should follow him.

"I am Captain Ari," said the male Fae, who dwarfed Edwin by at least three feet, including his long, curling horns. "You are Lord Edwin McGillicuddy?" His eyes switched between Edwin and Leo, unsure.

"Aye," said Edwin. "I'm your Huckleberry." That got a frown of confusion from Captain Ari.

These Fae. No sense of humor.

"Right then," Edwin sighed, waving to the captain. "Let's get on with Thunderdome, shall we?"

* * *

The stranger standing behind Tommy forcibly pushed him forward and then down into a nearby chair. From the raw strength in the person's hands, he thought it was a man, but he couldn't be certain of anything in his present state. It could be a woman. A female vampire.

He couldn't tell where he was or what was happening. He couldn't see a thing with the black hood tied loosely over his head.

"Sit and wait...and don't move," said his captor.

It was a woman.

"And if you try and run, I will kill you. Don't think I cannot, human. You'll be dead before you hit the floor."

"Don't run. Don't anger the vampiress," Tommy said all businesslike. "Got it."

Sitting quietly, Tommy assessed the situation both as a man and as a cop. He decided on a "wait and see" approach. Good sense and crisis training told him there was no point in fighting his captors. The vampiress manhandling him was stronger than twenty men, and he knew she could twist his head off his shoulders with the same effort he would use to twist the cap off of a bottle. Besides, he was in no position to stage an escape.

He put his hands on the table in front of him and stayed very still.

"Good boy," said the vampiress, petting his hooded head.

After a second or two, she pulled the hood off his head and glided back.

He was momentarily blinded by the lights in the unfamiliar room. He was also cold. He was dressed in just his shorts, undershirt, and a robe—what he had been wearing when he fell asleep on the sofa after Cesar left his apartment, looking very hurt after their row. He'd thought about calling him and telling him to come back, but he'd decided a little time and distance was good for them both. They needed to cool down, and Tommy needed time to re-assess the situation. He wanted both of their heads on straight before they proceeded.

The disquieting events of the day had taken their toll on Tommy's already precarious health, and he had fallen asleep in front of the TV. He'd had a surprisingly pleasant (even erotic) dream about Cesar, but then jerked awake when he felt someone pressing their gloved hand over his nose and mouth. He opened his eyes to a smeary figure looming over him. He tried to reach for his gun in its holster—then remembered his sidearm was across the room on the kitchen counter and out of reach. A rare moment of disappointment washed over him as he glanced at the nondescript face of the intruder standing over him. If he hadn't been taken by surprise, he knew he could have taken him…

But in the man's other hand he held an empty syringe. Ah.

The intruder's hand on his mouth loosened just a little, but Tommy could already feel the swimmy effects of the fast-acting drug coursing through his system, and he struggled just to open his mouth.

The intruder, a nondescript nobody, said, "Relax. If you don't struggle, you will not be harmed..."

Then things went black.

What followed were murmurs and bumps. He was vaguely aware of being transported, though where they were going and the identity of the architect of this kidnapping remained a mystery to him for some time. People he didn't know talked amongst themselves, but it was difficult to make out their words. Some didn't speak English at all.

Time passed. Tommy slid in and out of consciousness until he finally came fully awake in an unfamiliar and nondescript hospital bed.

Looking around, his first thought was that he was in hospice, or maybe he'd died and this was Heaven. Or that other place. His mind turned over the many possibilities. Maybe he wasn't dead and one of his past collars had done this to terrorize him—not that he was terrified. He couldn't seem to be arsed about being threatened, dead man walking that he was. (He chuckled.) Then a door shushed open, and before he could focus properly on the figure stalking toward him, someone threw a black hood over his head and forced him out of bed.

His captors weren't rough, exactly, but the way they manhandled him and the sheer brute strength behind their hold on his limbs indicated that they had no qualms about breaking his arm if he gave them any guff. He didn't, though. He was far too weak to fight. Instead, he went meekly and wordlessly with them, allowing them to steer him up and down a twist of corridors. They took several elevator rides, then it was more corridors.

Tommy, tired from all of the walking, was finally escorted into this room and told to sit. At least they took the black bag off his head; he could breathe much easier now. He only wished he was younger—and stronger. He might have been able to put up a fight. He might have had the courage to do so.

As it was, he was too tired from the simple ordeal of being walked down all those damned corridors to do more than sag in his seat. Besides, what was the point? Should he fight and possibly hurt himself badly only to die anyway—and possibly in a great deal of pain from his injuries? If this was a vendetta thing and they were going to kill him, they should just get on with it—and, he prayed, quickly and painlessly. He'd like that. He wasn't a man much interested in being put in pain and possibly messing himself.

Death didn't disturb him as much as the idea of dying in disgrace. He prayed to God that whatever happened to him in the next few minutes at least allowed him to retain his dignity. He didn't think that was too much to ask.

Slowly, he turned his head. The female vampire was standing sentinel against a wall. She was small, with reams of white dreads, small black eyes, and a lot of punkish black leather. Those eyes, masked in mascara like a raccoon's, narrowed when he looked her way.

"Don't look at me, human," she said, and he dutifully turned his head away.

Licking his lips nervously, he said in a surprisingly parched voice, "Whatever you people shot me up with...it's giving me a headache. I'd like some water, please, love. Some painkillers would be nice, as well."

"You won't be here long," she intoned. "And I'm not your 'love.'"

"Fair enough." He was about to ask further questions in an attempt to gather info about what this was about when the door shushed open again and a rather young voice said, "Thank you, Lady Claire. Please leave us now."

"Gladly," she grumbled. "I can go and wash the stink of dying human off my hands." She stomped out of the room.

"Rude," Tommy said, turning his head—but only a little this time. He was a tad afraid of the wrath of the unknown person in the room with him. He had no idea if he was rough and uncultured as he vampiress.

"I apologize for that. Lady Claire is a bit...salty." The newcomer came around and slid into his field of vision.

Tommy didn't have much interest in pop culture and celebrity gossip. He didn't watch much in the way of reality TV shows or follow celebrity politics. So it took him a moment to recognize the newcomer. On top of that, he was still muzzy from the roofie and it took his slow, stuttering mind a moment to catch up.

He'd seen an article or two, something about the progressive outlook on the world's future that the vampires were taking—which was just as hilarious as it sounded. The oldest creatures on Earth wanted to be taken seriously as leaders of humankind's future. Spearheading this ludicrous PR campaign was one of vampirekind's most famous members. He'd been interviewed multiple times and was an acting advisor to the President of the United States and the British PM.

"Fuuu..." Tommy stopped and cleared his throat. "Y-you're him...Foxley."

The creature stood unnaturally still and watched him, its head tilted slightly as if it was listening to something beyond the walls of the room. Its hands hung loosely at its sides. Its eyes moved not at all. It possessed few human mannerisms almost as if it was so old that it no longer even possessed a desire to appear vaguely human.

It stayed that way a long moment before suddenly becoming animate. When it did, it turned its head properly upright and stuck its hands in its pockets. The result was a shivery nightmare akin to a demonic, living toy.

"And you are Special Agent Thomas Quinn," said the vampire.

Tommy couldn't even grasp its accent. There was something there, but it was not an inflection he had ever encountered in his life. And it spoke in a monotone. Really, it acted like a big wooden marionette, something not quite right. Real Uncanny Valley shite. It made Tommy's skin crawl.

It also made him irrationally angry. For all the press that Foxley got, and all the accolades he attracted, Tommy still recognized a thug when he saw one. Foxley was an old vampire thug, nothing more. He was no better than the white-collar, corporate criminals Tommy had brought to justice for most of his life.

"Not Thomas. Tommy," he said just to be an ass.

All the pieces fell together like a weird jigsaw puzzle in his head. He realized he was not here to die, the victim of some angry felon he'd put away long ago. This was something entirely different. Something Worse.

He was on board the *Gypsy Queen*, Lord Foxley's gyro, and he was here to be interviewed for the part of Foxley's Heir.

Tommy, suddenly panicked by this revelation, began to struggle in his seat. "I know who you are and what's going on. I shouldn't be here. I didn't agree to this." He tried to lift his hands off the armrests of the chair he was sitting in, but he suddenly found himself stuck in place, unable to move any part of his body except for his head, and that only minimally.

Foxley smiled knowingly. "Don't fight it, child. Don't fight me. Fighting only makes it hurt." With that smile firmly in place, Foxley went on to say he was a bloodkinetic, quite a powerful one, and Tommy would not be able to move until his interview was over. Not until Foxley willed it so.

Tommy was breathing faster, harder. He realized he was edging close to a full-on panic attack. He had to swallow and remember his training to calm his runaway heart.

"N-no," he insisted, carefully breathing in and out. "I never agreed to this," he repeated. "This is Cesar's doing. He's behind this!"

Lord Foxley did not even attempt to deny it. "He and I have an understanding."

"I...I don't understand."

Foxley showed off his small, perfectly sharp teeth. "I am to interview you. And if you pass muster, child, you will become my latest...acquisition, if you will."

Shivers went up Tommy's spine at the news. "No...no! I want it noted that I am not in favor of this. I did not agree to this and am being forced against my will to participate in this ludicrous interview."

"It is noted," Foxley said, though Tommy noted that the Vampire Lord didn't seem to care.

Foxley, ignoring all of his pleas, proceeded to ask him a series of interrogation questions. They went deep psychologically and carefully highlighted a number of scenarios, some fairly outlandish. It reminded Tommy of his years training with the Feds.

Tommy refused to answer even one of the vampire's ridiculous questions, and as time passed, he found himself growing angrier and more self-destructive. He refused to be shoved around and forced into this lifestyle by some creepy vampire child! Near the end, Tommy finally spat on the front of Foxley's suit for the first time.

"Let me go now, you bloody monster!" he ranted. "I am an agent of the law, and I refuse to be treated like some criminal!" He struggled, though, true to what Foxley said, it hurt to do so. A lot.

Tommy wondered if Cesar was nearby and if he was watching the interview as he said he would. Tommy struggled to turn his head. He started calling for his lover, demanding that he show himself.

Cesar. This was *all* Cesar's doing.

As the despair crept into Tommy's heart, tears sprang to his eyes. This was not how he'd wanted to spend his last moments on Earth—a terrified captive being cornered by a monstrous vampire Lord. This was not how he envisioned the end. And it was all Cesar's doing.

Tommy was afraid, finally and completely, and it hurt him to know the lover he had given his heart to had done this to him, that he was so selfish as to subject Tommy to this small slice of hell. Why didn't he listen to his instincts when he first met Cesar at the restaurant? He should have walked out of that place and away from the vampire forever, never to look back.

Nothing good came from vampires. *Nothing.*

Foxley finally stopped asking his insipid questions and exited the room. He was gone for approximately five minutes, allowing Tommy some peace to cry out his frustration.

When he returned, Cesar was in tow. Tommy noted how close Foxley stood to Cesar and the way he put his hand on his arm. It was pretty clear that Foxley considered Cesar his property by the way he spoke to him and by his small, lingering touches.

Cesar looked at Tommy with pain-filled but hopeful eyes. He then glanced at Foxley nervously. Foxley nodded permission. Cesar stepped forward and leaned down to say excitedly, "You did it, Tommy! You didn't answer any of the questions. That means you passed."

Tommy's heart jumped in his throat. He looked back and forth between the two vampires, sniffing back his tears. "No…I…I told you! I don't want this. I don't want to be a vampire!" His voice was rising to a fever pitch, and he realized he was close to breaking down into hysterics, but he couldn't help himself. Whatever he'd felt for Cesar was ruined beyond repair. Burned up in an atomic blast—along with his heart. How could he possibly love someone who refused to respect his wishes, his body? His death? How could he be in love with a creature who wanted to twist him into a monster?

"Cesar," he sobbed, "Cesar...please!"

But Cesar continued to smile vacantly, unperturbed by Tommy's distress. After a moment, Tommy saw there was no reasoning with him. Abandoning him, he turned his attention back on Foxley, who was observing him keenly. He almost seemed to be enjoying Tommy's tears. "You have to help me," he begged. "Reason with Cesar! You have to let me go!"

"I believe that is what we are here to do," Foxley stated.

Panic finally broke Tommy's pride. "Bloody hell! You can't do this to me! I never agreed to it! I don't want it!" He tried to move, but his body felt like stone—as if someone had poured lead into his joints. He couldn't move at all.

Lord Foxley stepped forward. A small smile played upon his young lips.

Tommy fought in earnest to squirm away from the vampire, but trying to move his muscles resulted in exactly what Foxley said would happen—excruciating pain shot through his body in sparkling fireworks almost as if his blood was burning up. He didn't even mind the pain so much, would have endured even worse, but his body was weak from all of the damage the cancer had done, and even though he wanted to fight—*needed* to fight—he realized there was no way out.

There was no escaping Foxley when he put his small, glove-like hand on Tommy's shoulder and drew close enough to whisper something privately in his ear.

Tommy smelled the blood on the vampire's breath.

"Be still. This won't hurt at all. And fear not, child, you will get exactly what you want. Your lover doesn't know this, but I took a vow decades ago to never again make an Heir after Edwin. Tonight, I intend to keep my vow."

Tommy, breathing hard and in panicky spurts, tried to relax. He told himself to be brave and not to act like a fool now that he was at the end at last. But he couldn't help himself.

He felt Foxley's cool breath on his neck, followed by his smile—and then, finally, his teeth—hideously sharp but mercifully painless as they penetrated his flesh and began to feed upon him. Tommy whimpered, suddenly—wholly—terrified of dying. His eyes moved across the room and centered on Cesar, who was watching him in anticipation. He tried to beg Cesar for help with just his eyes—for life or for death, he wasn't sure.

As blood began gusting over Tommy's collar, Cesar slowly lost his smile. He looked suddenly concerned by the amount of blood pouring from Tommy's wound. But Tommy didn't care. He was dying at last, and he found he was no longer worried that Cesar was concerned for him. He no longer loved Cesar, and perhaps he never had.

Bloody vampires...

Foxley was correct. Tommy was getting exactly what he wanted.

And Foxley, true to his word for once, began the process of killing Tommy.

| X |

Ceremonial drums started up as he walked down the lighted corridor toward what the Fae called the "White Room." That sounded innocuous enough, Edwin thought. But near the end, as the sliding door slid open and the roars of a great many people penetrated the hallway he was standing in, he rethought that. Suddenly, he had a bad feeling about this whole thing.

With a shrug, he stepped into a huge, domed room the length and width of a football field. Elaborate Grecian columns held up the gracefully arching ceiling of the coliseum, and the floor was made of powdery white sand that Edwin feared might be bone dust. Far above was a clear dome that let in the first rays of morning. Edwin hesitated and looked up at the blinding light, reluctant to move into it.

Captain Ari stepped up beside him—either as a formal escort or a warden to ensure he didn't run, he reckoned. "Don't worry. The White Room is UV-protected. You may proceed, vampire."

"Have a lot of vamps hanging about, eh?"

Ari smiled, his teethy mouth splitting his face in half. "We have our fair share in here."

Edwin took a tentative step into the coliseum, then put his hand out and into a beam of morning light. He wiggled his fingers; he did not burn. Drums and flutes accompanied him as he moved cautiously toward the center of the room, which was packed with what had to be all of the occupants of the Sky Palace. Every type of Fae glared down at him in their unfriendly way from their tiered seats high above.

Raising his gaze, he spotted an elaborate royal box carved from white stone about fifty feet up. The Morrigan and her royal retinue, including her Prince Consort and their children, sat sternly by, not clapping, just watching him with their keen black eyes.

Meeting her gaze, he said, "We're here, mum. Let's get on with it, aye?"

The Morrigan laughed at his use of the royal "we." Then she stood up.

The musicians fell silent, as did the rest of the audience.

Leaning on the rail of her box, she proclaimed, "You are correct, Lord McGillicuddy. You are here. And we are impressed that you have come." She looked around the packed coliseum. The other Fae were murmuring low and nodding. "And, as you can no doubt imagine, you are not the first of your kind to find his fate in the White Room."

Edwin held her even gaze even though a small shiver went up his spine. "What happened to the other vampires?"

Captain Ari, stationed a few paces away (he reckoned in case Edwin made a break for it), drew his thumb in a sawing motion across his throat, his smile growing wider still. The others in the stand mimicked the gesture and began stamping their feet.

"Lovely," Edwin answered, turning back to the Queen of the Fae.

The Morrigan was smirking, her hands now pressed together like a little girl in the throes of some secret glee. She was really getting off on this. It reminded Edwin of how bad things had gotten between their two kinds. They were cousins, and yet, they were always trying to kill one another.

"Bloody family," he muttered to himself. Taking control of the proceedings, he raised his fist and cried, "Kill the vampire! Vampires suck! The Fae are the champions! Yay, the Fae! Now, bring on the Green Man!"

The Morrigan didn't look happy that he'd stolen her thunder. She turned, an embittered expression on what existed of her face, and motioned toward a door on the opposite side of the coliseum with one long, thin, white hand.

The great double doors were thrown open to the roars of everyone in the coliseum. The drums started up again, louder than ever—so loud that Edwin squinted from the barrage of sound as a very large, muscular being moved inward, swinging its arms. He had to move a little sideways through the doorway of the coliseum that was almost too small for him.

Edwin had expected a Fae—a rather large one, sure. But what he got was a Rock Giant.

He'd heard of them, of course. Everyone knew someone who knew someone who had seen one. But he'd never laid eyes on one himself. As far as he was aware, they were so rare as to never put in an appearance anywhere.

This one was ten feet tall and looked to be made quite literally from red and black lava rock. Its head was tiny, its arms—Edwin noted there were six of them—as thick around as saplings. It walked slightly hunched, a number of giant stone spines running down its back and along its short, stumpy tail. It eyed him coolly as it chugged at a leisurely pace to the center of the coliseum. There it stopped, stood as straight as it could, and raised all six arms into the air. It screamed a battle cry that was answered by every Fae that was present, including those in the royal box.

Edwin looked around, spotted Captain Ari grinning, then looked back at the Green Man. "Shite."

As the applause and whoops slowly died down, the Green Man turned away from his adoring audience and glared at Edwin—not a friendly look. After a moment, its tiny, piggish eyes grew smaller still. He expected it to talk like some muscle-headed dildo. Instead, when it turned to briefly speak to his queen, Edwin heard it say in a rough but surprising cultured voice, "May I ask who I am fighting today, my liege?"

It took Edwin a moment to recover from that.

The Morrigan said, "Lord Edwin McGillicuddy, the Fae Killer, also known as the Prince of Hell."

The Rock Giant grunted. "He doesn't look much like a prince, my liege."

She shrugged in an "it is what it is" gesture, then looked at them both. "The rules are simple. Two opponents, no weapons. The battle is over when one of you has fallen to the dust."

That didn't sound like too much fun.

The Rock Giant pulled himself upright and then turned to Edwin with a quizzical look on his face. "Wait. I know you. You write those books. The *Doctor Blood* adventures."

"Y-yeah?" Edwin answered uncertainly.

"I enjoy those books. Good reads. I always review them on Amazon." He stopped and made air quotes. "Dr. Blood is a typical Byronic hero, only without being invariably solitary."

"Uh...thanks, I guess?"

The Green Man nodded. "I regret that I will need to kill you today, Lord McGillicuddy."

Edwin swallowed hard. "Aye? Maybe we can—?"

Before he could finish, the Green Man charged him, moving much faster than he'd expected—so fast that he had a hard time even following it. Before he even knew what hit him, the Rock

Giant had thrown his arm out, his stone-hard shoulder smashing into Edwin's chest.

The impact tossed him back twenty feet, almost to the edge of the coliseum. He crashed down so hard onto the sandy ground that he felt the hard click of his shoulder as it was dislocated, and a spear of pain went up that side of his body, making him cry out. He coughed as he rolled over and sat up in a cloud of dust, clutching his injured shoulder. Getting his arm back into the socket was no trouble—he'd done this a time or two even whilst still alive—but it didn't happen without another wave of dizzying pain.

The coliseum erupted into screams of pleasure. The Rock Giant lifted his six arms high into the air and roared in response. He then turned back to Edwin. "Get up, little vampire. We're not done dancing, you and I."

Edwin climbed unsteadily to his feet, clutching his injured shoulder. His arm was numb and almost useless where it hung at his side. He raised his eyes to the Rock Giant, who was clenching all six of his massive fists and grinning. Raising one hand, he made a come-hither gesture. The muscles jumped in his arms in a disconcerting way.

"I thought you were the great 'Fae Killer?'" the Rock Giant teased. "You're about as tough as a newborn kitten, little vampire."

"A kitten who has claws," Edwin said, hoping that didn't sound as stupid as he thought it did.

"Meow."

Snorting in anger, Edwin kicked at the sand, undid his suit jacket, ripped it off, then dropped his braces as if he was about to catch a brawl in an English pub. The Rock Giant looked him up and down all wide-eyed before laughing at him. Meanwhile, Edwin knelt and powdered his hands from the sand on the floor.

"You are brave and persistent. I like that. I'm glad I've read your books, Lord McGillicuddy."

"Fark your compliments. Fight me, you big clod!" Edwin put up his fists defensively as if he was back in the Old Bell Tavern in Limehouse and nodded.

The Rock Giant grinned, showing off huge, peg-like teeth. "All right. Yes. We should dance again."

He started to circle Edwin, looking for an opening. Edwin stayed apace with his movements, always keeping his opponent in front of him. He wouldn't let the giant take him unawares again.

But it soon became obvious the Rock Giant had done this many times before. He sank low...then kicked a massive amount of dust into Edwin's eyes, the dirty bastard. And while Edwin was blinking and trying to recover, he charged him again. They clashed together hard.

Time slowed and all sound vanished into a long, low howl as they clenched. Edwin, blinded, tried to sink his fingers into one of the Rock Giant's ginormous arms. He knew if he could get a good grip, even as big as he was, he would still have the strength to toss him away. But his fingers just screeked off the hard, unfeeling skin. So he tried to kick the Rock Giant's legs out from under him instead. Unfortunately, he just wasn't fast enough. The Rock Giant punched him in the gut, a blow that would have killed a human, and Edwin slid backward in the dust, sending clouds of it up. He doubled over, then tried to rebound, but the Rock Giant charged him. Head down, he grabbed Edwin around the middle, lifted him, then squeezed his rib cage so hard that Edwin's breath went out in a puff and he just couldn't seem to suck in any more oxygen.

They turned like a couple waltzing, except this dance was going to end with one of them badly injured or dead. The Rock Giant squeezed even harder, so hard that Edwin felt his ribs strain and one of them pop. Fresh pain flooded his body. He tried to think what to do, but the pain stripped away his personality, made him more vampire than fighter, more animal than human, and he instinctively lunged forward, snapping his sharp teeth at the Rock Giant's exposed neck.

He was surprised when his teeth found root and sank in. The Rock Giant screamed in pain.

Blood, or what passed for blood in a Rock Giant, gushed into Edwin's mouth, over his lips, down his throat, and also down the front of his shirt. The Rock Giant, suddenly panicked, threw him away as if he was a leech that had suddenly attached himself to him, but as he did so, Edwin's teeth tore a sizeable chunk of rock flesh from his neck.

Edwin fell in a more controlled roll this time, came up on his knees, and twisted around, finding his feet. His face, shirt, and even his hair were covered in the weird, greenish blood of his opponent. It didn't taste good. Not by any means. But his kind were leeches by nature, and they were able to take nourishment and strength from almost anything—blood, fear, the very dying souls of their victims. The blood, though vile, was like a massive kick of caffeine to his system. He felt his heart knock harder against his ribs, and all of his muscles started jumping. He felt a warm surge of strength coursing through his normally cold body. His broken rib mended itself in seconds, and even the pain in his dislocated shoulder faded to silence.

The Rock Giant was walking in circles, one of his huge hands clamped over the open, gushing wound in his neck. The audience was booing and screaming for the Rock Giant to *"Kill the vampire! Kill the vampire!"* But just then, the Green Man did not look like he was in any shape to kill anyone.

"You bit me, you little bloodsucking shit!" the Rock Giant cried, outraged.

Edwin stood up and smiled, then wiped the blood off his mouth and licked his fingers. He hissed fearsomely at the Rock Giant, who jumped at the display.

After he got his fright under control, the Rock Giant touched his wound tentatively and said, "Am I going to be a vampire now?"

"It doesn't work that way." Edwin eyed the Rock Giant savagely, watching as he slowly recovered from his bite wound. "It's just a big hickey."

The creature looked angry as hell as he clenched his many fists and eyed Edwin like he wanted to destroy him. "For that, you die." Anger and pain dripped from his tongue. "Your books aren't that good." He started moving toward Edwin, but this time, Edwin stayed where he was. He'd had a strange thought.

Foxley was a powerful bloodkinetic, the most powerful that Edwin had ever encountered. Edwin had inherited some of that. He could manipulate his own blood when he needed to in order to create various weapons. But since meeting Eliza and exchanging blood with her, he'd discovered something else. When she was still struggling to walk on her own after her accident at Castle Whitby, he'd been able to help her maintain her balance when she was standing upright by manipulating her blood. It was more of a subconscious thing than anything else. He'd wanted her to be able to stand upright unassisted and she had. He'd thought at the time that it was only wishful thinking on his part, but now he wondered if he was in fact doing it.

As the Rock Giant sauntered toward him, growling a warning, Edwin turned sideways and raised his hand, extending his fingers outward in a "stop" gesture. The creature continued to approach him, but at a slightly slower pace as if suspicious.

Edwin clenched his hand into a fist and tried to direct his will into his hand—and, by extension of his power, into the Rock Giant's blood. His fist trembled and he licked his lips, savoring the bitter-tasting blood that he now had inside of him. Taking a very deep breath, he flashed his hand out.

The Rock Giant stopped dead in his tracks and looked at him quizzically. "What are you doing?"

Was it working? Edwin couldn't tell, but he forced all of his will into his hand and took a step forward, his hand fully outstretched.

The Rock Giant took a stumbling step back as if Edwin had pushed him from afar.

The small victory made Edwin smile. He took another step, forcing his power outward. He imagined it like a giant cloud with the ability to push his opponent down.

Gasping, the Rock Giant dropped to his knees. His six arms tensed and his rocky muscles quivered as he fought the force pushing him down to the ground. "What...are...you...doing?"

Edwin didn't answer. He had very little explanation for what was happening. He was just thankful he finally had an advantage. So he just kept forcing the pressure down until the Rock Giant was lying supine in the dust of the White Room. His entire mountainous body trembled, but he was unable to get to his feet.

Edwin had done it. "One...two...three!" he said as if he were calling it for a wrestling match. "You're done, mate."

Releasing his fist and, in turn, the pressure, he turned away and looked up at the Morrigan in her royal box. He expected some kind of approval like a Caesar watching a gladiator match, but she shook her head slowly back and forth.

"Mum?"

"It is to the death, vampire."

The Rock Giant collided with him, and the two of them crashed over each other and wound up on the ground in a grapple, the Rock Giant on top of Edwin. He snarled at Edwin as he raised four of his six arms, made fists, and punched downward. Edwin only narrowly missed each of his fists as the Rock Giant slammed them into the ground around him. The last one caught him in the spleen and he coughed and lashed out in pain, scratching at the Rock Giant's eyes with his fingernails.

The Rock Giant reared back at the last moment, Edwin's suddenly sharp fingernails screeking across his rock-hard face, and the two opponents turned over and over in the dust, finally scrambling to their feet. The Rock Giant, enraged by his pain and humiliation, didn't waste any time jumping on Edwin. He meant to crush Edwin with his sheer weight, but Edwin, much smaller and more maneuverable, slid sideways and came up and around the beast. He threw his forearm around the monster's neck.

The Rock Giant grunted and cursed him out, but Edwin didn't let go. He hung on as the Rock Giant stood up. Of course, he tried to shake Edwin off, but Edwin just tightened his arms, then brought his legs up and wrapped those too around the Rock Giant's massive neck. Edwin used all of his strength as a man, a vampire, and a lifelong brawler to hang on as the Rock Giant tried to buck him off.

The audience was going crazy now, screaming, though Edwin couldn't tell which side they were on anymore. Maybe even they didn't know.

The Rock Giant took a few stumbling steps, all six of his arms flailing but none of them landing any blows on Edwin in his current position. All the Rock Giant managed to do was hit himself a few times in the jaw as he took blind punches. Another few steps, and Edwin, now growling with determination, tightened his hold. He was strong. Stronger than the Rock Giant. He knew that even if it didn't seem so.

The bigger they are, the harder they fall...

The Rock Giant began to choke under the crushing hold Edwin had on his windpipe. He might be big, and his skin might be rock hard, but he, like everything, had his Achilles heel, and Edwin knew he'd just found it when his opponent began to wander in aimless circles, his footing more unstable.

"Gggg-grrrr..." growled the Rock Giant. He suddenly threw himself backward and collided with one of the Roman-style columns holding up the ceiling. As Edwin's back smashed into it, the whole coliseum trembled and Edwin felt a bone-snapping pain run up his back. It make him clench his teeth, but even so, he didn't let go, not even when the Rock Giant did it twice more, each time with a little less force as he weakened.

As he quickly lost strength, he began to weave. Edwin hung on for dear life.

Finally, after a few more grunts, the Rock Giant dropped to his knees, gasping.

"Sorry, big guy." Edwin hung on until all of the strength went out of the behemoth's body and he dropped to his face, this time fully out for the count.

Once Edwin was certain the creature wasn't going to suddenly rally, Edwin climbed off his unconscious foe and moved to the center of the coliseum. He dusted his hands and gave the Morrigan a nod and a wide smile before throwing his arms up in victory.

At first, nothing happened—not that that surprised him. Then, someone in the audience clapped. Someone else joined them. And, after a few tense seconds, the audience began to cheer their new champion of the White Room. They even stood up and started screaming their delight at his victory.

Edwin lifted his chin, stuck out his chest, and then turned to wink at the Morrigan, who seemed a bit disoriented by the collective shouts and stomping of her people, most of who were standing now. Finally, too embarrassed not to join in, the Queen of the Fae stood up and clapped in a more reserved manner.

Slowly, one by one, the Fae calmed down and grew quiet, taking their seats once more. When the room was mostly silent, she spoke.

"My people...after many years, it seems we have a new champion. A most peculiar one, at that. But I must bow my head to the rules of the White Room. I present to you your new champion: the new sentinel of the Fae race and our new Green Man...Lord Edwin Oliver McGillicuddy!"

Edwin put down his arm. He thought he hadn't heard right. "Wait...bloody *what?*"

* * *

After enduring nearly twelve thousand years of life, Lord Henry Foxley often found himself becoming bored. He had done everything he set out to do with his life, and there were few, if any, challenges left to overcome. There were only so many ways to take pleasure—blood, sex, power, death—and he had explored them all. He understood the mechanics of immortality, but if he was being honest with himself, he was more restless than usual these days, and that was mostly due to heartbreak.

He missed Edwin.

In the beginning, when his Heir first slipped out of his grasp, it was a fierce, biting pain that he'd spent years using vice to try to ignore and then overcome. And he'd thought that was the worst of it.

But he was wrong. It wasn't the initial pain of losing Edwin, the great love of his long life, that hurt so much. It was the time since, the long stretches of empty, emotional wandering that he did. The ways that he tried to fill the time and deaden the pain—and failed. No matter how many lovers he took, Poppets he bought, blood or drugs he indulged in, or humans he toyed with and destroyed, nothing eased the agony biting around the edges of his eternal life.

And the idea of it going on and on...he wasn't entirely certain he could endure it and remain sane.

So, these days, he found ways to forget. Ways to amuse himself, if even momentarily.

He called them his "little adventures." He would dress up (or dress down) and revisit the haunts that he and Edwin had frequented when they were on Earth together—the pubs, speakeasies, museums, cafes, lounges, and parks burned deep into his memory and his nostalgia. Sometimes, he just chose a city like New York and walked the streets aimlessly all night, pretending to be a lost child, his path always taking him past Edwin's townhouse—though he never knocked. He was no common stalker. Once, he went to London and bought the building where Club Mischief once gaily proclaimed itself the most Bohemian hidey-hole in the city. He then refurbished it to look exactly as it had the night Edwin left him. He invited the closest members of his Court and even had a Poppet stand in for Edwin, and, together, they partied for days.

Of course, it wasn't lost on him that every "little adventure" he took was somehow tied to Edwin in some way. Much like the one he was embarking on today.

He stood in his gigantic Grecian bathroom and clipped his hair short in the lighted mirror over the sink. The short, tousled blond hair falling into his eyes made him look even younger than his physical body was, which was exactly the effect he was going for tonight. He then patted on some light bronzer over his face and neck. It gave him an almost human coloring. Finally, he put in colored contacts to make his faded white-blue eyes look darker and warmer than they actually were.

From his vast walk-in closet—larger than most people's whole homes—he chose his favorite outfit, a British schoolboy uniform: Grey short pants, a deep, burgundy red jacket over a white shirt, and a striped tie. A large embroidered insignia for an exclusive academy that no longer existed was emblazoned on the left-hand breast pocket of the jacket. No one ever noticed that.

Edwin thought it was some sick fetish of his—these outfits. But the truth was, they were practical and helped him move about his world with more ease, considering his...physical challenges. Humans tended to get involved when they saw a child out by himself with no guardian. But one wearing a uniform was more invisible. He might be a child on his way to school or home, or he might even be on a school trip of some kind. Strangers tended to leave him alone and let him get on.

Once he was dressed and had checked his appearance one last time in the mirror, he exited his quarters and slipped by his security detail. It was easy enough. As a bloodkinetic, he could control any part of a human's anatomy because blood was, quite literally, the life—and it ran throughout a living body. All living bodies. He could make them go temporarily blind or even give them an aneurysm, if it pleased him.

Once he was alone, he took a lift down to the docking bay of the *Gypsy Queen*. He noticed Mr. Stephen in the hangar, talking to someone boarding a ship. Possibly, it was one of his many lovers, but when Mr. Stephen spotted him, he quickly detached himself and came up alongside Foxley.

"Another 'little adventure,' my Lord?" he asked.

He said it with a light inflection as if it was meant as a jest, but Foxley heard the concern in his personal secretary and Pleasure Poppet's voice. Mr. Stephen was a comely Poppet, well muscled and handsome of face, and his blood was one of the most delicious elixirs that Foxley had ever tasted, but he could be a tad clingy at times.

Foxley shrugged a shoulder under the weight of this slight annoyance. He had hoped to escape Mr. Stephen's keen observance of his comings and goings, but it was difficult. Mr. Stephen, much like Edwin's beloved little Poppet wife, was a Deaf. That is, he acted under his own will. He had a genius-level intellect and was frighteningly capable. He could not even be hypnotized correctly. Under normal circumstances, Foxley would have had such a Poppet destroyed as a security danger, but Mr. Stephen was so devoted to him that Foxley harbored no fears. He knew the Poppet would do anything he asked of him—even die for him.

It amused Foxley to no end.

Sometimes he thought about retiring Mr. Stephen to the lab, having him taken apart bit by bit to find out how the Deaf Poppets operated and had come about. But Mr. Stephen was so good at handling Foxley's personal business that he knew it would be hard to replace him, so Foxley took a more indulgent attitude

"No, Mr. Stephen," he lied, "merely getting some fresh air."

"Shall I accompany you, my Lord? I have the time if you require me."

"That won't be necessary." Foxley got into an empty Hummingbird and closed the cockpit while Mr. Stephen was still talking to him, pleading with him to take him along.

The Poppet stood there, looking in on him sadly like a little kicked puppy.

Foxley ignored him. Internally, he was rolling his eyes as he went to work on the preflight protocols. He'd invented the Hummingbird, and he knew how they worked inside and out. He never really worried about becoming stranded; he could fix or even dismantle and then put one back together in hours. He was, in addition to being an excellent shipbuilder and captain, a brilliant engineer and pilot, though that wasn't ego talking. It was a simple truth. He had invented everything aboard the *Gypsy Queen*, including the ship herself.

Without even waving goodbye, Foxley shuttled off. He flew fast and hard, pushing the craft to its limits. There was something exhilarating about flying faster than his kind was ever meant to do, and he enjoyed pushing everything, living or not, to its breaking point just to see what would happen to them.

He reached Scottish airspace by morning. The Hummingbird was outfitted with UV shields, so the rising sun was no concern to him. He was also old enough that even being caught out under the normally killing rays of the sun was, at best, an inconvenience. As he descended and cut a swath through the clouds toward the Sky Palace, he briefly reflected on the events of the evening before—another "little adventure" of his.

When Cesar first came to him with his request, he'd been neither offended nor particularly interested. He'd had no set plan for Cesar or his lover. He was merely acting on an internal compass that had never led him down before. The detective was connected to Cesar, who, himself, was connected to Edwin. It was yet another thread to reel in, one that might prove useful in the future, though Foxley couldn't see the use for it right at the moment.

The Sky Palace shimmered into view. He was close enough now to feel Edwin's presence aboard her. Not that he didn't feel him most of the time anyway—the ragged, lingering fragments of their bloodlink had never dissipated. But this close, his Heir's emotions cut him deeper and in a way he found infinitely more pleasurable. It felt like an orgasm that was always building, but one that never quite crested. Yes, Edwin was aboard. And, soon, he would be, as well.

In their years together, Edwin had always found him cagey, and he was correct in assuming that Foxley had many secrets, including some that he'd never revealed even to his favorite Heir. Among them was the ability to see through the eyes of his Heirs and Grand-Heirs and vicariously experience what they were experiencing when he was near them. Which was how Foxley knew the layout of the Sky Palace before he even began the docking procedure. He was also close enough now to physically manipulate the people aboard the gyro, which was how he got the officers of the hangar to clear him for landing and to open the docking doors so he could fly smoothly in and land the Hummingbird without alerting any of the Fae guards.

When he got out and finally stood within the rig's hangar, he saw the Fae personnel all rooted in place, their hands on the proper controls to let him through.

"What good little fairies you are," he told them as he waltzed up to the doors leading to the corridors beyond. A pair of royal guards stood there with some fierce-looking weapons crossed over one another, barring his way, but all they could move were their eyes. They couldn't even tremble as he approached them.

One said in a whisper, "C-can't get past security code."

Foxley looked the strange, angry-looking creature over. "Fairy, do you know who I am?"

He tried to shake his head but failed.

"Then I will tell you," he said in a soft, neutral voice and bared his fearsome smile of teeth. "I am your fucking god."

With a wave of his hand, the two guards bashed their own armored heads hard against the door, which made them slump down, their weapons skittering away. Foxley then turned to the security system on the door, which was complicated but in no way a challenge to him. The Floating Palace was a stationary gyro, but, first and foremost, a *gyro*, and he had invented the gyro that vampires and the other supernatural creatures used and lived on. There was no gyro in the world that did now owe its design or computer system to him in some way. He had, by extension, created them all.

And all of them came with an override command line that he had written long ago to take control of them all.

The command line was long, but Foxley had an eidetic memory. He quickly inputted it and the doors shushed open for him, their creator. A little animated fairy in pixels even showed up on the control pad and greeted him by name. He walked through and started down the suspiciously empty corridors. Most of the Fae, even the guards, were up in the White Room, enjoying the day's bloody festivities.

He found a lift to take him to the top level of the ship where the coliseum was located. It was easy enough; there were signs everywhere written in the complicated Fae language. A language, consequently, that he had invented thousands of years ago when the Fae—and, indeed, most intelligent beings—were little more than grunting sapient beings wallowing in mud.

Another Fae guard was waiting at the door that led to the White Room. That one he made go blind long before he reached him, and while the guard stumbled about, terrified and confused, Foxley casually inputted his command override and let himself into the Fae's coliseum. As the door closed behind him, he waved his hand, boiling the blood in the blind Fae's body.

Seeing the glory of the White Room, he felt a surge of excitement that he hadn't known since Emperor Commodus's "bread and circuses" insanity at the end of the Pax Romana. He chose a seat near the top of the Greek-inspired steppes and settled in to watch the battle unfold. Just the smell of the blood in the sand at the bottom of the coliseum was enough to give Foxley an all-over tingle. And when his beloved Edwin came out to fight the six-armed Rock Giant, well, Foxley thought he would simply orgasm right then and there.

It was a lovely, brutal battle. It left Foxley on the literal edge of his seat, and when it was done, and only Edwin remained standing,

Foxley found he was more in love with his Heir than ever before. He even opened a small bit of their bloodlink toward the end and suggested that Edwin use his weak bloodkinetic powers to turn the fight in his favor. Edwin, thinking it was his own idea, listened and did as Foxley suggested. Foxley might even have given him a little extra kick of power to bring the Rock Giant to his knees. But when Edwin finished the brute off by squeezing the consciousness out of him, that was one hundred percent the Prince, Foxley's prize Enforcer. Foxley had no hand in that.

And then Edwin stood over his fallen opponent, his fist raised in victory, and Foxley was the first to clap. Foxley pushed the others to follow, and very soon, the whole coliseum was cheering their new champion—their new Green Man.

The Morrigan, the Queen of the Fae, actually flew down out of her box and walked with her retinue of royal guard to the center of the coliseum to congratulate Edwin herself. Foxley got up and excitedly pushed his way down to the front to better watch the proceedings.

Edwin looked confusedly at her and her royal guards. "I...I don't understand. How in bloody hell can I be the Green Man?"

"It is an honorary position given to the greatest champion to fight in this arena. You are our now our Green Man, Lord McGillicuddy. The defender of the Fae race."

Edwin looked horrified by the news—though Foxley knew this little detail about the battle. He had seen plenty of Green Men come and go over the long centuries, and he found the Fae were depressingly pragmatic and redundant in their proceedings.

But Edwin didn't know that and threw up his hands. "I don't have the time to be your Green Man, mum! I have a Court to care for...a Congress! And a wife to save!"

But the Morrigan wasn't listening. She was motioning for Captain Ari to bring forth the Coronet of Branches, a huge crown of twisted, Fae magic-infused vines, branches, and flowering greenery. The giant Fae commander stepped forward, the whole crown thing slithering in his hands with sentience.

On seeing it, Edwin backed away, appalled, a hand held up to ward it back. "Erm...uh, that's quite all right, mum."

The Morrigan looked disappointed. "But you must. You are now our Green Man. Who will stand between my Unseelie Court and the modern world?"

Foxley held his breath and waited to see how Edwin would handle this new challenge. Most people assumed his Heir was all brawn and no brains, but Foxley knew better. Edwin had an astute and calculating mind. He was frighteningly clever and shockingly compassionate in his decision-making. It was what made him a good Vampire Lord and leader. He just didn't make a show of such things—and that often worked to his advantage because his enemies consistently underestimated him.

After a long moment's thought, Edwin lowered his hands, then took a step forward and extended one hand to the Fae queen as an idea came to him. "Here's a better offer, mum. Join my Congress and I will defend not just your Unseelie Court, but your entire species."

The Morrigan stopped and looked at his hand, then up at his eyes, her head tilted slightly as if she was trying to assess whether he was lying. "You wish to defend the Fae species, Fae Killer?"

Edwin swallowed nervously, though his eyes were solid and determined. "That's correct. And I am not a killer of the Fae. I killed Sleepwalkers laying siege to a town that didn't deserve such treatment. Fae that would have brought the Darkness down upon us all, vampire and Fae alike. Surely you, mum, can see the difference?"

It was pretty typical of Edwin to turn things around, to take control of the situation this way.

The Queen of the Fae pursed her lips. "You make a sound argument, Lord McGillicuddy. You understand you will need a very large and powerful Congress to defend not only the Unseelie Court but all of our kind?"

"I have wolves. Werewolves. A whole pack of them," Edwin insisted.

"But werewolves are the enemy of the Fae kind," she pointed out.

"I have werewolves that are loyal to me and act under my command. And, with your help, mum, my Congress can be the most powerful the world has ever seen."

"Still...you have a small Vampire Court. Few followers," the Morrigan insisted, and she wasn't wrong.

"Untrue," Foxley finally spoke up and felt the eyes of the whole audience turn to him in confusion. This was like the situation with Cesar and his lover. Foxley had no clear plan or even a notion as to why he was getting involved, but, suddenly, he was inspired. He wanted—*needed*—to do this for Edwin and his Congress. He realized that this was the reason for his "little adventure" all along.

Ignoring the Fae watching him so closely, Foxley pushed through the crowd until he reached the sandy edge of the coliseum and could present himself to the queen. She looked at him with curiosity, momentarily confused as to who he was. Edwin looked plain taken aback by his sudden appearance.

"Bloody hell, what are you do—?"

Foxley held up his hand to silence his Heir. He turned his full attention on the Morrigan. "My lady, may I introduce myself..."

"That," she interrupted when she suddenly recognized him under the makeup and affectations, "won't be necessary."

"I take it you know who I am?"

Her jaw dropped open, but she quickly recovered. "I do...Lord Foxley."

"Then you are familiar with my Court and my gyro, the *Gypsy Queen*. The grandest gyro to ever exist...aside from the Floating

Palace, of course. I have recently handed Edwin the keys to her." The words just tumbled out of his mouth. He didn't think too hard about them. He was on a path, and he wanted to see where this took him. And, after all, the *Gypsy Queen* was merely a ship. A lifetime's dream, yes, but still. Even in all of her glory, his beautiful floating world could not fully compare with the love he felt for Edwin.

The Morrigan glanced back and forth between him and Edwin as if trying to make sense of the whole unusual situation. "You gave Lord Edwin your ship? This is…highly unusual."

Edwin was watching but quickly glomped onto the opportunity as Foxley knew he would. Turning to the queen, he stated, "Aye, that's correct, mum. I am the sitting Lord-at-Court of the *Gypsy Queen* and her crew. I also command the *Queen Anne's Revenge II*. Surely, that is power enough to protect you and your people?"

The Queen of the Fae, looking dubious, turned to speak to her general and retinue in a little huddle. While she was doing that, Edwin shifted closer to Foxley and said, "What in hell are you doing here?"

"Helping you negotiate terms with the Queen of the Fae."

"Why?"

Foxley gave him a droll look. "My Heir, never look a gift horse in the mouth. Here." He snaked his hand out and deposited the key to the *Gypsy Queen* that he always wore around his neck into Edwin's hand.

When the Morrigan turned back around, Edwin held the key up. The Fae queen looked impressed. "We have agreed it is in our best interest to join your Congress, Lord Edwin. But we do have a request. Two, actually."

"I'll allow it," Edwin said imperiously.

The Morrigan held up her long, thin, white finger. "First, as a sign of good faith on your part, you shall send the selkie women to us so we might reunite them with their people. As the Fae portion of your Congress, we should handle all Fae-related transactions anyway. It is better and safer that way." She put up a second finger. "And, second, we the Unseelie Court hold the keys to your gyros as a sign and sigil that we may visit whenever we wish. If you are agreed to those terms, we will draw up the contract."

Edwin hesitated only a moment. "Fine. Agreed." He held out the key to the queen.

xi

One thousand years from today

He wakes from a deep, dreamless sleep full of vivid shadows and corroded memories.

Opening his eyes, he recognizes the rounded, honeycombed chamber he is sleeping in, though it takes him a moment to place where he is. Oh, yes. He is at the base of one of the four Galilean moons—which one, he isn't entirely sure. His is a life of travel, and he frequently finds himself waking on many different moons, satellites, and space gyros. Work has sent him as far out as the Kuiper belt, a cold, remote station that greatly appealed to his aesthetic with its isolation and remote beauty.

He realizes the shush of the chamber door has awakened him, and he sits up in his hyperbaric, UV-protected sleep chamber and hits the command prompt to decompress the impenetrable plastic capsule. It slides open with a hiss of cool air.

The other has returned.

He swings his legs over the edge of the bed and says to his lover, "Did you bring the chrysanthemums I asked you to?"

The other looks at him curiously, his head tilted slightly. "I'm sorry. I forgot. You should have mind-texted me a reminder."

"I thought I did."

"You may have. It is possible. But that was so long ago."

He has to think about the last time he talked to the other, either by mind text or in person. It has been some weeks, he realizes. Perhaps longer. And he realizes he requested the chrysanthemums months ago. No wonder the other forgot.

He hangs his head. "I'm sorry. It was stupid of me."

"Not at all," the other says, moving to sit beside him on the edge of the bed. "Time is a malleable thing, is it not? Ever-changing." The other touches his cheek and gives him a long, lingering kiss of hello, their first in months. Maybe years. He can't recall. Time ceased to mean anything centuries earlier.

He kisses the other back, reveling in the familiarity of the kiss, though the lips—indeed the whole body—is once again different. It's the same for him. Work has taken them both in different directions and made it necessary to rearrange their molecules many times over. They have been all sorts of people—Black, White, male, female, genderless, even alien. Yet, despite whatever form they are presently in, they always manage to recognize one another. The gift of the Chimerian.

As they make out, relearning each other's bodies with their hands and their lips, he suddenly recalls something that Lord Foxley told him long, long ago. The ancient vampire once promised him that he would protect him from any advances made by the remaining Chimera. Lord Foxley lied about that as he has lied about almost everything in his entire long life. Despite Foxley's vow, the Chimera found him in time and took him away. Foxley did not intercede, though he suspects the ancient one probably never had the power to do so anyway. Or, honestly, the interest.

He resisted at first, of course. He believed that the Chimera meant to do him harm, even death. But, over time, the other's motives became clearer to him and his confidence and sense of self improved. He stopped fearing the other centuries ago, though it was a long time, and an even longer pursuit before they came to mean something to each other. It was a journey that came with pain and with many hardships on both their parts.

In the end, he learned that the Chimerian played the long game. They have the patience to wait, the stamina to pursue, and a very long memory.

The other draws back and strokes his face. "I like this body. I like the way your skin feels. I like its color."

He blushes at the other's compliment. "Thanks. Yours is nice, too."

Because they are one entity now, they do not use names. In fact, he has trouble remembering what his name used to be from so long ago. He can barely summon or even properly recall his original form. That was lost several centuries ago—though "form" is an ambivalent thing for creatures such as they are. They are male, female, Black, White, a combination of things. All things. Nothing.

It is the same for the other. He has said many times over the years that he has no clear memories of what he was before he became what he is now. He isn't even entirely sure he was a "he" at the beginning. The other feels that he has always been this malleable thing.

It is something he finds himself contemplating often as he grows older, more ancient, and becomes less a "he" and more a "them." Was there ever a "him" before? Perhaps he was born this thing?

No, no. There was a time…long ago…

Though he is not sure about the details of his own past, he recalls his master and maker—Lord Edwin McGillicuddy. His touch. His kiss. And that brings with it a flood of painful memories that leave him chilled and feeling nauseated if he concentrates on them too hard. He has not crossed paths with Lord Edwin in centuries, not since their parting, which happened much earlier than any Lord or Heir should experience.

He knows his former master took to the stars some centuries before with his Bride and his Congress. He is widely regarded as the most powerful and long-lived vampire in current existence, a record formerly held by Lord Foxley, who disappeared eons ago.

Again, he feels vaguely ill as he recalls these small details...

The other jumps up as if ready to run off to another mission.

"Where are you going?" he asks, standing as well.

"To get you those chrysanthemums, darling."

"Don't," he insists, holding up his hands. He looks at them in an attempt to recall his current form. He realizes they are small and feminine, and his skin is very dark and of a bluish hue. "It's not important. It's...it's something I can't recall now. Stay with me. Make love with me. It's been so long."

The other thinks about that. "Has it? All right." Sitting down again, he entwines his fingers with his lover's and draws him into his lap for a kiss. "But we must be quick about it. We have work ahead of us."

"Another job?" he asks the other, feeling a stab of disappointment. They have both only recently returned from missions. It strikes him with great annoyance that the High Vampire Courts they work for plan to send them back out without so much as rest period. The Courts always divide them. Apart, of course, they cover more ground and finish more missions that way.

The other smiles. "I know what you are thinking, but this is a special case. The High Courts want us together on this one."

That makes his heart feel lighter. It has been ages—literally—since the High Courts have sent them on a joint mission. But it also concerns him. That the vampires who control Earth want two Chimera on a mission means only one thing—a hard target. This will be dangerous. They both may not even make it back.

"Who's the mark?" he asks worriedly.

The other's smile grows. "You will enjoy this greatly, I think. The High Courts have decided that Lord Edwin McGillicuddy's Congress has grown too great in power. They are requesting that we retire the good Lord and break down his Congress."

He starts at the news. "They want us to kill Lord Edwin?"

The other pulls him closer so only their breaths separate them. "A challenge, yes? Lord Edwin is no easy target. But is it a problem for you, darling? I know you have a history..."

He thinks about that for a long moment. "No, but it may prove dangerous. Lord Edwin is wily and very good at surviving all manner of attacks on his person. I know this firsthand."

"You know him better than all of us," the other says and kisses him on the cheek. "That is why it will fall to you to deliver the killing blow, my darling. He will never see you coming."

* * *

Back to the present

"My lady, you look gorgeous!" Brianna announced as she worked small, white roses into Eliza's voluminous hair.

Eliza stood before the three-way mirror in her bedroom and stared vapidly at herself, then up at the clock on the wall. One hour before her Red Wedding.

Her wedding gown was slim and white, and its Chantilly lace covered her from just below her chin to her feet. It itched like hell and was nothing like the gown Edwin had designed for her one true marriage just over a year ago. That one was more of a crazy Celtic design, and it didn't hobble her.

This one looked and felt like the prison it was.

"I tested the fabric for the great reveal," Brianna explained, grinning broadly in the mirror. "You may test it if you like, my ladyship."

Oh, yes. That.

In years past, when a vampire took a Bride, the Bride wore white (whether it was a man or a woman), and after the ceremony, the vampire would publicly feed on his or her new Bride to change the poor, unfortunate soul. There was a lot of blood involved, and the vampire purposely let it flow down the Bride's white clothes as a symbol of their covenant. The Bride's wedding clothes were then packaged up as an heirloom and became part of the new vampire's Inheritance. But times had changed, and vampires no longer made such huge public messes. It was considered tacky these days. But the tradition remained, so some damned soul invented fabric that changed colors under the right circumstances, and it soon became all the rage to throw a grand Red Wedding. As the Bride was changed into an Heir, the fabric changed color with them, going from pure white to crimson red.

She pinched the sleeve of the dress and saw its molecule structure change subtlety to red before resetting itself to white. She wanted to cry.

The dress made all of this so real. This was really happening.

In just one hour, she was going to belong to Summersfield—mind, body, and soul. His to use, his to control. His to keep or to dispose of, if that was his decision.

She looked up at her miserable, tear-stained face in the mirror.

Brianna clucked over her. "No need to be nervous, my lady. You are going to be perfect. You will make the master a beautiful vampire Bride."

She thought about screaming at Brianna, telling her she didn't want this. She'd never had a choice. And now she was doomed. Damned.

Lost.

She had put her faith in Edwin coming back for her and saving her, but it had been weeks, and there was no word, no Edwin. She realized now that she'd been a fool to trust him. She could have tried to escape on her own as she had the first time with Derek. She could have tried to fight Summersfield even if she died. She could have done *something*. Anything to avoid this. But she'd chosen to wait for him and to protect Dahlia.

She was a fool. Dammit, she was crying all over herself.

"My lady?" Brianna said, finally understanding that something was very wrong with her mistress.

She was about to tell Brianna to get out, to go to hell and let her cry herself blind, when she heard a disturbance from the adjacent room where Dahlia was being dressed by Brianna's assistant.

"No…no, stop it!" came Dahlia's strained cry. "You can't have him!"

Eliza immediately sucked in her tears, centered herself, and raced to the next room. Brianna followed, calling after her. Brianna's assistant David had gotten Dahlia into her bridesmaid's dress and was trying to wrest her Mr. Snoop away from her. Dahlia was crouched in the corner of her room, clutching her stuffed dog and screaming. But the moment she spied Eliza, her eyes went wide.

"Leeza….Leeza, don't let them take him, pleeeeeease…!"

Eliza moved toward the distraught girl, trying not to look too threatening. "Dahlia, it's okay!"

"No! No one is going to take Mr. Snoop!" Dahlia insisted, but David interrupted her.

He looked as miserable as she was. "Lord Summersfield said no toys. He was very insistent."

"Surely we can come to some compromise!" Eliza insisted.

"He isn't firing me. Or worse!" David leaned down and ripped Mr. Snoop away from Dahlia. Dahlia began to wail in earnest.

The sound was giving Eliza a migraine. And then all at once, all her pent-up frustration broke. Eliza turned on the designer. "You listen to me! You will not talk to Dahlia that way! And you will not take her toy!" She snatched at it, but David backed away, keeping it just out of her reach. The lights in the room flickered in tandem with Eliza's anger. David looked around in alarm.

Eliza pursued him, the beat of the lights matching her own rising, erratic heart rate. The fear on David's face was palatable. When Eliza passed Dahlia's standing mirror, she thought she saw a faint zigzag of electricity passing over her arms and shoulders, and her eyes almost seemed lighted from within, but she couldn't be sure. Her only prerogative was to get the toy back for Dahlia.

"I can't let her have this," David insisted, gritting his teeth and backpedaling blindly. "If I disobey Summersfield, he'll kill me! He wants everything perfect for today!"

The weeks of horror had worn her down, and as Eliza backed the man into a corner, she found she couldn't control herself. Couldn't care less if he killed David. She put out her hands, the ambient electricity in the air of the gyro dancing over her fingers and then jumping off them and out at him.

David screamed and dropped the stuffed toy. Some of Mr. Snoop's fluff burst from him, and the toy started to burn. Eliza rescued it from off the floor and beat at the flames eating at it with the hem of her dress. By the time she was done, her wedding dress was burned black at the hem.

Brianna, standing a few feet away, looked at her with her mouth wide open. "My lady! You're to be married in less than an hour!"

"Find another dress!" she roared at Brianna, electricity arcing all over her as if she were some appliance with a bad short. Raising both hands, Eliza caused the angry crackles of electricity to jump to the walls over their heads, cracking the wainscoting. "And both of you get out!"

The two designers scrambled to exit the room.

As soon as they were gone, Eliza lowered her hands and took a few deep breaths to get her temper under control. The last thing she needed to do was to set the room on fire—or even crash the gyro. She glared sharply at Dahlia's door and it shushed closed on them, locking. Let them run. Let them scramble to find her a new dress. Let them *talk*. In the meantime, she gingerly picked up the toy and approached Dahlia, who had collapsed into a corner.

"It's okay, baby. He's fine, see?" She knelt to show Dahlia the slightly burned but otherwise intact Mr. Snoop.

Dahlia dropped her hands and stared at Eliza with wildly terrified eyes. She didn't touch the toy.

"Dahlia..." Eliza said, trying to give her back her stuffed dog, but the girl had melted into a terrifying silence. She almost looked catatonic.

"He's going to kill me, Leeza," she said. Her voice was so soft that Eliza almost couldn't hear her. "I know. I heard him say."

Eliza frowned. "What do you mean?"

"Heard him say." She clutched herself. "He's going to kill me tonight after you are married." Tears and snot poured down the girl's face, ruining her makeup. "It's okay, though. It's okay so long as I have Mr. Snoop." She suddenly clutched the toy to her tear-stained cheek and then started sucking her thumb.

Slowly, Eliza stood up. She looked down at the girl.

Of course. After tonight, Summersfield didn't need Dahlia hanging around. After tonight, she would be Summerfield's Heir. And as his Heir, she would be unable to harm him or escape him...she'd be unable to live without him. She would be his completely. No need to keep her in line by threatening Dahlia.

Dahlia was...collateral damage.

Eliza felt a wave of sickness.

She didn't even think about her next move. She simply pulled Dahlia up from off the floor. "Come with me and bring Mr. Snoop."

Dahlia nodded and, still sucking her thumb, followed Eliza to drag her into the adjoining room.

First, Eliza kicked off her shoes and tore her dress so she had more range of motion. Next, she glanced around the chamber, but there was nothing she could use for a weapon. Summersfield did not allow her to keep utensils in her room—not even scissors. She had nothing except...perhaps...the white wedding parasol she was expected to carry for the photoshoot after the wedding. She grabbed it up, found Dahlia a coat to cover her thin little bridesmaid dress, and another for herself to cover her wedding gown. She pulled the roses from her hair and, still holding Dahlia's hand, moved to her door. She put her ear to it.

She could hear Brianna and David arguing in the hallway outside about what they were going to do about "Summersfield's bitch." Brianna wanted to fetch Summersfield, but David was terrified their Lord would go on a rampage.

Eliza swallowed hard, her panic edging up a notch. She had no allies here. No one who would help her. Turning to Dahlia, she whispered, "We're going to go on an adventure, baby. But it's a secret adventure and you can't make a sound. Not even to cry. Can you do that for me? Can you stay absolutely silent?"

Dahlia swallowed her tears and nodded. "Yes, Eliza."

"Good." She steered Dahlia back into her adjoining room. Eliza then tightened her hold on Dahlia's hand. "We're going to run really fast, all right? All the way to the hangar downstairs."

She knew if they could only make it to a Hummingbird, Eliza could override the system and use it to make their escape. She had done so when she was running from Foxley two years ago. But the plan hinged on Dahlia being able to hold it together just long enough for them to navigate the long warren of corridors to get to the docking bay.

"Dahlia?"

"Okay." Finally, Dahlia sounded interested, her eyes bright even though there was snot running out of her nose.

Kissing Dahlia's hand, Eliza took off down the hallway, dragging the girl after. It intersected the hallway where Brianna and David were still arguing, but she hoped that she and Dahlia flew by so quickly that the two never noticed.

Eliza stopped at the end of the hall where the lifts were. A keycard was required to activate them, but she had dealt with this system in the past. She put her hand on the command pad and summoned the lift. The system beeped and turned green on her command. Unfortunately, it took forever for the lift to arrive, and she kept glancing back, certain that Brianna and David would be there, shouting at them to stop.

Nothing happened except that the lift arrived. Once she and Dahlia were inside, she looked at the electronic prompt and programmed in the level where the docking bay was located. The command blinked yellow as if it was thinking about it, then went red. The letter "K" appeared on the pad. It took Eliza a moment to realize it was asking for a keycard. So, she put her hand on the pad and commanded the lift to take them down to the docking bay immediately.

The lift started down, then jarred slightly. Eliza felt her heart skip a beat. Was there a failsafe engaged? Or was someone jamming the lifts? Had someone noticed the two of them were gone from their rooms? But then, after a moment, the lift started down again. She had to calm her panicked heart and concentrate to get the lift to obey.

They started to descend again.

"Leeza…I'm scared."

"I know, baby," she said and gathered Dahlia against her and stroked her hair.

The lift shuddered down level by level, much too slowly for Eliza's liking. By the time it settled and the doors shushed open, she was certain the two designers upstairs knew that she and Dahlia were gone. From here on out, she had to assume they were being hunted.

They started down an identical corridor, then hit an intersection. Eliza read the signs. She realized they hadn't descended far enough, and they were at the mess hall level where the kitchens and employee cafeteria were located. She had made some error in the lift, probably because she was as frightened as Dahlia and not thinking clearly.

Casual voices emanated from behind them, so Eliza opted not to turn back. The kitchen staff weren't stupid. They would easily recognize her and Dahlia as Pleasure Poppets and wonder what they were doing in a part of the ship where they weren't allowed.

Eliza forged ahead, racing down one corridor after another with Dahlia in tow, hoping to find another lift. Following one route almost took them into the main industrial kitchen where all of the cooks were working. Eliza had to double back and pick their path across the vast, confusing floor plan until she spied a set of doors leading to some industrial fire stairs.

"You still with me, baby?" she said to Dahlia, who was starting to stumble.

"Yes, Eliza," Dahlia panted, not complaining at all.

They burst through the doors and onto a landing. Eliza directed the girl down the stairs, hoping they were at least close to the hangar floor, but then suddenly stopped, pulling Dahlia up short. She could hear some Security Poppets down below talking and futzing about. They were guarding the landing and speaking into their comms. They sounded anxious.

Eliza turned on the stairs and pulled Dahlia back up. Dahlia was struggling in her high heels, so Eliza stopped and dropped down just long enough to pull them off. Together, the two of them took the staircase in their stockinged feet to the floor above. Eliza hoped to find a lift there *somewhere*. Dahlia was panting by then, really starting to struggle. She was smaller than Eliza, and Summersfield had been draining her in place of Eliza. She didn't have the stamina that Eliza had.

They stopped on the landing above, and Eliza leaned down to watch the guards take the doors into the mess hall floor. They were definitely being hunted.

"Dammit," she breathed, trying not to panic and make any stupid mistakes. They needed to get to the docking hangar. Then Eliza remembered that Summersfield had a private helipad on the roof, if they could get to it. There would probably be at least one Hummingbird there.

Hefting the wedding parasol up, she threw it down into the stairwell, where it bounced round and round until it hit a floor farther down. As she suspected, the guards emerged from the landing door and started pounding down the stairs as they chased after the parasol.

She started going up, but Dahlia squeezed her hand and stopped her.

"Eliza!"

She turned and saw Dahlia staring in horror where Mr. Snoop was tumbling down the stairs to the next floor. The girl started down after him, but Eliza couldn't risk Dahlia intersecting the guards. She grabbed the girl by the arm. "Dahlia, no!"

"But Mr. Snoop!"

"We can't. The bad men are down there. We have to go *up*."

Dahlia whimpered, looking down.

"Shhh...it's okay, baby. We'll come back for him," she lied. She scooted down and looked Dahlia in the eye. "Mr. Snoop will be okay in the meantime. The guards don't want him."

After a moment, a teary-eyed Dahlia nodded her head. Thankfully, the girl trusted her enough to listen.

Taking her little hand, Eliza started climbing to the next level. When they reached the landing, Eliza put her ear to the heavy metal door. She heard frantic voices talking, so she took Dahlia to the next level, which sounded quieter and less occupied. They burst through the doors and started down a long, empty corridor on an unknown floor. All the doors were closed, and Eliza had no idea which level they were on. These could be employee apartments or business suites, for all she knew.

Up ahead, she spotted a lift. Her heart, still thundering in her chest, suddenly burst with hope. With a sudden spurt of energy, they lunged ahead, both making it to the end of the long hall without anyone emerging from the many closed doors.

The lift doors were closed, so Eliza raised her hand, conducting the power in the gyro to it and demanding the machinery obey her. This time, it gave her no problem. The light on the control pad turned green and the doors opened...

...on Lord Summersfield. He was dressed in a tuxedo, though his top button and his cuffs were undone. His blood-red satin bowtie for the wedding ceremony hung around his neck. His face was contorted into a wolfish rage, and his eyes were small and black and full of fury.

"Elizaaaaa..." he said, snarling through elongated incisors, "...what are you doing?"

Eliza couldn't help herself. She screamed. She screamed in rage and horror and pure frustration. Dahlia screamed with her. She threw both arms up and commanded the doors to slide shut on Summersfield before he could exit the lift. The lights in the corridor blinked frenetically and the lift doors started to close, but he came anyway. He came like a juggernaut, tearing through the lift doors and tossing the dented bits of metal aside as if they were weightless pieces of paper. They clanked as they hit the walls. The sound he made in his throat as he lunged at them both made her hair stand on end.

No! Focus! You have to get away!

Still holding Dahlia's hand, Eliza spun around and started running full-tilt down the long hallway back to the stairwell. She and Dahlia ran as fast as they possibly could. They pounded down that hallway even as the electric wall sconces on the walls flickered erratically, perhaps in sympathy for her panic.

She'd never run so hard or so fast in her life. She ran *for* her life. For her eternal life.

They made it halfway to the door before Summersfield reached them.

But he didn't take her. He took Dahlia.

She felt Dahlia's little hand as it was yanked out of her own. She heard—and felt—her friend's animalistic screams of panic as Summersfield dragged her forcibly back into his arms. Skidding to a halt, Eliza turned, nearly slamming into a wall.

Summersfield had Dahlia. He had her ragged little body pinned to the front of his tuxedo like he was wearing her. He carried her with no trouble at all as he pounded after Eliza, his eyes pinned on her face.

"Please..." Eliza cried, backing away. "Please, master...please, please..."

"Please...*what?*" Summersfield roared as he closed in on her. "What is it you want, Eliza? Mercy? Freedom? I gave you everything I had! I planned to make you my Bride!"

Eliza backed away, cowering. She was quickly losing all will to continue and nearly fell to the floor in fear. But she couldn't afford to give in to her panic. She had to play this right. She had to save Dahlia. So, instead of giving up, she slowed down and held up her hands in pure supplication.

"Please...let Dahlia go, master. I brought her here. It's all my fault."

"Yes, Eliza, it is," he said. He was grinning as he continued toward her, but he was going slower now. Dahlia mewed in his powerful grip. "You've turned against me, Eliza. You've turned Dahlia against me!"

She cried out at the way he shook Dahlia. "Take me...just take me!"

Summersfield continued to stalk forward down the hallway, and Eliza continued to take blind steps backward. Eventually, she felt the door to the stairwell at her back. Felt it give. Then they were standing in the stairwell, all three of them.

Eliza took one more step back and her back hit the safety rail.

Summersfield stopped in front of her. His eyes were locked on hers, all blackity black. Vampire black. But as he leaned forward, boxing her in, he also lifted a whimpering Dahlia into the air over his head.

"Please take me!" Eliza begged, her eyes tracking Dahlia's tearful, terrified face. She sobbed long and hard as she collapsed to her knees on the floor and raised her arms to him. "Please, my Lord! I'm yours! I'm all yours!"

He looked long and hard at her in the seconds before he threw Dahlia over the edge of the safety rail. "Yes," he affirmed, "you are."

Eliza screamed as Dahlia fell. She couldn't look. She just couldn't. She didn't have that kind of courage.

Thankfully, by some dark miracle, Dahlia's screams stopped the moment she landed in the stairwell dozens of floors before. Eliza supposed, even hoped, the impact had killed her instantly.

The silence that followed was deafening and all consuming.

She didn't feel a thing—not even when Summersfield came for her next, grabbed her by the throat, and lifted her up off the floor. She couldn't breathe. Couldn't speak or scream. She could do nothing but hang there and grip his powerful hands compulsively, not that she could ever break his hold, she knew. She choked as he raised her higher, and then higher. Her feet pedaled the air uselessly.

He looked deep into her eyes when he said, "You little, disobedient bitch. You will never leave me again."

She hoped he would drop her next. She hoped he meant to kill her. At least this way, her pain would be over. All of this would end. But he denied her even that. Instead of letting her die the true death, he yanked her forward and buried his teeth in the side of her neck.

Eliza's white wedding gown turned crimson.

| xii |

Chrysanthemums.
All they had in the damned gift shop were fucking boring white chrysanthemums. Cesar hunted high and low for something better, nicer, but the merchandise in the shop was all religious icons, cheap trinkets, and stuffed animals. Nothing spoke to him. In the end, he snatched up the chrysanthemums and went up to the checkout desk. Strangely, the clerk refused to take his money, saying he was welcome to the flowers. Rather than argue with her, he stepped out of the gift shop and took the corridor to the lift in the hospital ward of Foxley's ship.

As he rode the lift to the Intensive Care Unit, he started to feel sick again. By the time the doors opened on the surprised faces of a couple wanting to board the lift, he was nearly vomiting. He raced past them to the nearest restroom, threw himself down, and choked his breakfast out into the toilet.

Dizzy, he sat back. The smell from the toilet was awful. Throwing up as a vampire was just about as bad as it sounded.

Getting up, he flushed, picked up his fallen flowers, and went to the sink to splash cold water on his face. His eyes looked haunted, and sleepless black pits surrounded them. Foxley had offered him the use of the presidential suite in one of his many posh hotels while his staff prepared a wing of his private residence for Cesar to move into, but despite the ultra-soft king-sized bed and a quiet room full of whatever conveniences he needed—all there for free—he'd gotten no sleep at all.

Part of it was the fact that being aboard the *Gypsy Queen*, his day-to-night rhythm was getting all screwy from the lack of real sunlight or moonlight. But a bigger part of it was the simple fact that he couldn't stop thinking about what he'd done, the mistakes he'd made. He kept contemplating the many ways he could have handled things better. And how he could now do nothing about the situation.

If he could fix what he'd done, he'd do it in a heartbeat. And if he had to give up everything to do so, he would. He'd even give up Tommy and walk away, never to speak to him again.

But he had no answers—no idea how to fix this. Maybe Edwin would know. Miss Eliza would certainly know. But he wasn't wise like Edwin or smart like Miss Eliza. And both were off, dealing with their own crises, so he had no one to talk to about this.

He was alone.

Sighing and trying not to sob, he splashed some cold water from the sinks over his swollen eyes so he didn't look like he'd been crying all night, then picked up the bouquet, now worse for wear, and exited the washroom. The signs on the walls told him where to go.

When he got to the nurse's station, he started to worry. Tommy likely did not have him down for a contact. But when the nurse checked, she confirmed that he was on Tommy's contact list. His was the only name. Cesar realized that Tommy must have put him down as a contact when he started his plans for hospice care. He'd told Cesar he wanted him there at the end.

"Please go ahead, Mr. Schultz. You have an omnipass. No need to check in with any nurses from now on," she said, smiling broadly at him and in a decidedly funny way.

"What's an omnipass?" he asked.

The night nurse looked confused. "You're Lord Foxley's Enforcer. You can access any part of any building or the hangar of the *Gypsy Queen*. No need to ask permission from anyone."

He felt a strange numbness pass through his body.

The nurse looked confused. "Mr. Schultz, are you all right?"

"Y-yeah," he said before he upset her. "Th-thanks."

Passing her, he went into the ward divided by plastic walls. He looked at the names on the partitions until he found Tommy's bed.

The man in the bed didn't look like Tommy. The man hooked up to multiple machines looked shrunken and weak, a large bandage covering one whole side of Tommy's neck. This wasn't the Tommy he knew, the one who had taken down a major drug dealer only a few months ago. Confused and agitated, he started glancing around for a vase for the stupid flowers. A few seconds later, the ward nurse rushed over to provide him with one, as well as a seat and her hospitality.

"If you need anything, let me know," he said, making eyes at Cesar.

He could tell the nurse wanted a quick hookup. But even though he was the most drop-dead gorgeous man in the ward, Cesar wasn't in the mood. "I would like to see the doctor attending Mr. Quinn."

"Of course. I'll fetch her."

He was gone in a flash. Cesar sat down at Tommy's bedside to wait.

The doctor, an attractive Indian woman in her mid-fifties, appeared a few minutes later. He wondered if she had abandoned her duties to fly to his side, seeing how he was Foxley's new Enforcer. The thought wasn't flattering; instead, it was just fatally depressing.

"Mr. Schultz!" she said cheerily, then stopped herself. "Or is it Lord Schultz?"

"No. Not yet."

Nodding, she went on at length about Tommy's condition. It wasn't the blood loss that had caused him to slip into a coma but the trauma of the bite. That surprised Cesar. Tommy had a weak heart, probably due to the extensive damage to his body from his cancer. She was surprised he survived the surgery that repaired his carotid artery, but it was unlikely he would come out of his coma. She said it was probably for the best anyway.

"What do you mean?"

She showed him some scans and explained that Tommy's entire digestive system was compromised. Even if he woke up, he'd remain on a drip, and even then, his body wouldn't tolerate it without massive pain management drugs, vitamins, and probably dialysis. "He has zero quality of life, Mr. Schultz," she said in conclusion. "He'd require so many meds to control his pain level that he wouldn't be lucid. But that's unlikely now. We will keep him on a morphine drip until…the end."

Her prognosis felt like a collection of knives sinking deep into Cesar's heart. He glanced over at Tommy's withered form in the seemingly too big bed. He felt cold. "He did this, you know. Foxley. He did this to Tommy. He fed off a man dying from cancer."

"I wouldn't know anything about that," the doctor said in a neutral, almost robotic voice. "I'm an oncologist treating him for late-stage cancer, Mr. Schulz. However, I hope his care is to your approval."

Of course she wasn't going to raise a complaint against her employer, Cesar thought. She was probably terrified of Foxley's retribution.

"As long as you are doing everything to keep him pain-free, then I'm happy," he said.

She smiled broadly just as the nurse had. "Of course. We value all of our patients here at Bleeding Heart."

"Heh. That's an appropriate name for Foxley's hospital."

She didn't respond. Just stood at soldierly attention as she waited for his next command.

He looked her up and down, hating her. Hating all of this.

Himself, most of all.

"I'm going to say with him."

"Of course. I can arrange a private room, if you like."

"Yes, I'd like that."

He got Tommy a whole private suite of the hospital, with nurses that walked softly as they came and went, attending to Tommy's needs. All of them were alert to Cesar's commands. Tommy, though, continued to just lie there. Cesar joked to himself that Tommy was too tough to die, but he knew it was stupid—and inevitable. Tommy was dying, just in a way that would probably take longer and leave him with fewer and fewer dignities.

What's not to understand? Tommy's voice from seemingly long ago. *I want to spend my remaining time with you, but when it's my time, it's my time.*

That's what Tommy said the night of their argument. And it was one of the last things he had said to Cesar before everything went to hell in a handbasket. He doubted that Tommy even wanted him in the room, considering what he'd done, but he couldn't bring himself to leave Tommy's side. He was the reason that Tommy was here.

***

The days came and went. Tommy continued to breathe slowly in and out with the aid of machines.

The chrysanthemums slowly withered in their glass vase. Cesar watched them turn brown and the fragile white flowers fall apart, making a mess on the nightstand. Cesar couldn't bring himself to remove or replace them; he'd decided they had come to represent his and Tommy's relationship. Short-lived, broken, rotten...

Tommy's dying took a painfully long time.

After a full week of sitting there, listening to the ventilator, Cesar found himself begging God (or Whoever was running the universe at this point) to just take Tommy already. Let him go and be free to be with Maggie. He prayed for it over and over. But as morning dawned once more over the UV-protected windows of Tommy's suite, there was no change. Tommy continued to lie there, growing gaunter by the day, withering but not dying. It all reminded him of his Uncle Luis.

Cesar asked for all kinds of details from the staff, including the overly kind doctor, but she didn't have any satisfying answers. "We just don't know, Mr. Schultz. He might come out of his coma. He might never come out. Or he might come out...damaged. However, we can't just let him go. He never completed the paperwork for his DNR. All we can do is wait."

"Wait for what?" Cesar cried, startling her. His eyes had turned all black, he knew, and his teeth rasped dangerously against his tongue. He couldn't help himself. He grabbed the vase of chrysanthemums and threw them at the wall beside the doctor. The vase shattered, and brown water, dried flowers, and water splashed across the floor. "Wait for him to turn into a skeleton?"

She backed away slowly, her face unusually pale. She looked at the mess, then at him. It took her a moment to find her words. "All we can do is wait for a change in his condition." She turned and raced from the room.

Cesar sank to the floor, sobbing. God, it never should have been like this. How had his whole life become this fucking bag of shit?

He sat on the floor for a long time, maybe a day or more. He wasn't sure. Time had ceased to have any meaning. He thought about his Uncle Luis. Cesar was very young when he visited his uncle in the hospital, but he remembered him giving him the green Jell-Os that came with his meals and telling him stories about the old country.

Eventually, Cesar picked up his phone and called his sister.

"Hey, Iz. It's me," he said when she answered.

An awkward silence followed, and then, "Cee? Is it really you?"

"Yeah. I...I was thinking of you and wanted to call. Are you okay? How is the fam?"

"Yeah...I mean, Dad's being Dad. You know. But otherwise, things are good."

They talked for almost an hour. He got all the gossip about the family. Isabella said she and her husband were well. So were the kids, who were getting big. Mom was okay. She still talked about him, which upset Dad.

He avoided talking about himself, and Iz tactfully didn't ask for any details. She didn't disapprove of his lifestyle, exactly, but he knew she had to keep the peace in the family, and his parents, good Roman Catholics, did not approve of vampires.

They talked at length about the video games they had played as children and the movies they had seen at the drive-in before it closed. Innocent stuff. For a while, he was almost happy. Then she said she had to go, and Cesar had a feeling deep in his gut that told him this was the last time he would ever speak to his family. He couldn't know that, of course, but it was a razor-edged certainty grinding away at his already tired and battered soul.

But he knew. After Tommy was gone, Foxley would move in to claim him, body and soul, and his life would be radically different from what he'd known at Edwin's Court.

He thought about saying deep things, telling her he loved and missed her, but he didn't. He didn't want to worry her. They hung up and he looked at the phone.

Another regret.

* * *

It was day eleven when Tommy coded.

"Please, sir, if you will, wait outside," said the nurse with the crash cart.

He did, his back to the wall of Tommy's suite. He felt like such a coward. He should have used his status to stay and be there for Tommy's final moments. But he'd decided he couldn't bear it. He was there when Uncle Luis died. He didn't remember all of it, of course, just a flurry of people and shouting and his mom crying. Someone pushed him back so hard he almost hit the wall. Then a nurse said in her robotic, health-care voice, "He's gone, Mr. and Mrs. Schultz. I'm sorry."

It happened so fast.

But not this time. As Cesar leaned stiffly against the wall, holding his breath, time seemed to move both too quickly and much too slowly. All he had was his breathing and his memories for a while. After an indeterminate amount of time, the doctor came out to talk to him.

"We managed to get Mr. Quinn stable, Mr. Schultz. You can see him now, if you like."

He's still alive. Oh, god...when was this fucking nightmare going to end?

He thought about going to his knees at Tommy's bedside and begging God to take him, but what was the point? He was a goddamn vampire. It wasn't like God was going to listen to him.

He felt the need to scream, to pound the walls, but he was so well mannered and unwilling to make a scene, that all that came out was, "O...okay. Thank you."

When he went back inside, he saw that Tommy was hooked up to more machines and there was a new, ugly, grey and white tube going down his throat.

Why are you doing this to me? I just wanted to save you...

He went up to the wall opposite the bed, leaned against it, and screamed like a wolf with its leg stuck in a trap. A nurse promptly appeared to see what was happening, but when he turned to glare at her, her face turned as white as paper at the sight of him and she fled from the room in the same state of fright as the doctor had when he threw the chrysanthemums at her.

Sliding bonelessly to the floor, Cesar lay with his head against the wall, not sobbing. Empty.

For the first time, he missed Edwin. Missed him horribly. He needed his master. Needed his strength. How in hell was he going to drag himself through this hell? He wanted to call Edwin just to hear his voice, but his pride wouldn't allow for it. Edwin would probably just tell him he deserved it, that he'd made this mess and deserved to wallow in it, and he wouldn't be wrong. He had put himself into this hell.

Slowly getting to his feet, Cesar went to Tommy, leaned over the bed, and took Tommy's limp, cool hand in his. His teeth were already fully extended. It wouldn't take much. A small wound in the right spot and it would be over before either of them even realized it. Last year, Lord Severn had even taught him how to put a suffering animal down during the debacle a Whitby Hall.

Tommy couldn't go on this way. Just couldn't.

But in the end, Cesar didn't do it. Instead, he brought the heel of his own hand to his lips and bit into the flesh. He looked at the blood swimming to the surface of his pale skin—it looked darker than human blood, but not by much. He painted Tommy's mouth with his blood, then massaged his throat until Tommy swallowed compulsively.

He repeated the process several times. Afterward, he resumed his place in the chair. He noticed that some thoughtful nurse had replaced the dead chrysanthemums with fresh new ones, also white.

Eventually, he nodded off to sleep through sheer exhaustion. He slept deeply but fitfully. Tommy was in his dreams, but always standing at a distance across a vast field or lost in a dense, dark forest. He kept motioning to Cesar to find him, and Cesar did his best to seek him out in the shadows, cutting wildly through the underbrush, but he never found him.

He might have slept forever, except a shrill, high-pitched screaming jarred him awake.

* * *

At first, what he knows is a tearing, all-consuming pain—like someone is extracting his soul through a ragged hole in his throat. Afterward, though, there is a warm darkness he finds himself floating in. He can't see or speak, but sometimes he hears voices very far away, as though he is hearing them from deep underwater. Crying and praying. Mumbling. The strangely bitter scent of flowers.

The darkness carries on...beautifully. Wondrously.

He likes the darkness. In the darkness, there is no pain, no panic. No sense of self that can be lost. Ahead, he spies a light, dim at first, but over time, it grows in brightness and beauty. The light reminds him of home. He starts to swim through the darkness toward it, but he never quite seems to reach it. Maybe if he tries harder, swims harder, hopes harder for it?

In time, the light seems to stabilize and he's able to move closer to it. It takes a great deal of work, and he is dreadfully tired by the time he reaches it. There it is. Just up ahead. Perhaps a hundred feet away. He hovers in place, his heart filling with hope.

Within the welcoming light, he can see living shapes, many of them familiar. His parents...his brother who died in a boating accident when he was fourteen...even a past lover or two. He sees his wife, though he has to think about her name for a moment. *Maggie.*

Maggie, I am coming, he thinks to her as he swims steadily toward the light, now fighting with all of his remaining strength for every inch he achieves. It's so difficult, and she still seems much too far away.

She is beautiful like she was on the day they married. *Oh, my love*, she seems to say. She reached out to him with both hands. *I've missed you, and I've waited forever...*

Her voice galvanizes him. He swims faster and faster to her. He is inches away now. He has almost reached her when...

...something tears him away from her outstretched hand. It trawls him backward like a great monster from the deep carrying him away. He screams in rage and frustration. He was so close!

But the darkness that has its claws in him now and drags him back relentlessly, unkindly. It carried him away even as he continues to scream and beg to be let go. But the creature that has him is heartless in its determination. He eventually stops screaming. He can do nothing as he's pulled down and down, which strikes him as odd, as he was formerly going up and up and...

He opens his eyes. The light is absolutely blinding, and he wonders if this is Heaven or even just some approximation. But before he can even look around and determine where he is, pain fills his body, making him gasp. Tears fill his eyes. The pain is carnivorous, eating through every part of his body. He's never felt such pain. Such a...

Hunger.

Sitting up, he pulls frantically at the wires and tubes attached to his body, the things keeping him pinned down to the bed. In the course of it, he spies his skinny hand, his atrophied arm. He can breathe better this way, with the tubes out, but the pain—the biting, primitive hunger—has him in its teeth, and that makes him issue a low, desperate growl in his skeletal chest. Looking around, he realizes he is in a hospital ward of some kind. A large, chilly room, it is empty save for the figure sitting in the chair beside him.

Turning his stiff, clickety neck, he zeroes in on the figure. A living thing full of blood and flesh. The sheer *aliveness* of the creature attracts him as nothing else ever has. Climbing carefully from the hospital bed, he slinks forward on his painfully emaciated limbs to the edge of the bed and sniffs at the man.

He is indeed alive. But there is something wrong with this man, something cold and *erased* about him. Something that stinks of the dead. Looming over the creature, he sniffs closely at it again, taking its scent deep into his lungs. His scent is familiar, and his presence reminds him oddly of Maggie, though he isn't sure why that should be. This was someone of importance to him once. Someone once a part of him. Or he was a part of the man.

He can't quite figure it out. So, he reaches out to touch the man's sleeping face, stopping less than a hair's breadth away, his monstrous fingertips hovering over the man's pale cheek.

Such a pretty face. He feels a relentless and abiding tenderness for this man. He wants to kiss the man—but he also wants to bite him. He even tries to—tries desperately to bite the man—but his hungry jaws just won't click shut on the pretty young face. He loves this man too deeply, and on a primal level that makes it impossible for him to act against him. It's a feeling even the hunger cannot overcome, so he withdraws and sniffs the air around him for other prey.

Yes, there are others. Warm-blooded. Close by. He can feel them moving about in the hallways outside his room.

Unable to walk properly, he drops to the floor and moves that way. He has to crawl like an animal. He hasn't even reached the door when it is pushed open by one of the warm-blooded creatures stepping into the room. Such luck!

The moment he sees her, he loves her. He wants her. But it's not the same as the man sleeping in the chair. With her, he feels no restraint.

She looks at him curiously, perhaps too shocked or full of questions to react. It helps him move closer to her. It helps him zero in on the warmth of her skin. By the time she understands the danger, it is too late.

He springs at her. He takes her arm. He bites into it—savagely. He has to do something to abate this hunger or he knows it will tear his sanity apart.

She screams as she attempts to retreat, but he has her now, and he cannot afford to let her slip away. She rips her arm free of his hold, leaving bloody tears in her flesh, but he pursues her to the door and then out into the hallway. She is a terrified prey animal on the run, but he is fast. A true predator. And long before she reaches the end of the hallway, he is upon her.

* * *

The screaming drove Cesar up and out of his chair. Disoriented, he stumbled around for a few moments to get his bearings before looking at the bed.

Empty. Sheets tangled and lying on the floor...

Tommy's bed was empty!

Another scream erupted from the hallway, this one even shriller than the first. Then the sound was truncated, and only a long, low gurgling sound followed.

Wasting no time, Cesar flew into the hallway and found it was total bedlam. This being midday, there were people all up and down the corridor—patients, nurses, doctors, visitors. Some were fleeing in random directions, while others seem to be wired to the walls, trying to make themselves small and invisible to the dangerous predator in their midst.

Bodies littered the tiled floors. All looked like they had been attacked by a ravenous wolf. Skin and hair were torn mercilessly from the dead bodies. Blood was smeared across the floor in long, shining streams, and bloody handprints marred the painted beige walls and even the boring watercolor paintings.

His military training immediately kicked in, and Cesar stopped and assessed the danger on both sides of him. Though he saw people running away, he didn't see the perpetrator. He wished he had a weapon. Then he recalled that he was a vampire He was, literally speaking, a weapon. Whatever had done this, as grotesque as it was, was most certainly not stronger than he was.

Smelling blood down the hallway to the right heading to the visitor's lounge, he turned in that direction. Seconds later, a man's scream rang out.

The corridor took him past several hospital rooms before he reached the lounge, which was outfitted with vending machines and a large TV on the wall scrolling the weather report. A man lay on the floor beside an overturned wheelchair, one of its wheels still spinning. He was gargling through his own blood as someone—some *thing*—crouched over him, ravaging his throat.

The monster was thin, skeletal, and twisted at strange angles. Cesar stopped short in the doorway and felt a cough of vomit rocket up his throat, which was stupid. Since meeting Edwin, he had dealt with vampires, werewolves, demonic fairies, and all manner of undead. This should not have thrown him, and yet it had.

The man lying on the floor was dead, or very soon to be. He lay there, staring sightlessly up at the ceiling, while the bizarre, undead-looking creature worried the gigantic wound in his throat.

Cesar choked back a sob at the sight, recognizing the creature even in its terrible, half-decayed state. It glanced up at him with a dry, grey, almost mummified face and burning black eyes.

"T-Tommy..." Cesar managed to squeak out.

The creature, on hearing his name, growled at him from his crouched position. There was blood all up and down Tommy, on his face and in his hair. Blood drenched his hospital gown. He snarled a warning at Cesar like a dog whose meal has been rudely interrupted. He bared long, peg-like, blood-yellowed teeth that were neither human nor vampiric.

Whatever Tommy had become wasn't like a vampire. No vampire would do this level of devastation so quickly and mindlessly. It was almost as if he was caught in an in-between state. A revenant. A zombie.

Ghoul...

Cesar shook all over and then dropped to his knees in the blood on the floor. Behind him, he heard shouts, police-ban radio, and the tapping of feet as security made its way into the room. "T-Tommy...Tommy!" It was all he could manage to scream.

Tommy, growling out a warning, launched himself at Cesar.

| xiii |

The sudden jolt of awakening stole Edwin's breath away. Pain squirmed its way through his body from top to bottom, and he swore he could hear his own blood crashing in his ears. For a moment, he was completely blind. Then the darkness parted and he realized he was lying on Leo's bed in the captain's stateroom.

Leo wasn't there, and neither was Marco, the helpful Poppet who had offered Edwin his blood last night after Edwin returned from fighting the Green Man aboard the Floating Palace. At the time, Edwin knew he looked like several shades of death, and even Leo had commented on it before leaving Marco to attend to Edwin's needs.

Edwin started saying Eliza's name—Eliza, who normally wound up his heart in the morning—but when the darkness finally parted, he recalled his beloved Bride wasn't here. Instead, a nightmare waited for him: He found Foxley sitting on the side of the bed, looking down at him in loving concern. He was putting the literal key to Edwin's heart back under his shirt.

Edwin was too startled to move. "What are you doing here aboard Leo's ship?"

Foxley smiled, patting the key like it was his most beloved possession. With the makeover he'd given himself, Edwin could tell he was trying to appear more human. As if he ever was. "I gave you my ship. The least you could do is let me hitch a ride on this little adventure of yours." He tilted his head as he considered. "Besides, I could use a lift back to the *Gypsy Queen*."

Slowly, Edwin pushed himself up on his elbows. "Don't you have a Hummingbird? I'm pretty sure that's how you got aboard the Faes' rig."

Foxley made that little dismissive expression that they used to call a moue a hundred years ago. "Sometimes, I feel like you want me to go away, my Heir. Like you don't like me at all."

Edwin rolled his eyes.

"I helped you with the Rock Giant."

Edwin grunted in acknowledgment. He figured Foxley had had something to do with him winning the tournament that secured his place as the new Green Man. "Aye, likely so. But the question is *why*? What's your end game, Foxley? And don't tell me you don't have one. Because you always do."

Foxley gave him that facetiously hurt look that he always had on standby. "All this time, and still you don't trust me, my Heir."

"I've never trusted you." Edwin tried to push himself into a sitting position on the bed, but Foxley reached out and touched his cheek, stopping him. The touch of his master's hand sent shivers of danger and revulsion in equal parts through Edwin's body. If he lived a thousand years, or even a million, he would never get used to how bloody creepy Foxley was, inside and out.

As if sensing his thoughts, Foxley withdrew his hand. "Captain Leo asked me to tell you that while you were sleeping, the *Queen Anne's Revenge* was boarded by a rather large collection of werewolves. It appears your pet wolf and his pack have arrived."

Malcolm! Finally, good news.

Then a disturbing thought occurred to Edwin. "How long have you been here in this room?"

Foxley, looking oh so innocent, said, "Just long enough to wind up your heart."

"And that's it. You didn't do anything else to me?"

"Such as?"

Edwin didn't know how to answer that.

Getting up suddenly, Foxley turned and said, "Leo also informed me that inside the next hour, we will be within hailing frequency of the *Marie Antoinette*. I assume, as our acting Lord, you want to do the honors of contacting her."

As he sat up on the edge of the bed and oriented himself, Edwin felt a slight tremor of fear at the news. And that fear had absolutely nothing to do with Foxley's proximity. "Aye. I plan to challenge Summersfield for his holdings. All of them. The ship. His crew. Including Eliza."

"Ballsy move," his master mused.

Edwin met Foxley's eyes, a thing he knew very few living creatures were capable of. "Well...you know me."

"I do," said Foxley, his voice full of admiration. "You never back down. You never surrender. And you just might be madder than I am."

Edwin couldn't help it. He laughed at that.

Foxley looked ridiculously delighted—and perhaps a little sad. "Seeing you in that ring yesterday brought back such memories," he mused. "If I was different..." He ran a hand down the front of his suit. "...if this body was different..."

Edwin told the truth. It was time he heard it. "You would still be a monster. And I would have still left you, Foxley."

Foxley shuddered slightly as if Edwin had struck him an invisible blow. For the first time in nearly forever, his face showed real emotion, real regret, not the theater he usually showed the press, his

Court, and the rest of the world. Edwin had wounded him deeply and in a way he would never fully recover from.

He never imagined Foxley's obsession was this bad.

Before Foxley left the stateroom, he turned to address his Heir one last time, that wistful expression still on his young, pained face. "You know, when you left me, Edwin, you didn't just betray me. You ripped out my heart. You bled me in a way no one ever has. You will never know how much it pains me that we are apart."

Edwin, dumbstruck, waited until Foxley was gone, then let out his breath. Bloody Foxley.

He groaned as he rolled out of bed. He was still a mite sore from his battle the day before, though all of his wounds had to have healed by now. Shrugging off the pain, he looked over the suits hanging in Leo's closet. He recalled that they were the same size and wore the same types of clothes, though Leo had quite an eclectic collection of modern suits these days.

The one he chose was what he felt a Lord-at-Court would wear, a deep burgundy jacket sequined with a lot of the hardware that was popular in fashion today—watches, cogs, chains, and the like—and black trousers. He paired it with a shirt and bowtie that he hoped Eliza would approve of, then topped it off with a formal top hat and shiny shoes with brass toes.

While he brushed his teeth and then his hair in the bathroom, he thought about what was to come. He didn't have time or patience for whatever foolish drama Foxley was stirring up. But he also knew Foxley could also be a powerful ally in this if he played his cards right. Foxley was a wanker, all right, but a wanker hopelessly in love with him, and Edwin wasn't too proud to use that to his advantage.

Before he left the stateroom, he looked at himself in the mirror. It was quite a change from the funny T-shirts, braces, and golf pants he usually favored. He looked, to put it bluntly, like the Vampire

Lord he was. He just hoped it was enough to impress Summersfield and help him save Eliza.

Out in the narrow hallway, Hugo the werewolf was bouncing around like an excited puppy. Edwin assumed it had something to do with all of the other werewolves on board the *Queen Anne's Revenge II*.

"The wolves downstairs...they your wolves?" he asked hopefully. "I mean, you're their Lord, right?"

"They are mine," Edwin said. "And I am their Lord, aye."

Hugo looked him up and down with awe. "Wow. I don't know a single vampire who commands werewolves."

"What about Captain Leo?"

"Nah." Hugo shook his big head. "We're his crew. But he's not our Lord. This ain't the same thing as what you're doing." He was virtually vibrating with excitement. "The first Congress in half a century!"

Edwin started to shrug it off. He'd always hated High Court formality and all the stupid rules attendant thereon. But then he thought better of the gesture. In the next few hours, the way he presented himself to his new Congress, Leo's crew, and, ultimately Summersfield and his Court, would shape his rule as a Vampire Lord of status. He couldn't come off as some insipid, casual bloke or no one would respect him—including his enemies.

So, instead of palling around with Hugo as he'd intended, he held out his hand rather formally in the way of the High Courts. It took Hugo a moment to catch on, but when he did, he took it. Hugo went to one knee and bowed over it before standing again. It was a brief gesture, but it meant a lot. Hugo was acknowledging him as his leader and Lord.

"The wolves downstairs..." Hugo started to say, then stopped.

"They could be your mates, Hugo."

Suddenly, Hugo looked shyly down at his feet. "It's been a long time since I was part of a pack. What if they don't like me?"

"Why don't we find out together?"

Hugo, brightening up, led him down to the landing bay but stayed very quiet and to the side as Edwin strode in to meet with his new Congress.

Bloody hell, he thought. Here we go.

* * *

Before bedding down for the night, Edwin had asked Leo to see to everyone's arrival and to assemble his new Court down in the loading bay, including the Fae and the wolves that would shortly be boarding the *QAR2*. He wasn't disappointed. As he approached the rather large and eclectic collection of mixed beings, he realized Leo had fulfilled his request with great formality and precision. He felt his mechanical heart jump a little inside of him.

It was a lot of people to address, and up until now—up until Eliza's capture—things such as impressing others had never really appealed to Edwin. He was a lone wolf by nature, and after years of being an Enforcer, he wasn't interested in shoving people about. But now things were changing. Things were in flux. He was a Vampire Lord in charge of the first Congress to exist in five hundred years.

He stepped into the hangar with a fake it till you make it attitude.

The Fae representing the Floating Palace were clustered together, while Malcolm stood at attention at the forefront of a collection of strange werewolves that Edwin did not know. The Fae were standoffish, as to be expected, but Malcolm turned to greet him with bright eyes and a smile. With him was a gorgeous and immensely tall black woman that Edwin immediately identified as a high-ranking alpha female.

Since this was the first time they were meeting and he had no idea if she trusted him, Edwin approached the female alpha wolf cautiously. He was happy he'd taken the time to dress properly. He wanted to make a good impression on the wolves and their queen.

She watched him as he closed in on her, nostrils slightly flared.

"Madam," Edwin said, taking her hand. Normally, he would have bowed over it, but that was a greeting between a human gentleman and a lady. He was a Vampire Lord and she was the mate of his Dog of War. So, he held it out stiffly before him and waited for the proper response.

He let her weigh the strength of his hand.

"Lord Edwin McGillicuddy," she announced, "I am Anjou La Croix, Queen Wolf of the Youngbloods."

He smiled but kept it tight-lipped to appear friendly. Any show of teeth could be misinterpreted as a threat. "I welcome you to my Congress, Anjou La Croix, and I welcome the Youngbloods." He nodded to the other wolves, who were murmuring amongst themselves. "As the sitting Lord-at-Court of this Congress, I extend my umbrella of protection to you and your people." He couldn't remember the exact formal words, but he knew they went something like that and he hoped she got the gist of it.

She moved a bit closer and sniffed him. He allowed for it.

When she finally stepped back, he saw her face was placid. "Malcolm told me you are a good man and a fierce but fair leader." She smiled. "I believe him. You smell of blood, but I suspect it is the blood of battle and the blood of your enemies, not the blood of innocents."

He smiled at that. "You would be correct." And, throwing tradition to the wind—he decided he was going to do this thing his way anyway—he leaned down to kiss her hand. "Thank you, milady."

She turned to Malcolm, blushing profusely. "He's charming. And he has good manners."

"I told you," Malcolm said. He moved toward Edwin.

He smelled a great deal like Anjou. Edwin had the impression that they were already mated. They'd probably been fucking like jackrabbits while he was away. But Malcolm looked happy, and that was all Edwin cared about. It made Edwin happy to see his Dog of War so happy for a change.

Malcolm started sinking to one knee to renew his vow of loyalty, but Edwin moved forward and embraced the big, hairy lug. Malcolm tentatively returned the gesture. It felt good and strangely *complete* to hold Malcolm in his arms. Edwin realized he was on the verge of tears. Aye, he was going to do this Congress thing *his* way, and the rules be damned. "It's good to see you, my friend. I've missed you."

When he finally drew back, he saw the unshed tears in Malcolm's eyes.

"You as well, my Lord. My heart is glad to see you." Malcolm lost his smile. "Is she safe?"

Edwin bit his lip. "I don't know, my friend."

Nodding, accepting that (for he had no other choice), Malcolm moved aside and went about the business of introducing his new pack—actually, Edwin's new pack. The Youngbloods were a baker's dozen of young punks, rough, street-hardened wolves, and they were understandably a bit wary, but Edwin liked them immediately. They were his kind of people. Once he had taken the hand of every pack member, and every wolf had bent a formal knee, Malcolm gathered the pack around him and Edwin was allowed to move on to the Fae Court.

But before he did, he called Hugo to his side and told Malcolm to make the engineer welcome. Hugo looked at the large collection of werewolves with more than a touch of fearful excitement, but Edwin slapped him on the shoulder. "You'll be fine, mate."

The Morrigan was pretty conspicuous in her absence. But Narissa was here and stepped forward. She still looked angry and hurt from her encounter days ago, and her eyes were red-rimmed and swollen from crying, but she threw her shoulders back and met Edwin toe to toe as a warrior should.

"Lord McGillicuddy, my queen has asked me to represent her," she said, though her voice quavered uncertainly. "I am to speak in her stead and relay messages between her and you. Additionally, when this mission is complete, I am to formally join your Congress, seeing how I don't..."

She meant to say, "Since the Unseely Court won't have me." But he could see she was choking up. Instead, she backtracked and said, "...formally join your Congress if you'll have me." She looked away, clearly unhappy with her lot. He could feel the pain in her speech. The betrayal. He had no idea what she must be feeling.

"That's good, chit," he told her, taking her hand, which was large and dwarfed his own.

"It is?"

Edwin decided to be kind. "I accept your offer and I welcome you to my Congress, Narissa of the Fae. I extend my umbrella of protection to you and any Fae who travels with me."

Tears filled her eyes. "I know this is not what you probably thought was going to happen," she mumbled.

"But it's exactly as I would have it. I trust you. I didn't trust *her*."

Narissa sniffed and her small mouth made a kind of brief half-smile. "I am to act as her proxy since she cannot be away from the Floating Palace." She glanced behind her. "Me and some of her royal guard." She indicated the Fae behind her, a dozen guards evenly divided between male and female, including Captain Ari.

Edwin was impressed. The Fae Royal Guard were some of the best-trained warriors in existence. Moving toward them, he got the name and rank of every one of them before returning to Narissa.

"You're very ki—" She looked away before she started to cry again.

To save her embarrassment, Edwin turned to look at Leo, who had been standing off by himself this whole time. He realized that he, Leo, and Foxley were the only vampires aboard. "Where's Cesar?"

Foxley suddenly appeared from somewhere and joined Leo. The two of them—and Edwin—represented the vampire part of the Congress. "Ah, that," Foxley explained, sounding bored. "Your Enforcer is currently on board the *Gypsy Queen*. There has been a...development."

Edwin felt a chill. "What did he do?"

Foxley shrugged. "It's rather complicated. Best you speak to your Heir about it when this business is concluded."

He didn't like the sound of that, but at the moment, he didn't have time for Cesar's drama. He turned away and sighed. He was down one Enforcer, which would not look good when he hailed the *Marie Antoinette*. He glanced at Leo, but the vampire got his meaning and immediately shook his head.

"As the captain of the *QAR2*, and considering the work we do aboard her, I can't risk making myself so public to the Courts."

Dammit. He started looking around for someone who could step in as a temp, but no one jumped out at him. Then his greatest fear was realized when Foxley immediately stepped forward. "I will be your acting Enforcer."

Edwin gave him a droll look. "Get off it, Foxley. You know an established Lord can't act as an Enforcer."

"A Lord can do anything he wishes. I wish to be your Enforcer...for today."

He wished he had more options, but there were no vampires or any other high-ranking inhumans with clout enough to act as his Enforcer, and time was running out for Eliza. He had no choice.

"Fine," he said, looking his Congress over in its glorious entirety. "Foxley, Malcolm, Narissa...you're with me and Leo. Let's go shake up the *Marie Antoinette*."

* * *

"Sir, a gyro is hailing us," said the Security Poppet who had stepped cautiously into Summerfield's private suite.

Summersfield didn't allow for intrusions except for under the direst of circumstances—fire, a ship-wide disaster, or an imminent attack. And although he knew this must be pretty serious for the timid little Poppet to creep in here uninvited, he was also very annoyed by the interruption.

Pushing himself up from where he'd been crouched over his bed, worrying his Poppet Nathalie's throat with his teeth, he turned his head and glared at the stupid creature standing there, staring at him with his bottom jaw almost on his chest in surprise.

"And?" Summersfield said. His voice sounded funny because his mouth and throat were clotted with Nathalie's blood. It was all over his face and clothing, and the bed was soaked through with crimson. Nathalie, though, was as white a ghost under him. She'd expired more than fifteen minutes ago.

It took the Security Poppet a moment to compose himself and look away from the dead Pleasure Poppet. The scar over his eye pulsed erratically. Summersfield had given him that scar a few years ago. "A-and...and, it's...it's..."

"It's what?" Summersfield roared so loudly that he managed to splatter the Security Poppet with Nathalie's blood from ten feet away.

The Security Poppet cringed and Summersfield smelled the distinct odor of the Poppet's bladder letting go into his uniform. "A-a-and it's important you respond, sir!" he blurted out the words.

Summersfield sat back on his haunches and narrowed his eyes. He rubbed the blood between his fingers. "Why?"

It took the Security Poppet a long time to get the words out, but the gist of it seemed to be that there was an enemy gyro hailing the *Marie Antoinette*. Unprovoked, it was threatening to fire upon her.

"Why?" Summersfield demanded, appalled that another Vampire Court would have the gall to threaten him. "And what gyro?"

The Poppet began stuttering again, so Summersfield got off the bed and swiftly closed the distance between him and the Poppet. The creature could not even react when Summersfield grabbed him by his uniform and tossed him over his shoulder and onto the blood-splattered floor as if he weighed nothing.

He decided to go investigate himself. But before he left the room to get on a lift, he shouted, "Clean up that mess!"

The bridge was a place he rarely went. Had had staff to handle the day-to-day minutia of running his gyro. But when he arrived, he saw the Security Poppet hadn't underestimated the danger. The bridge was in chaos, every flight station filled with well-trained, high-ranking soldiers ready for defensive maneuvers. All of his best people were waiting for him, including security and flight experts, even engineers, and they only ever appeared when there was an issue with the ship.

Someone started saying, "High Lord on the bridge..." but Summersfield cut him off.

"What is going on?" he demanded, pacing to the main screen. "What ship is hailing us?"

The navigator, looking nervous, said, "It's the *Queen Anne's Revenge II*, sir. She has threatened us with direct fire. The Lord aboard her wants to speak to you immediately." He added tentatively, "I...don't think he's bluffing, sir."

"Who is 'he?'"

"It's...well, it's Lord Edwin McGillicuddy, sir."

"McGillicuddy?" Summersfield screeched.

It took Summersfield one whole moment to remember what ship he was looking at or who it belonged to. The *QAR II*, as far as he was aware, was a floating casino that Lord Foxley owned...no, no, that wasn't correct. Foxley *had* owned it, but it was stolen maybe sixty or seventy years ago and refurbished as one of the few Jolly Rogers that hunted the skies over Earth, stealing goods and crew from other, law-abiding gyros. A hive of scum and villainy, if ever there was one. But, so far, the High Courts had chosen not to do anything about her. Mostly because they were a bunch of useless old gits.

The navigator showed him the screen and instructed him in how to respond to the hail.

"What is the meaning of this?" Summersfield hissed into a mic. "Who the hell is this?"

Slowly, a picture formed on the huge screen hanging over the console.

Summersfield saw an unfamiliar vampire standing on the bridge of the ship, surrounded on both sides by his crew. One crewmember might have been a werewolf, one was certainly one of those bizarre, alien-like Fae, and the third looked suspiciously like Lord Foxley.

Summersfield was confused by the whole setup but figured the vampire in the middle was likely Edwin McGillicuddy. Still, he chose not to address him. "Foxley, what the bloody hell is the meaning of this?" Summersfield demanded.

Foxley, in a soft, sibilant, and extremely controlled voice, said, "Calm yourself, Michael, or I will send the *Gypsy Queen* to slap you out of the sky. And you know I *can* and *will* do it."

Summersfield bristled but ultimately held his tongue. Foxley was just unpredictable enough to do it, and for no other reason than because he woke up today in a bad mood. And the *Gypsy Queen* was huge and very well armed. That he knew, too.

Foxley presented the vampire beside him. "This is my master, Lord Edwin McGillicuddy, the sitting Lord-at-Court aboard the *Queen Anne's Revenge II*, and he has a proposal for you. I suggest you listen to it."

The little bugger's words made no sense. Summersfield was about to demand clarification when Edwin McGillicuddy straightened up to address him. Summersfield remembered the little toerag from a handful of encounters over the years, none of them pleasant. He was small potatoes, always more of a nuisance than a threat, and Summersfield remembered asking the kitchen staff to count the silverware after the upstart left his company.

McGillicuddy was barely more than a baby, and yet, today, he carried himself like a Vampire Lord a thousand years steeped in his power. That made Summersfield even angrier—and raised his concerns.

"Summersfield, mate," said the vampire in a truly appalling Cockney accent, "I am Edwin Oliver McGillicuddy, Lord-at-Court of the *Queen Anne's Revenge II*, and…bloody hell, what in blazes happened to you?"

Summersfield looked down at all of the blood on his hands and spattered down the front of his shirt, then up at the upstart demanding his time and attention. He smiled to show the blood also on his teeth, hoping he was just off-putting enough that Lord Edwin might just fuck right off.

Instead, Lord Edwin looked concerned. Enraged. "Is Eliza all right? What did you do to my Bride, you monster?"

Summersfield laughed. "Yours, Lord Edwin? I'm afraid you're too late. She's not your Bride any longer, and she doesn't want you anymore. Also, she is quite fucking *dead*."

A darkness passed across Edwin's face and slid behind his eyes, turning them black. In half a second, he'd gone from a cocky upstart with questionable fashion sense to something that looked like it had crawled out of the deepest pit of hell. Summersfield slid back a step as if the other vampire had reached for him through the screen.

It was stupid and irrational, and he couldn't understand why he should be wary of a two-hundred-year-old vampire baby with a pet dog and a Fae. The notion was ridiculous, and yet, Summersfield had the distinct impression that, like his master, Lord Foxley, Lord Edwin was a vampire who was quite mad and might do anything.

It took Edwin a moment to compose himself, but even after he did so, his eyes remained black. His teeth were unnaturally, even freakishly, long in his mouth when he spoke next. "I want her back, Summersfield. I want my wife back—dead or alive."

The threatening nature of Lord Edwin's demand made Summersfield's hair stand on end, and his sudden fear turned to anger. "She's not yours to have, you cur! She was never yours! I should be the one threatening you. You stole my property!"

Growling, Edwin bared his fearsome fangs. "She was never your property! Or anyone's! She is a human being, you pathetic excuse for a man. And I demand you send her to me aboard the *Queen Anne's Revenge II*. Otherwise, I'll have the *Gypsy Queen* tear your tin can of a ship apart."

Summersfield forced a smile that felt far more strained than it should. "You talk a good game, pup, but I don't believe you have the power or authority to make good. I think you are bluffing. The *Gypsy Queen* firing on the *Marie Antoinette* would be an act of war."

"As a Congress, my people and I have more than enough power to take your vessel, Summersfield. I am merely being a gentleman Lord is offering you a peaceful surrender."

"A Congress? You must be joking! There hasn't been a Congress in hundreds of years."

"And yet..." Edwin lifted both hands, indicating his werewolf and his Fae. He pointed to someone off-screen, who changed the camera angle so Summersfield could see the rather impressive corps waiting in the wings of the bay, both wolf and Fae.

"Vampires...werewolves...Fae..." came Lord Edwin's voice as the camera panned across his crew. "I also have all of the soldiers aboard the *Gypsy Queen and* the Floating Palace in reserve. As you can see, I have formed the first Congress in five hundred years. We are also armed to the teeth and can blow your gyro out of the sky in minutes."

The camera flipped back to Edwin, who was leaning forward and growling into the camera. "Surrender, Summersfield, and prepare to be boarded."

Summersfield stuttered on a response. He didn't know for certain if the *Queen Anne's Revenge II*, the *Gypsy Queen*, or the Floating Palace had the resources to make good on the threat, but he knew just enough about Edwin McGillicuddy to know the sod was crazy enough to try. Plus, there was Foxley's presence. That concerned Summersfield. A lot.

He indicated to the navigator that he should cut the camera for a moment, then leaned forward and took a deep breath. Losing the *Marie Antoinette* wasn't optimal, but he knew he would survive it.

Foxley was a wildcard, though. He was part of the High Courts and had the ear of most of the world's most powerful leaders, both vampire and human. He could pull strings and have Summersfield thrown off the High Court. Summersfield wasn't sure he would survive *that*. If he was stripped of his power, perhaps even his Court, he'd have nothing. Life would not be worth living in that case.

It didn't take him long to figure out what to do. He could resolve this and make himself even wealthier and more powerful if he played his cards right. He indicated that the navigator should re-open the hail.

Standing proudly, Summersfield puffed out his chest a little. "Fight me for the *Marie Antoinette*, Lord Edwin. If you win, you get her and everything—and every*one*—aboard her. But if you lose, I get your Congress. The *Queen Anne's Revenge II*, and the Floating Palace. And the *Gypsy Queen*, too." He smirked Foxley's way.

Lord Edwin considered that. Being a shrewd vampire by nature, he pointed out, "We have more leverage than you do, Summersfield."

Keeping his poker face in place, Summersfield said, "That may be so, but I could self-destruct the *Marie Antoinette* to keep her out of your grubby little hands. Kill my whole ship and your Eliza. Because the only way you will ever see Eliza again is if you literally go through me first. Do we have a deal or not?"

Lord Edwin stuttered on a response as Summersfield thought he would. He could feel the vampire's intentions—his special talent, so to speak. It had served him well for just over a thousand years. He knew what Lord Edwin wanted more than he did, and it was painfully obvious.

The little upstart didn't want the *Marie Antoinette*. He could care less about Courts or Congresses or power. All of this was for *Eliza*.

"Navigator," Summersfield started to say, glaring at Lord Edwin, "cut the comm—"

"You're on!" Edwin said quickly as Summersfield knew he would. "Prepare to receive me, Summersfield. We'll settle this as men…and as vampires."

Summersfield narrowed his eyes and licked the dried blood on his lips. "I simply cannot wait."

| xiv |

After Edwin had the comm shut down, Foxley gave him a worried look.

"He was bluffing. He would never destroy his ship."

"Maybe," Edwin said. He hated the uncertain quaver in his voice. It wasn't very Lordly, he felt. "But I can't take that risk with Eliza aboard."

"He is playing you, my Heir."

"Probably."

"How are you going to fight something like Summersfield?"

Edwin swallowed thickly. "With my fists? The way I did the Green Man?"

"Summersfield is not the Green Man, Edwin my boy. Summersfield has never lost a fight in all the centuries I have known him. He never loses."

Edwin closed his eyes and swallowed thickly. He knew Foxley could smell his fear. "I know. I'll figure something out. Don't worry. I won't lose you your ship."

"I'm not worried about my ship," Foxley said, surprising Edwin. "If I lost the *Gypsy Queen*, I could build a new ship. But Summersfield is going to kill you. He is older, madder, and far more experienced than you are, and he will anticipate your every move even before you do."

"I know that."

"So, again, I ask: How will you defeat him, my Hair? Or, let me rephrase: How are you going to keep him from killing you?"

For once, Edwin had no answer. He hadn't been thinking that far ahead. Despite the brave face he put up, talking to Summersfield had left him with a stone of dread burning in his stomach that he hoped Summersfield didn't register. And it only got worse when Summersfield said those things about Eliza being dead. Was he afraid of the older vampire? You betcha. Was he going to back down? How could he? Summersfield was probably bluffing. But there was no way he was letting Eliza languish at that monster's hands.

So, he put on his brave face as he always had and said, "I'll think of something. I always do. You know that." He forced a smile. "I always had a solution as your Enforcer."

Foxley seemed to think about that for a long moment before nodding to himself and stepping aside. "I believe it is time I take my leave. I refuse to stand here and watch you kill yourself for the sake of a Poppet."

The others watched Edwin uncertainly. Their lack of confidence in him didn't make him feel any better, but he sniffed and stood tall as their Lord. *Fake it until you make it, boyo*, he reminded himself as he headed to the lift that would take him down to the docking bay.

* * *

As was customary among the Vampire Courts, Summersfield's Enforcer was supposed to meet Edwin in the docking bay of the *Marie Antoinette*. His or her job was twofold, to act as his guide and also to size him up, so Edwin was surprised when he found the head of the Security Poppets there instead.

"What happened to Summerfield's Enforcer?" he asked the uniformed man.

The guard swallowed hard. "He doesn't have one. Well, he did, once, but our Lord ended him."

"Summersfield ended own Heir? He killed his own Enforcer?"

The Security Poppet nodded. There were scars on his face. "Our Lord has a very short temper. But that was a long time ago, before my time. Please follow me."

Edwin, suppressing a shiver, walked behind the Security Poppet. The hangar of the *Marie Antoinette* was huge, but not as busy as the *Gypsy Queen's* was during a normal day of business, with people flying on and off the ship. Then Edwin remembered that the *Marie Antoinette* did not host outside corporations, hotels, or have much in the way of tourism or commerce. Summersfield's gyro was one of the more introverted Courts—a Black Box, as they called it.

The Security Poppet and a small retinue of three guards in uniform escorted Edwin up a series of lifts to a huge, dim, vaulted chamber somewhere in the middle of the ship. The remnants of what looked like a wild party lingered. Long trestles still held a bounty of food, chairs were pushed around everywhere, some overturned, and a large dais was set up with string instruments lying abandoned on chairs. Streamers and black and white balloons puffed up as he crossed the floor. Edwin recognized it as the same ballroom where he had surprised Eliza all those weeks ago. That seemed like a lifetime ago now.

"Can you tell me where Eliza is?" Edwin asked the Security Poppet. But then he realized he probably wouldn't know.

The soldier turned and gave him a sad look. "I suppose Lady Eliza in our Lord's private quarters."

His answer lifted Edwin's heart. He had hoped that Summersfield was bluffing when he said Eliza was dead. "Do you know if she is well?"

"I can't really say, Lord McGillicuddy. Security Poppets are not normally allowed in our Lord's private quarters. I'm sorry."

Edwin nodded, feeling disappointed but not hopeless. "Thanks, mate."

The Security Poppet gave him a long, worried look.

Edwin said, "Is there something you want to ask me?"

The man nodded in return and rubbed at the scars on his face. "If you win this battle against Lord Summersfield, that means you'll be the new Lord of the *Marie Antoinette*, right? And everyone on board her?"

"That's correct."

"I pray to god you win."

Edwin started to ask why and then noticed a motion near the center of the darkened ballroom. He went in that direction. The lights were out but he saw clearly the huge aquarium set up there and the creature inside it clinging to the glass, trying to get his attention by motioning to him.

He'd heard of sirens but had never seen one in the flesh before. He stopped in front of the tank and instinctively put his hand on the glass.

The siren inside looked grey and mottled, her skin sloughing off her body. He could tell she wasn't very well cared for. The moment she aligned her hand with his, he heard her voice in his head like some beautiful but mournful song.

You have come.

"Aye?"

You have come at last to awaken her. Our champion.

He looked deep into her faded, sea-green eyes and saw her sorrow and her pain. He passed his gaze over her gaunt body. Her scales and skin were flaking, and there were premature lines on her face. She was dying, and that made him sad and angry. "I don't understand."

I told her you would come. That you would set her free. She did not believe me in the end...

"Who? Eliza...?"

Eliza...she will save us all...

He saw her eyes widen in fear and desperation. He tried to ask her more questions. He wanted to get more answers from her. But she suddenly darted away from the tank and went to hide in some dark recess of her prison. He turned to see what had scared her so badly.

Summersfield stood in the shadows of the ballroom, taking in the size of him.

Edwin turned on his heel and faced his opponent squarely for the first time. In his mind, Summersfield was this huge, terrifying monster. Perhaps that perception had come about through Eliza's description of him. But now, finally, Edwin realized the monster wasn't any bigger than he was. He was perhaps a hair more muscular, but Edwin felt he more than made up for that with his wit and wily ways. And, though Summersfield radiated a bestial ruthlessness, Edwin decided they weren't that badly matched after all.

Summersfield wore a tuxedo jacket without the shirt or tie, probably to better aid his moves in battle. And maybe because his shirt had been heavily caked with blood. But there was still plenty of it all over his Brioni tux. It was on the sides of his face and in his carefully jelled dark hair. His eyes were all black as he took his first step.

Edwin straightened and smiled cockily in response even though fear was gnawing around the edges of his self-confidence. *Fake it till you make—*

"You little Cockney punk, get the hell off my ship!" Summersfield said in a low growl, his large hands clenching into fists.

Edwin turned sideways to minimize himself as a target. "No," he stated imperiously. "Make me, old man."

Summersfield bared his glistening, dagger-like incisors, and the retinue of guards scrambled back and out of sight, leaving Edwin alone. "You toerag. How old are you? You dare threaten me?" He circled Edwin casually as he spoke.

Edwin turned with his opponent to keep him always in front of him. "A young pup, aye. And, yet, I preside over a Congress. I have thousands of beings under my sigil. What have you built, Michael, except this empire of fear?" He indicated the room. He liked the speech he was giving. He thought it was clever. "Even your own people hate you and are praying for your defeat."

He thought that would be enough to provoke the other vampire into attacking, but Summerfield stopped and laughed at him. "You are sad and pathetic, Edwin. Do you think I'm some brainless dote in a pub in the East End? That you'll incite me into a rage and then pummel me to the floor? You don't have much experience outside the filthy streets and alleyways of old London, do you? You think I'm easy. I promise I am not."

The move had worked on many an opponent back then, and it annoyed Edwin that Summersfield knew what he was doing. So he changed tactics and simply lunged at his enemy. He moved so fast that he was able to snatch the front of his tux. He thought for sure that Summerfield would never see it coming—surely not something so forward—but the vampire moved evasively to one side to avoid a collision while simultaneously delivering a punch to the back of

Edwin's head. Only Edwin's speed prevented Summersfield from literally knocking his head off with his great strength.

The punch was bad, though, and Edwin lurched to the floor, disoriented for a moment. Then he was up, rounding on Summersfield, who had turned to head him off. Summersfield caught him at the shoulders and threw him back down so hard that he felt the Spanish tile crack under the impact of his skull. Edwin groaned and stared up at the ceiling.

Summersfield slid backward almost like he was gliding on air. It was uncanny. He looked down at his torn tux coat, then ripped the fabric off his naked shoulders and threw it aside. He spread his wings—huge, demonically devilishly things that kicked up a hard wind as he centered himself for battle.

Edwin stood up a little uncertainly. He shucked off his own coat and dropped his braces. Summersfield tensed, and Edwin thought the other vampire might dive at him, but Summersfield was on the offense now, and he was far from stupid. With a flick of his wings, he glided upward like a demonic kite. Edwin watched him float on the air. Then, like a black nightmare, Summersfield dived right at him, knocking Edwin's legs out from under him.

Edwin never saw it coming. Again, he smashed into the floor. He snarled and leaped to his feet, reaching for Summersfield as the vampire rocketed upward. He managed to grab Summerfield, who was now several feet off the floor, by the ankle. Or tried to. The bastard was slippery and skirted away from him. Suddenly, Summersfield was behind him, not in front. Edwin turned, but Summersfield clocked him across the face before retreating once more into the air.

Summersfield packed a hideously powerful blow. Edwin slid the full length of the banquet hall on his ass before the back of his head slammed into the aquarium, making the whole structure quiver.

Edwin coughed up blood and teeth onto Summersfield's floor. He tried to get up, but he was seeing double at the moment. He decided to stay down—at least until the room stopped spinning. Behind him, he heard the siren speak.

He can anticipate your every move, vampire.

"No fucking shite."

You must do better than this.

Edwin bristled. "I'd like to see you do better."

The siren—Moira, her name was, he quickly learned—started to whisper into Edwin's head.

Edwin listened, then nodded. "Not good news for you, darling."

Don't worry about me, vampire. I can endure anything. Just do it.

With a grunt, Edwin got to his feet, though he wavered uncertainly.

Summersfield hovered in the center of the ballroom under the disco ball, watching him. He looked like a sparkly angel up out of hell. "Are we done here, baby vampire? Do you concede? I have important matters to attend to."

"Fuck off, cuntwaffle," said Edwin. "Is that all you've got?"

Summersfield laughed and started circling him again, moving with the fluid grace that only the really old ones could achieve. "You really are stupid, aren't you? You cannot defeat a Vampire Lord a thousand years steeped in his power. What's wrong with you, Lord Edwin? You must be some kind of stupid." Grinning wickedly, Summersfield added, "You can't even fly, can you?"

Edwin spat blood onto Summersfield's formally clean floor. "I don't have to fly to turn your face into black pudding, mate. Come down here and face me man to man, you shit-face sparklepire."

"No," Summersfield cooed. "I am not a man. I am not bound by those rules of honor and chivalry that you follow. You should not be, either. But I can tell you cling to your humanity. Has it helped you, Lord Edwin? Have it made you powerful?"

Grumbling, Edwin bit into his thumb and let his blood flow into the black blood-manriki he favored for situations such as these. He flicked it and it hissed obediently across the floor. "Is this powerful enough for you, Michael?"

"*That* is a parlor trick. What are you, the Marquis de Sade? Going to tickle me with that?"

Edwin let the whip fly, but Summersfield easily evade the bite of his weapon, and Edwin only managed to slap at open air. Summersfield, somehow moving at inhuman—and *invampire*—speed, got behind him, knocking him down on his face. Pain smashed through his face as more of his teeth broke and his nose was shattered, speckling the floor with his blood. Edwin lost his concentration and the whip melted away.

Summersfield, hovering, chuckled at him. "You have something on your face," he said in response to all of the blood all over Edwin's face. He even threw Edwin the handkerchief from his trouser pocket.

This wasn't working. Edwin's face and body felt lighted from within with pain. Summersfield was just playing with him.

As he pushed himself into a half push-up, Edwin experienced his first gnawing doubts. He had to do something different. Summersfield was no common enemy.

He looked up and tried to blank his thoughts, which, it turned out, was more difficult than it seemed. So, instead, he turned his thoughts to Eliza and away from the battle before him. He saw Summersfield's expression change subtlety as he struggled to read Edwin's intentions. But Edwin wasn't thinking about destroying Summersfield. He didn't care about him at all.

Summersfield had been moving, making an increasingly smaller spiral around him. Edwin saw that now. He wasn't quite within reach yet when Edwin, on impulse, reached out and used his unbelievable strength to drive his fingers into a tile on the floor. Ripping it loose, he tossed the heavy stone like a discus at the vampire, clocking him in the jaw. The blow knocked Summersfield back half the length of the room.

"Cheers!" Edwin said as Summersfield crash-landed near the wall, his wings askew. It took him a few seconds to recover and orient himself, which was good because it gave Edwin a chance to scuttle toward him across the floor, which was something he hadn't planned to do—and something Summersfield didn't see coming.

But it did little good in the end. For a tall man, Summersfield moved like a ghost and was as slippery as an eel. Though Edwin had momentarily grounded him, he had trouble grappling him even when he acted on impulse instead of planning his moves out. The bloody vampire twisted and turned, slamming his wings into Edwin's face, tearing gouges in his skin. Finally, roaring with rage, Edwin grabbed a wing and, with a burst of strength and rage, simply tore it right out of Summersfield's wing root, which sent the vampire spinning into the wall.

"You bastard!" Summersfield roared, precious blood spurting from his grievous shoulder wound.

Edwin stood up, throwing the ragged remnants of Summersfield's right wing aside. He snarled and Summersfield snarled back. Both of them were now in so much pain, they were more vampire than men. After that, both moved quickly. An onlooker—such as the guards were—likely had trouble following the battle. Edwin and Summersfield clashed together and started trading punches and kicks, scratching and biting like two rabid animals. They shredded each other's clothes and tore gouges in each other's skin.

At one point, Summersfield grabbed Edwin, hugging him close and pinning his arms. He lifted Edwin off his feet. With a roar, he threw Edwin against the nearest wall. The impact made the whole room shudder, and Edwin felt a sharp pain in his hip as the plaster cracked down to the studs. He tried to stand and failed. He couldn't sustain his weight on his shattered joint. Edwin dropped to the floor, groaning and gurgling in pain.

"You little shit..." Summersfield growled, blood and drool dripping from his jaws and ragged, shark-like teeth. "You're pathetic. What did your master ever see in you, eh? What did Eliza?"

Edwin, clutching his hip, rolled into a sitting position. "At least I had a master. At least I wasn't made by accident and left in a hole on a forgotten battlefield to rot like the mistake I was." Edwin tried to get up again, but his leg buckled. His hip was good and broken, and without blood, it wasn't likely to heal anytime soon.

Summersfield weaved in place, looking ridiculous with one wing. It took him a moment to gain his balance, but then he closed in on Edwin, going slowly so he could savor his victory. Edwin hissed and lashed out at him, but Summersfield grabbed his arm and, grinning, twisted it slowly at a bad angle, breaking it at the elbow. The popping noise made Edwin sick to hear. He screamed compulsively. Summerfield laughed and grabbed him by the throat, lifting him up off the floor.

Edwin choked, wondering how in hell's bells he was going to get out of this mess. That's when the Security Poppet that had escorted Edwin to this room suddenly appeared and jumped on Summersfield's back. He never knew the Poppet's name, but the man locked an arm around Summersfield's throat, applying the more-than-human Poppet strength he possessed to pinch his windpipe closed. Summersfield gasped and dropped Edwin in a heap to address the new threat.

"You!" Summersfield sputtered, grabbing at the Poppet's arms.

"Fuck you!" the Security Poppet said and inclined his head. He couldn't let go or risk sliding down Summersfield's back, so he bit into the side of Summerfield's neck. It was a sloppy bite with human teeth not made for the job, but Summersfield choked in pain and rage all the same and began thrashing side to side, but he couldn't quite get the Poppet off his back. The two twisted and turned, taking them farther away from Edwin. The violent motion tore an increasingly larger hole in Summersfield's throat.

Edwin heard their struggle, but he was having trouble recovering. He lay against the wall, panting, his breath rattling out of his half-crushed throat. He coughed and more blood he couldn't afford to lose came up like a geyser and splattered the front of his shirt.

"Here," someone said, pressing his wrist to Edwin's mouth. He looked up and saw one of the other Security Poppets offering his blood. Edwin was in no position to question the gift. He reached up to clutch the man's arm as he bit into the flesh and began to feed off the blood. Behind him, the other soldiers were lining up and rolling up their sleeves, ready to contribute their life force to this endeavor. Edwin found it both touching and terrifying—the total lack of loyalty these Poppets had for their master.

Meanwhile, Summersfield was thrashing and smashing the Poppet back against the walls so hard that one of the banners fell down. Every time he drove the soldier's body into the wall, Edwin heard a new sickening crunch and flinched from the sounds of the brutal blows. After three or four blows, the soldier's grip on Summersfield slipped and he began to slide free, but Summersfield wasn't finished with him. He whipped around, his eyes black and wild, and grabbed his Security Poppet by the throat in a stranglehold.

Carrying the man in his fist, he charged forward until he reached a random trestle table and smashed him down so hard that the trestle rocked and the Poppet's entire body crackled like kindling. The man's breath escaped from his lungs in a pathetic squeak as he died.

"Traitor!" Summersfield growled and proceeded to drive the dead Poppet's body into the table over and over again until the whole table collapsed in a heap.

Edwin, having taken a little blood from the three remaining Security Poppets, got shakily to his feet. He noted that the Security Poppet on the table had died with a smile on his face, his eyes pinned on Edwin, who was now standing.

"Thanks for the blood, mates," Edwin said to the guards. He was weaving as if he was drunk, but he quickly got his newly healed body under rigid control. It was the least he could do for the man who had given his life to buy him recovery time. "But you go now. Get out of here."

The other soldiers swallowed nervously, nodded, and made for the door while Edwin turned to face Summersfield, his face stony except for a tic in one corner of his mouth. "Michael," he said. "Michael, turn and face me, you bloody git."

Summersfield did. He was grinning maniacally, a blood-slathered animal. "Ready for more, you little shit?"

"Your move, old man." Edwin forced himself to relax, hands at his sides. Then, suddenly inspired, he went down on one knee on the floor. He bowed his head slightly and cleared his mind of all thoughts. If he relaxed enough, he really could feel Summersfield rummaging around in his brain, looking for his next move. After a second or two, a thought entered his head, but it was a silly one. An old Cockney pub song he hadn't heard in fifty-some-odd years. He closed his eyes and gave himself over to the ditty.

"Knees up Mother Brown

Knees up Mother Brown

Under the table you must go..."

An overconfident Summersfield grabbed a decorative broadsword off the wall of the ballroom. With a mad gleam in his eye, he surged toward his enemy kneeling on the floor, the blade angled toward his head.

Edwin heard him coming but forced himself to stay utterly still.

"Ee-aye, Ee-aye, Ee-aye-oh
If I catch you bending
I'll saw your legs right off..."

Summersfield had reached him. He was looming over Edwin, bringing the broadsword down over his shoulder as he prepared to cleave Edwin's head off his body. Edwin ducked and moved slightly left, flinging Summersfield off his shoulder. Summersfield went down hard, cracking the tiled flood under his weight. His sword skittered away.

Edwin stood up and slowly turned, moving fluidly.

"Knees up, knees up
Don't get the breeze up
Knees up Mother Brown..."

Snarling, blood and foam on his mouth from where he'd broken his teeth, Summersfield pushed himself up. He finally looked shaken. "Stop fucking singing and fight me, you cur...!" He whipped around in an arc and tried to attack Edwin from the back, his signature move. Even with just one wing, he flowed like black water.

Edwin, though, was ready for him. He started the pub ditty from the beginning, concentrated on it, and, as Summersfield fell upon him, he turned, randomly delivering an uppercut to Summersfield's chin that knocked him back onto the floor. Summersfield, who, ironically, was nothing if not predictable, tried to kick Edwin's legs out from under him.

But Edwin had found an inner calm within himself, and, spreading wide his arms and wings, he narrowly averted contact as he floated over Summersfield's body like he imaged an angel of death might. He had decided to treat the whole experience like a big, extra-slow kung fu move. He achieved hang for one long second before returning to earth with a massively powerful dropkick that drove Summersfield's body across the room and into the aquarium tank with such force that a crack appeared...and then another.

Just as Moira had asked him to do.

The impact knocked Summersfield's breath out of him and his body crumpled up like an insect in the seconds before the gigantic tank exploded around him.

The sudden gush of seawater slammed into Edwin, carrying him like a cannonball across the hall and into the corridor beyond. He finally hit a wall. The impact stunned him and left him sliding to the floor, coughing and floundering. It hurt, but what was happening to Summersfield was far, far worse.

Moira, finally freed from her prison, had gotten her clawed fingertips into Summersfield's flesh. She fell upon Summersfield like a hungry lion on prey, scratching and biting. Summersfield screamed as Moira began the process of ripping her enemy apart alive and screaming.

Once on his feet again, Edwin stumbled back into the ballroom. But what was happening was hard to watch, even for Edwin, and he'd seen some pretty bloody messed up things in his time as an Enforcer. Blood and bits of flesh flew everywhere.

As the water flowed away, Moira began to choke. She couldn't breathe outside the tank of water, and after a few minutes, she began to flounder and her attacks grew weak, though no less savage. Summersfield, still screaming in pain and rage, took advantage of her struggles and grabbed her by the throat.

Moira choked and her eyes started to roll back in her head.

Summersfield, panting through his pain and injuries, squeezed harder and harder until Edwin heard the sound of delicate neck bones snapping. Moira flopped and wriggled on the floor, but he could tell it was just her body reacting to her suddenly truncated life. She was already gone.

Roaring, Summersfield threw her body aside and scrambled in all of the glass and blood and water to find his feet. Part of his face on one side had been bitten away by Moira, and Edwin could see his teeth all the way back to the pointed molars. His skin had also been peeled away to a place just above his left eye, which rolled blindly, damaged, like a white egg in his head. Blood poured like black ink from the grievous wounds in his neck.

Snarling and choking, the wounded vampire stumbled to find his balance, falling again and again. He seemed to realize he was losing. Dying. Finally, he clawed at the nearby wall to stand upright, then turned to the door of the ballroom and extended his hand in a come-hither gesture, screaming, *"My Heir...come to me...!"*

Edwin cringed. Summersfield screamed out of his mouth but also out of the side of his face. His heart banged at the sound. At the words. Slowly, he turned to look at what Summersfield had summoned from the shadows.

It took a moment or two, but a female figure darkened the doorway to the ballroom. He saw her eyes first—bright reddish-brown and wild as they sought their master out. Then Eliza stepped into the room.

Edwin felt his heart stop inside him. She was dressed in a red wedding gown, her hair snarled into a black halo around her weirdly grey face. She moved robotically, at a stumbling walk almost like she was having trouble getting her body under control. Once she was fully inside the ballroom, she stood there, ignoring Edwin and looking at Summersfield as if she were confused and awaiting directions.

Edwin weaved and then dropped to his knees at the sight. He was finally destroyed. Utterly and completely.

Nothing Summersfield had done to him thus far hurt as much as this.

Summersfield, doddering into an upright position, pointed to Edwin. "Kill him, my Heir! Kill Lord Edwin!"

Eliza, his Eliza, slowly turned her head to look at him with those wild red eyes. They looked glassy and crazed with life, and they didn't seem to recognize him at all.

"E-Eliza..." Edwin began, but then his voice failed him.

Everything he went through...and still he was too late...

Summersfield had been telling the truth, he realized. He had killed Eliza...

Eliza, struggling with her new undead body, took a stumbling step toward him, moving with that queer mechanical gait. As she grew closer, she dropped her mouth open and growled at him, showing off her needle-sharp teeth. She spread her black wings wide, her eyes full of pain and rage.

Hunger more than anything else.

Edwin knew immediately what Summersfield had done. He had made her. And then he had starved her like a dog being beaten into submission. He had turned her into the perfect weapon to destroy him.

Seconds later, Eliza the starving Vampire Bride threw herself at Edwin.

| XV |

She had no control over her body and no idea what was happening to her. She only knew that her master was in pain. The pain dug deep into her body like a set of sharp knives, making her groan as she rolled over on the floor of the cell in Summersfield's bedroom. It seemed to enter her very being, animating her. Even though she was weak from blood loss, hunger, and her recent transformation, she managed to sit upright. Hunger tore at her with small, precise teeth—the worst hunger she had ever experienced in her life. Even so, it didn't compare with what was happening to her master.

Eliza...Eliza...come to me. I need you!

Her master's voice filled her head and pulled at her, actually lifting her up off the floor as if she was on wires. It animated her even though she felt like a soulless rag doll. Stepping up to the door of the cage where her master had placed her, she took the bars in her hands and ribbed the door off as if the whole structure was made of fragile sticks.

Seconds later, she was flying down the corridors, pulled along by her master's pain and all of that horrific and invisible wirework. She was far from unaware. In fact, she was painfully lucid, but she had never felt anything like this in her life. Not even Edwin's pain felt like this, and they'd shared a bloodlink as vampire and Bride.

No, this bloodlink was not like that, or it was, but with the volume turned all the way up.

She stumbled into the ballroom, panting and growling with exertion and the pain pulsing through every cell of her body. There she halted and looked to find her master. She spotted Edwin, and she certainly recognized him. She knew who he was, and she felt both exalted that he was here and ashamed that he should see her like this. But even though she was aware of these things, she couldn't *feel* anything for him.

Searching the room, she saw her master struggling on the floor in the shadows near the massively broken tank where Moira used to live. She saw Moira on the floor, dead and motionless, but she couldn't feel anything for her friend, either. All Eliza could feel was her master's pain. It was All. And it was Everything.

Summersfield, weaving dangerously into a semi-upright position, his face half-shaved away, pointed to Edwin. "Kill him, my Heir! Kill Edwin!"

No! Please, master! she begged him with just her eyes. *Please, just stop this pain. Or just end me.*

Either resolution was preferable. But Summersfield only jerked her invisible wires tighter. And when he pointed, she instinctively turned and looked at Edwin, who, though also wounded, looked to have fared considerably better in the battle.

Edwin looked at her. Her Edwin. He looked appalled. "Eliza..." he began, but it didn't stop her. Summersfield propelled her on. The pain drove her to the very edge of her sanity.

Please, don't. I don't want to hurt him! I love him!

She didn't want to...god help her, she'd rather die. Still, Eliza threw herself at him. She had to kill him. She had to kill Edwin and obey the will of her master. Then this pain would end.

***

Eliza grabbed Edwin by the shoulders and, growling like a wounded animal, threw him down on the floor. He was shocked at the power in her small hands. As a newborn vampire, she shouldn't have been that powerful. But then he realized what was different: She wasn't just a vampire. She was also a Poppet, genetically enhanced to be stronger and more durable to endure her master's restless hunger and endless cruelty. She was stronger than any vampire he had ever encountered. She was probably stronger than he was.

"Eliza!" he shouted. "Lovey!"

She didn't hear. She *couldn't* hear. He knew enough about what being a vampire was to know she was under her master's thrall. And it wasn't her fault. It was the way of things. Baby vampires were entirely dependent on their masters. And they were naturally conditioned to do whatever they said. It was a bond that no one could break, not even Edwin. Not even love.

Summersfield made her. She belonged to her master. She belonged to Summersfield.

All he could do was throw his arms up as she fell upon him, snapping her teeth compulsively, trying to get at his throat. Not knowing what else to do, he shoved his forearm into her mouth to hold her at bay. Her teeth went deep into his flesh like steel needles. Like an industrial machine. The pain was excruciating, made all the worse because he knew she was feeling it all through the remnants of their bloodlink. She was suffering and hurting even as she tried to kill him.

She tried to scratch at him, but she was wild and confused, with little coordination. Her nails sank into the tiled floor, breaking it out in pieces. She screamed and snapped and worried his forearm like a rabid dog. His blood from his wound splattered his face and over his clothes.

"Eliza..." he begged, his voice growing weaker. "Eliza, please, I can't kill you, lovey, I just can't...!"

This was the one thing he couldn't do. The one act he could never perform.

He couldn't kill her. He loved her too much.

She didn't hear. She only growled and shook her head from side to side, trying to get him to lower his arm so she could tear the red life from his throat. After a few minutes, he realized this whole thing was killing her slowly and in agonizing pain. Sighing, he made the decision to lower his arm and let her at him. It was better than to let her suffer. And even though he didn't want her trapped in this living hell with Summersfield, he knew he wasn't strong enough, tough enough, to kill her. He just wasn't.

Taking a deep breath to steady himself, he flung both arms out and looked her in her large, mad, all-black eyes. "It's all right," he said softly and smiled.

Eliza stopped, momentarily confused by his resignation.

Moments ticked by. He didn't fight her. He held her eyes while he waited for his death.

Pitch-black tears flowed down both of Eliza's cheeks. Her eyes were so black they looked like mirrors into eternity. "I'm sorry," she finally said, and her voice sounded strained like it was full of ground glass. "Edwin...I don't want to do this."

"I know," he told her. He even reached up to stroke a lock of her hair. "I don't blame you, my love. I should have come sooner. I didn't. None of this is your fault."

"I didn't lose faith," she sobbed. "I didn't!"

"I know."

"I don't want to do this!"

He reached up and rubbed the tears off her face. "I forgive you, Eliza. None of this is on you."

He was aware that Summersfield was standing over them both, grinning his ghoulish, blood-slathered grin like some madman. "Eliza, I told you to kill Edwin."

"I know." She choked out a sob. "I will."

"Kill him now."

She shook her head, splattering Edwin with her tears. "Edwin, I'm sorry. I can't...I can't..."

Her whole body began to shake violently as she worked to resist her master's prerogative.

"I understand," he told her. "You have to obey him. I get it, lovey."

A low, almost subliminal hum had begun to fill the room. In his prone position, Edwin had to angle his head down slightly to see that Eliza's hands, buried in the tiles on the floor, were glowing with a peculiar blue light. He could feel a charge building all around her.

He looked back up into her eyes. No vampire he had ever known had been able to resist a summons by their master. But then he reminded himself that long before she was Summersfield's, she was his. His wife. His Bride. He looked at her hands and then back up at her face. She was using her queer kinetic power to try to resist her master's summons. He nodded his understanding.

"I don't know if I can do this," she sobbed. "I don't know if I'm strong enough."

Summersfield, thinking she meant something else, started shouting, "Of course you can kill him! I'm commanding you, Eliza!"

But that wasn't what she meant. She was testing the limits of her and Edwin's bloodlink as vampire and Bride.

The humming increased. The charge grew, the light now so brilliant it looked like a halo surrounding Eliza. Summersfield even took a concerned step back, his nostrils flaring at the scent of ozone on the air. The charge in the air made the hair on Edwin's head and arms stand on end.

Edwin, fully understanding, whispered, "You can do this. You *will* do this."

"Command me."

"Lovey…"

"Command me!" she shouted, and little sparks of electricity skipped over her shoulders and through her hair. It landed on Edwin, biting like wasps.

Holding his Bride's blinkless gaze, he reached up, grasped her face in his hands, and said, "Eliza, I command you to kill Summersfield."

"Yes, master," she said in a hush, and then, with a throat-tearing shout, Eliza turned and heaved the massive halo of electrical energy she was generating at Summersfield like a weapon.

Summersfield screamed as if he'd been struck with lightning—which was apropos, Edwin figured. The charge from Eliza's hands threw him all the way across the room and high up against the far wall, where it pinned him for several seconds. He convulsed, and the smell of his hair and flesh burning filled the whole hall with a bitterly sweet stink. Then he slid slowly down, tearing down several banners and decorative weapons along the way.

Eliza turned back to Edwin. Her eyes were still black, but now she was grinning, her cattish teeth fully extended. Edwin almost expected her to attack him, to bite out his throat, but it was obvious she was under his thrall now. She was his to command.

And he did. He told her what to do. In detail.

She threw herself off him and crossed the room in seconds to where Summersfield lay broken. He seemed to be slightly on fire.

Edwin sat up and watched as Eliza dragged her former master's singed body up slightly so he was resting against the front of her blood-splattered bridal gown. She looked like a beautiful and awful nightmare as she dragged his head to one side to expose the remnants of his throat.

"E-E-Eliiiiiizaaaaa..." Summersfield begged in the seconds before she sank her teeth into his burned and blackened flesh and began drinking him to the final death.

***

Edwin caught Eliza just before she passed out and dropped to the floor. Her mouth was roughed in her dead master's blood, and it gave her face a kind of frightening, lifelike color, but she lay bonelessly in his arms. He couldn't even hear if she had a heartbeat.

A spike of panic ripped through him. He immediately swung around and hurried out into the corridor where the Security Poppets were half hiding.

"I need to get to the infirmary now!" he barked, probably harsher than he needed to.

The Poppets jumped into action immediately. "Y-yes, sir, Lord McGillicuddy," one said, the de facto leader now that the head of security was dead. His arm was still bleeding from Edwin's bite, but he ignored his injury, turned, and hurried down the corridor toward a lift. Edwin followed.

To Edwin's surprise, a whole team of doctors and nurses were waiting for him in the infirmary. The new head of security must have called down ahead of them.

"Is this the woman in need of medical care, sir?" one of the doctors demanded, rolling out a gurney.

"Yes, she's my...my..." Edwin wasn't sure what to call her. "My...wife...my Bride..." He gently set Eliza down on the gurney. She hardly weighed anything, and she was such a bloody mess. He wiped a bit of blood away from her cheek and moved a lock of black and white hair aside. She was barely breathing.

"I need you to take very good care of her. She's important to me," he told the staff. "Treat this as if your lives depend on it."

In seconds, they wheeled her through a pair of swinging doors, speaking rabid medspeak back and forth to each other. He started to follow, but a male nurse stood in his way.

"I understand you want to come in, but you'd be in the way," he said. And then he added, "Sir."

Their behavior confused him. They were treating him as if he was important. Then he recalled that he was the brand new Lord-at-Court of the *Marie Antoinette*. He was the Lord and they were his Court. He could push through this big fellow if he wanted to.

But he didn't want to get in their way. So, he grabbed the nurse's shoulder and look into his eyes. "Don't let her die."

He nodded, then vanished through the doors, leaving Edwin to try to decide what to do. He couldn't think straight, couldn't make any kind of decision until he knew Eliza was going to live. So, he turned, slid down the wall of the infirmary, and just sat there on the floor for a long, long time. He thought about praying to God for Eliza's wellbeing, but though he always considered himself a good Catholic boy, he realized he was no longer sure if he truly believed.

* * *

As word quickly spread across the ship, staff appeared in the corridor outside the infirmary where Edwin waited to hear word of what was happening with Eliza. One brought him a comfortable chair. Another hovered over him, asking him if he needed anything. He shook his head as he waited…and waited.

Hours passed.

The Security Poppets returned. The new Head of Security, a man named Robert, according to the badge on his uniform, halted in front of him, went to one knee, and bowed his head. "We wanted to take a moment to acknowledge you, my Lord." He looked up at Edwin with fiery, determined eyes. "And we want to formally offer our services. We are yours to command."

Edwin had no idea what to say to that. He'd never had Security Poppets before. He'd never had a gyro or even a formal Court. But now he was a Vampire Lord presiding over a vast Congress, and the word was spreading on board the ship—and probably beyond it.

"Th-thanks, mate," he muttered, fairly convinced that wasn't the proper response. Unfortunately, he had no education in these things. He was strictly winging it now.

The Security Poppets smiled, not offended by his lack of knowledge of proper etiquette. After they were gone, the Pleasure Poppets visited him next. There were maybe ten of them, all strangely bruised and tired looking, with black rings under their eyes and terrifying scars and even burn marks on their faces and bodies. Sascha, the male in the front—the de factor leader, he reckoned—stepped up and made the same gesture and said the same words.

"If you need us for nourishment or sex, we are at your disposal, Lord McGillicuddy," he said.

Edwin looked at the young man who was kneeling there. He was barely more than a child. His hatred for Summersfield, even though the wanker was dead, grew even stronger. "Not Lord McGillicuddy. Lord Edwin," he said, hating how formal his Congress was being with him. "And...you're free. Go to Earth...or wherever you want to go."

The Pleasure Poppet stood back up and turned to look at the others in confusion.

After a moment, Edwin realized his mistake. They probably thought he was unhappy with their services. Being Pleasure

Poppets, they had no skills beyond what they had been taught to help them survive the world. No family to take them in. They had no one. This was all they knew.

So, he amended his words by saying, "If that's what you want, I mean. If not, then you are welcome to stay aboard. But you won't be forced to do anything. In fact, I command you to do nothing you don't consent to."

His words pleased the Poppets and they brightened collectively. The head of the little entourage smiled widely at him. "Thank you, my Lord!"

He was happy they were happy. But he was even happier when they had gone.

Several of the board members from Summersfield's corporation visited him next. One of his new attorneys informed him that the deed to Summersfield's holdings, including the gyro and everything belonging to his Court, had already been transferred to Edwin's name. He'd been what they called "deeded." No need to sign anything. It was the tradition of the High Vampire Courts. To the winner go the spoils and all that.

He thought about telling them that Eliza was the one who had defeated Summersfield. It was she who deserved to be the new Lady of the *Marie Antoinette*, but they probably wouldn't understand. He decided he would sort that out with her later, assuming she survived all of this.

Sometime later, a random server passed down the hallway but turned to look at him oddly. He smiled.

Edwin turned his head to follow the employee. On impulse, he got up out of his chair and followed the server down the hallway.

They passed through a large number of corridors before they reached the mess hall where the medical staff took their breaks. The server continued out onto the parapet. Edwin followed.

It was near midnight, the sky full of tiny stars. The *Marie Antoinette* was moving now, making good speed in the headwind. It was rendezvousing with the *Gypsy Queen* and ETA was seven hours, one of the Security Poppets informed him earlier. Even though the gyro didn't move quickly, it still kicked up quite a wind, and Edwin grasped the safety rail to anchor himself.

They were alone on the parapet, he and the server.

"I know who you are," Edwin said. "Your lot always smells like old blood to me."

The server turned to face him, raised his sleeve, and sniffed himself. "Eh. Must work on that."

And just like that, the server seemed to shimmer, to break apart, and then reconstitute itself into a new being, all of its web-like cracks full of white light. It was almost fascinating to watch, this transformation. And when it was done, the person standing before Edwin was Foxley, not the random server. He thought that was an odd choice for the Chimera to choose.

The creature said, "I felt if I chose Eliza, you might get a bit rough with me."

"I don't plan to get rough," Edwin said evenly. He looked the creature over, searching for flaws, but it was perfect. The creature was beyond talented. "I intend to kill you like the cockroach you are. You set all of this in motion. All of it. And because of that, Eliza may die."

The Chimera didn't even make a show of looking confused. Staring unblinkingly at Edwin, it said, "You took my other from me. Consider it recourse." It tilted its head back slightly as if it were admiring the night sky and smiled nastily with Foxley's catty little teeth. "Did you think that what you did would go unanswered, Lord Edwin?"

"You started this all those decades ago when you first came after me," Edwin insisted. He narrowed his eyes and bared his teeth. "*You* killed your other. Not me."

For the first time, the Chimera, his ancient enemy, actually bristled. "I was hired by the High Courts—by *Foxley*—to bring you back, Lord Edwin. And so I did. And then you ran away and caused me to pursue you once more. It is not on me—"

"No one told you to send your other after me two years ago!" Edwin said, referring to the time when the other Chimera hunted him down in Poppettown, forcing him to kill it. "You *chose* to do that. Your other?" he snored. "You sent your mate to do the dirty work for you. You sent your lover to their death, chum. You killed him…or her…or whatever you aberrations are. Not me. Your pride and your laziness killed your other."

With a growl, the Chimera suddenly lunged, stopping a mere centimeter from Edwin's face. Even though they were practically nose to nose and he could smell the rotten death on the creature's breath, Edwin never flinched. He had long ago figured out that the remaining Chimera didn't want him dead. Far from it. If he was dead, he couldn't suffer. And that was the whole purpose behind this creature's existence now. The reason all of this had happened in the first place. To make him suffer.

"You will know my pain, Lord Edwin," it said in a low, breathy growl. "You will suffer the way I suffer. You will lose everything you hold dear, and when you are alone, and in despair, you will take your own life. *Then* I will have satisfaction."

Edwin thought about grabbing the creature by the throat, trying to end its damnable existence, but surely it would just melt away like the nightmare it was. It would be like trying to hold black water in his arms.

So, instead, he merely said, "You better play a good game, aberration. A *better* one. Because this web you've spun is getting pretty thin, chum."

The creature snarled, covering him in spit. It morphed once more, this time into Cesar. The sight of him gave Edwin an awful pang. But before he could react, the Chimera spread its wings and let the powerful nighttime winds lift it skyward like a dark kite. Edwin watched the creature drift up and up.

The Chimera grinned, almost glowing in the moonlight. "Lord Edwin, you have yet to discover how much you have lost," it said before the wind ripped it away.

* * *

The ship's doctor was waiting in the hallway when Edwin got back to the infirmary.

His pace slowed until he came to a full stop ten feet away from the frightening, white-coated figure. Despite everything he had faced in the last few days, this was the most terrifying.

The doc held up Eliza's chart. And then he smiled.

Edwin's heart, which had seemingly stopped for a moment, started beating again.

"She is well, my Lord," he announced. "She is awake and asking for you."

Edwin let out his breath in relief, then noticed the doctor's confused expression. He shuffled forward. "What's wrong?"

The doctor looked at his clipboard, then adjusted his glasses. "Well...it's all very strange, my Lord. When she first came in, we were certain your Bride was a newly turned vampire. Now, though..."

"What?"

He looked up and down, first at Edwin and then down at the chart. He adjusted his glasses again. "Er...uh, she doesn't seem to be any longer. A vampire, I mean. Her blood work shows that she is a human. But I'm not sure how that's possible. I mean, I admit her whole case is unusual, including her pregnancy. Though perhaps that is a factor. Her body may have rejected the infusion of vampire blood simply because her pregnancy could not continue if she wasn't alive..."

He gulped, clearly dismayed. "Frankly, sir, we aren't sure of anything. I studied vampire physiology in medical school, of course, but there is still so much we don't know about how your kind works, and most of the High Courts are secretive about such things..."

Edwin hardly heard the man's speech. His brain had shut down at the word "pregnancy." Taking another step toward the man, he blurted out, "Sh-she's with child?"

It took the doctor a moment to register the question. Then he said, "You didn't know? About your Poppet...uh, I mean your Bride?"

"She's not a Poppet. She's a fucking human being," Edwin said more angrily than he'd intended. God, he hated the term "Poppet."

The doctor cowered a little at his outburst, which didn't make him feel any better. He was feeling ragged and raw from everything, and his temper was exceeding short. Taking a deep breath, he said in a calmer voice, "Forgive me. I'm not blaming you, and I appreciate everything you are doing. I'd like to see my wife now."

"This way, please, my Lord." The doctor turned but glanced at him over one shoulder as if Edwin might jump him. After a few tense seconds, he escorted Edwin into the ward and down a long hallway.

They had put Eliza in a private VIP room to rest. She was tucked into a large hospital bed with the covers drawn up to her chest, but Edwin finally noticed the small changes in her body—things he had not registered until. Lying there, she looked tired and pale, but at least she no longer had that ghastly grey cast to her face and hands, and someone had washed her face and combed her hair into a semblance of semi-tamed curls.

The doctor quickly scurried away.

Edwin stopped just inside her door and looked his wife over, afraid to approach her. He had no idea if Summersfield, though dead, had any lasting hold on her through the bloodlink they had shared. Technically, she should not even be alive right now. Mostly newly turned vampires couldn't even function without their masters, and if their Lord died, the newly turned Heirs often died with them. But then he reminded himself that through some bizarre miracle of either science or vampire magic, Eliza's body had rejected her vampirism.

Turning her head slightly, Eliza spotted him, and her eyes lit up. "Ed..." she began but seemed too weak to even speak.

He rushed to her bedside. "Don't talk. You don't have to, lovey. I know everything the doctor said, and I was there earlier, when you...well, that doesn't matter now." He looked her over. She looked the way she was supposed to. Like his Eliza. He glanced down at her stomach under the covers, but she wasn't showing just yet.

Pregnant. How in bloody hell could she be...? And who was the father, then?

She saw his look. "S-sorry...I..."

"I know," he answered for her so she wouldn't have to struggle to explain. "You didn't tell me because you didn't want to worry or distract me."

She gave a weak nod.

He didn't want to ask her this, not now, but he knew he couldn't live without knowing if there was some small part of Summersfield still between them. "Is it...his?"

The moment just before she responded seemed to last an eternity. Then she shook her head.

A weight seemed to come off him. He moved to encircle her with his arms.

"Edwin..."

"We'll discuss everything later on when you're stronger," he said. "Can I just hold you for now?"

She nodded, and he slid into the hospital bed beside her. She laid her head on his chest and closed her eyes. He stroked her hair, saying nothing. And they stayed that way, nestled in each other's arms, for the rest of the night.

* * *

By morning, Eliza felt strong enough to get up and walk a few steps, though, as in the past, she needed Edwin's help to dress. She was still weak from lack of proper nutrition, and her fingers were a little too shaky to get her buttons through the loopholes.

"I remember when you did this for me after Whitby Hall," she sighed, looking upon him miserably. He knew how much it pained her to let him help. She was a very independent woman. "I seem to keep winding up your burden, don't I?"

"You are never a burden," Edwin told her, finishing the last button and pulling her close to kiss her on the forehead.

She looked like she might cry again. He knew she was still processing everything that had happened. Hearing the news about Nathalie's death made her cry all over again even though she said they didn't like each other. She also told him that she would never get over Dahlia even if she lived a thousand years, which she just might, according to the doctor who was still running tests on her. He didn't even know what to make of her at this point; she seemed to possess DNA for both human and vampire—though, according to him, Eliza's vampire DNA was recessive or perhaps dormant at present.

Over the course of the following day, Edwin took pains to explain everything she had missed and everything that had happened to him—and her. She seemed grateful for that because there was so much she admitted she couldn't remember, like the whole debacle in the ballroom. She might have killed Summersfield, but, she said, she had no recollection of anything after he attacked her in the stairwell.

The doctor wanted to keep her for at least a week, but he said there was nothing wrong with Eliza going on a little walk and seeing something other than her private room—assuming she didn't overdo it, of course. As they were leaving the infirmary, Edwin pushing her in a wheelchair, Eliza said, "Can I speak with Captain Leo?"

He looked down at her. "Of course."

She gave him a small, wistful smile. "I've missed you."

"I missed you more," he admitted. "I don't think my heart beat the whole time we were apart."

***

Edwin's words stunned her. They were uncharacteristically romantic of him.

When they were in the lift on the way down to the docking bay, he said, "We have to be sneaky, love. The whole crew is celebrating Summersfield's passing, and I don't want anyone ambushing us. It seems the people on board this pile like to chase me around."

Eliza reached out and put her hand on his arm. "You're very important to them, Edwin. You're their new Lord."

He shrugged self-consciously. "That's going to take some getting used to."

She nodded at that. "I know you've got this. How does it feel to be the first Lord to be so young and be in charge of a Congress and a gyro?"

Edwin fell speechless. She saw the fear pass behind his eyes and realized her husband was going to need a lot of support to survive this. Edwin was a good leader, but he wasn't experienced in these matters. He had no real ambitions. She was going to have to help him, she knew. Thankfully, she was getting stronger by the hour, though she had no clear idea why that should be. Maybe something to do with her unique condition.

She rubbed at her belly, then glanced up at the lighted buttons as they slowly descended to the bay level. "You haven't said anything about...you know...since last night. How...how do you feel about...you know...?"

"The baby?" he said.

She nodded. She desperately hoped he wasn't appalled by her condition. She had given this a lot of thought last night, and she had decided that she might like to try things as a mum. But what if Edwin didn't want it? "The doctor said he has no idea if it will survive—or even what it will be. I don't even know how this is possible..."

He smiled a little crookedly and put a finger on her lips to stop her rambling. "We'll just have to find out, lovey."

"I know, but...I mean, is it something you want?"

He surprised her by crouching down so they were eye to eye. He cupped her face in his two big hands and kissed her deeply even as the doors of the lift opened on all of their waiting friends and crew, who cheered suddenly at the sight of the two of them. While they were shouting their glee, Edwin pushed his face close to her ear and said, "Yes, I want our baby. Whatever it is."

She smiled at him, relieved.

Standing, he pushed her out of the lift, and the large crowd of people immediately absorbed the two of them. Eliza was hugged, kissed, and squeezed (very gently) by a large variety of friends. When Malcolm stepped up to her, accompanied by a beautiful woman with golden eyes, she saw the look of love and relief in his eyes. He went to one knee to kiss her hand as the "Queen Mother" of their Congress. His mate, Anjou, gave Eliza a tentative welcome hug and then pulled her aside to gossip with her for a bit.

While they were getting to know one another better, Eliza kept glancing over, looking for Cesar, but he didn't seem to be in attendance, which saddened her. She missed him so much. She did notice Captain Leo standing at a reserved distance.

The last prince of Russia, she thought as he cautiously approached her. He bowed to her very formally, and after they had exchanged introductions, she asked him if the many wild stories Edwin had told of his exploits were true.

"They are, madam," he said and went on to explain about his ship, the *Queen Anne's Revenge II*. He explained what Edwin had gone through to get back to her.

"He never told me about you," she said, feeling a little hurt about that.

"Lord Edwin is not my master any longer. And I'm no longer his Heir. We...performed a very painful ceremony to sever our bloodline."

More vampire secrets, she thought with a sigh. She felt nervous about asking Edwin's former Heir a favor, but Leo assured her that he was at her service, seeing how she had rid the world of one more corrupted vampire.

"It's about Moira." She had to stop and suck up the tears in her nose. She kept thinking about Moira and Dahlia and everyone else that Summersfield had destroyed so flippantly. It seemed almost impossible, and unbearable, that they were gone, the last victims of Summersfield's wrath. Her heart broke each time she let her thoughts drift to them. She hadn't known any of them very long, but they had all become her family.

"Moira belonged to the sea, and I'd like to see her body returned, if that's possible."

"Say no more. I shall have my crew return her forthwith to her people," he promised.

She bit back the tears in her throat. "Thank you. I know that's what she would want."

They passed a few more words, and Captain Leo even added a few funny anecdotes about Edwin before she turned to find her husband. She didn't want him getting too embarrassed.

She saw Edwin off at a distance, approaching Cesar, who had finally arrived, having been couriered over to the *Marie Antoinette* from the *Gypsy Queen*. Foxley was with him. All three vampires passed a few words and then disappeared into the hallway. She thought about following them—she hated how cagey vampires could be—but she had a bad feeling somewhere under her heart that things were about to take a bad turn.

Besides, her new friend Anjou was waving to get her attention, and she had some delicious punch in glasses she was holding up.

* * *

Cesar was uncharacteristically silent on the walk to the private room in the docking bay. When Edwin stepped into it, he saw it was a large depot half full of mostly dry goods that the kitchens used. But in one corner stood a rather large cage covered in a tarp. Some living thing clanked around inside, but Edwin was more interested in talking to Cesar at the moment.

Edwin closed the door and turned to find his Heir standing with his head down and his hands clasped behind his back, looking defeated. He wished Foxley would fuck right off, and, to his surprise, he did disappear, though not before giving Cesar a small, private nod that made Edwin's stomach flip-flop. Most of the tragedies in his life could be traced back to Foxley in some way.

Now that they were alone, Edwin let out his breath in a puff. "Mind telling me what you're doing with Foxley?"

Cesar continued to stare at the floor for a long time while he gathered his courage and his words.

After too many moments of uncomfortable silence, Edwin's thoughts turned to what the Chimera said before it flew away. He said in a whisper, "Cesar, what did you do?"

Cesar raised his chin and met Edwin's eyes. He appreciated that Cesar wasn't cowering, at least. Taking a deep breath, he let it out before saying, "I found out why vampires who are not Lords don't make other vampires."

Edwin had had a feeling this was going to happen. At the same time, he'd had so much to concern him that he hadn't been in the right mind to hold Cesar's hand. He realized now that that was a mistake. He should have kept Cesar with him.

He should have been a better Lord to him.

"Explain," Edwin said. He kept his voice soft, but he didn't say it nicely. He had vowed to be a better Lord over his Congress than most vampires were, but that didn't mean he could afford to be some pushover.

Cesar wrung his hands while he told his story. He told Edwin about his row with Tommy Quinn, as well as what he'd done afterward to try and save him. His contract with Foxley, and what Foxley had done—and not done. He told Edwin about the long hours at Tommy's bedside, and, ultimately, what it all led to. What he was responsible for doing.

"Tommy turned on me, Edwin...well, I thought he did," Cesar explained. "Maybe he did. But then he stopped. You said a vampire can't attack his master? His maker?"

Eliza had attacked her master—killed him, in fact—but Eliza was a strange case, he reminded himself. "Aye. And then what happened?"

"I restrained him. I was going to...to end Tommy. But I just couldn't do it." Cesar stopped wringing his hands and went to stand by the cage. "It isn't his fault. All this is on me. All of this is my doing." He pulled away the tarp.

They had put Tommy in restraints. He was very thin and grey-faced, but Edwin knew how strong a ghoul could be—especially when it was underfed. His skinny arms were chained over his head, and he hung in them with defeat, looking frightened and almost contrite. The front of his hospital Johnny was covered in blood and gore. It was pretty obvious that Cesar had been feeding him...something. He looked so sad as he hung there, gently rattling his chains. He didn't speak. Edwin wasn't sure if he had the presence of mind to do that. But his eyes followed him. There was an uncanny awareness in them that was disconcerting.

"I failed you twice, Edwin," Cesar said in a small voice. "First, by disobeying you. Then again when I couldn't help Tommy. Couldn't end him. I know what I've done, and I'm sorry."

Edwin approached the cage and looked in on Tommy.

Tommy's eyes moved to take him in. He cowered slightly as if Edwin might strike him.

"He's still in there, isn't he?" Cesar said. He sounded defeated and his voice broke on a near-sob.

Edwin nodded. "I think so, aye."

Slowly, Cesar slid to his knees beside the cage. He clutched Edwin's legs and rested his face against them. "It probably doesn't mean much to you at this point, but I'm just...I'm so sorry. I was so angry...I felt like you didn't care...I..."

Cesar started to sob. "And now I don't know what to do with Tommy. Foxley offered to...to dispose of him. But I just can't let that monster have him, Edwin. I need you." He looked up with pleading eyes. "I'm not strong enough to do this. I need my master to take care of this for me."

Edwin searched Tommy's pale, roaming eyes. There was something there...a small spark...but he wasn't sure if it was enough. He looked down at Cesar's miserable face. "Will you accept my judgment on the matter? I mean without question or argument?"

Cesar nodded frantically. "Yes. Whatever you say, I'll do."

Most of the decisions that Edwin had made in his life had been pretty sudden and flippant. He seldom had to think things through, but this was different.

He thought about his options for a long moment before deciding. "Leave Tommy with me. Let me handle him."

Cesar looked confused and rubbed at his tears. "Are you going to end him for me?"

Edwin wasn't sure, but he felt there was something here—a path to take. "I'm going to work with him. See what I can salvage, but..." He looked back down at Cesar. "I can't have you together. I don't want you two together right now."

Nodding, accepting that, Cesar climbed slowly to his feet. "Whatever you command...my Lord."

Edwin nodded. "I'll also talk to Foxley about breaking your contract. I—"

Cesar held up his hand to stop him. "That I've already made a decision about."

Edwin hesitated. "You aren't going to go with him?"

His Heir slowly straightened his shoulders. He swallowed hard. "You were right about something. I am immature and impetuous. I made a mess of things while you were gone, and I intend to clean my mess up myself. And if that takes me two hundred years to do so, then so be it."

Edwin stared at Cesar long and hard. Maybe he hadn't heard right? "You're going to work for Foxley?"

Cesar swallowed again, then nodded. "I'm going to fulfill my contract. So...yes."

"You don't have to—"

"I want to. I need to," Cesar interrupted him. His eyes were cool. Different. Edwin felt he was catching a glimpse of the vampire Cesar was destined to become one day.

"I need to be...worthy of you. I'm not. Not now. But I will be." Cesar nodded. "One day, I'll be the Enforcer you deserve."

"Cesar," Edwin said, his voice breaking. "He's a monster! He'll turn you into a monster..."

Cesar nodded at that, too. "Yeah, well, turns out I'm pretty much already there. I've made a lot of really crappy life decisions while you were gone, Edwin. And I think...no, I know...I need him. I need him to be an example of what I want to *not be* one day."

This was insane! "Well, I'm not letting you go" Edwin insisted. He clutched Cesar's sleeve. "You're *my* Heir and *my* Enforcer. I have attorneys now. I'll..."

Cesar was shaking his head. Edwin realized after a moment that it was futile.

His Heir had made up his mind.

Cesar smiled, finally, and reached out to set his hands on Edwin's shoulders. "I'm contracted to him, Edwin. We—you and I—don't have a contract. He tells me that trumps what we have."

It took Edwin a long moment to wrap his head around Cesar's decision. That he was willing to submit himself to this insanity. But after a few moments of silence, he reached up and cupped his Heir's face. "Is this really what you want?"

Cesar shook his head. "No, but it's what I need."

Edwin sighed.

"I mean, *you* are my master, Edwin. You always will be. And I still love Eliza—and even that big hairball. But, yeah, this is what I need to do right now."

"He won't make your life easy."

"I know." Cesar's confidence in his decision infuriated Edwin. "I want that, too. I don't want things easy anymore."

Before they parted—Cesar would be leaving with Foxley in the next few minutes to return with him to the *Gypsy Queen*—Edwin pulled him close, kissed him passionately and with great hunger and terror, and held his Heir a long, silent moment, their foreheads touching.

You have yet to discover how much you have lost.

Chimera. Goddamn the bastard.

* * *

When he returned alone to the party, he saw Eliza sitting there in her wheelchair with all of his crew and her friends surrounding her. Malcolm, Anjou, and their pack, Narissa—who had decided to stay aboard the *Marie Antoinette* as a liaison for the Morrigan—the Security and Pleasure Poppets that Eliza had freed from Summersfield's control...everyone. It was quite an eclectic Congress.

There was even a band, and it started playing a formal tune as the new Lord-at-Court of the *Marie Antoinette* stepped into the room to assume his duties.

Eliza saw him and motioned him forward. "They say it's customary for the Lord and his Bride to have a formal dance after taking control of a dead Lord's Court," she whispered with regret. "I wish..."

Edwin swept her out of her chair and into his arms as if she weighed nothing, then twirled her around as the band played a waltz and the strobe lights followed them across the dance floor.

She smiled. "You're supposed to be all formal. You really don't have a handle on this Lord business yet, do you?"

"Not yet," Edwin told her as he moved to the center of the room to dance with his Bride. "But with you, lovey, I will."

ABOUT THE AUTHOR

K.H. Koehler is the bestselling author of various novels and novellas in the genres of horror, SF, dark fantasy, steampunk, and young and new adult. She is the owner of KH Koehler Books and KH Koehler Design, which specializes in graphic design and professional copyediting. Her books are widely available at all major online distributors and her covers have appeared on numerous books in many different genres. Her short work has appeared in various anthologies, and her novel series include *The Kaiju Hunter, A Clockwork Vampire, Planet of Dinosaurs, The Nick Englebrecht Mysteries,* and *The Archaeologists*. She is the author of multiple Amazon bestsellers and was one of the founders and chief editors of KHP Publishers, which published genre fiction from 2001 to 2015. She has over fifteen years of experience in the publishing industry as a writer, ghostwriter, copyeditor, commercial book cover designer, formatter, and marketer. Visit her website at https://khkoehler.net.

www.ingramcontent.com/pod-product-compliance
Lightning Source LLC
LaVergne TN
LVHW030317070526
838199LV00069B/6476